Arlo Bates

The Puritans

Arlo Bates

The Puritans

ISBN/EAN: 9783743305823

Manufactured in Europe, USA, Canada, Australia, Japa

Cover: Foto ©ninafisch / pixelio.de

Manufactured and distributed by brebook publishing software
(www.brebook.com)

Arlo Bates

The Puritans

CONTENTS

THE PURITANS

I

AFTER SUCH A PAGAN CUT
Henry VIII., i. 3

"WE are all the children of the Puritans," Mrs.
Herman said smiling. "Of course there is an ethical
strain in all of us."

Her cousin, Philip Ashe, who wore the dress of a
novice from the Clergy House of St. Mark, regarded
her with a serious and doubtful glance.

"But there is so much difference between you and
me," he began. Then he hesitated as if not knowing
exactly how to finish his sentence.

"The difference," she responded, "is chiefly a matter of the difference between action and reaction.
You and I come of much the same stock ethically.
My childhood was oppressed by the weight of the
Puritan creed, and the reaction from it has made me
what you feel obliged to call heretic ; while you, with
a saint for a mother, found even Puritanism hardly
strict enough for you, and have taken to semi-monasti-
cism. We are both pushed on by the same original
impulse : the stress of Puritanism."

She had been putting on her gloves as she spoke,
and now rose and stood ready to go out. Philip looked
at her with a troubled glance, rising also.

"I hardly know," said he slowly, "if it 's right for

me to go with you. It would have been more in keeping if I adhered to the rules of the Clergy House while I am away from it."

Mrs. Herman smiled with what seemed to him something of the tolerance one has for the whim of a child.

"And what would you be doing at the Clergy House at this time of day?" she asked. "Wouldn't it be recreation hour or something of the sort?"

He looked down. He never found himself able to be entirely at ease in answering her questions about the routine of the Clergy House.

"No," he answered. "The half hour of recreation which follows Nones would just be ended."

His cousin laughed confusingly.

"Well, then," she rejoined, "begin it over again. Tell your confessor that the woman tempted you, and you did sin. You are not in the Clergy House just now; and as I have taken the trouble to ask leave to carry you to Mrs. Gore's this afternoon, more because you wanted to see this Persian than because I cared about it, it is rather late for objections."

Philip raised his eyes to her face only to meet a glance so quizzical that he hastened to avoid it by going to the hall to don his cloak; and a few moments later they were walking up Beacon Hill.

It was one of those gloriously brilliant winter days by which Boston weather atones in an hour for a week of sullenness. Snow lay in a thin sheet over the Common, and here and there a bit of ice among the tree-branches caught the light like a glittering jewel. The streets were dotted with briskly gliding sleighs, the jingle of whose bells rang out joyously. The air was full of a vigor which made the blood stir briskly in the veins.

Philip had not for years found himself in the street
with a woman. Seldom, indeed, was he abroad with
a companion, except as he took the walk prescribed
in the monastic régime with his friend, Maurice
Wynne. For the most part he went his way alone,
occupied in pious contemplation, shutting himself stub-
bornly in from outward sights and sounds. Now he
was confused and unsettled. Since a fire had a week
earlier scattered the dwellers in the Clergy House, and
sent him to the home of his cousin, he had gone about
like one bewildered. The world into which he was
now cast was as unknown to him as if he had passed
the two years spent at St. Mark's in some far island
of the sea. To be in the street with a lady; to be on
his way to hear he knew not what from the lips of a
Persian mystic; to have in his mind memory of light
talk and pleasant story; all these things made him
feel as if he were drifting into a strange unknown sea
of worldliness.

Yet his feeling was not entirely one of fear or of
reluctance. Sensitive to the tips of his fingers, he felt
the influences of the day, the sweetness of his cousin's
laughter, the beauty of her face. He was exhilarated
by a strange intoxication. He was conscious that more
than one passer looked curiously at them as, he in his
cassock and she in her furs, they walked up Beacon
Street. He felt as in boyhood he had felt when about
to embark in some adventure to childhood strange and
daring.

"It is a beautiful day," he said involuntarily.

"Yes," Mrs. Herman answered. "It is almost a
pity to spend it indoors. But here we are."

They had come into Mt. Vernon Street, and now
turned in at a fine old house of gray stone.

"Is there any discussion at these meetings?" he asked, as they waited for the door to be opened.

"Oh, yes; often there is a good deal. You'll have ample opportunity to protest against the heresies of the heathen."

"I do not come here to speak," he replied, rather stiffly. "I only come to get some idea of how the oriental mind works."

He felt her smile to be that of one amused at him, but he could not see why she should be.

"I must give you one caution," she went on, as they entered the house. "It's the same that the magicians give to those who are present at their incantations. Be careful not to pronounce sacred words."

"But don't they use them?"

"Oh, abundantly; but they know how to use them in a fashion understood only by the initiated, so that they are harmless."

They passed up the wide staircase of Mrs. Gore's handsome, if over-furnished house. They were shown into the drawing-room, where they were met by the hostess, a tall, superb woman of commanding presence, her head crowned with masses of snow-white hair. Coming in from the brilliant winter sunlight, Philip could not at first distinguish anything clearly. He went mechanically through his presentation to the hostess and to the Persian who was to address the meeting, and then sank into a seat. He looked curiously at the Persian, struck by the picturesque appearance of the long snow-white beard, fine as silk, which flowed down over the rich robe of the seer. The face was to Philip an enigma. To understand a foreign face it is necessary to have learned the physiognomy of the people to which it belongs, as to comprehend their speech it is necessary to have mastered their language. Ashe knew not whether the countenance of the old man attracted or repelled him more, and could only decide that at least it had a strange fascination.

Suddenly Ashe felt his glance called up by a familiar presence, and to his surprise saw his friend, Maurice Wynne, come into the room, accompanied by a stately, bright-eyed woman who was warmly greeted by Mrs. Gore. He wondered at the chance which had brought Maurice here as well as himself; but the calling of the meeting to order attracted his thoughts back to the business of the moment.

The Persian was the latest ethical caprice of Boston. He had come by the invitation of Mrs. Gore to bring across the ocean the knowledge of the mystic truths contained in the sacred writings of his country; and his ministrations were being received with that beautiful seriousness which is so characteristic of the town. In Boston there are many persons whose chief object in life seems to be the discovery of novel forms of spiritual dissipation. The cycle of mystic hymns which the Persian was expounding to the select circle of devotees assembled at Mrs. Gore's was full of the most sensual images, under which the inspired Persian psalmists had concealed the highest truth. Indeed, Ashe had been told that on one occasion the hostess had been obliged to stop the reading on the ground that an occidental audience not accustomed to anything more outspoken than the Song of Solomon, and unused to the amazing grossness of oriental symbolism, could not listen to the hymn which he was pouring forth. Fortunately Philip had chanced upon a day when the text was harmless, and he could hear without blushing, whether he were spiritually edified or not.

The Persian had a voice of exquisite softness and flexibility. His every word was like a caress. There are voices which so move and stir the hearer that they arouse an emotion which for the moment may override reason; voices which appeal to the senses like beguiling music, and which conquer by a persuasive sweetness as irresistible as it is intangible. The tones of the Persian swayed Ashe so deeply that the young man felt as if swimming on a billow of melody. Philip regarded as if fascinated the slender, dusky fingers of the reader as they handled the splendidly illuminated parchment on which glowed strange characters of gold, marvelously intertwined with leaf and flower, and cunning devices in gleaming hues. He looked into the deep, liquid eyes of the old man, and saw the light in them kindle as the reading proceeded. He felt the dignity of the presence of the seer, and the richness of his flowing garment; but all these things were only the fitting accompaniments to that beautiful voice, flowing on like a topaz brook in a meadow of daffodils.

The Persian spoke admirable English, only now and then by a slight accent betraying his nationality. He made a short address upon the antiquity of the hymn which he was that day to expound, its authorship, and its evident inspiration. Then in his wonderful voice he read: —

THE HYMN OF ISMAT.

Yesterday, half inebriated, I passed by the quarters where the vintners dwell, to seek the daughter of an infidel who sells wine.

At the end of the street, there advanced before me a

damsel, with a fairy's cheeks, who in the manner of a pagan
wore her tresses dishevelled over her shoulders like a sacer-
dotal thread. I said: "O thou, to the arch of whose eyebrow the new moon is a slave, what quarter is this, and
where is thy mansion?"

She answered: "Cast thy rosary to the ground; bind on
thy shoulder the thread of paganism; throw stones at the
glass of piety; and quaff from a full goblet.

"After that come before me that I may whisper a word
in thine ear;—thou wilt accomplish thy journey if thou
listen to my discourse."

Abandoning my heart, and rapt in ecstasy, I ran after
her until I came to a place in which religion and reason
forsook me.

At a distance I beheld a company all insane and inebriated, who came boiling and roaring with ardor from the
wine of love.

Without cymbals or lutes or viols, yet all filled with
mirth and melody; without wine or goblet or flagon, yet
all incessantly drinking.

When the cord of restraint slipped from my hand, I
desired to ask her one question, but she said: "Silence!

"This is no square temple to the gate of which thou canst
arrive precipitately; this is no mosque to which thou canst
come with tumult, but without knowledge. This is the
banquet-house of infidels, and within it all are intoxicated;
all from the dawn of eternity to the day of resurrection lost
in astonishment.

"Depart thou from the cloister and take thy way to the
tavern; cast off the cloak of a dervish, and wear the robe
of a libertine."

I obeyed; and if thou desirest the same strain and color
as Ismat, imitate him, and sell this world and the next for
one drop of pure wine!

The company sat in absorbed silence while the reading went on. Nothing could be more perfect than the

listening of a well-bred Boston audience, whether it is interested or not. The exquisitely modulated voice of the Persian flowed on like the tones of a magic flute, and the women sat as if fascinated by its spell.

When the reading was finished, and the Persian began to comment upon the spiritual doctrine embodied in it, Ashe sat so completely absorbed in reverie that he gave no heed to what was being said. In his ascetic life at the Clergy House he had been so far removed from the sensuous, save for that to which the services of the church appealed, that this enervating and luxurious atmosphere, this gathering to which its quasi-religious character seemed to lend an excuse, bred in him a species of intoxication. He sat like a lotus-eater, hearing not so much the words of the speaker as his musical voice, and half-drowned in the pleasure of the perfumed air, the rich colors of the room, the Persian's dress, the illuminated scroll, in the subtile delight of the presence of women, and all those seductive charms of the sense from which the church defended him.

The Persian, Mirza Gholân Rezâh, repeated in his flute-like voice: "'O thou, to the arch of whose eyebrow the new moon is a slave;'" and, hearing the words as in a dream, Philip Ashe looked across the little circle to see a woman whose beauty smote him so strongly that he drew a quick breath. To his excited mood it seemed as if the phrase were intended to describe that beautifully curved brow, brown against the fair skin, and in his heart he said over the words with a thrill: "'O thou, to the arch of whose eyebrow the new moon is a slave!'" Half unconsciously, and as if he were taken possession of by a will stronger than his own, he found himself noting the soft curve

and flush of a woman's cheek, the shell-texture of her
ear, and the snowy whiteness of her throat. She sat
in the full light of the window behind him, leaning as
she listened against a pedestal of ebony which upheld
the bronze bust of a satyr peering down at her with
wrinkled eyes; her throat was displayed by the backward bend of her head, and showed the whiter by contrast with the black gown she wore. Philip's breath
came more quickly, and his head seemed to swim.
Sensitive to beauty, and starved by asceticism, he was
in a moment completely overcome.

Suddenly he felt the regard of his friend Maurice
resting upon him with a questioning glance, and it was
as if the thought of his heart were laid bare. Philip
made a strong effort, and fixed his look and his attention upon the speaker, who was deep in oriental mys-
ticism.

"It is written in the Desâtir," Mirza Gholân Rezâh
was saying, "that purity is of two kinds, the real and
the formal. 'The real consists in not binding the
heart to evil; the formal in cleansing away what appears evil to the view.' The ultimate spirit, that inner
flame from the treasure-house of flames, is not affected
by the outward, by the apparent. What though the
outer man fall into sin? What though he throw
stones at the glass of piety and quaff the wine of
sensuality from a full goblet? The flame within the
tabernacle is still pure and undefiled because it is
undefilable."

Ashe looked around the circle in astonishment,
wondering if it were possible that in a Christian
civilization these doctrines could be proclaimed without rebuke. His neighbors sat in attitudes of close
attention; they were evidently listening, but their

faces showed no indignation. On the lips of Wynne
Philip fancied he detected a faint curl of derisive
amusement, but nowhere else could he perceive any
display of emotion, unless — He had avoided looking
at the lady in black, feeling that to do so were to
play with temptation; but the attraction was too
strong for him, and he glanced at her with a look
of which the swiftness showed how strongly she affected him. It seemed to him that there was a faint
flush of indignation upon her face; and he cast down
his eyes, smitten by the conviction that there was an
intimate sympathy between his feeling and hers.

"This is the word of enlightenment which the damsel, the personification of wisdom, whispered into the
ear of the seeker," continued the persuasive voice of
the Persian. "It is the heart-truth of all religion.
It is the word which initiates man into the divine
mysteries. 'Thou wilt accomplish thy journey if thou
listen to my discourse.' Life is affected by many accidents; but none of them reaches the godhead within.
The divine inebriation of spiritual truth comes with
the realization of this fact. The flame within man,
which is above his consciousness, is not to be touched
by the acts of the body. These things which men call
sin are not of the slightest feather-weight to the soul
in the innermost tabernacle. It is of no real consequence," the speaker went on, warming with his theme
until his velvety eyes shone, "what the outer man may
do. We waste our efforts in this childish care about
apparent righteousness. The real purity is above our
acts. Let the man do what he pleases; the soul is
not thereby touched or altered."

Ashe sat upright in his chair, hardly conscious where
he was. It seemed to him monstrous to remain ac-

quiescent and to hear without protest this juggling with the souls of men. The instinct to save his fellows which underlies all genuine impulse toward the priesthood was too strong in him not to respond to the challenge which every word of the Persian offered. Almost without knowing it, he found himself interrupting the speaker.

" If that is the teaching of the Persian scriptures," he said, " it is impious and wicked. Even were it true that there were a flame from the Supreme dwelling within us, unmanifested and undefilable, it is evidently not with this that we have to do in our earthly life. It is with the soul of which we are conscious, the being which we do know. This may be lost by defilement. To this the sin of the body is death. I, I myself, I, the being that is aware of itself, am no less the one that is morally responsible for what is done in the world by me."

Led away by his strong feeling, Philip began vehemently; but the consciousness of the attention of all the company, and of the searching look of Mirza, made the ardent young man falter. He was a stranger, unaccustomed to the ways of these folk who had come together to play with the highest truths as they might play with tennis-balls. He felt a sudden chill, as if upon his hot enthusiasm had blown an icy blast.

Yet when he cast a glance around as if in appeal, he saw nothing of disapproval or of scorn. He had evidently offended nobody by his outburst. He ventured to look at the unknown in black, and she rewarded him with a glance so full of sympathy that for an instant he lost the thread of what the Persian, in tones as soft and unruffled as ever, was saying in reply to his words. He gathered himself up to hear and to

answer, and there followed a discussion in which a
number of those present joined; a discussion full of
cleverness and the adroit handling of words, yet which
left Philip in the confusion of being made to realize
that what to him were vital truths were to those about
him merely so many hypotheses upon which to found
argument. There were more women than men present, and Ashe was amazed at their cleverness and
their shallow reasoning; at the ease and naturalness
with which they played this game of intellectual gymnastics, and at the apparent failure to pierce to anything like depth. It was evident that while everything
was uttered with an air of the most profound seriousness, it would not do to be really in earnest. He
began to understand what Helen had meant when she
warned him not to pronounce sacred words in this
strange assembly.

When the meeting broke up, the ladies rose to exchange greetings, to chat together of engagements in
society and such trifles of life. Ashe, still full of the
excitement of what he had done, followed his cousin
out of the drawing-room in silence. As they were de-
scending the wide staircase, some one behind said:—

"Are you going away without speaking to me,
Helen?"

Ashe and Mrs. Herman both turned, and found
themselves face to face with the lady in black, who
stood on the broad landing.

"My dear Edith," Mrs. Herman answered, "I am
so little used to this sort of thing that I didn't know
whether it was proper to stop to speak with one's
friends. I thought that we might be expected to go
out as if we'd been in church. I came only to bring
my cousin. May I present Mr. Ashe; Mrs. Fenton."

"I was so glad that you said what you did this afternoon, Mr. Ashe," Mrs. Fenton said, extending her hand. "I felt just as you did, and I was rejoiced that somebody had the courage to protest against that dreadful paganism."

Philip was too shy and too enraptured to be able to reply intelligibly, but as they were borne forward by the tide of departing guests he was spared the need of answer. At the foot of the stairway he was stopped again by Maurice Wynne, and presented to Mrs. Staggchase, his friend's cousin and hostess for the time being; but his whole mind was taken up by the image of Mrs. Fenton, and in his ears like a refrain rang the words of the Persian hymn: "O thou, to the arch of whose eyebrow the new moon is a slave!"

II

THAT afternoon at Mrs. Gore's had been no less
significant to Maurice Wynne than to Philip Ashe.
His was a less spiritual, less highly wrought nature,
but in the effect which the change from the atmosphere of the Clergy House to the Persian's lecture
had upon him, the experience of Maurice was much
the same. He too was attracted by a woman. He
gave his thoughts up to the woman much more frankly
than would have been possible for his friend. She
was young, perhaps twenty, and exquisite with clear
skin and soft, warm coloring. Her wide-open eyes
were as dark and velvety as the broad petals of a
pansy with the dew still on them; her cheeks were
tinged with a hue like that which spreads in a glass
of pure water into which has fallen a drop of red
wine; her forehead was low and white, and from it
her hair sprang up in two little arches before it fell
waving away over her temples; her lips were pouting
and provokingly suggestive of kisses. The whole face
was of the type which comes so near to the ideal that
the least sentimentality of expression would have
spoiled it. Happily the big eyes and the ripe, red
mouth were both suggestive of demure humor. There
was a mirthful air about the dimple which came and
went in the left cheek like Cupid peeping mischievously from the folds of his mother's robe. A boa of

long-haired black fur lay carelessly about her neck, pushed back so that a touch of red and gold brocade showed where she had loosened her coat. Maurice noted that she seemed to care as little for the lecture as he did, and he gave himself up to the delight of watching her.

When the company broke up Mrs. Staggchase spoke almost immediately to the beautiful creature who so charmed him.

"How do you do, Miss Morison," Mrs. Staggchase said; "I must say that I am surprised that cousin Anna brought you to a place where the doctrine is so far removed from mind-cure. My dear Anna," she continued, turning to a lady whom Wynne knew by name as Mrs. Frostwinch and as an attendant at the Church of the Nativity, "you are a living miracle. You know you are dead, and you have no business consorting with the living in this way."

"It is those whom you call dead that are really living," Mrs. Frostwinch retorted smiling. "I brought Berenice so that she might see the vanity of it all."

Mrs. Staggchase presented Maurice to the ladies, and after they had spoken on the stairs with one and another acquaintance, and Maurice had exchanged a word with his friend Ashe, it chanced that the four left the house together. Wynne found himself behind with Miss Morison, while his cousin and Mrs. Frostwinch walked on in advance. He was seized with a delightful sense of elation at his position, yet so little was he accustomed to society that he knew not what to say to her. He was keenly aware that she was glancing askance at his garb, and after a moment of silence he broke out abruptly in the most naïvely unconscious fashion : —

" I am a novice at the Clergy House of St. Mark."

A beautiful color flushed up in Miss Morison's dark cheek ; and Wynne realized how unconventional he had been in replying to a question which had not been spoken.

" Is it a Catholic order ? " she asked, with an evident effort not to look confused.

" It is not Roman," he responded. " We believe that it is catholic."

" Oh," said she vaguely ; and the conversation lapsed.

They walked a moment in silence, and then Maurice made another effort.

" Has Mrs. Frostwinch been ill ? " he asked. " Mrs. Staggchase spoke of her as a miracle."

" Ill ! " echoed Miss Morison ; " she has been wholly given up by the physicians. She has some horrible internal trouble ; and a consultation of the best doctors in town decided that she could not live a week. That was two months ago."

" But I don't understand," he said in surprise. " What happened ? "

" A miracle," the other replied smiling. " You believe in miracles, of course."

" But what sort of a miracle ? "

" Faith-cure."

" Faith-cure ! " repeated he in astonishment. " Do you mean that Mrs. Frostwinch has been raised from a death-bed by that sort of jugglery ? "

His companion shrugged her shoulders.

" I don't think it would raise you in her estimation if she heard you. The facts are as I tell you. She dismissed her doctors when they said they could do nothing for her, and took into her house a mind-cure woman, a Mrs. Crapps. Some power has put her on her feet. Would n't you do the same thing in her place?"

Wynne looked bewildered at Mrs. Frostwinch walking before him in a shimmer of Boston respectability. He had an uneasy feeling that he was passing from one pitfall to another. He was keenly conscious of the richness of the voice of the girl by his side, so that he felt that it was not easy for him to disagree with anything which she said. He let her remark pass without reply.

"For my part," she went on frankly, "I don't in the least believe in the thing as a matter of theory; but practically I have a superstition about it, because I 've seen Cousin Anna. She was helpless, in agony, dying; and now she is as well as I am. If I were ill " —

She broke off with a pretty little gesture as they came within hearing of the others, who had halted at Mrs. Frostwinch's gate. Wynne said good-by absently, and went on his way down the hill like a man in a dream.

"Well," Mrs. Staggchase said, "you have seen one of Boston's ethical debauches; what do you think of it?"

"It was confusing," he returned. "I could n't make out what it was for."

"For? To amuse us. We are the children of the Puritans, you know, and have inherited a twist toward the ethical and the supernatural so strong that we have to have these things served up even in our amusements."

"Then I think that it is wicked," Maurice said.

"Oh, no; we must not be narrow. It is n't wrong

to amuse one's self; and if we play with the religion of the Persians, why is it worse than to play with the mythologies of the Greeks or Romans? You would n't think it any harm to jest about classical theology."

Wynne turned toward her with a smile on his strong, handsome face.

"Why do you try to tangle me up in words?" he asked.

Mrs. Staggchase did not turn toward him, but looked before with face entirely unchanged as she replied : —

"I am not trying to entangle you in words, but if I were it would be all part of the play. You are undergoing your period of temptation. I am the tempter in default of a better. In the old fashion of temptations it would n't do to have the tempter old and plain. Then you were expected to fall in love ; now we deal in snares more subtle."

Maurice laughed, but somewhat unmirthfully. There was to him something bewildering and worldly about his cousin; and he had come to feel that he could never be at all sure where in the end the most harmless beginning of talk might lead him.

"What then is the modern way of temptation?" he inquired.

"It shows how much faith we have in its power," she replied, as they waited on the corner of Charles Street for a carriage to pass, "that I don't in the least mind giving you full warning. Did you know the lady in that carriage, by the way?"

"It was Mrs. Wilson, was n't it?"

"Yes ; Mrs. Chauncy Wilson. You have seen her at the Church of the Nativity, I suppose. She is one phase of the temptation."

" I don't in the least understand."

" I did n't in the least suppose that you would.
You will in time. My part of the temptation is to
show you all sorts of ethical jugglery, the spiritual
and intellectual gymnastics such as the Bostonians
love; to persuade you that all religion is only a sort
of pastime, and that the particular high-church sort
which you especially affect is but one of a great many
entertaining ways of killing time."

" Cousin Diana ! " he exclaimed, genuinely shocked.

" I hope that you understand," she continued unmoved. " I shall exhibit a very pretty collection of
fads to you if we see them all."

" But suppose," he said slowly, " that I refused to
go with you ? "

" But you won't," returned she, with that curious
smile which always teased him with its suggestion of
irony. " In the first place you could n't be so im-
polite as to refuse me. A woman may always lead a
man into questionable paths if she puts it to his sense
of chivalry not to desert her. In the second, the
spirit of the age is a good deal stronger in you than
you realize, and the truth is that you would n't be left
behind for anything. In the third, you could hardly
be so cowardly as to run away from the temptation
that is to prove whether you were really born to be a
priest."

" That was decided when I entered the Clergy
House."

" Nonsense ; nothing of the sort, my dear boy. The
only thing that was decided then was that you thought
you were. Wait and see our ethical and religious
raree-shows. We had the Persian to-day ; to-morrow
I 'm to take you to a spiritualist sitting at Mrs.

Rangely's. She hates to have me come, so I must n't miss that. Then there are the mind-cure, Theosophy, and a dozen other things; not to mention the semi-irreligions, like Nationalism. You will be as the gods, knowing good and evil, by the time we are half way round the circle, — though it is perhaps somewhat doubtful if you know them apart."

She spoke in her light, railing way, as if the matter were one of the smallest possible consequence, and yet Wynne grew every moment more and more uncomfortable. He had never seen his cousin in just this mood, and could not tell whether she were mocking him or warning him. He seized upon the first pretext which presented itself to his mind, and endeavored to change the subject.

"Who is Mrs. Rangely?" he asked. "A medium?"

"Oh, bless you, no. She is not so bad as a medium; she is only a New Yorker. Do you think we'd go to real mediums? Although," she added, "there are plenty who do go. I think that it is shocking bad form."

"But you speak as if" —

"As if spiritualism were one of the recognized ethical games, that's all. It is played pretty well at Mrs. Rangely's, I'm told. They say that the little Mrs. Singleton she's got hold of is very clever."

"Mrs. Singleton," Maurice repeated, "why, it can't be Alice, brother John's widow, can it? She married a Singleton for a second husband, and she claimed to be a medium."

"Did she really? It will be amusing if you find your relatives in the business."

"She was n't a very close relative. John was only my half-brother, you know, and he lived but six months after he married her.   She is clever enough and tricky enough to be capable of anything."

"Well," Mrs. Staggchase said, as they turned in at her door, "if it is she it will give you an excellent chance to do missionary work."

.They entered the wide, handsome hall, and with an abrupt movement the hostess turned toward her cousin.

"I assure you," she said, "that I am in earnest about your temptation.   I want to see what sort of stuff you are made of, and I give you fair warning. Now go and read your breviary, or whatever it is that you sham monks read, while I have tea and then rest before I dress."

Maurice had no reply to offer.   He watched in silence as she passed up the broad stairway, smiling to herself as she went.   He followed slowly a moment later, and seeking his room remained plunged in a reverie at which the severe walls of the Clergy House might have been startled ; a reverie disquieted, chan-ging, half-fearful ; and yet through which with strange fascination came a longing to see more of the surpris-ing world into which chance had introduced him, and above all to meet again the dark, glowing girl with whom he had that afternoon walked.

III

AS FALSE AS STAIRS OF SAND
Merchant of Venice, v. 2

It was cold and gray next morning when Maurice took his way toward a Catholic church in the North End. He had been there before for confession, and had been not a little elated in his secret heart that he had been able to go through the act of confession and to receive absolution without betraying the fact that he was not a Romanist. He had studied the forms of confession, the acts of contrition, and whatever was necessary to the part, and for some months had gone on in this singular course. To his Superior at the Clergy House he confessed the same sins, but Maurice had a feeling that the absolution of the Roman priest was more effective than that of his own church. He was not conscious of any intention of becoming a Catholic, but there was a fascination in playing at being one; and Wynne, who could not understand how the folk of Boston could play with ethical truths, was yet able thus to juggle with religion with no misgiving.

This morning he enjoyed the spiritual intoxication of the confessional as never before. He half consciously allowed himself to dwell upon the image of the beautiful Miss Morison to the end that he might the more effectively pour out his contrition for that sin. He was so eloquent in the confessional that he admired himself both for his penitence and for the words in which he set it forth. He floated as it were in a sea of mingled sensuousness and repentance, and he hoped that the penance imposed would be heavy enough to show that the priest had been impressed with the magnitude of the sin of which he had been guilty in allowing his thoughts, consecrated to the holy life of the priesthood, to dwell upon a woman.

It was one of those absurd anomalies of which life is full that while Maurice sometimes slighted a little the penances imposed by his own Superior, he had never in the least abated the rigor of any laid upon him by the Catholic priest. It was perhaps that he felt his honor concerned in the latter case. This morning the penance was satisfactorily heavy, and he came out of the church with a buoyant step, full of a certain boyish elation. He had a fresh and delightful sense of the reality of religion now that he had actually sinned and been forgiven.

Next to being forgiven for a sin there is perhaps nothing more satisfactory than to repeat the transgression, and if Maurice had not formulated this fact in theory he was to be acquainted with it in practice. As he walked along in the now bright forenoon, filled with the enjoyment of moral cleanness, he suddenly started with the thrill of delicious temptation. Just before him a lady had come around a corner, and was walking quietly along, in whom at a glance he recognized Miss Morison. There came into his cheek, which even his double penances had not made thin, a flush of pleasure. He quickened his steps, and in a moment had overtaken her.

"Good morning," he said, raising his ecclesiastical hat with an air which savored somewhat of worldliness. "Isn't it a beautiful day?"

She started at his salutation, but instantly recognized him.

"Good morning," she responded. "I did n't expect to find anybody I knew in this part of the town."

"It is n't one where young ladies as a rule walk for pleasure, I suppose," Maurice said, falling into step, and walking beside her.

"I am very sure that I don't," Miss Morison replied with a toss of her head. "I do it because I was bullied into being a visitor for the Associated Charities, and I go once a week to tell some poor folk down here that I am no better than they are. They know that I don't believe it, and I have my doubts if they even believe it themselves, only they would n't be foolish enough to prevaricate about it. Oh, it 's a great and noble work that I 'm engaged in!"

There was something exhilarating about her as she tossed her pretty head. Wynne laughed without knowing just why, except that she intoxicated him with delight.

"You don't speak of your work with much enthusiasm," said he.

"Enthusiasm!" she retorted. "Why should I? It 's abominable. I hate it, the people I visit hate it, and there 's nobody pleased but the managers, who can set down so many more visits paid to the worthy poor, and make a better showing in their annual report. For my part I am tired of the worthy poor; and if I must keep on slumming, I 'd like to try the unworthy poor a while. I 'm sure they 'd be more interesting."

She spoke with a pretty air of recklessness, as if

she were conscious that this was not the strain in which to address one of his cloth. There was not a little vexation under her lightness of manner, however, and Wynne was not so dull as not to perceive that something had gone amiss.

"But philanthropy," he began, "is surely " —

"Your cousin," she interrupted, "declares that only the eye of Omniscience can possibly distinguish between what passes for philanthropy and what is sheer egotism."

He laughed in spite of himself, feeling that he ought to be shocked.

"But what," he asked, "has impressed this view of things upon you this morning in particular?"

His companion made a droll little gesture with both her hands.

"Of course I show it," she said; "though you need n't have reminded me that I have lost my temper."

"I beg your pardon," began Maurice in confusion, "I" —

"Oh, you have n't done anything wrong," she interrupted, "the trouble is entirely with me. I 've been making a fool of myself at the instigation of the powers that rule over my charitable career, and I don't like the feeling."

They walked on a moment without further speech. Maurice said to himself with a thrill of contrition that he would double the penance laid upon him, and he endeavored not to be conscious of the thought which followed that the delight of this companionship was worth the price which he should thus pay for it.

"This is what happened," Miss Morison said at length. "I don't quite know whether to laugh or to

cry with vexation. There's a poor widow who has had
all sorts of trials and tribulations. Indeed, she's been
a miracle of ill luck ever since I began to have the
honor to assure her weekly that I'm no better than
she is. It may be that the fib is n't lucky."

She turned to flash a bright glance into the face of
her companion as she spoke, and he tried to clear
away the look of gravity so quickly that she might
not perceive it.

"Oh," she cried; "now I have shocked you!
I'm sorry, but I could n't help it."

"No," he replied, "you did n't really shock me.
It only seemed to me a pity that you should be working with so little heart and under direction that
does n't seem entirely wise."

"Wise!" she echoed scornfully. "There's a
benevolent gentleman who insisted upon giving this
old woman five dollars. It was all against the rules
of the Associated Charities, for which he said he
did n't care a fig. That's the advantage of being a
man! And what do you think the old thing did?
She took the whole of it to buy a bonnet with a red
feather in it! The committee heard of it, though I
can't for my life see how. There are a lot of them
that seem to think that benevolence consists chiefly in
prying into the affairs of the poor wretches they help!
And they posted me off to scold her."

"But why did you go?"

"They said they would send Miss Spare if I did n't,
and in common humanity I could n't leave that old
creature to the tender mercies of Miss Spare."

"What did you say?"

The face of Miss Morison lighted with mocking
amusement.

"That's the beauty of it," she cried, bursting into a low laugh which was full of the keenest fun. "I began with the things I'd been told to say; but the old woman said that all her life long she had wanted a bonnet with red feathers, but that she had never expected to have one. When she got this money, she went out to buy clothing, and in a window she saw this bonnet marked five dollars. She piously remarked that it seemed providential. She's like the rest of the world in finding what she likes to be providential."

"Yes," murmured Maurice, half under his breath; "like my meeting you."

Miss Morison looked surprised, but she ignored the words, and went on with her story.

"She said she concluded she'd rather go without the clothes, and have the bonnet; and by the time we were through I had weakly gone back on all the instructions I'd received, and told her she was right. She knew what she wanted, and I don't blame her for getting it when she could. I'm sick of seeing the poor treated as if they were semi-idiots that couldn't think without leave from the Associated Charities."

The whole tone of the conversation was so much more frank than anything to which Wynne was accustomed that he felt bewildered. This freedom of criticism of the powers, this want of reverence for conventionalities, gave him a strange feeling of lawlessness. He felt as if he had himself been wonderfully and almost culpably daring in listening. He wondered that he was not more shocked, being sure that it was his duty to be. There was about the young man's mental condition a sort of infantile unsophistication. The New England mind often seems to inherit from bygone Puritanism a certain repellent quality

through which it takes long for anything savoring of
worldliness or worldly wisdom to penetrate. When
once this covering is broken, it may be added, the result is much the same as in the case of the cracking
of other glazes.

After he had parted from Miss Morison, Maurice
walked on in a blissful state of conscious sinfulness.
He understood himself well enough to know that before him lay repentance, but this did not dampen his
present enjoyment. He had not so far outgrown his
New England conscience as to escape remorse for sin,
but he had become so accustomed to the belief that
absolution removed guilt that there was in his cup of
self-reproach little abiding bitterness.

That afternoon he accompanied Mrs. Staggchase to
the house of Mrs. Rangely with a confused feeling as
if he were some one else. His cousin wore the same
delicately satirical air which marked all her inter-
course with him. She carried her head with her accustomed good-humored haughtiness, and her straight
lips were curled into the ghost of a smile.

"This is the most stupid humbug of them all," she
remarked, as they neared Mrs. Rangely's house on
Marlborough Street. "You'll think the deception too
transparent to be even amusing, — if you don't become
a convert, that is."

"A convert to spiritualism?" Wynne returned
with youthful indignation. "I'm not likely to fall so
low as that. That is one of the things which are too
ridiculous."

She laughed, with that air of superiority which
always nettled him a little.

"Don't allow yourself to be one of those narrow
persons to whom a thing is always ridiculous if they

don't happen to believe it. You believe in so many impossible things yourself that you can't afford to take on airs."

The tantalizing good nature with which she spoke humiliated Wynne. She seemed to be playing with him, and he resented her reflection upon his creed. He was, however, too much under the spell of his cousin to be really angry, and he was silenced rather than offended. They entered the house to find several of the persons whom he had seen at Mrs. Gore's on the day previous; and Wynne was at once charmed and disquieted by the entrance a moment later of Miss Morison, who came in looking more beautiful than ever. It gave him a feeling of exultation to be sharing her life, even in this chance way.

The preliminaries of the sitting were not elaborate. Mrs. Rangely, the hostess, impressed it upon her guests that Mrs. Singleton, the medium, was not a professional, but that she was with them only in the capacity of one who wished to use her peculiar gifts in the search for truth.

"She does not understand her powers herself," Mrs. Rangely said; "but she feels that it is not right to conceal her light."

Maurice was too unsophisticated to understand why Mrs. Rangely's talk struck him as not entirely genuine, but he was to some extent enlightened when his cousin said to him afterward: "Frances Rangely has the imitation Boston patter at her tongue's end now, but she is too thoroughly a New Yorker ever to get the spirit of it. She rattles off the words in a way that is intensely amusing."

The shutters of the small parlor in which the company was assembled had been closed and the gas lighted. There were about a dozen guests, and all had the air of being of some position. While the hostess went to summon the medium, Maurice asked in a whisper if the master of the house was present, and was answered that Fred Rangely was too clever to be mixed up in this sort of thing. Wynne caught a satirical glance between his cousin and Miss Morison, and more than ever he felt that the meeting was a farce in which he, vowed to a nobler life, should have had no part.

His musings were cut short by the entrance of Mrs. Rangely with the medium. He recognized Mrs. Singleton at a glance, and was struck as he had been before by the appealing look of innocence. She was a slender, almost beautiful woman, with exquisite shell-like complexion, and delicate features. An entire lack of moral sense frequently gives to a woman an air of complete candor and purity, and Alice Singleton stood before the company as the incarnation of sincerity and truth. Her face was of the rounded, full-lipped, wistful type; the sensuous, selfish face moulded into the likeness of childlike guilelessness which of all the multitudinous varieties of the "ever womanly" is the one most likely to be destructive.

Had it not been that Maurice was acquainted with her history, he could hardly have resisted the fascination of this creature, as tender and as innocent in appearance as a dewy rose; but he was thoroughly aware of her moral worthlessness. Yet as she stood shrinking on the threshold as if she were too timid to advance, he could not but feel her attractiveness and the sweetness of her presence. He watched curiously as in response to a word from Mrs. Rangely she came hesitatingly forward, bowed in acknowledgment to a general introduction, and sank into the chair placed for her in the centre of the circle. She was clad in black, but a little of her creamy neck was visible between the folds of lace which set off its fairness. Her arms were bare half way to the elbows, and her hands were ungloved. Maurice wondered if she would recognize him; then he reflected that he sat in the shadow, out of the direct line of her vision, and that it was years since she had seen him.

"We will have the gas turned down," Mrs. Rangely said; and at once turned it, not down, but completely out, leaving the room in absolute darkness.

There followed an interval of silence, and Maurice, whose wits were sharpened by his knowledge of the medium, and who was on the lookout for trickery, reflected how inevitable it was that this breathless silence, coupled with the darkness and the expectation of something mysterious, should bring about the frame of mind which the medium would desire. The silence lasted so long that he, not wrapt in expectation, began to grow impatient. He put out his hand timidly in the darkness and touched the chair in which Miss Morison was sitting, getting foolish comfort from even such remote communion. He fell into a reverie in which he felt dimly what life might have been with her always at his side, had he not been vowed to the stern refusal of all earthly companionship.

His reflections were broken by a loud, quivering sigh seeming to come from the medium, and echoed in different parts of the room. There was another brief interval of silence, and then the medium began to speak. Her tone was strained and unnatural, and at first she murmured to herself. Then her words came more clearly and distinctly.

"Oh, how beautiful!" she whispered. Then in a voice growing clearer she went on: "Bright forms! There are three, — no, there are five; oh, the room is full of them. Oh, how bright they are growing! They shine so that they almost blind me. Don't you see them?"

The room rustled like a field of wheat under a breeze.

"There is one that is clearer than the others," went on the voice of the medium in the electrical darkness. "She is all shining, but I can see that her hair is white as snow. She must have been old before she went into the spirit world. She smiles and leans over the lady in the armchair. Oh, she is touching you! Don't you feel her dear hands on your head?"

Maurice felt the chair against which his fingers rested shaken by a movement of awe or of impatience. He flushed with indignation. It was Miss Morison to whom the medium was directing this childish impertinence. He longed to interfere, and even made so brusque a movement that Mrs. Staggchase leaned over and whispered to him to remain quiet.

"There are many spirits here," the medium went on with increasing fervor, "but none of them are so clear. She is speaking to you, but you cannot hear her. She is grieved that you do not understand her. Oh, try to listen so that you may hear her message with the spiritual ear. She is so anxious."

The audience seemed to quiver with excitement. Simply because a woman whom Maurice knew to be capable of any falsehood sat here in the darkness and pretended to see visions, these men and women were apparently carried out of themselves. It seemed to him at once monstrous and pitifully ridiculous.

" It must be your grandmother," spoke again the voice of Mrs. Singleton, now thick with emotion. " Yes, she nods her head. She is so anxious to reach through your unconsciousness. Wait! she is going to do something. I think she is going to give you some token. Let me rest a moment, so that I can help her. She wants to materialize something."

Heavy silence, but a silence which seemed alive with excitement, once more prevailed. Maurice began himself to feel something of the influence pervading the gathering, and was angry with himself for it. Suddenly a cry from the medium, earnest and full of feeling, broke out shrilly.

" Oh, she has something in her hand. Try to assist her. She will succeed in materializing it fully if we can help her with our wills. I can see it becoming clearer — clearer — clearer! Now she is smiling. She is happy. She knows she will succeed. Yes; it is — Oh, what beautiful roses! They are changing from white to red in her hands. She holds them up for me to see; she is lifting them up over your head. Now, now she is going to drop them! Quick! The light!"

The voice of Mrs. Singleton had risen almost to a scream, and bit the nerves of the hearers. As she ended Maurice heard the soft sound of something falling, and felt Miss Morison start violently. The gas was at once lighted, and there in the lap and at the feet of Berenice, who regarded them with an expression of mingled disgust and annoyance, lay scattered a handful of crimson roses.

The company broke into expressions of admiration, of belief, of awe. Mrs. Singleton had played to her audience with evident success. Miss Morison gathered

up the flowers without a word, and held them out to
the medium, who lay back wearied in her chair.

"Don't give them to me," Mrs. Singleton said in a
faint voice. "They were brought for you."

"How can you bear to give them up?" a woman
said. "It must be your grandmother that brought
them."

"My grandmother was in very good health in
Brookfield yesterday," Berenice responded. "I hardly
think that they come from her."

The tone was so cold that Mrs. Singleton was vis-
ibly disconcerted.

"Of course I don't know the spirit," she said.
"But are both your grandmothers living?"

"She nodded her head, you know," put in another.

To this Miss Morison did not even reply; but the
awkwardness of the situation was relieved by Mrs.
Rangely, who broke into conventional phrases of admiration and wonder.

"Yes, Frances," Mrs. Staggchase observed dryly,
"as you say, it couldn't be believed if one hadn't
seen it."

Her manner was unheeded in the flood of praise
and congratulation with which Mrs. Singleton was
being overwhelmed.

"It is what I've longed for all my life," one lady
declared, wiping her eyes. "I never could have confidence in professional mediums, but this is so perfectly satisfactory. Oh, I *do* feel that I owe you so
much, Mrs. Singleton!"

"Yes, this we have seen with our own eyes," another
added. "It is impossible for the most skeptical to
doubt this."

To this and more Maurice listened in amazement,

until he rather thought aloud than consciously
spoke : —

"But it all depends upon the unsupported testimony of the medium."

Mrs. Rangely drew herself up with much dignity.

"That," she said, "I will be responsible for."

"It is n't unsupported," chimed in one of the ladies.
"Here are the roses."

At the sound of Maurice's voice Mrs. Singleton had
turned toward him, and he saw that she recognized
him. She looked around with a glance half terrified,
half appealing.

"It is so kind in you to believe in me," she murmured pathetically. "I don't ask you to. I only tell
you what I see, and " —

Maurice rose abruptly and strode forward.

"Alice," he exclaimed, "what do you mean by this
humbug? Don't you see that they take it seriously?
Tell them it 's a joke."

Again Mrs. Singleton looked around as if to see
whether she had support.

"It is manly of you to attack me," she answered,
evidently satisfied with the result of her survey. "I
cannot defend myself."

"Do you mean to insist?" he demanded, with growing anger.

"If the roses do not justify what I said," responded
she, sinking back as if exhausted, "it may be that I
saw only imaginary shapes."

A sharp murmur ran around the room. The be-
lievers were evidently rallying indignantly to the support of their sibyl, and cast upon Wynne glances of
bitter reproach. He looked at Mrs. Staggchase, but
it was impossible to judge from her expression whether

she approved or disapproved of what he had done. He was suddenly abashed, and stood speechless before the rising tide of outraged remonstrance. Then unexpectedly came from behind him the clear voice of Miss Morison.

"It is unfortunate that the roses should have been given to me," she said, "for by an odd chance I saw them bought a couple of hours ago on Tremont Street."

There was an instant of hushed amazement, and then the medium fled from the parlor in hysterics.

IV

"O thou to the arch of whose eyebrow the new
moon is a slave!"

Philip Ashe colored with self-consciousness as the
words came into his mind. He felt that he had no
right to think them, and yet as he looked across the
table at his hostess it seemed almost as if the phrase
had been spoken in his ear by the seductive voice
of Mirza Gholân Rezâh. He sighed with contrition,
and looked resolutely away, letting his glance wander
about the room in which he was sitting at dinner.
He noted the panels of antique stamped leather, and
although he had had little artistic training, he was
pleased by the exquisite combination of rich colors
and dull gold. Some Spanish palace had once known
the glories which now adorned the walls of Mrs.
Fenton's dining-room, and even his uneducated eye
could see that care and taste had gone to the decoration of the apartment. Jars of Moorish pottery, few
but choice, and pieces of fine Algerian armor inlaid
with gold were placed skillfully, each displayed in its
full worth and yet all harmonizing and combining in
the general effect. Ashe knew that the husband of
Mrs. Fenton had been an artist of some note, and so
strongly was the skill of a master-hand visible here
that suddenly the painter seemed to the sensitive
young deacon alive and real. It was as if for the

first time he realized that the beautiful woman before
him might belong to another. By a quick, unreasonable jealousy of the dead he became conscious of how
keenly dear to him had become the living.

Ashe had met Mrs. Fenton a number of times during the week which had intervened since the Persian's
lecture at Mrs. Gore's. He had seen her once or twice
at the house of his cousin, with whom Mrs. Fenton
was intimate, and chance had brought about one or
two encounters elsewhere. He had until this moment
tried to persuade himself that his admiration for her
was that which he might have for any beautiful
woman; but looking about this room and realizing so
completely the husband dead half a dozen years, he
felt his self-deception shrivel and fall to ashes. With
a desperate effort he put the thought from him, and
gave his whole attention to the talk of his companions.

"Yes, Mr. Herman is in New York," Mrs. Herman
was saying. "He has gone on to see about a commis-
sion. They want him to go there to execute it, but I
don't think he will."

"Does n't he like New York?" asked Mr. Candish, the rector of the Church of the Nativity, who
was the fourth member of the little company.

Mrs. Herman and Mrs. Fenton both laughed.

"You know how Grant feels about New York,
Edith," the former said. "If anything could spoil his
temper, it is a day in what he calls the metropolis of
Philistinism."

"I never heard Mr. Herman say anything so harsh
as that about anything," Candish responded. "Do
you feel in that way about it?"

"The thing which I dislike about the place is its

provincialism," she answered. "It is the most pro-
incial city in America, in the sense that nothing
really exists for it outside of itself. If I think of
New York for ten minutes I have no longer any faith
in America."

"Then I should n't think of it, Helen," put in
Mrs. Fenton.

"Then you would n't go with your husband if he
went there to do this work, I suppose," Mr. Candish
observed.

"I should go with him anywhere that he thought it
best to go. I fear that you have n't an exalted idea
of the devotion of the modern wife, Mr. Candish."

Ashe watched with interest the rector, who flushed
a little. He knew of him well, having more than
once heard the awkwardness and social inadaptability
of the man urged as reasons of his unfitness to be
placed at the head of the most fashionable church in
the city. Philip saw him glance at the hostess and
then cast down his eyes; and wondered if this were
simple diffidence.

"That is hardly fair," Mr. Candish said, somewhat
awkwardly. "The clergy, not having wives, are poor
judges in such a matter."

"That might be taken as an argument for the marriage of the clergy," she responded with a smile.

"How so?"

"If they had wives they would be better able to
sympathize with the trials and joys of their parishioners."

"I never thought of that," murmured Mrs. Fenton.

Mr. Candish flushed all over his homely, freckled
face.

"By the same reasoning you might hold that a

clergyman should have committed all the sins in the decalogue, so that he should have ready sympathy with all sorts of sinners."

"I'm not sure that he wouldn't be more useful if he had," Mrs. Herman answered with a smile; "at least a man who hasn't wanted to commit a sin must find it hard to sympathize with the wretch that hasn't been strong enough to resist temptation. Still, I hope that sin and marriage are not put into the same category."

"Oh, of course not," Mrs. Fenton interpolated. "Marriage is a sacrament."

"It has always seemed to me inconsistent," Mrs. Herman went on, "that the church should exclude her priests from one of the sacraments."

Ashe saw a faint cloud pass over the face of the hostess. He was himself a little shocked; and Candish frowned slightly.

"The church admits her priests to this sacrament in a higher sense," he said with some stiffness.

Helen smiled.

"Now I have shocked you," was her comment. "I beg your pardon."

"I can never accustom myself to a familiar way of handling sacred things," he returned. "It is to me too vital a matter."

"I am afraid that that is because you are still so young," she retorted. "It is, if you'll pardon me, the prerogative of youth to find all views but its own intolerable."

The manner in which this was said deprived the words of their sting, but Mrs. Fenton evidently felt that they were getting upon dangerous ground, and she interposed.

" We shall ask you to define youth next, Helen," she threw in.

" Oh, that is easy. Young people are always those of our own age."

In the laugh that followed this the question of the marriage of the clergy was allowed to drop ; but to all that had been said Philip had listened with a beating heart. He felt the air about him to be charged with meanings which he could not divine. He had somehow a suspicion that the hostess was more interested in this talk than she was willing to show ; and with what in a moment he recognized as consummate and fatuous egotism, he felt in his heart the shadow of a hope that there might be some connection between this and her interest in him. Then a fear followed lest there might be things here hidden which would make him miserable did he understand.

" Mrs. Herman insists that she is a Puritan," Mrs. Fenton said a moment later. " You see how she proves it by the position she takes on all these questions."

" Of course I am a Puritan," was the answer. " I was born so. There is nothing which I believe that would n't have seemed to my forefathers good ground for having me whipped at the cart's tail, but I am Puritan to the bone."

" I don't see what you mean," Candish said.

" I mean that I inherit, like all of us children of the Puritans, the way of looking at things without regard to consequences, of feeling devoutly about whatever seems to us true, and of realizing that individual preferences do not alter the laws of the universe ; is n't that the essence of Puritanism ? "

" Perhaps," he answered ; " but are the unbelievers of to-day devout ? "

Ashe looked at his cousin as she paused before answering. He felt that the question must baffle her. He did not comprehend what was behind her faint smile.

"Certainly not all of them," was her reply. "The age is n't greatly given to reverence. I am a Puritan, however, and I must say what I think. I believe that there is a hundredfold more devoutness in the infidelity of New England to-day than in its belief."

Ashe leaned forward in amazement, half overturning his glass in his eagerness.

"Why, that is a contradiction of terms," he exclaimed.

Mrs. Herman's smile deepened.

"Not necessarily, Cousin Philip," returned she. "It is possible for belief to degenerate into mere conventionality, while sincere doubters at least must have a realization of the mystery and the awe which overshadow life."

Mrs. Fenton put up her hand in a pretty gesture of deprecation.

"Come," she said, "I don't wish to be despotic, but I can't let Mrs. Herman lead you into a discussion of that sort. We 'll talk of something else."

"Am I to bear the blame of it all?" demanded Helen. "That I call genuinely theological."

"Worse and worse," the hostess responded. "Now you attack the cloth."

"It seems to me," observed Mr. Candish, coming out of a brief study in which he had apparently not heard Mrs. Fenton's last words, "that you leave out of account the matter of desire. The believer at least longs to believe, and surely deserves well for that."

"I don't see why. Certainly he has n't learned the

first word of the philosophy of life who still confounds what he desires and what he deserves."

" Come, Helen," put in Mrs. Fenton; " I would n't have suspected you of trying to pose as a belated remnant of the Concord School."

Ashe easily perceived that the hostess was becoming more and more uneasy at the course of the discussion. He could see too that Mr. Candish was growing graver, and his sallow face beginning to flush through its thin skin. It was evident that Mrs. Fenton saw and appreciated these signs, and wished to change the subject of conversation. Philip wondered that she took the matter so gravely, but cast about in his own mind for the means of helping her. Before he could think of anything to say his cousin had started a fresh topic.

" By the way," she asked, " who is to be bishop?"

Candish shook his head with a grave smile.

" We should be relieved if we knew," was his answer.

" There's a great deal being done to defeat Father Frontford," Ashe added; " but the lay delegates have n't been chosen."

" The friends of Mr. Strathmore are working very hard," observed Mrs. Fenton. " It would be a great misfortune if they were to succeed."

" But I suppose the friends of Father Frontford are at work too?" returned Helen.

Ashe thought that he detected a faint trace of satire in her voice, and he turned toward her with earnest gravity.

" It is not to be supposed," he answered, " that the friends of the church are idle at a time of so much importance. Mr. Strathmore is really little better than a Unitarian; or at least he is so lax that he gives the world that opinion."

He felt that this was a reply which must end all inclination to raillery on her part. He began to feel fresh sympathy with the disturbance of Mr. Candish earlier in the dinner. The matter now was to him so vital that he could not talk of it except with the greatest gravity. He watched Helen closely to discover if she were disposed to smile at his reply. He could detect no ridicule in her expression, although she did not seem much impressed with the weight of the charge he had brought against Mr. Strathmore, the popular candidate for the bishopric of the diocese, then vacant.

"Mrs. Chauncy Wilson is doing a good deal," Mrs. Fenton remarked, glancing smilingly at Helen.

"Oh, yes," responded the other. "I remember now that she declined to be on a committee for the picture-show because, as she said, she had to run the campaign for the bishop."

"The expression," Candish began, rather stiffly, "is somewhat" —

"It is hers, not mine," Helen replied. "I should not have chosen the phrase myself."

"It is singular," Mrs. Fenton said thoughtfully, "how little general interest there is in this matter of the choice of a bishop."

"And what there is," Mrs. Herman put in with a faint suspicion of raillery in her tone, "comes from the fact that Mr. Strathmore is popular as a radical."

"It is natural enough that the general public should look at it in that way," Mr. Candish commented. "Mr. Strathmore has all the elements of popularity. He is emotional and sympathetic; and religious laxity presented by such a man is always attractive."

"The infidelity of the age finds such a man a living excuse," Ashe said, feeling to the full all that the words implied.

Mrs. Fenton smiled upon him, but shook her head.

"That is a somewhat extreme view to take of it, Mr. Ashe. I think it is rather the personal attraction of the man than anything else."

The talk drifted away into more secular channels, and Ashe in time forgot for the moment that he was already almost a priest. Youth was strong in his blood, and even when a man has vowed to serve heaven by celibacy the must of desire may ferment still in his veins. A youthful ascetic has in him equally the making of a saint and a monster; and until it is decided which he is to be there will be turmoil in his soul. His newly realized love for Mrs. Fenton threw Ashe into a tumult of mingled bliss and anguish. The heart of the most simple mortal soars and exults in the sense that it loves. It may be timid, sad, despairing, but even the smart of love's denial cannot destroy the joy of love's existence. Philip felt the sting of his conscience; he looked upon his passion as no less hopeless than it was opposed to his vows; he was overshadowed by a half-conscious foresight of the pain which must arise from it; yet he swam on waves of delight such as even in his moments of religious ecstasy he had never before known. He felt his cheeks flush, and when his cousin glanced at him he dropped his eyes in the fear that they would betray his secret. He dared not look openly at Mrs. Fenton, yet from time to time he stole glances so slyly that he seemed almost to deceive himself and to conceal from his conscience the transgression.

Yet, too, he struggled. He realized at moments what he was doing, and his cheek grew pale at the idea that he was juggling with his conscience and his soul. He tried to attend to the talk, and could only succeed in listening for the sound of her voice. He kept no more hold on the conversation than was sufficient to allow him to put in a word now and then to cover his preoccupation. The instinct of simulation asserted itself as it springs in a bird which flies away to decoy the hunter from its nest. He feigned to be interested, to be as usual, but all his blood was trembling and tumbling with this new delirium ; and all struggles to forget his passion only increased its intensity.

At moments he was astonished at himself. He could not understand what had taken possession of him. He even whispered a desperate question to himself whether it might not be that he had been singled out for a special temptation of the devil, — a distinction too flattering to be wholly disagreeable. Then he glanced again at his hostess, fair, sweet, and to his mind sacred before him, and felt that he had wronged her by supposing that the arch fiend could make of her a temptation. He had for a moment a humiliating fear that he might have eaten something that after the spare diet of the Clergy House had exhilarated him unduly. He felt that at best he was a poor thing; and he seemed to stand outside of his bare, empty life, pitying and scorning the futility of an existence unblessed by the love of this peerless woman.

The evening went on, and Ashe struggled to conceal the wild commotion of his mind, feeling it almost a relief to get away, so fearful had he been of losing control of his tumultuous emotions. It would be bliss to be alone with his dream.

As he and Mrs. Herman were going home, Helen
said : —

"I do wonder" —

"What do you wonder?" he asked.

"Did I say that out loud?" she responded. "I
did n't mean to. I was thinking that I could n't help
wondering whether Edith Fenton will ever marry Mr.
Candish."

The first thought of Ashe was terror lest his secret
had been discovered; his second was a memory of
the way in which he had seen Mrs. Fenton look at the
rector at dinner. He was overwhelmed by a rush of
hot anger against his rival.

"Mr. Candish!" he echoed. "Why, he is an or-
dained priest!"

His own words cut him like a sword. He had himself pronounced the death sentence of his own hope.
It was with difficulty that he suppressed a groan, and
what reply or comment Mrs. Herman made was lost
in the tumult of an inner voice crying in his heart:
"O thou, to the arch of whose eyebrow the new
moon is a slave!"

V

VOLUBLE AND SHARP DISCOURSE
Comedy of Errors, ii. 1

ON the morning after the dinner at Mrs. Fenton's, Philip Ashe and Maurice Wynne met on the steps of Mrs. Chauncy Wilson's. The house was on the proper side of the Avenue, with a regal front of marble and with balconies of wrought iron before the wide windows above, one of especially elaborate workmanship, having once adorned the front of the palace of the Tuileries. Pillars of verd antique stood on either side of the doorway, as if it were the portal of a temple.

"Good morning, Phil," Maurice called out as they met. "Are you bound for Mrs. Wilson's too?"

"Yes," was the answer. "I had a note last night."

"Well," Wynne said gayly, as they mounted the steps, "if the inside of the house is as splendid as the outside, we two poor duffers will be out of place enough in it."

Ashe smiled.

"You may be a duffer if you like," he retorted, "but I'm not."

"Here comes somebody," was the reply. "For my part I'm half afraid of Mrs. Wilson. They say"—

But the door began to move on its hinges, and cut short his words.

Wynne might have concluded his remark in almost any fashion, for there were few things which had not been said about Mrs. Wilson. Although she had been born and bred in Boston, one of the most common comments upon her was that she was " so un-Bostonian." Exactly what the epithet "Bostonian" might mean would probably have been hard to explain, but it is seldom difficult to defend a negation; it was at least easy to show that the lady did not regard the traditions in which she had been nourished, and that she had a boldness which was as far as possible from the decorous conventionality to be expected of one in whose veins ran the blood of the most correctly exclusive old Puritan families.

There was a general feeling that Mrs. Wilson's marriage was to be held accountable for many of her eccentricities; although, as Mrs. Staggchase remarked, if Elsie Dimmont had not been what she was she would not have chosen Chauncy Wilson. Wellborn, wealthy, pretty, and not without a certain cleverness, Miss Dimmont had had choice of suitors enough who were all that the most exacting of her relatives could desire; yet she had disregarded the conviction of the family that it was her duty to marry to please them, and had chosen to please herself by selecting a handsome young doctor whom she met at the house of a cousin in the country. He was of some local eminence in his profession, it is true, although as time went on he gave less attention to it; he was handsome, and astute, and amusing; but he was a man without ancestors or traditions. He seemed born to justify the saying that nothing subdues the feminine imagination like force; and although the stormy times which were liberally predicted at the marriage of two creatures so strong-willed had undoubtedly marked their marital career, it was in the end impossible not to see that Dr. Wilson had secured and held command of his household.

It is impossible for two to live together, however, without mutual reaction, and Elsie had unquestionably lost something of the fineness of the breeding which was hers by right of birth. For a time after her marriage she had been excessively given up to gayety. She had figured as a leader in the fastest of the "smart set," as society journals called it. She rode well, owned a stud which could not be matched in town, and raced for stakes which startled the conservative old city. It was even affirmed by the more credulous or more scandalous of the gossips that it was only the stand taken by the managers of the County Club which prevented her on one occasion from riding as her own jockey; and short of this there was little she did not do.

All this, however, was in the early days of the marriage, before Dr. Wilson had become accustomed to his position as husband of the richest woman in town and a member of what was to him the sacred aristocracy. When the time came that he had found his place and entered his veto upon these wild doings, there was an instant and determined revolt on the part of his wife. Elsie fought desperately to maintain her position as head of the family. By way of humiliating her husband she flirted with an openness which won for her a reputation by no means to be envied, and she wantonly trampled on his wishes. Given a husband, however, with an iron will and a fibre not too fine, with a good temper and yet with a certain ruthlessness in asserting his sway, and there

is little doubt that in the end he will triumph. If a
clever, handsome, good-humored man does not subdue a wild, headstrong wife, it is almost surely owing
to over-delicacy; and Chauncy Wilson was never
hampered by this. Elsie plunged and reared when
she felt the curb,—to use a figure which in those
days might have been her own,—but she was by a
judicious application of whip and spur taught that
she had found her master. The result was that she
became not only manageable, but devotedly fond of
her husband. No woman was ever mastered and
treated with kindness who did not thereupon love.
Dr. Wilson was too good-natured to be unkind, and
for the most part he allowed his wife to have her way,
fully aware that he had but to speak to restrain her;
and thus it came about that the household was on a
most peaceful and satisfactory basis.

Mrs. Wilson, however, craved excitement, and ethical amusements she laughed to scorn. She did, it is
true, take up high-church piety, which she treated, as
Mrs. Staggchase did not hesitate to say, as a play-
thing; but her interest in church matters was chiefly
in the line of politics. She took charge of the affairs
of the Church of the Nativity with a high hand which
abashed and disquieted the devout rector. She liked
Mr. Candish, although she did not hesitate to jest at
his unpolished manners and rather unprepossessing
person, and it was inevitable that she should be unable to appreciate his self-denying devotion. On one
or two occasions she had found him to have a will
not inferior to her own; and although she resented
whatever balked her pleasure, she was yet a woman
and respected power in a man.

Mr. Candish was of all men the one least resembling the traditional pastor of a fashionable church, and had nothing of the caressing manner dear to the souls of self-pampered penitents. Fashionable women found little to admire in this man with the air of a bourgeois and the simplicity of a babe. He had, however, a strong will, and a sure faith which was not without its effect upon his parishioners. Ladies whose religion was largely an affair of nerves found comfort in relying upon his simple and untroubled devotion. They were piqued by being treated as souls rather than bodies, but this was perhaps one of the secrets of his influence. Every woman of his flock had unconsciously some secret conviction that to her was reserved the triumph of subduing this intractable nature, hitherto unconquered by the fascinations of the sex. An ugly man may generally be successful with women if he remains sufficiently indifferent to them. His unattractiveness, suggesting, as it must, the idea of his having cause to be especially solicitous and humble, imparts to his attitude in such a case an all-subduing flavor of mystery. The instinctive belief of the other sex is that he is but protecting his sensitiveness, and each longs to tear aside the veil of dissimulation. The rector, it may be added, was an eloquent preacher, and he intoned the service wonderfully. His voice in speaking was somewhat harsh, but when he intoned, it melted into a beautiful baritone, rich, full, and sweet, which, informed by his deep and earnest feeling, thrilled his hearers with profound emotion. Mrs. Wilson was proud of the effect which the service at the Nativity always had, and she took in it the double pleasure of one who claimed a share in religious enthusiasms and who had something of the glory of a manager whose tenor succeeds in opera.

Into the contest over the election of a bishop to fill
the place recently left vacant Mrs. Wilson had thrown
herself with characteristic vigor. There were but
two candidates now seriously considered, the Rev.
Rutherford Strathmore and Father Frontford. The
former, a popular preacher of liberal views, was
regarded as the more likely to receive the appointment, but the High Church party contested the point
warmly, supporting the claims of the Father Superior
of the Clergy House which was the home of Maurice
Wynne and Philip Ashe. The political side of the
matter was exactly to Mrs. Wilson's taste. A woman
has but to be rich enough and determined enough to
be allowed to amuse herself with the highest concerns
of both church and state; and Mrs. Wilson lacked
neither money nor determination. Her vigor at first
disconcerted and in the end outwardly subdued the
clergy. If she actually had less influence than she
supposed, she was at least thoroughly entertained, and
that after all was her object. She interviewed influential persons, she wrote letters, some of them sufficiently ill-judged, she sought information in regard to
the character and circumstances of the clergy in the
diocese, and did everything with the zeal and dash
which characterized whatever she undertook.

"Have you any idea what Mrs. Wilson wants of
us?" Wynne asked of Philip, as they waited in the
luxurious reception-room.

"I only know that Father Frontford said that we
were to put ourselves under her orders," was the reply. "Of course it is something about the election."

Maurice looked at him keenly.

"Old fellow," he said, "you look pale. What's
the matter with you?"

"I did n't sleep well," Ashe answered with a flush. "I went to Mrs. Fenton's to dine, and the indulgence was n't good for me. It 's really nothing."

Maurice did not reply, but sank into an easy-chair and looked about him. The room was a charming fancy of the decorator, who claimed to have taken his inspiration from the American mullein. The ceiling was of a pale, almost transparent blue, a tint just strong enough to suggest a sky and yet leave it half doubtful if such a meaning were intended; the walls were hung with a rough paper matching in hue the velvety leaves of the plant, here and there touched with conventionalized figures of the yellow blossoms. This contrast of green and yellow was softened and united by a clever use of the clear red of the mullein stamens sparingly used in the figures on the walls, in the cords of the draperies, and in the trimmings of the velvet furniture. The decorator had used the same simple tone for walls, furniture, and curtains; and the effect was delightfully soothing and distinguished.

Wynne felt somehow out of place in this room which bore the stamp of wealth and taste so markedly. He smiled to himself a little bitterly, recalling how alien he was to these things. Descended from a family for generations established in a New England town, he had in his veins too good blood to feel abashed at the sight of splendors; but he had in his life seen little of the world outside of lecture-rooms or the Clergy House. Born with the appreciation of sensuous delight, with the instinctive desire for the beautiful and refined, he felt awake within him at contact with the richness and luxury of the life which he was now leading tastes which he had before hardly been aware of possessing. He was being influenced by the joy of worldly life, so subtly presented that he did not even appreciate the need of guarding against the danger.

His reflections were cut short by the entrance of a servant who conducted the young men to a private sitting-room up-stairs. The halls through which they passed were hung with superb old tapestry, interspersed with magnificent pictures. On the broad landing it was almost as if the visitors came into the presence of a beautiful woman, lying naked amid bright cushions in an oriental interior. As he dropped his eyes from the alluring vision, Maurice saw in the corner the name of the artist.

" Fenton," he said aloud. " Did he paint that?"

His companion started, regarding the picture with widening eyes. The English footman, whom Wynne addressed, turned back to say over his shoulder : —

" Yes, sir ; they say it's his best picture, and some says he painted his best friend's wife that way, with nothing on, sir."

" It is a wicked picture !" Ashe said with what seemed to Maurice unnecessary emphasis.

The footman regarded the speaker over his shoulder with a smile.

" Oh, that's owin' to your bein' of the cloth, sir," was his comment. " They don't generally feel to own to likin' it ; but they mostly notices it."

A superb screen of carved and gilded wood stood before an open door above. When this was reached, the footman slipped noiselessly behind it, and they heard their names announced.

" Show them in," Mrs. Wilson's voice said.

The lady met them in a wonderful morning gown which seemed to be chiefly cascades of lace, with bows

of carmine ribbon here and there which brought out
the color of the dark eyes and hair of the wearer.
Maurice could hardly have told why he flushed, yet
he was conscious of the feeling that there was something intimate in the costume. To be met by this
beautiful woman, her hand outstretched in greeting,
her eyes shining, her white neck rising out of the
foam of laces ; to breathe the air, soft and perfumed,
of this room ; to be surrounded by this luxury, these
tokens of a life which stinted nothing in the pursuit
of enjoyment ; more than all to appreciate by some
subtle inner sense the appealing charm of femininity,
the suggestions of domestic intimacies ; all this was to
the young deacon to be exposed to influences far more
formidable to the ascetic life than those grosser temptations with which a stupid fiend assailed St. Anthony.
Wynne drew a deep breath, wondering why he felt
so strangely moved and confused ; yet unconsciously
steeling himself against owning to his conscience
what was the truth.

"It is so good of you to come early," Mrs. Wilson
said brightly. "I hope you don't mind coming upstairs. I wanted to talk to you confidentially, and we
might be interrupted. Besides, you see, I am not
dressed to go down."

The young men murmured something to the effect
that they did not in the least mind coming up.

"Didn't mind coming up!" she echoed. "Is that
the way you answer a lady who gives you the privilege
of her private sitting-room ? Come, you must do
better than that. If you can't compliment me on my
frock, you might at least say that you are proud to be
here."

The two deacons stood awkwardly in the middle of

the room, abashed at her raillery. Maurice saw the lips of Ashe harden, and he hastened to speak lest his companion should say something stern.

"You should remember, Mrs. Wilson," he said a little timidly, yet not without a gleam of humor, "that our curriculum at the Clergy House does not include a course in compliment."

"It should then," she responded gayly. "How in the world is a clergyman to get on with the women of his congregation if he can't compliment? Why, the salvation or the damnation of most women is determined by compliments."

The visitors stood speechless. Mrs. Wilson broke into a gleeful laugh.

"Come," cried she; "now I have shocked you! Pardon me; I should have remembered — *virginibus puerisque!* Sit down, and we will come to business."

Both the young men flushed at her half-contemptuous, half-jesting phrase, but they sat down as directed. Mrs. Wilson took her seat directly in front of them, and proceeded to inspect them with cool deliberation.

"I am looking you over," she observed calmly. "I must decide what work you are fitted for before I can assign anything to you."

Two young men do not live together so intimately, and care for each other so tenderly as did the two deacons without coming to know each other well; and Maurice was so fully aware of the extreme sensitiveness of Ashe that he involuntarily glanced at his friend to see how he bore this inspection. He resented the impertinence of the scrutiny far more on Philip's account than his own. Ashe's pale face had on it the faintest possible flush, and his always grave manner had become really solemn; but otherwise he made no sign. Wynne had a certain sense of humor which helped him through the ordeal, and there was a faint gleam of a smile in his eye as he confronted the brilliant woman before him; but he was ill-pleased that his friend should be made uncomfortable.

"Do you judge by outward appearances," he asked, "or have you power to read the heart?"

"Men so seldom have hearts," she retorted, "that it is not worth while to bother with that branch." Then she added, as if thinking aloud, and looking Ashe in the face: "You are an enthusiast, and take things with frightful seriousness. You must see Mrs. Frostwinch. You'll just suit her."

Maurice could see his companion shrink under this cool directness, and he hastened to interpose.

"But Mrs. Frostwinch," he said, "is absorbed in Christian Science or something, is n't she?"

"Oh, dear, yes," Mrs. Wilson answered, toying with the broad crimson ribbon which served her as a girdle. "There is a horrid woman named Trapps, or Grapps, or Crapps, or something, that has fastened herself upon cousin Anna, and is mind-curing her, or Christian-sciencing her, or fooling her in some way; but Mrs. Frostwinch is too well-bred really to have any sympathy with anything so vulgar. She takes to it in desperation; but she really detests the whole thing."

"But," Ashe began hesitatingly, "does her conscience" —

Mrs. Wilson laughed, making a gesture as if sweeping all that sort of thing aside.

"I dare say her conscience pricks her, if that's what you mean; but it's so much easier to endure the sting of conscience than of cancer that I'm not surprised at her choice."

"Besides," Maurice put in, "this is all done nowadays under the name of religion. It isn't as if it were called by the old names of mesmerism or Indian doctoring."

"That's true enough," assented she. "At any rate Anna is mixed up with this woman, who gets a lot of money out of her, and earns it by making her think that she's better. However, Cousin Anna must be made to see that it's her duty in this case to use her influence to prevent the election of a man who would subvert the church if he could."

"But if you are her cousin," Ashe began, "would it not"—

"Be better if I went to see her myself? Not in the least. She entirely disapproves of my having anything to do with the election. Besides, nobody can successfully talk religion to a woman but a man."

Maurice smiled in spite of himself at the air with which this was said, but he none the less felt that Mrs. Wilson was flippant.

"What influence has Mrs. Frostwinch?" he asked.

"Well," Mrs. Wilson answered, leaning back to consider, "I don't know whether to say that she controls three votes in the upper house of the Convention, or four."

The two young men regarded her in puzzled silence.

"There are at least three clergymen in the diocese that are dependent upon her," Mrs. Wilson explained. "There is Mr. Robbins: he married her cousin,— not a near cousin, but near enough so that Anna has half supported the family, and the family is always increasing. I tell Anna that they have babies just to work on her compassion. I think it's wrong to

encourage it, myself. Then there is Mr. Maloon; he
depends on Mrs. Frostwinch to support his mission.
Then there's Brother Pewtap, — did you ever know
such a lovely name for a country parson? — he just
lives on her with a family bigger than Mr. Robbins's.
He's really a Strathmore man, but he would n't dare
to vote against her wishes. She might manage all
those votes. Besides, there's a Mr. Jewett somewhere
near Lenox that she's helped a good deal; but I
have n't found out about him yet."

She rose as she spoke, and went to a writing-table
fitted out with all the inventions known to man for
the decoration of the desk and the encumbrance of
the writer.

"I have here a list of all the clergy of the diocese,"
she said, taking up a book bound in red morocco and
silver. "I've marked them down as far as I've
found out about them. It's necessary to be system-
atic. I've done just as they do in canvassing a city
ward."

Maurice regarded Mrs. Wilson with ever-increasing
amazement, but, too, not without increasing amusement. He was somewhat shocked by the business
way in which she treated the subject, but his heart
was set on the election of Father Frontford; he was
honest in feeling that the church would be injured by
the election of Mr. Strathmore, and he was too completely a man not to be half-unconsciously willing that
for the accomplishment of an end he desired a woman
should do many things which he would not do himself.
The three went over the list together, the young men
giving such information as they possessed, Maurice all
the time strangely divided in his mind between disapprobation of Mrs. Wilson and admiration. Her

breath was on his cheek as she bent over the book, the perfume of her laces filled faintly the air, now and then her hand touched his. He was not conscious of the potency of this feminine atmosphere which enveloped him; he did not so much think personally of Mrs. Wilson, beautiful and near though she was, as he felt her presence as a sort of impersonation of woman. He thought of Miss Morison, and warmed with a nameless thrill of longing. Then he recalled the remark of Mrs. Staggchase that he was undergoing his temptation, and his heart sank.

"You see," Mrs. Wilson was saying, when he forced his wandering attention to heed her words, "men are really elected before the convention. The work must be done now. You two can, of course, do a lot of things that it would n't be good form for a regular clergyman to do. Of course you would n't be able to manage the directing, but there is a good deal of work that is in your line."

"Of course we are glad to do what we can," Maurice responded, smiling.

He glanced at Ashe and saw that his friend's face was stern.

"I knew you would be," the lady went on. "Mr. Ashe is to see Mrs. Frostwinch. You can't be too eloquent in telling her the consequences of Mr. Strathmore's election. If you can get her to write to the men I 've named, she can secure them. It won't be amiss to flatter her a little; and above all don't abuse the faith-cure business."

"But if she speaks of it," Ashe returned hesitatingly, "what am I to do?"

"Oh, she 'll be sure to speak of it; but you must manage to evade. Let her say, and don't you contra-

, dict. She 'll say enough, I 've no doubt. Very likely she 'll abuse it herself; but don't for goodness' sake make the mistake of falling in with her. If you do, it 'll be fatal."

"But I know Mrs. Frostwinch so slightly," Philip objected, "that I do not see " —

"Come!" she interrupted; "there is to be none of this. You are under my orders. I 'll give you a letter to Cousin Anna now."

" But " —

"But! But what?" she cried, laughing. "Do you mean that you distrust your leader so soon? Do I look like a woman to fail?"

She spread out her arms in a gesture half imploring, half jocose, her laces fluttering, her ribbons waving, the ringlets about her face dancing. Her eyes were brimming with mocking light, and however poorly she might seem to represent ideas theological she certainly did not personify failure.

Maurice laughed lightly and glanced at his friend. Ashe did not smile, but he bowed as if in resignation to the command of a leader.

"You are to go to Mrs. Frostwinch's this very afternoon," Mrs. Wilson declared. "It won't do to lose any time. If once her votes get pledged to the other party, there 's an end to that. That 's your work. Now you," she continued, turning to Wynne, " are to go to Springfield and the western part of the State."

" The western part of the State?" Maurice ejaculated in astonishment. " Do you work there too?"

"Of course we have to cover the whole diocese," she returned vivaciously. "Did you suppose we left everything but Boston to the enemy?"

He could only reply by a stare. He had never in his life encountered anything like this woman, and he was bewildered by her audacity, her alertness, her beauty, and the dash with which she carried everything off.

"You will go to-morrow," she went on, "and I will send you the list of the men you have to see. I'm sorry not to go over it with you, but I have an engagement this morning, and I shall be late now. You are staying with Mrs. Staggchase, are n't you?"

"Yes; she is my cousin."

"So much the better for you. It's a liberal education to have a cousin as clever as that. Good-by. Thank you both for coming."

She rang as she spoke, and handed the young men over to the maid who appeared; the maid in turn handed them over to the footman, and by him they were seen safely out of the house. As they turned away from the door, Ashe sighed deeply, while Wynne was smiling to himself.

"What a — a — what a woman!" Philip said fervently. "She 's amazing!"

"Oh, yes," his friend laughed; "but what do you or I know about women anyway?"

VI

As Philip Ashe, his eyes cast down in earnest thought, approached Mrs. Frostwinch's gate that afternoon, he looked up suddenly to find himself face to face with Mrs. Fenton. She was dressed in dark, heavy cloth, set down the waist with small antique buckles of dark silver; and seemed to him the perfection of elegance and beauty.

"Good morning, Mr. Ashe," she greeted him, smiling. "I did not expect to find you coming to hear Mrs. Crapps."

"To hear Mrs. Crapps?" he echoed. "Who is Mrs. Crapps?"

Mrs. Fenton turned back as she was entering the iron gate which between stately stone posts shut off the domain of the Frostwinches from the world, and marked with dignity the line between the dwellers on Mt. Vernon Street and the rest of the world.

"Do you mean," asked she, "that you did n't know that Mrs. Crapps, the mind-cure woman, is to lecture here this afternoon?"

Ashe drew back.

"I certainly did not know it," he answered. "I was coming to speak to Mrs. Frostwinch about the election."

"It 's the last of three lectures," Mrs. Fenton explained. "Mrs. Crapps, you know, is the woman that has been curing Mrs. Frostwinch."

Ashe stood hesitatingly silent in the gateway a
moment.

"I should like to see her," he said thoughtfully.
"Not from mere curiosity, but because I cannot understand what gives these persons a hold over intelligent men and women."

"The thing that gives her a hold over Mrs. Frostwinch is that she has raised her up from a bed of sick-
ness. Come in with me, and see her. I should like
to see how she strikes you. You can speak to Mrs.
Frostwinch after the lecture."

He hesitated a moment, and then followed her, saying to himself with suspicious emphasis that the fact
that the invitation came from her had nothing to do
with his acceptance. He soon found himself seated
in the great dusky drawing-room of the Frostwinch
house, an apartment whose very walls were incrusted
with conservative traditions. It was furnished with
richness, but both with much greater simplicity and
greater stiffness than he had seen in any of the houses
he had thus far been in. The chief decoration, one
felt, was the air of the place's having been inhabited
by generations of socially immaculate Boston ancestors. There was a savor of lineage amounting almost
to godliness in the dark, self-contained parlors; and
if pedigree were not in this dwelling imputed for
righteousness, it was evidently held in becoming reverence as the first of virtues. There are certain
houses where the atmosphere is so completely im-
pregnated with the idea of the departed as to give
a certain effect as a spiritual morgue; and in the
drawing-room of Mrs. Frostwinch there was a good
deal of this flavor of defunct, but by no means departed, merit. Grim portraits stared coldly from the

walls, Copleys that would have looked upon a Stuart as parvenu; the Frostwinch and Canton arms hung over the ends of the mantel; while the very furniture seemed to condescend to visitors. Ashe could not have told why the place affected him as overpowering, but he none the less was conscious of the feeling. The company was apparently nearly all assembled when he came in, and he sank down into a chair in a corner, glad to escape observation.

The speaker of the afternoon was already in her place when he entered, and he examined her with curiosity. She was a woman who might have been forty years of age, with a hard, eager, alert face; her forehead was narrow, her lips thin and straight, her nostrils cut too high. Her eyes were bold and sharp, dominating her face, and fixing upon the hearers the look of a bird of prey. Mrs. Crapps's hair was tinged with gray, and in her whole appearance there was a sharpness which seemed to speak of one who had battled with the world. Ashe was struck by the personality of the woman, yet strongly repelled. She was evidently a creature of abundant vitality, and exultantly dominant of will. The bold, black eyes sparkled with determination, and he could at once understand that Mrs. Crapps was one to establish easily an influence over any nature naturally weak or debilitated by disease.

Ashe listened with curiosity to the opening of the address. The voice of the speaker had much of the vivacity of her glance. She spoke with an air of candor and frankness, and yet Philip found himself distrusting her from the outset. He said to himself that it was because he was prejudiced, that he doubted; but he yet felt that her manner would in

any case have begotten repulsion. She had that air
of insistence, of determination to be believed, which
belongs to the speaker who is absorbed rather in the
desire to prevail than in the wish to be true. He felt
that her air of conviction was no proof of her conception of the truth of what she was saying; she protested too much. He was at first so absorbed in
watching the woman that he paid little heed to her
theories; but he soon began to flush with indignation.
This woman, with her bold air and masculine domi-
nance, sat there talking of herself as a present incarnation of Christ; of Christ as the incarnation of
the human will; of disease as a sin; and of death as
a mere figment of the imagination. The paganism of
the Persian as he had heard it at Mrs. Gore's seemed
to him less offensive than this. He moved uneasily
in his seat, his cheeks flushing, and his lips pressed
together. Presently he felt the glance of Mrs. Fenton, who sat near him, and looking up he encountered
her eyes. She seemed to him to show sympathy with
his feeling, but to remind him that this was not the
time or place for protest. He regained instantly his
self-control, and perhaps from that time on thought
less of Mrs. Crapps than of his neighbor.

The talk of Mrs. Crapps was commonplace enough,
and hackneyed enough, could Ashe but have known
it. There was the usual patter about spiritual and
physical freedom, about faith and perfection, "the
Deific principle as a rule of health," a jumble of
things medical and things physical, things profane
and things holy mingled in a strange and unintelligible jargon. By the time that the eager-eyed speaker
had talked for an hour Ashe felt his mind to be in
confusion, and he could not but feel that not a few

of the hearers must be in a state of utter mental bewilderment if the address had impressed at all.

"The end of the whole matter is," Mrs. Crapps said in closing, " that mankind has for ages submitted to this cruel superstition of death. We have bowed ourselves beneath the wheels of this Juggernant; we have sent to the dark tomb our best loved friends ; we crouch and cower in awful fear of the time when we shall follow. We hear ever thrilling in our ears the quivering minor chord of human woe, voice of the burning heart-pain of the race, launched rudderless upon a troubled sea of woe, and undrowned even by the throbbing march-beats of the progression of man down the vista of the ages. And yet there is no death. This fear is only the terror of children frightened by ghosts of their own invention. What we dread has no existence save in the fevered and fancyfed fear of blinded men. O my hearers, why can we not seize upon the hem of this truth which the Messiah came to teach ! Death is but sin ; and sin has been removed by atonement ; the holiness of the soul is immortal. There is, there can be no death ! Receive the glad tidings, and cry it aloud ! There is no death ! Let all the earth hear, until there is none so base, so low, so poor, so ignorant, so sinful that he shall not be immortal. It is his birthright, for we are all born to eternal life."

The voice of Mrs. Crapps took on a more persuasive inflection as she delivered this peroration ; and it was easy to see that she had affected the nerves if not the minds of her audience. There was a deep hush as she concluded. She lifted for a moment her sharp black eyes toward heaven, and then dropped her glance to earth, as if overcome by feeling, or as if with

awe she had caught sight of sacred mysteries which
it was not lawful to look upon. In a moment more
she raised her eyes, and invited any of her hearers to
question her about anything connected with the subject
which troubled them. For a breathing time there was
silence, and then a lady asked with a puzzled air : —

" But do you Christian Scientists deny " —

" I beg your pardon," Mrs. Crapps interrupted,
leaning forward with a deprecatory smile, " but I am
not a Christian Scientist."

" I mean do you Faith Healers " —

" That is not our title," Mrs. Crapps said with
gentle insistence.

" Are you called Mind Curers, then ? "

" No," the priestess responded, with an air lofty yet
condescending ; " with those forms of error we have
no dealing or sympathy. It is true that those who
teach faith-healing, mind-cure, or any sort of religious
rejuvenance, have in part taken our high tenets ; but
they have in each case obscured them by errors and
follies of their own. We are the Christian Faith
Healed, — not healers, you will observe, because we
believe that all mankind are really healed, and that
all that is needed is that they recognize and acknowledge this precious truth."

The ladies present looked at one another in some
confusion, and Ashe caught in the eyes of Mrs. Staggchase, who sat half facing him, a gleam of amusement.
This emboldened him to repeat the question which
had been abandoned by its first asker, who had evidently been overwhelmed by the delicacy of the distinction of sects made by Mrs. Crapps.

" Do you then," he asked, " deny the existence of
death ? "

" Utterly," the seeress returned, bending upon him a bold look as if to challenge him to differ from what she asserted. " It is as amazing as it is melancholy that mankind should have submitted to the indignity of death so long."

" How can they submit to that which does not exist ? "

" It exists in seeming, but not in reality."

A murmur ran through the company, and Philip met the eyes of Mrs. Fenton, who shook her head slightly, as who would say that discussion was futile.

" But — but how " — one hearer began falteringly, and then stopped, evidently too overwhelmed by the astounding nature of the proposition laid down to be able even to frame a question.

" Indeed," Mrs. Crapps said, taking up the word, " we may well ask how. It transcends the incredible that the monstrous delusion of death should ever have been entertained for an instant. The explanation lies in sin. Death is but the projection of a sin-burdened conscience upon the mists of the unknown. Thank God that it has been given to our generation to tear away the veil from this falsehood, and to recognize the absolute unreality of the phantom which the ignorance and superstition of guilty humanity have conjured up."

The smooth, deliberate voice of Mrs. Staggchase broke the silence which this declaration produced.

" It is then your idea that death comes entirely from the belief of mankind ? "

" What we call death undoubtedly has that origin," Mrs. Crapps answered.

" How then could so extraordinary a delusion have had a beginning ? "

A faint shade crossed the face of the seeress, but it merged instantly into a smile of patient superiority.

" That is the question unbelief always asks," she said. " It seems so difficult to answer, and yet it is really so simple. The idea of death of course arose from a distorted projection of the condition of sleep upon the diseased imagination. With sin came the bewilderment of human reason, and the delusion followed as an inevitable morbid growth."

" Then the earlier generations of mankind were immortal ? "

" Undoubtedly. We have traces of the fact in all the old mythologies."

" But what became of them ? "

" Once the idea of death had entered the world," Mrs. Crapps said impressively, " it spread like the plague until it had infected all mankind. Even those who had lived for ages to prove it false were not able to resist the prevalence of the thing they knew to be untrue, — any more," she added, dropping her eyes, and speaking in a tone sad and patient, " than we who to-day understand that there is no such thing as death can resist the overwhelming power of the belief of the masses of the race. The might of the will of the majority, directed by an appalling delusion, compels us to submit to that which we yet know to be an unreality."

Again there was a hush. The woman was appealing to the most fundamental facts of human experience and the most poignant emotions of human life, and boldly denying or confounding both. It seemed to Ashe that the only possible answer to such talk was an accusation either of madness or blasphemy. The silence was once more broken by Mrs. Staggchase.

"But if there is no such thing as death," she observed, with the faintest touch of irony perceptible in her well-bred voice, "of course you do not really die; and since you do not share the general delusion in thinking yourselves to be dead, it would seem to follow that although you may be dead for the world in general, you are still immortal for yourselves and each other."

The black eyes of Mrs. Crapps sparkled, but she controlled herself, and shook her head with an air of gentle remonstrance.

"It proves how strong is the hold upon mankind of this delusion," she said, "that what I tell you appears incredible. The truth is always incredible, because the blind eyes of humanity can see only half-truths except by great effort. I have tried to enlighten you, and I can do no more. It is for you and not for myself that I speak."

She rose from her chair, which seemed to be the signal for the breaking up of the assembly, and that her cleverness in securing the last word was not without its effect was apparent by the murmurs of the company. In another moment, however, Ashe heard as at Mrs. Gore's the exchange of greetings and bits of news, the making of appointments for shopping or theatre-going, and all the trivial chat of daily life. He stood aside until the crowd should thin, and in the mean time had the felicity of being near Mrs. Fenton. He began to feel himself almost overcome by the delight of being so near her, of meeting her clear glance, frank and sympathetic, of hearing her voice, of noting the ripples of her hair, the curve of nostril and neck. He was like a boy in the first budding of passion before reason has softened the extravagance of his feeling.

The talk of the afternoon, his indignation at the words of Mrs. Crapps, his feeling that he had been assisting at a sacrament of impiety, were all forgotten as he stood talking to his neighbor.

"Come," she said at length, "I must speak to Mrs. Frostwinch before I go."

He bent forward to remove a chair which was in her way, and her gloved hand brushed against his. He covered the spot with his other hand as if he would preserve the precious touch.

"I found Mr. Ashe at the door," Mrs. Fenton said to the hostess, "and I would not let him turn back. I was too much interested in his errand."

"I am sorry if he needed urging to come in," Mrs. Frostwinch responded with graceful courtesy; "but what was the errand?"

"Mrs. Wilson asked me to see you in relation to the election," Ashe answered.

"Elsie is having a beautiful time managing this election," commented Mrs. Frostwinch. "She has n't been so amused for a long time. She thinks Father Frontford is a puppet in her hands, while he knows that she is one in his."

"I hope," Mrs. Fenton put in, "that you may be able to help Mr. Ashe. I can answer for it that he is not making the matter one of amusement."

Ashe could not help flushing. He thanked her with a glance, and turned again to Mrs. Frostwinch.

"I do not know or like the electioneering of such affairs," he said gravely; "but since there is a strong effort being made on the other side it certainly seems necessary to do whatever can be done fairly."

A few last visitors who had been chatting among themselves now came forward to say good-by. Mrs.

Fenton also took leave, and Ashe found himself alone with his hostess and Mrs. Crapps.

"Mrs. Crapps, Mr. Ashe," Mrs. Frostwinch said.

It seemed to him that there was in the manner of Mrs. Frostwinch something of condescension, as if the Faith Healed was a sort of upper servant. He had himself not outlived the ingenuous period wherein a youth feels that the preservation of truth in the world depends upon his not covering his impressions, and he was accordingly extremely cold in his manner.

"Ah, a new disciple to our faith, I trust," Mrs. Crapps said, fixing upon him her keen, bold eyes.

"I have never even heard of your doctrine until to-day," he answered.

"But surely it must strike you at once," she responded, with a manner evidently meant to be insinuating.

He hesitated. He remembered that he had been expressly warned not to say anything against the vagaries with which Mrs. Frostwinch was concerned; but his conscience would not allow him to evade this direct challenge.

"It struck me as being blasphemous," he responded with unnecessary fervor.

Mrs. Crapps raised her eyes to the ceiling, and uttered a theatrical sigh.

"Oh, sacred truth!" she exclaimed.

"Come, Mrs. Crapps," Mrs. Frostwinch interposed almost sharply, "you know that Mr. Ashe is right. It is blasphemous, and I feel as if I'd allowed my house to be used for a sacrifice to false gods. If you will excuse us, I wish to speak with Mr. Ashe on business. Will you kindly come to the library, Mr. Ashe."

As he followed, Philip caught sight in a mirror of the face of Mrs. Crapps. It wore a singular smile, but whether of anger or contempt he could not tell.

" I dare say, Mr. Ashe," Mrs. Frostwinch remarked, as soon as they were seated in the library, " that it seems strange to you that I have that woman speak in my parlors. Of course I don't mean to apologize, but I am sorry that you should hear things that shocked you."

" Dear madam," he answered, leaning forward in his eagerness, " what I heard does not matter; but it does seem to me a pity that such things should be said, and said under your protection."

He was too much in earnest to be self-conscious, even when she regarded him in silence a moment before replying.

" You are perhaps right," she said at length, " although you exaggerate the influence of such things."

" I do not pretend to know whether they are influential or not," he returned simply. " It is only that they do not seem to me to be right. If they are wrong, they are wrong."

She smiled and sighed.

" Life is not so simple as that," was her reply. " The woman has saved my life. I should have been in my grave months ago but for her. My physician insists now that I haven't any real right to be out of it. I cannot refuse to allow her to say the thing that she believes, since that thing has a certain proof in my very life."

Philip shook his head.

" It is not for me to judge," said he, " but the way in which all sorts of heresies and strange doctrines are taught and played with in Boston seems to me monstrous. The persons of influence who lend their names and aid " —

He broke off suddenly, recalled by the half-smile in her eyes to the fact that he was condemning her.

" There is much in what you say," Mrs. Frostwinch assented. " I suppose that the difficulty is that we have ceased to recognize any authority in matters of belief."

" But the church ! "

" Yes, there is the church," she said doubtfully, " but to many it has ceased to be an authority, and modern thought allows so much individual freedom. Our church has never claimed to be infallible like the Catholic ; and individual freedom of conscience has come pretty generally to mean freedom from conscience."

" Then it is a pity that the authority which is exercised in the Roman church is not exercised in ours."

" Ah, Mr. Ashe, you reckon without the spirit of the age in which we live. But tell me what I can do for you in the matter of the election."

Mrs. Frostwinch was a devout churchwoman in her way, although she was now in appearance following after strange gods. She readily promised her aid in favor of Father Frontford.

" I agree with you, Mr. Ashe," she said, " that everything possible should be done to stem the tide of laxness which seems advancing everywhere. The mental reservations of Mr. Strathmore are certainly so broad that they may cover anything. I know women who go to his church and simply say the beginning of the creed : ' I believe in God ; ' and who do not hesitate in private to explain that by the name

God they mean whatever force it is that moves the universe, whether it is intelligent or not."

"How dreadful!" Philip exclaimed. "How can the church endure if this goes on?"

They talked for some time longer, and Mrs. Frostwinch assured him that she would do her best to secure the votes of the clergymen who were her pensioners. Ashe left her with a pleasant feeling in his heart that he had accomplished his mission without sacrificing his convictions. Yet perhaps more potent still in warming his heart was the remembrance of the pleasant words which Mrs. Fenton had spoken in his behalf. The memory colored all his thoughts of elections, of bishops, and of creeds, as a gleam of rosy light tinges all upon which it falls.

VII

"I KNEW that she was to send me tickets," Maurice Wynne said, standing with an open note in his hand. "She insisted upon that; but why should she send parlor-car checks too?"

"It is all part of your temptation," Mrs. Staggchase responded, smiling. "Of course if you go as the representative of Mrs. Wilson it is fitting that you go in state. If you were to represent the church now" —

"If I don't go as a representative of the church," he responded, as she paused with a significant smile, "I go as nothing."

"Oh, I thought that it was Elsie that was sending you. However, it's no matter. The point is that you are becoming acquainted with the luxuries of life. You are being tried by the insidious softness of the world."

He regarded her with some inward irritation. He had a half-defined conviction that she was mocking him, and that her words were more than mere badinage. He was not without a suspicion that his cousin was sometimes histrionic, and that many things which she said were to be regarded as stage talk. He did not know how far to take her seriously, and this gave him a feeling at once confused and uncomfortable. To be played with as if he were not of discernment ripe enough to perceive her raillery or as if he were not of consequence sufficient to be taken seriously, offended his vanity; and the man whom the devil cannot conquer through his vanity is invulnerable. Wynne had no answer now for the words of Mrs. Staggchase. He contented himself with a glance not entirely free from resentment, at which she laughed.

"I wonder, Cousin Maurice," she said, "if you realize how completely you have changed in the ten days you have been here. It is like bringing into light a plant that has been sprouting in the dark."

He did not answer for a moment, trying to find it possible to deny the charge.

"The fact that you know me better makes me seem different," he answered evasively.

"How much has the fact that you don't know yourself so well to do with it?"

"What do you mean?"

"Oh, anything you like. I merely suspect that you are not so sure of your vocation as you were in the Clergy House. Even a deacon is human, I suppose; and if life is alluring, he can't help feeling it. Are you still sure that the clergy should be celibate, for instance?"

He felt her eyes piercing him as if his secret thoughts were open to her, and he knew that he was flushing to his very hair. He hastened to answer, not only that he might not think, but that she might not perceive that he had admitted any doubt to his heart.

"More than ever," he responded. "It is impossible not to see that a clergyman who is married must have his thoughts distracted from his sacred calling."

Mrs. Staggchase leaned back in her chair and regarded him with the smile which he found always so puzzling and so disconcerting.

"You did that very well," she said, "only you shouldn't have put in the word 'sacred.' That made it all sound conventional. However, you probably meant it. She is distracting."

The hot blood leaped into his face so that he knew that it was utterly impossible to conceal his confusion.

"I don't know what you mean," he stammered.

Instantly his conscience reproached him with not speaking the truth. He responded to his conscience that it was impossible in circumstances like these to say the whole, and that what he had said was not untrue. He could not know what his cousin meant by her pronoun, and if the thought of Miss Morison had come instantly into his mind, it by no means followed that it was she of whom Mrs. Staggchase was thinking. Life seemed suddenly more complex than he had ever dreamed it possible; and before this remark the unsophisticated deacon became so completely confused that for the instant it was his instinctive wish to be once more safely within the sheltering walls of the Clergy House, protected from the temptations and vexations of the world. He was after all of a nature which did not yield readily, however, and the next thought was one of defiance. He would not yield up his secret, and he defied the world to drag it from him. His companion smiled upon him with the baffling look which her husband called her Mona Lisa expression, and then she laughed outright.

"My dear boy," she said, "you are no more a

priest than I am; and you are as transparent as a piece of crystal. Well, I am fond of you, and I'm glad to have a hand in proving to you that you are not meant for the priesthood before it's too late."

"But it hasn't been proved to me," he cried, not without some sternness.

"Oh, bless you, it's in train, and that's the same thing. 'Not poppy, nor mandragora, nor all the drowsy syrups of the east' could put you to sleep again in the dream you had in the Clergy House. It will take you a little longer to find yourself out, but the thing is done nevertheless."

As she spoke, a servant came to the door to announce the carriage. Mrs. Staggchase held out her hand.

"Good-by," she said, as Maurice rose, and came forward to take it. "I hope that we shall see you again in a couple of days. I have still a good deal to show you."

He had recovered his self-possession a little, and answered her with a smile: —

"You make it so delightful for me here that I am not sure you are not right in saying that you are my temptation."

"Oh, I've already given up the office of tempter," she responded quickly. "I found a rival, and that I never could endure. You'll have your temptation with you."

It seemed to Maurice when he came to take his seat in the parlor car that his cousin was little short of a witch. In the chair next to his own sat Berenice Morison. She greeted him with a friendly nod and smile.

"Mrs. Wilson told me that you were going on this

train," she said, " and she got a chair for you next to
mine so that you should take care of me."

He bowed rather confusedly, but with his heart full
of delight.

" I shall be glad to do anything I can for you," he
answered, vexed that he had not a better reply at
command.

He saw the dapper young man across the aisle regard him curiously, and a feeling of dissatisfaction
came over him as he reflected upon the singularity of
his garb, and the incongruity between the clerical
dress and the squiring of dames. Religious fervor is
nourished by martyrdom, but it is seldom proof against
ridicule. It is not impossible that the faint shade
of amusement which Maurice fancied he detected in
the eyes of the stranger opposite was a more effective
cause for discontent with his calling than any of the
influences to which he had been exposed under the
auspices of Mrs. Staggchase.

He could not help feeling, moreover, that there was
a gleam of fun in the clear dark eyes of Miss Morison.
She was so completely at ease, so entirely mistress of
the situation, that Wynne, little accustomed to the
society of women, and secretly a little disconcerted
by the surprise, felt himself at a disadvantage. It
touched his vanity that he should be smiled at by the
trimly appointed dandy opposite, and that he should
be in experience and self-possession inferior to the
girl beside him. He began vaguely to wonder what
he had been doing all his life; he reflected that he
had not in his old college days been so ill at ease, and
it annoyed him to think that two years in the Clergy
House should have put him so out of touch with the
simplest matters of life. He said to himself scorn-

fully that he was a monk already; and the thought, which would once have given him satisfaction, was now fraught with nothing but vexation and self-contempt. He had a subtile inclination to give himself up to the impulse of the moment. He felt the intoxication of the presence of Miss Morison, and he yielded to it with frank unscrupulousness. He resolved that he would repent afterward; yet instantly demanded of himself if this were really a sin. He was after all a man, if he had chosen the ecclesiastic calling. If indeed he were transgressing he told himself half contemptuously that as he did penance doubly, once that imposed by his own spiritual director and again that set by the Catholic at the North End, he might be held to expiate amply the pleasure of this hour. He at least was determined to forget for the once that he was a priest, and to remember only that he was a man, and that he loved this beautiful creature beside him. He noted the curve of her clear cheek and shell-like ear; the sweep of her eyelashes and the liquid deeps of her dark eyes. He let his glance follow the line of her neck below the rounded chin, and became suddenly conscious that he was fascinated by the soft swell of her bosom. The blood came into his cheeks, and he looked hastily out of the window.

The train was already clear of the city, and was speeding through the suburbs, rattling gayly and noisily past the ostentatious stations and the scattered houses. Maurice felt that his companion was secretly observing him, although she was apparently looking at the landscape which slid precipitately past. He wished to say something, and desired that it should not be clerical in tone. He would fain have spoken, not as a deacon, but as a man of the world.

" Are you going to New York ? " he asked.

" I shall not have the pleasure of your company so far," she returned with a smile.

" No," he responded naïvely. " I am going only to Springfield."

" Ah," she said, smiling again ; and too late he realized that she had meant that she was not going through.

He was the more vexed with himself because he was sure that his confusion was so plain that she could not but see it, and that it was with a kind intention of relieving his embarrassment that she spoke again.

" I am going to visit my grandmother in Brook-field."

He replied by some sort of an unintelligible murmur, and was doubly angry with himself for being so shy and awkward. He glanced furtively at the trim young man opposite, and was relieved to find that that individual was reading and giving no heed. He wondered why he should be so completely thrown out of his usual self-possession by this girl, so that when he talked to her, and was most anxious to appear at his best, he was most surely at his worst. There came whimsically into his head a thought of the wisdom of training the clergy to the social gifts and graces, and he remembered the flippant speech of Mrs. Wilson about the need of their being able to pay compliments.

" I seem to be specially stupid when I try to talk to you," he said with boyish frankness.

Miss Morison looked at him curiously.

" Am I to take that as a compliment or the reverse ? " she asked.

" It must be a compliment, I suppose, for it shows how much power you have over me."

He was reassured by her smile, and felt that this was not so badly said.

" The power to make you stupid, I think you intimated."

" Oh, no," he responded, with more eagerness than the occasion called for; " I did n't mean that."

She smiled again, a smile which seemed to him nothing less than adorable, and yet which teased him a little, although he could not tell why. She took up the novel which lay in her lap.

" Have you read this ? " she inquired.

He shook his head.

" You forget," he answered, " that I am a deacon. At the Clergy House we do not read novels."

" How little you must know of life," returned she.

There was a silence of some moments. The train rushed on, past fields desolate under patches of snow, and stark, leafless trees; over rivers dotted with cakes of grimy ice; between banks of frost-gnawed rock. The landscape in the dim January afternoon was gray and gloomy; and as day declined everything became more lorn and forbidding. Maurice turned away from the window, and sighed.

" How disconsolate the country looks ! " said he. " I am country bred, and I don't know that I ever thought of the sadness of it; but now if I see the country in winter it makes me sigh for the people who have to live there all the year round."

" But they don't notice it any more than you did when you lived in it."

" Perhaps not; but it seems to me as if they must. At any rate they must feel the effects of it, whether they are conscious of it or not."

Miss Morison looked out at the dull, sodden fields and stark trees.

"I am afraid that you were never a true lover of the country," said she thoughtfully. "You should know my grandmother. She is almost ninety, but she is as young as a girl in her teens. She has lived in the finest cities in the world, — London, Paris, St. Petersburg, and of course our American cities. Now she is happiest in the country, and can hardly be persuaded to stay in town. She says that she loves the sound of the wind and the rain better than the noise of the street-cars."

"That I can understand," he answered; "but I am interested in men. I don't like to be away from them. There is something intoxicating in the presence of masses of human beings, in the mere sense that so many people are alive about you."

She looked at him with more interest than he had ever seen in her eyes.

"But I don't understand," she began hesitatingly, " why " —

" Why what?" he asked as she paused.

"I don't know that I ought to say it, but having begun I may as well finish. I was going to say that I could not understand how one so interested in men and so sensitive to humanity could be content to choose a profession which cuts him off from so much of active life."

"It was from interest in men, I suppose, that I chose it. I wanted to reach them, to do something for them. Although," Maurice concluded, flushing, "I don't think that I realized at that time the feeling of being carried away by the mere presence of crowds of living beings."

There was another interval of silence, during which they both looked out at the cold landscape, blotted and marred by patches of snow tawny from a recent thaw.

"I doubt if you have got the whole of it," Miss Morison said thoughtfully, turning toward him. "Dear old grandmother is as deeply interested in the human as anybody can be. She always makes me feel that my life in the midst of folk is very thin and poor as compared to hers. She has known almost everybody worth knowing. Grandfather was minister to England and Russia, and she of course was with him. Yet she's content and happy off here in Brookfield."

"Perhaps," Wynne returned hesitatingly, "there's something the matter with the age. I don't suppose that at her time of life she has anything of this generation's restless " —

He broke off abruptly.

"Well?" his companion said curiously.

He smiled and sighed.

"I don't know why I am talking to you so frankly," replied he. "As a matter of fact I find that I'm more frank with you than I am with myself. I've always refused to own to myself that there was anything restless in my feeling toward life; yet here I am saying it to you."

"One often thinks things out in that way. Hasn't that been your experience?"

"Yes," he responded thoughtfully; "although I don't know that I ever realized it before. I see now that I've often reasoned out things that bothered me simply by trying to tell them to my friend, Mr. Ashe."

"Is he your bosom friend and confidant? It is usually supposed to be a woman in such a case."

"Oh, no," was his somewhat too eager rejoinder; "I never talked like this to a woman. I never wanted to before."

A look which passed over her face seemed to tell him that the talk was taking a tone more confidential than she liked. He was keyed up to a pitch of excitement and of sensitiveness; and a thrill of disappointment pierced him. He became at once silent; and then he fancied that she glanced at him as if in question why his mood had changed so suddenly. The train rolled into the station at Worcester, and he went out to walk a moment on the platform, and to try to collect his thoughts. He had forgotten now to question his right to be enjoying the companionship of Miss Morison; he gloated over her friendly looks and words, thinking of how he might have said this and that, and thus have appeared to better advantage, and resolving to be more self-controlled for the remainder of the ride. The open air was refreshing; and a great sense of joyousness filled him to overflowing. When again he took his seat in the car he could have laughed from simple pleasure.

The chat of the latter part of the journey was more easy and unconstrained than at the beginning. It was not clear to Wynne what the change was, but he was aware that he was somehow talking less self-consciously than before. They spoke of one thing and another, and it teased the young man somewhat that when now and then his companion mentioned a book he had seldom seen it. The things which he had read of late years he knew without asking that she would not have seen. Even the names of current writers of fiction were hardly known to him, and an allusion to what they had written was beyond him. In spite of a word which now and again brought out the difference between his world and hers, however, Maurice thoroughly enjoyed the talk. Now and then he would reflect in a sort of sub-consciousness that the delight of this hour was to be dearly paid for with penance and repentance, but this provoked in him rather the determination at least to enjoy it to the full while it lasted, than any inclination to deny himself the present gratification.

It has been remarked that the ecclesiastical temper is histrionic; and Wynne was not without a share of this spirit. He would have gone to the stake for a conviction, and made a beautifully effective death-scene for the edification of men and angels, not for a moment aware that there was anything artificial in what he was doing. Now he was not without a consciousness that he was playing the rôle of a lover and a prodigal, sincere in his love and devotion ; yet none the less subtly aware how much more interesting is repentance when there is genuine human passion to repent, is renunciation when there is real love to sacrifice; of how much more effective is saintliness set off against a background of transgression. It was a real if somewhat childish joy to be able to sin actually yet without going beyond hope ; of being dramatically false to his vows without crossing the line of possible pardon.

" We shall be in Brookfield in ten minutes," Miss Morison said, beginning to look about for her belongings. " We pass the New York express just here."

Hardly had she spoken when suddenly and without warning there was an outburst of shrieks from the

whistle of the engine, answered and blended with
that of another.　Before Maurice could realize what
the outburst meant, there followed a horrible shock
which seemed to dislocate every joint in his body.
Berenice was thrown violently into his arms, flung as
a dead weight, and shrieking as she fell against his
breast.　Instinctively he clasped her, and in the terror
of the moment it was for a brief instant no more to
him that his embrace enfolded her than if she had
been the veriest stranger.　A hideous din of yells, of
crashing wood and rending iron, of shivering glass, of
escaping steam, of indescribable sounds which had no
resemblance to anything which he had ever heard or
dreamed of, and which seemed to beat upon his ears
and his brain like blows of bludgeons wielded by the
hands of infuriate giants.　The end of the car before
him was beaten in ; splinters of wood and fragments
of glass flew about him like hail ; it was like being
without warning exposed to the fiercest fire of bat-
teries of an implacable enemy.　A woman was dashed
at his very feet torn and bleeding, her face mangled
so that he grew sick and faint at the sight ; pinned
against the seat opposite, transfixed by a long splinter
as with a javelin, was the dapper young man, horribly
writhing and mowing, and then stark dead in an instant, staring with wide open eyes and distorted face
like a ghastly mask.　Moans and shrieks, grindings
and roarings, howlings and babbling cries that were
human yet were piercingly inarticulate filled the air
with an inhuman din which drove him to a frenzy.　It
seemed as if the world had been torn into fragments.

　　Yet all this was within the space of a second.　Indeed, although all these things happened and he saw
and heard them clearly, there was no pause between

the first alarming whistle and the overturning of the
car which now came. He was lifted up; he saw the
whole car sway with a dizzying, sickening motion, and
then plunge violently over. Fortunately it so turned
that he and Miss Morison were on the upper side.
He fell across the aisle, striking the chair opposite,
but somehow instinctively managing to protect Berenice from the force of the concussion. She no longer
cried out, but she clung convulsively about his neck,
and as they swayed for the fall he saw in her eyes a
look of wild and desperate appeal. He forgot then
everything but her. The desire to protect and save
her, the feeling that he belonged absolutely to her and
that even to the death he would serve her, swallowed
up every other feeling. As they went over a vise-like
grip caught his arm, and amid all the infernal confusion he somehow connected that despairing clutch
with a succession of shrill and piercing shrieks which
rang in his ear, seeming to be close to him. He remembered that in the chair behind his had been a
young girl, and he felt a pity for her that choked him
like a hand at his throat. Then as they went down
he instinctively but vainly tried to shake off the hold,
which was as that of a trap. It was like being in
the actual grip of death.

All sorts of loose articles fell with them from the
upturned side of the car to the other; they were
part of a cataract of falling bodies, involved as in a
crushing avalanche. Wynne found himself in this
falling shower crumpled up between two chairs, one
of his feet evidently thrust through a broken window
and the other still held by that convulsive clasp.
Miss Morison was half above him, partly supported
by a chair which still held by its fastenings to the

floor. He could not see her face, and his body was so twisted that he could not move his head with freedom. Berenice was evidently insensible, but whether stunned from the shock or more seriously hurt he could not tell. He struggled fiercely to free himself, straining her to his breast. There were still movements in the car after it had overturned. It rocked and settled; for some time small articles continued to fall. He drew the face of the unconscious girl more closely into his bosom to protect it. As he did so he was aware that his arm was hurt. A burning, biting pain singled itself out from all the aches of blows and contusions. He seemed to remember that a long time ago, some hours nearer the beginning of this catastrophe which had lasted but a moment, he had felt something rip and tear the flesh; but he had been so absorbed in the attempt to shield Berenice that he had not heeded. Now the anguish was so great that it seemed impossible to endure it. He set his teeth together, determined not to cry out lest she should hear him and think that he lacked courage. Then it seemed to him that he was swooning. He struggled against the feeling; and for what seemed to him an interminable time he wavered between consciousness and insensibility. It was either growing darker or he was losing the power to see. He could not distinguish clearly any longer that human hand, smeared with blood, sticking ludicrously in the air from amid a pile of bags, coats, and all sorts of things thrown together just where the position of his head constrained him to look. He had been seeing that hand for a long time, it seemed to him, and only now that the darkness had so increased as to cut it off from his sight did he realize what it was and what it must mean.

He still retained a consciousness of the face of Berenice, warm against his bosom, and with each wave of faintness he struggled to keep his senses that he might protect her. The din of noises seemed far away, the cries somewhere at a distance ever increasing. The moans that had seemed to him those of the girl who clutched his arm grew fainter, until they were lost in the buzz and whirr of a hundred other sounds. Then the clasp which held him relaxed as suddenly as if a rope had been cut away. It came into his mind with a wave of horror that the girl who had held him was dead. The thought that Berenice might be dead also followed like a flash, and aroused his benumbed senses. He spoke to her; he tried to move; to release her from her position. He seemed buried under a mound of débris, and she gave no sign of life. He exhausted himself in frantic attempts to escape; to get his arms free; to turn his head far enough to see her face; to thrust back the rubbish which had fallen against them. The anguish to his arm was so great that he could not continue; he could do nothing but suffer whatever fate had in store for him. He tried to pray; but his prayers were broken and confused ejaculations.

All at once he distinguished amid the chaos of noises roaring and singing in his ears something which made his heart stand still; which pierced to his dulled consciousness like a stab. It was the cry of "Fire!" He had once seen a servant with her hair in flames, and instantly arose before him the picture of her shriveling locks and the terror of her face. He seemed to see the dear head on his bosom — The thought was more than he could bear, and for the first time he cried out, shouting for help in a

transport of frenzied fear. He was so absorbed in
his thought of Berenice that he had forgotten himself; but the realization of his own peril revived as a
waft of smoke came over him, choking and bewildering. He was then to die here, stifled or wrapped in
the torture of flame. Then the wild and desperate
thought sprang up that at least if he must die he
should die with her on his bosom, clasped in his arms.
He might give himself up to the delirium of that joy,
since there was no more of earth to contaminate it.
But the horror of it! The anguish for her as well as
for him! Not by fire! His thoughts whirled in his
brain like sparks caught in a hurricane. He scarcely
knew where he was or what had happened to him.
Only he was acutely aware of the acrid smoke, of how
it increased, constantly more dense and stifling.

However the mind may for a moment be turned
aside from its usual way by circumstances, habit is
quick to reassert itself. The habitual constrains men
even in the midst of events the most startling. The
mind of Wynne had been too long bred in priestly
forms not to turn to the religious view here in the
face of death. His conscience cried out that he might
be responsible for the peril and disaster which had
come upon them. With the unconscious egotism of
the devotee, he felt that heaven had been avenging the
impiousness of his sin. He had dared to trifle with
his sacred calling, to look back to the loves of the
world and of the flesh, and swift destruction had overtaken him. And Berenice had been crushed by the
divine vengeance which had so deservedly fallen on
him. He groaned in anguish, seeming to see how she
had perished through the blight of his passion. Not
by fire, O God! Not by fire! How long would it

be possible to breathe in this stifling reek, heavy with unspeakable odors? It was his crime that had brought her to this death. He, a man set apart and consecrated to the work of God, had turned from heaven to earth, and heaven had smitten with one blow him and the woman who had been unwittingly his temptation. And she so innocent, so pure, so sacred! Through his distraught mind rushed a pang of hatred against the power that could do this. He was willing to suffer for his sin, but where was the justice of involving her in his ruin? It was because this was what would hurt him most! It was the work of a devil! Then this thought seemed to him a new transgression which might lessen the chances of his being able to save her, and he tried to forget it in prayer, to atone by penitence. He offered his own life amid whatever tortures would propitiate the offended deity, but he prayed that she might be spared.

All this time — and whether the time were long or short he could not tell — he had heard continued cries and groans. He had now and then been dully aware of a change in the noises. Now it would seem as if all else was swallowed up in the sound of tremendous blows, as if the car were being struck again and again by a mighty battering-ram. Then a chorus of shouting went roaring up, as if an army cried. Noise and physical sensation were too intimately blended to be separated; his brain struggled in confusion, emerging now and then for a moment of consecutive thought and sinking back into semi-unconsciousness as a spent swimmer goes down, fighting wildly for life. He knew that a light had come into the car. He saw it amid the smoke, and his first thought was that it was flame. Dulled and half asphyxiated, he said to himself now almost with indifference that the end had come. Then with a thrill which for a moment aroused all his energies he recognized that it was the glow of a lantern. He was aware that rescuers were close above him, climbing down through the windows over his very head. He cried to them in a paroxysm of appeal : —

"Save her! Save her!"

Whether he was heeded amid the babble of cries and all the noises which seemed to swell to drown his voice, he could not tell, but in another instant he felt that friendly hands had seized Miss Morison, and were endeavoring to lift her insensible form. He strove to loosen his hold, but the effort gave him agony so intolerable that he could do nothing. A thousand points seemed to rend and tear him as he tried to move, and when a voice somewhere above him shouted : "We'll have to try to lift them together!" he experienced a strange sort of double consciousness as if he stood outside of himself and heard others talking of him. He felt himself grasped under the arms, and the pain of being moved was too horrible to be endured. He shrieked in mortal agony, and then in a whirl of dizzying circles seemed to go down in a tide of blackness sparkling with millions of sharp scintillations.

VIII

PHILIP ASHE found himself less and less able either to understand or to sympathize with the politics of Mrs. Wilson. He believed in the righteousness of her cause, and was keenly alive to the peril of the appointment of Mr. Strathmore to the vacant bishopric. It is an inevitable and necessary condition of enthusiasm that it shall be narrow; and religious fervor would be impossible to a mind open to conviction. To accept the possibility of any opposed truth is to be secretly doubtful of the creed which one holds; and tolerance is of necessity the child of indifference. Had Ashe been able to perceive that the church would go on much the same no matter which of the rival candidates was chosen, it would have been impossible for him to be so deeply concerned for the success of Father Frontford. As it was he was as much in earnest as Mrs. Wilson, and thus he felt forced to acquiesce in the strangeness of her methods of work. He said to himself that he supposed this electioneering to be a necessity, no matter how unpleasant; and he added the reflection that in any case it was not in his power to prevent it.

Other feelings were, moreover, completely absorbing his mind. Although he was not yet conscious that anything had come between him and the church, priesthood in which had been his highest earthly ideal, the truth was that his passion for Mrs. Fenton waxed steadily. Chance threw them together. Mrs. Fenton had been appointed to a committee on charities, and it happened that Ashe was a visitor in the North End in a region which the committee were making an especial field of labor. He was called into consultation with her, and sometimes they even went together to visit some of the poverty-stricken families which evidently existed chiefly to be subjects for philanthropic manipulation. Day by day Ashe felt her speak to him more easily and familiarly; and although their talk was strictly impersonal and unemotional, none the less did it feed his growing love.

The nature which does not sometimes try to deceive itself is an abnormal one; and Ashe was not behind his fellows in devising excuses for the joy which he found in Mrs. Fenton's presence. He dwelt in his musings upon her devotion to the church, her good works, her visitings of the poor and sick. He assured himself with a vehemence too feverish not to be fallacious that he was instigated only by entirely disinterested feelings; by the desire to assist in deeds of Christian helpfulness, and by pleasure in the society of one whose devotion to godliness was so marked. He argued with himself as eagerly as if he were struggling to convince another, protesting to his own secret heart as earnestly as he would have protested to a friend.

A man seldom really deceives himself, however, save in thinking that he can deceive himself. There were moments in which his inner self rose up and laughed him to scorn; moments in which his sin glowed before him in colors blood-red. He saw himself apostate, false to his vows, drawn away by his earthly

lusts and beguiled. There were nights when he cast
himself upon the ground in an agony of self-abase-
ment, beating his breast and praying in a passion of
remorse; times when by the cruelty of his self-accus-
ings he involuntarily sought to do penance for the
sweet sin which festered in his bosom.

Worse than all was the color which was imparted
to his passion by the self-imposed prohibitions which
he was violating. The insistence upon the earthly
side of love which is an inevitable accompaniment to
the idea that woman is a temptation, cannot but degrade the relation of the sexes in the mind of the
professed celibate. To keep before the thoughts the
theory that passion is a snare and a pollution is to
render it impossible to love with purity and self-
abandonment. Poor Philip, endowed at birth with
a nature of instinctive delicacy, could not free himself from the taint of his training; yet he shrank as
from hot iron from the blasphemy of connecting any
shadow of earthliness with the woman who had become his ideal. His only resource was to take refuge
in repeating to himself that he did not love Mrs.
Fenton; but even in denying it he felt that he was
defending himself from a charge which was a degradation to her as well as to himself. He fell into that
morbid state of mind where whatever he tried as a
remedy made his disease but the worse; where the
idea of love was the more horrible to him the more it
possessed and pervaded his whole being.

Mrs. Herman was not unobservant of his condition,
although she was far from understanding his state of
mind. She felt that there was little use in forcing
his confidence, but she gave him now and then an
opportunity to confide in her, feeling sure that he
would be the better for freeing his heart in speech.

She was sitting one afternoon alone in the library
when Ashe came home from a missionary expedition.
The day was gray and gloomy, and the early twilight
was shutting down already, so that the fire began to
shine with a redder hue. Mrs. Herman was taking
her tea alone, and as it chanced, she was thinking of
her cousin.

"You are just in time for tea," she greeted him.
"It is hot still."

"But I seldom take tea," he answered, seating himself by the fire with an air of weariness which did not
escape her.

"That is so much more reason that you should
take it now. It will have more effect. I can see
that you are tired out. One lump or two?"

He yielded with a wan smile, and, resuming his
seat, sat sipping his tea in silence for some moments.
At length he sighed so heavily that she asked with a
smile : —

"Is it so bad as that?"

"Is what so bad?" he returned, looking at her in
surprise.

"You sighed as if all life had fallen in ruins about
your feet, and I could n't help wondering if there
were really no joy left to you."

He smiled rather soberly, and did not at once reply. The fire burned cheerily on the hearth, noise-
less for the most part, but now and then purring like
a cat full of happy content; the shadows showed
themselves more and more boldly in the corners,
daring the firelight to chase them to discover their
secrets. The colors of the room were softened into
a dull richness; the dim gilding on the old books
which had belonged to Helen's father, dead since

her infancy, caught now and then a gleam from a tongue of flame which sprang up to peer into the gathering dusk; the copper tea equipage reflected a red glow, and gave to the picture a certain suggestion of comfort and cheer.

"I was thinking how comfortable it is here," Philip said at length.

"And that made you sigh?"

"Yes; I'm ashamed to say that it came over me how far away from me all this is."

"If it is," she returned slowly, "it is simply because you choose that it shall be."

He turned his face toward her as if about to protest; then looked again into the fire. The conversation seemed ended, until Mrs. Herman spoke again as if nothing had been said.

"You have been slumming this afternoon?"

"I do not like the name, but I suppose I have."

"It isn't a cheerful day to go poking about alone among the tenement houses."

"I was not alone," Ashe answered with a hesitation which she could not help noting and with a significant softening of voice. "Mrs. Fenton was with me."

"Ah!"

The exclamation was involuntary. In an instant there had flashed upon Helen's mind a suspicion of the true state of things. The despondency of her cousin, the reflection upon the comfort of domesticity, connected themselves in her thought with trifling incidents which had before come under her observation; and his manner of speaking brought instantly to her mind the conviction that Ashe was thinking of Mrs. Fenton with more than the friendliness of acquaintanceship. When Philip looked up with a question in his eyes, however, she was already on her guard.

"The weather is so doleful," she hastened to add, "that I should think that even philanthropy might lose its power of amusing."

"Cousin Helen," returned he, with some hesitation, "I do not like to hear you speak in that way of what is part of my life work."

She smiled; then sighed and shook her head.

"My dear Philip," replied she, "I had certainly no intention of wounding you; and if you'll let me say so, I think you are going out of your way to find cause of offense. Philanthropy isn't a thing so sacred that it is not to be spoken of with a smile."

"No; but"—

"But what?"

He did not answer at once. He put down his empty cup absently, and then sat staring into the fire as if he were trying there to read the solution of the riddle of existence.

"Come," Helen observed, after waiting for a little, "you have something on your mind. What is it? It will do you good to tell it, even if I'm not clever enough to help you."

"I am sure that you could help me," he began eagerly; and then in a changed voice he added, "if anybody could."

She left her place behind the tea-table and came nearer to him, sitting directly before the fire. The light fell on her convincing face and on her wavy hair. She folded her hands in her lap, and looked at him.

"Well?" she said.

"I do not know how to say it," Philip responded

slowly. "I am afraid that you have not much sympathy with my views of life."

"I probably have more than you realize. It's true that I do not believe as you do, but we are both Puritans at heart, so that in the end our theories come to much the same thing."

He looked up with evident inability to follow her meaning.

"I don't understand," he said.

"Very likely I could n't make myself clear if I tried to explain. Suppose we give up abstractions and come to the concrete. What is the especial thing in which you think that my theories are different from yours?"

"I do not think," he answered, hesitating more than ever, "that you have much sympathy with asceticism."

"None whatever," she declared uncompromisingly. "Nobody could have more honor for a sacrifice to principle than I have; but I believe that a sacrifice to an idea is apt to be the outcome of nothing but vanity or policy."

"But what is the difference?"

"Why, an idea is a thing that we believe with the head; don't you know the way in which we think things out while we secretly feel altogether different?"

"I do not think I follow you; but surely self-denial is a sacrifice to principle."

"Not necessarily. I'm afraid I may seem to you profane, Philip, but I must say that it seems to me that asceticism is one of the worst plague-spots which ever afflicted humanity. The root of it is the pagan idea of propitiating a cruel deity by self-torture."

"How can you say so!" he cried. "It is the pure

devotion of a man to the good of his higher nature
and to the good of the race."

"As far as the race goes, vicarious suffering can't
be anything, so far as I see, except an effort to pla-
cate an unforgiving deity. As for the devotion of a
man to his higher nature, you will never convince me
that to go against nature and to indulge in morbidness
is improving to anything. But here we are, swamped
in a bog of great moral propositions again. We can't
agree about these things, and the thing which we
really want to say will be lost sight of entirely."

He turned his face away from her again, either
troubled by what she had been saying or unable to
find words and confidence to go on with the confession of his trouble.

"Is it," Helen inquired, "that you have found that
you have yourself a doubt of the value of asceticism ?"

"No, not that," he answered, dropping his voice;
"but — but I begin to doubt myself."

She leaned forward in her chair. Some power outside of her own will seemed to constrain her.

"Philip," she said, bending over and touching his
hand, "has love made you doubt ?"

The question evidently took him entirely by surprise. She wondered what impulse had made her
speak and how her question would affect him. He
flushed to his forehead, and cast at her a look so full
of pathetic appeal that she felt the tears come into
her eyes. It was the look of a hunted creature which
sees no way of escape, yet which has not the fury of
resistance, which pleads its own weakness. She knew
that Philip could not equivocate and that the secret
of his heart lay bare before her. She shrank from

what she had done, and a flood of pity and sympathy
filled her mind.

He gave her no more than a single look, and then
buried his face in his hands.

"I have betrayed my high calling," he exclaimed
in a voice of bitter suffering. "I have put my hand
to the plough and looked back. I am too weak to be
worthy to " —

"Stop," she interposed brusquely, although she was
deeply touched. "I can't listen to that sort of talk.
It is n't wholesome and it is n't manly. If you have
fallen short of your ideal, your experience is that of
the rest of the race. I suppose the secret of our
making any progress is the power of conceiving things
higher than we can reach. It keeps us trying."

"But I devoted myself to " —

"My dear boy," she interrupted him again, "you
are like the rest of us. You told yourself that you
would be above all the passions and emotions of common humanity, and you are discouraged to find that
you 're human after all. That 's really the whole of
it."

"But to allow yourself to love " —

It was not necessary for her to interrupt him now.
He stopped of his own will, casting down his eyes and
blushing like a school-boy. It seemed to her that it
might be better to try raillery.

"To allow yourself, O wise cousin!" she cried.
"Men do not allow or disallow themselves to love.
It 's deeper business than that."

"But I should have had strength not to yield."

"Is there anything discreditable in loving?" she
demanded.

"There is for a priest."

" If there were, you are not a priest."

" In intention I am; and that is the same in the sight of Heaven."

She could not repress a gesture of impatience. She felt at once an inward annoyance and a secret admiration. The temper of his mind was exasperatingly like her own in its tenacity of conviction. He would not excuse himself by any shifts, no matter how convincing they might seem to others. The matter must be met fairly and frankly, and she must reach his deepest feelings if she would move him. She reflected how best to deal with him, and with her thoughts mingled the question whether Edith Fenton could return Philip's love. The young man was well made and sufficiently good-looking, although paled by study and austerities. He was of good birth and property, and from a worldly point of view not entirely an unsuitable match for the widow, should she think of a second husband. He was somewhat younger than Mrs. Fenton; and Helen was not without the thought that this passion might be on his part no more than the inevitable result of his coming in contact with a beautiful woman after having been immured in the monastic seclusion of the Clergy House; a passion which would pass with a wider acquaintance with the world. The whole matter perplexed and troubled her, and yet she earnestly longed to help her cousin.

" Dear Philip," she said, " I can't tell you how I enter into your feeling. I don't agree with you, but we are not so far apart in temperament, if we are in doctrine. I'm afraid that you'll think that I'm merely tempting you when I say that it seems to me that your conscientiousness is entirely right, and that your conviction is all wrong."

"Of course I know that you do not hold the same faith that I do."

"But one of your own faith might remind you that your own church upholds the marriage of the clergy."

"Yes," he assented with apparent unwillingness, "but my conscience does not."

"Do you mean that you find your conscience a better guide than the church? That seems to put you on my ground, after all."

"Oh, no, no! Certainly I do not put myself above the authority of the church."

"The eagerness with which you disclaim any common ground with me is n't polite," she retorted, glad of a chance to speak more lightly and smilingly; "but it 's sincere, and that is better."

"I was n't trying to disclaim thinking as you do; but to insist that I do not set myself above the church."

"Then I repeat that the church sanctions the marriage of the clergy. If you don't agree, I don't see why you do not really belong in the Roman Catholic Church."

There was a long pause, during which she watched her cousin narrowly. He seemed to be thinking deeply, with eyes intent on the fire. She was so little prepared for the direction which his thought took that she was startled when he said at last with a sigh : —

"I do sometimes find myself envying the absolute authority with which the Roman Catholic Church speaks."

"Authority!" she repeated indignantly. "Do you mean that you wish to give up your individuality?"

"No; not that; but it must be of unspeakable comfort in times of mental doubt to repose on unquestioned and unquestionable authority."

Helen rose from her place by the fire and walked to the window. She felt that she was on very delicate ground, and she would gladly have escaped from the discussion could she have done so without the feeling of having evaded. She stood a moment looking out into the darkening street, dusky in the growing January twilight, bleak and dreary. Then with a sudden movement she went to her husband's desk and took up a picture of her boy, a beautiful, manly little fellow of three years, of whom Philip was especially fond. Crossing to her cousin, she put the picture in his hand, at the same time turning up the electric light behind him.

"See," she said, with feminine adroitness. "I don't think I've shown you this picture of Greyson."

He looked at it earnestly, and sighed.

"It is beautiful," said he. "Greyson is a son to be proud of and to love."

"Well?" she asked significantly.

"What do you mean?" returned he. "What has Greyson's picture to do with what we were talking about?"

She took the photograph from his hand, extinguished the light, and walked back toward the desk. The room seemed darker than before now that the firelight only was left. Suddenly she turned, with an outburst almost passionate : —

"O Philip!" she exclaimed. "Can't you see? My son! Surely if there is anything in this world that is holy, that is entirely pure and noble, it is parentage. Do you suppose that all the churches in the world, with authority or without it, could make Grant and me feel that there is anything higher for us than to take our little son in our arms and thank God for him!"

He did not answer, and she controlled her emotion, smiling at her own extravagance, while she wiped away a tear. She kissed the picture, and put it in its place; then she returned to her chair by the fire.

"I don't expect you to understand my feeling," she said. "You never can until you have a son of your own. If a little cherub like Grey puts his baby hands into your eyes and pulls your hair, you'll suddenly discover that a good many of your old theories have evaporated."

"But, Cousin Helen," he began hesitatingly, "certainly there is often sin" —

She interrupted him indignantly.

"There is no sin in faithful, loving, self-respecting marriage," she insisted. "That is what I am talking about. It is the holiest thing on earth. Anything may be degraded. I've even heard of a burlesque of the sacrament. I don't see why I should n't speak frankly, Philip. You are in a state of mind that is morbid and self-tormenting. If you love a woman, tell her so honestly and clearly; and if she is a good woman and can love you, go down on your knees, and thank God."

He leaned his forehead on his hands, as if he were struggling with himself. The firelight shone on his rich hair, auburn like her own. Helen watched him anxiously, wondering if she had said too much, and whether she were taking too great a responsibility in the advice she gave. Certainly anything must be good that took him out of his unhealthy mood.

"Come," she said, rising, and turning on the electric light again. "It is time for Grant to be at home, and for me to be dressing. We are to dine at the Bodewin Rangers to-night."

He put up his hand to arrest her, and said in a tone that wrung her heart: —

"But, Cousin Helen, I cannot speak of love to a woman until I am ready to give up for her my priestly calling."

"Until you are willing to give up your unwholesome idea of celibacy and asceticism, you mean."

"It would be sacrificing a principle to a passion."

Helen sighed.

"I could reason with you," she returned, half-humorously, "but how shall I get on with all the Puritan ancestors who prevail in you and me! The thing that I say is n't that you are to give up your notions about the celibacy of the priesthood in order to marry, but because they are unwholesome and abnormal. The thing that most closely links you to humanity is the thing that best fits you to be of use in the world."

He regarded her with a glance of painful intensity.

"But suppose," he suggested, "that the woman I loved could not love me? Then I should come back to the church, and lay on the altar only a discarded and worthless sacrifice."

"Come back to the church!" she echoed. "You don't leave it. If marriage takes you out of the church, then the sooner such a church is left the better! Do you realize what you are doing, Philip? Do you remember that you insult the good name of your mother by the view you take of marriage? I

am sick of all this infamous condemnation of what to
me is holy! If the church cannot rise to a noble and
pure conception of it, the sooner the church is done
away with, the better for mankind!"

"But you wrong the church," he interrupted
eagerly. "The church makes marriage a sacrament;
it recognizes its purity; it" —

"Then what are you doing," she burst in, "with
your exceptions to the theory of the church? It is
you who degrade it — Pardon me, cousin," she added
in a calmer voice, coming to him and laying her
fingers lightly on his shoulder. "I am speaking out
of my heart. I have the shame of knowing that I
once failed to realize how high and how noble a thing
marriage is. I am older than you, and I have suffered
as I hope you may never have to suffer; the end of it
all is that I have learned that there is nothing else on
earth so blessed as the real love of husband and wife.
Of course," she concluded, as he would have interrupted, "I talk as a woman, and I cannot decide what
you are to do. Only I would like you to believe that
I would help you if I could, and that what I say of
marriage is the thing which seems to me the truest
thing on earth."

Then without waiting for reply, she went away and
left him to his thoughts.

IX

"Who is Mr. Rangely?" Ashe inquired one morning at breakfast.

Mrs. Herman looked at her husband as if she expected him to reply, although the question had been addressed to her.

"Fred Rangely," Grant Herman answered, "is a writer. He writes for the magazines and is a newspaper man. He's written one or two novels, and the first one was pretty successful. He's written plays too."

Helen smiled.

"Grant is too good-natured to tell you what you really want to know," she commented. "Mr. Rangely was once in some sort a friend of his, in the old days when there was still something like an artistic brotherhood in Boston, and he can't bear to say things that are not to his credit. Now I should have answered your question by saying that Fred Rangely is a warning."

"A what?" Ashe asked, while Herman sighed.

"A warning. A dozen years ago he was one of the most promising men about. He had made a good beginning, he was clever and popular, and both as a novelist and as a playwright we hoped for great things from him."

"And now?"

"Now he is a failure."

Herman looked up almost reprovingly.

"I don't think he would recognize that," he observed.

"No, he wouldn't; and that's the worst of it. Ten years ago if anybody had said of Fred Rangely: 'Here's a fellow that has started out to do good work, but has found that there's more money in sensationalism; who despises the popular taste and caters to it; who writes things he doesn't believe for the newspapers and spends the money in running after society,' he would have pronounced such a fellow a cad. Now he would say: 'Well, a man must live, you know; and the public will only pay for what it wants.' It's lamentable."

"You put it rather worse than it is," her husband responded. "We are all in the habit of judging men as if their degradation was deliberate, which as a matter of fact I suppose it never is. Rangely hasn't coolly accepted the choice between honesty and Philistinism. It's all come gradually."

"Like learning to pick pockets," she interpolated.

"Besides," Herman continued, "we over-estimated in the beginning both his character and his talent. He found he couldn't do what was expected of him, and he was weak enough to do then what was most comfortable instead of what seemed to him highest. It is what nine men out of ten do."

"Of course," Helen assented, "but after all it has come about by his giving in on one thing after another. There was always a good deal that is attractive about him, but he never showed much moral stamina. He could never have married as he did if he had possessed fine instincts."

" And his wife ? " Ashe inquired.

" Oh, he married a New York girl, who " —

" There, there," broke in Herman good-naturedly.
" It is just as well not to go into a characterization of
Mrs. Rangely. I own that there is n't much good to
be said of her ; so it is as well to let her pass."

" Well, so be it," his wife assented, smiling. " I
have only to say," she added, turning to her cousin,
" that when Grant declines to have a woman discussed it is equivalent to a condemnation more severe " —

" Nonsense," protested Herman. " Don't believe
her, Ashe. As for Mrs. Rangely, it 's enough to say
that she is merely an imitation in most things, and
that she has called out the worst of her husband's
nature instead of the best. I 'm sorry to say it, but
I 'm afraid it 's true."

Mrs. Herman looked at him with a smile which
seemed to tease him for having been betrayed into
saying a thing so much more severe than were his
usual judgments. Then with true feminine instinct
she brought the talk back to its most significant point.

" Why did you ask about his wife ? " she inquired
of Philip.

" I — I did not know," he returned, so evidently
disconcerted that she did not press the matter.

Had Helen been a gossip she might have added
that Rangely had acquired the reputation of being
always philandering with some woman or other.
Before his marriage he had been the slave of Mrs.
Staggchase, and now, after devotion to all sorts of
society women, he had come to be counted as one
of the train of admirers who offered their devotion at
the shrine of Mrs. Wilson. Where a Frenchwoman

prides herself on the intensity of the devotion of some
man not her husband, an American of the same type
glories in the number of slaves that her charms en-
snare.   In either case the root of the matter is vanity
rather than passion. The American fashion is at
once the more demoralizing and the less dangerous.
Mrs. Wilson in the early days of her married life
had tried to make her husband jealous by allowing
the desperate attentions of a single lover. She never
repeated the experiment. The lover went abroad to
recover from the sting of having been made hopelessly ridiculous, and Mrs. Wilson learned that in
marrying she had found a master. Fortunately she
had married for love, and no woman loves a man less
for finding him able to control her. In these days
Mrs. Wilson amused herself by having a troop of
admirers, and perhaps prided herself upon being able
to outdo the wiles of the other women of her set in
securing and holding her captives; but she discussed
them with her husband with the utmost frankness,
mocking them to their faces if they made a step
across the line which she drew for them. They were
kept in a state of marked but respectful admiration.
It was expected of them that they should pretend to
be consumed by a passion as violent as they might
please, but always a passion which was hopeless, which
asked for no reward but to be allowed to continue;
which found in mere admission to her presence joy
enough at least to keep it alive.

It may be that Rangely had more vanity than the
rest of Mrs. Wilson's followers, or it may be that he
was more resolute. Certain it is that he was more
presuming than the rest, and that his devotion had
not failed to produce a good deal of talk. Little as

Mrs. Herman was accustomed to pay attention to social gossip, she had not failed to hear tattle about Elsie Wilson; and while she probably did not much heed it, she was at heart too conscientious not to feel shame and irritation. That a woman in the position of Mrs. Wilson should allow herself to give rise to vulgar gossip moved her to deep disapproval; while she could not but feel contempt for the man who neglected his own wife to wait upon the caprices of one whom Helen looked upon as a heartless and vain creature.

Behind the question which Ashe had asked about Rangely lay an incident which had occurred the day previous. He was now called upon to see Mrs. Wilson frequently in relation to matters connected with the election, and with that instinct which was inborn she had carelessly exercised upon him her arts of fascination. There is a certain sort of woman in whom the mere presence of anything masculine awakens the rage for conquest. It is as impossible for such women not to exert their fascinations as it is for a magnet to cease to attract. It is the destiny of woman to love, and dangerous is she who is inspired only with the desire to be loved, the woman who instead of loving man loves love. Elsie was saved from being such a monster by the fact that she had a husband strong enough to subdue and control her nature; but nothing could prevent her from trying her wiles on every man she met.

Philip was too completely unsophisticated to understand, and too much absorbed by his passion for another woman to respond to the cunning attractions of Mrs. Wilson; yet it is not impossible that she so far influenced him as to render him unconsciously jealous of another man. He had surprised Rangely kissing the hand of that lady with an air of devotion so warm that the blood of the young deacon rose in resentment which he supposed to be entirely disapproval. He was in a state of mind which made him especially sensitive to any suggestion of love; and the sight of any man caressing the hand of a beautiful woman could not but set his heart throbbing with disconcerting rapidity. In his world even the touch of a woman's fingers was almost a forbidden thing, and to kiss them an act not to be so much as imagined. Philip dared not think, or to define to himself what significance he attached to this incident. An unsophisticated man is often suspicious from the simple fact that he is forced to distrust his judgment. He is unable to estimate the value of appearances, and in the end often falls the victim of errors which might seem to arise from malevolence or low-mindedness, when in reality they are the inevitable fruit of ignorance.

As Philip stood confronted with Mrs. Wilson after Rangely had left the room it seemed to him that he read unspeakable things in her glance. His clerical bias with its unholy blight of asceticism, his ignorance of the world, made him a victim of a misapprehension which brought the blood to his cheeks. His hostess looked at him curiously, and then burst into a laugh.

"Upon my word," she cried, "I believe you are shocked! You are really too delicious!"

He flushed hotter yet, and there came over him a helpless sense of being alike unable to understand this brilliant creature or to cope with her.

"But — but," he stammered, "I — I" —

"Well?" she demanded, her eyes dancing. "You what? You saw Mr. Rangely kiss my hand. You may kiss it too, if you like; though I doubt if you can do it half so devotedly. He's had a lot of practice with a lot of hands."

Ashe stared at her with wide open eyes.

"But has he a wife?" he asked gravely.

"Meaning to remind me that I have a husband?" she gayly returned. "Yes; we are both of us married. To think," she continued, spreading out her hands and appealing to the universe at large, "that such simplicity exists! Where have you been all your life? Did you never kiss a lady's hand — or a lady's lips, for that matter?"

"I think you forget, Mrs. Wilson," Ashe said with real dignity, "that I am a priest."

She regarded him with lifted brows for a moment. Then she moved to a seat.

"Come," said she; "sit down and talk to me. Where have you passed your life? You cannot have been brought up in a monastery, for we don't have them in our church."

"It is a great pity," responded Philip, obeying her command, and seating himself in a large arm-chair near her.

"Do you really mean it?" was her reply. "Yes, I believe you do! You were evidently born to be a monk. Oh, how *triste* it must be to be made without an appreciation of us!"

He remained silent, his face more grave than ever.

"Well," she went on, settling herself comfortably in the corner of her sofa amid a pile of sumptuous cushions, "tell me something about your life. It may be that you were designed by fate to introduce a new order of monks."

"There is not much to tell," he responded stiffly and almost mechanically. "I was brought up in the country by a widowed mother. I went through Harvard and the Divinity School, and since then I have lived at the Clergy House."

She regarded him closely. Her glance seemed half mocking, and yet to search into the very secrets of his heart, as if she were asking him questions which he would not have dared to ask himself. Her eyes suggested impossible things; they demanded if he had not known of forbidden cups which held wine deliriously enticing. He cast down his glance, no longer able to endure hers, yet not knowing why he was thus abashed.

"But don't you know anything of life?" she questioned. "How could you go through Harvard without seeing something of it? What were your amusements?"

"I rowed some, and I walked. The only thing that was a real pleasure outside of my work was to be with Maurice Wynne. I do not remember that I ever thought about needing to be amused. Of course I knew a few fellows. I never knew a great many of the men."

"And no women?"

"None except the boarding-house keeper."

She looked at him rather incredulously. Then she once more threw out her hands in a gesture of amusement and amazement.

"Good heavens!" declared she; "there are just two things which might be done with you. You should be put in a glass case as a unique specimen of

otherwise extinct virtue; or you should be sent to
Paris to learn to be a real man. However, it's not
my place to take charge of you, so that may pass."

There burned in the cheek of Ashe a spot of crimson which was perhaps too deep not to betoken something of the nature of earthly indignation.

"Mrs. Wilson," he said, "I came here to discuss
church interests, and not to be myself the subject of
remarks which you certainly would not think of making to other gentlemen who call on you."

She clapped her hands.

"Bravo!" she cried. "There's the making of a
man in him. It's a thousand pities you can't go to
Paris and learn the fun of life."

He rose indignantly.

"If you wish only to talk lightly of evil things,"
said he, "I do not see that it is necessary for me to
take up more of your time."

"Well," she responded, smilingly unmoved, "I'll
confess that if there is one thing for which I am especially grateful to Providence it is for its having spared
me the ennui of having to live in a virtuous world!
But sit down, and I'll talk as if that blessing had not
been granted to us. As for the salutation of Mr.
Rangely which so shocked your reverence, that was
part of the campaign. He had just promised to write
an article for the 'Churchman' advocating Father
Frontford from the point of view of a layman; and of
course until that is in print it is necessary to be gracious to him. The trouble with you is that you've
seen so little of life that you exaggerate the most
innocent things. You really are rather insulting to
me, if you think of it; but I pardon it because you
don't know what you were doing. I suppose you

never wanted to kiss a woman's hand or to write a
sonnet to her eyebrow?"

Ashe felt the blood rush into his face in so hot a
tide that he involuntarily turned away from his tor-
mentor and walked toward the door. The question
would in any case have been disconcerting, but it was
made doubly so by the word which recalled the phrase
from the Persian hymn which was in his mind so
closely associated with Mrs. Fenton : " O thou, to the
arch of whose eyebrow the new moon is a slave ! "
He had taken but a step, however, before Mrs. Wilson sprang from her seat, clapping her hands again.
She interposed between him and the door, her face
radiant with fun and mischief.

" Oh, what a blush ! " she cried. " Upon my word,
there 's a woman ; there is a woman even in that ice-
box you keep for a heart ! "

She burst into a peal of laughter, while he stood
confounded and speechless, trying to look unconscious,
and vexatiously aware of how completely he failed.
Mrs. Wilson laid the tips of her slender fingers on
his arm, and peered up into his eyes.

" I would n't have believed it, St. Anthony ! Come,
make me your mother confessor, and I 'll give you
good advice. It 's part of my mission to take charge
of the love affairs of the clergy. Only yesterday I
spent half the afternoon trying to find out how deeply
Mr. Candish is smitten with a pretty widow."

Ashe started in amazement and alarm. The words
of Mrs. Herman connecting the name of Mrs. Fenton
with that of Candish flashed into his mind, and seemed
to supply what Mrs. Wilson left unspoken. The
jealous pang which he felt at this confirmation of the
interest of Candish in the woman he loved was doubled

by the resentment he felt that this mocking torment
before him should dare even to think of Edith. Almost without knowing it he broke out excitedly into
protest.

" How dare you meddle with her affairs? " he cried.

Mrs. Wilson stared at him an instant in amazement,
evidently taken completely aback. Then a light of
cunning comprehension flashed into her sparkling eyes.

"Ah!" exclaimed she. "You too! Is Mrs. Fenton so irresistible to the ecclesiastical heart? "

He confronted her in silence. A wave of misery,
of helplessness, of weakness, swept over him. He
had no right even to be Mrs. Fenton's defender. He
was, as Mrs. Wilson intimated, not a real man, but a
priest. The very tone of the whole conversation this
morning showed how far she was from regarding him
as one having any part in her world. He had only
injured Mrs. Fenton by his ill-judged outburst, and
given this creature who so delighted in baiting him
one more opportunity. Worse than all else was the
fact that he had given her a chance to jest about the
woman whom he loved. The tears rushed to his eyes
in the intensity of his feelings, and the beautiful face
before him, with its teasing brightness and dancing
fun, swam in his vision. He hated its laughter, and
he expected fresh mockery for the emotion which he
could not help betraying. To his surprise, however,
Mrs. Wilson again laid her hand on his arm, and her
face lost its gayety.

" You poor boy," she said, with genuine feeling in
her tone, " is it so real as that? I would n't have
hurt you for the world, if I had known. What business had you to be meddling with vows and renunciation until you knew what they meant? "

She moved back to her seat as she spoke, motioning Ashe to resume his place. He was too deeply moved to obey her.

"If you will excuse me," he said, "I will see you to-morrow in regard to those delegates. I — I am not quite myself."

"But you shall not go without saying that you forgive me for my teasing. Really, I am sorry and ashamed. I never intend to hurt you, but I see that my teasing may be taken more seriously than it is meant."

There was real gentleness and pity in her smile, and as she rose to stand looking into his face with a winning smile of apology he forgot all his bitterness.

"The trouble is with me," he said. "I do not understand the world, and I should keep out of it."

"Oh, not at all," she retorted briskly. "You should learn how to live in it."

A spark of mischief kindled in her glance as she spoke, and she extended to him the back of her hand. Her smile challenged him, and he had been won and moved by the sympathy of her voice. The hand, too, was so beautiful, so slender, so feminine; he had so keen a longing to be comforted, to be soothed by womanly softness, and to assuage his loneliness by woman's sympathy, that it seemed impossible to resist the invitation of those delicate fingers. He took her hand, and raised it half way to his lips. Then he dropped it abruptly, letting his own arm swing lifelessly to his side.

"No," he said bitterly. "I am a priest!"

X

THE first sensation which returning consciousness brought to Berenice Morison, after the shock of the collision and the feeling that the whole train had been hurled confusedly into space, was that of coming into fresher air as if she were emerging from the depths of the sea. Opening her eyes without comprehending where she was or what had happened, she found herself on the side of an overturned car. Around her were dreadful noises, yells, groans, cries, shouts; her nostrils were filled with the reek of burning stuffs; the light of lanterns and of torches blinded her eyes; a sense of horror oppressed her; appalling calamity which she could not understand seemed to have overtaken her; and she shuddered with terror unspeakable. Her first impulse was to shriek and to attempt to flee from the fearful things which surrounded her; but instantly the self-control of returning reason made itself felt.

Berenice found herself supported by a couple of men, and it became clear to her in an instant that she had just been lifted from that pit below where she could see the glint of flame and the blinding smother of smoke, and from which came such heartrending cries that she instinctively tried to cover her ears. In the movement she realized that beside the hold which her rescuers had of her, she was grasped by other arms; that she was in the embrace of a man apparently dead. In the dim light her dazed sense did not recognize him, and she struggled to release herself from the hold of this corpse.

"Take him away from me!" she shrieked hysterically in mingled terror and repulsion.

"Gently, gently," said one of the men who held her. "He's got killed tryin' to save yer."

"If this cut in his arm was in your back," remarked the other, who was unlocking the hands so strongly clasped behind her, "it'd 'a' been a finisher."

Her head reeled, and she nearly swooned again; but somehow she found herself released, and passed down from the car into the arms of more men.

"For God's sake, hurry," one of them said. "It's getting too hot to stand here."

A blistering puff of smoke enwrapped her as she went down. She saw a face blackened and ghastly advance in the flaring light of a lantern. Hands that seemed to come out of a cloud and a great darkness helped and sustained her, until she was out of the instant press beside the burning car. When once she was free and stood upon her feet, she regained something like self-possession. Her head swam, but she realized the situation and felt that she was able to help herself.

"I am not hurt," she said to those who would have assisted her. "Don't mind me."

As she spoke, the body of a man was passed out of the smoke close to her, and she saw that it was Wynne. Instantly she remembered being flung into his arms, although what followed she could not recall. She looked at him now with a piercing conviction that he was dead. His cassock hung about

him in rags, his face was smeared with blood and
grime, his arm hung limp and bleeding. The words
of the rescuer on the car-roof came to her, and she
saw in the disfigured form of the young deacon the
body of the man who had given his life for hers.
Instantly all her powers rallied to help and if possible
to save him.

"Bring him this way," she said, stepping forward
eagerly, her weakness forgotten. "I'll take care of
him."

She moved out of the smoke without any clear
idea where she was going or what she could do. The
hurt man was brought after her, one of the many
that were being carried as dead weights among the
confused and agonized crowd. At a short distance
from the track there were hastily arranged car-
cushions, coats, and loose coverings thrown down on
a bank half covered with snow. Here the bearers
laid Wynne, hurrying back to their work with a pre-
cipitancy which seemed to Berenice heartless.

The scene which Berenice took in at a glance was
so wild and terrible that it stamped itself on her brain
in a flash. Lanterns were burning all about, dancing
and flitting to and fro like fireflies in a mist. The
eye caught everywhere glimpses by their light of disordered groups, dim and dreadful as a nightmare.
Close about her were the victims heaped as if from a
battlefield, the wounded moaning in pain, the women
wailing over the dying or the dead, each with cruel
egotism intent upon her own, and seizing upon any
helper with terrible eagerness of despair. A hundred
feet away, lighted by the flames which were beginning
to thrust quick tongues through the smoke and the
darkness, was a long heap of shapeless wreck, about

which dark figures were swarming like midges about a bonfire. She could distinguish in the middle of the line the two locomotives silhouetted against the darkness, standing half on end like two grotesque monsters rearing in deadly conflict. Every moment the flames became fiercer, and the hurrying lanterns moved more wildly.

It was Wynne, however, that claimed her attention. One swift glance took in the awful picture, and then she sank down on her knees beside him as he lay, bleeding and insensible, perhaps dead. For a moment she was ready to cast herself down on the snow in helplessness and in terror at the horrors of the situation; but the grit of stout Puritan ancestors was in her fibres, the moral endurance which finds in the sense of a duty to be done an inspiration that lifts above all difficulties. Her work was before her; to abandon it impossible.

The flames of the burning car brightened with appalling rapidity. Shrieks arose so piercing that they wrung her heart as if with a physical agony. It was the car from which she and Wynne had been taken which was now that hell of fire. Its glare lit up the pale and bleeding face beside her, and she realized that at that minute they might have been in that awful agony. She began to sob wildly, but she began, too, to try to bring Wynne back to consciousness. She took snow in her hands and put it to his forehead; she twisted her handkerchief about his arm to stop its bleeding. She tried to recall what she had heard at Emergency Lectures, with a strong determination forcing herself to remember. Kneeling in the snow, in the light of the burning car, her heart torn by the cries of the suffering, trembling with excitement, fear, and the shock she had undergone, sobbing almost hysterically, she yet constrained herself to do her best, binding up his arm with strips of her clothing, and trying to bring back his senses.

A physician came to her without her knowing until he was at her side. He bent to examine Wynne, and Berenice tried to repress her sobs that she might talk to him, and take his directions. The life of Wynne might depend upon her calmness. She caught up more snow, and pressed it to her own temples.

" Is he much hurt ? " she asked feverishly.

" It is not dangerous as far as I can judge," the doctor answered hurriedly. " Get him away from here as soon as you can."

She looked after him as he hurried on to other patients, and her first feeling was one of indignation. Then it occurred to her that his going so soon must mean that her patient was less hurt than she had feared. But why was Wynne so long insensible? She knelt beside him again, and as she did so he opened his eyes.

" Where am I ? " he cried feebly.

He tried to start up, but fell back with a groan.

" There has been an accident," she said hurriedly. " It 's all right now. You are safe. Are you in much pain ? "

" Are you hurt ? " he demanded almost fiercely.

" No, no; never mind me."

He struggled again to rise, but fell back with a groan. She put her hand on his shoulder.

" Lie still," she commanded authoritatively. " I 'll see what can be done. Lie still while I look about."

A second car was burning, and the whole place was aglare with yellow light. The wild groups stood out

black against the trodden and dingy snow, while overhead rolled clouds of sooty smoke. It occurred to
Berenice that the accident had taken place so near
Brookfield that many persons must have come from
the town. She seized a respectable-looking man by
the arm, and asked him if he knew of any way in
which she could get an injured friend to Brookfield.
He stared at her a moment as if it was impossible at
such a time to receive words in their ordinary meaning, but when the question had been repeated he
answered that there were some hackmen from town
in the crowd. He helped her to find one, and as Mrs.
Morison was well known, Berenice had little further
difficulty. Wynne submitted to being half led, half
carried through the crowd, and when at last with the
assistance of the hackman Berenice got him into the
carriage he fainted again.

Singular and frightful to Berenice was that ride.
The terrors through which she had passed, the shock,
mental and physical, which she had undergone, had
almost prostrated her. As soon as she was in the
carriage she broke out into hysterical tears. The
fainting of her companion, however, called her attention from herself, forcing her to think of him. She
supported his head on her shoulder, lifting his wounded
arm on to her lap ; and into her heart came that thrill
of interest and compassion which is the instinctive response of a woman to the appeal of masculine helplessness. A woman's love is apt to be half maternal,
and she who nurses a man is for the time being
in place of his mother. Berenice's thoughts were in
a whirl, but pity for the hurt man at her side was
her most conscious feeling. She remembered the
words of her rescuer, and endowed Wynne with the

nobility which belongs to him who risks his life for
another. What had happened she could not tell.
She remembered the awful terror of the collision, and
mistily of being hurled into his arms; but after that
came a blank until the moment of her rescue. It was
evident that Wynne had in some way been hurt in
protecting her, and the very vagueness of the service
he had rendered made the deed loom larger in her
imagination. She felt his breath warm on her cheek,
and suddenly into her dispassionate musings there
came a fresh sense, which made her face grow hot.
She was angry at the absurdity of flushing there in
the dark, and asked herself why the mere breath on
her cheek of an insensible and wounded man should
set her to blushing like a self-conscious fool! Then
she remembered how he had held her in his arms, and
she grew more self-conscious still. A jolt made her
companion moan, and in a twinkling all else was forgotten in the anxiety of getting to shelter and aid.

When the carriage stopped before the house of
Mrs. Morison, the old lady and a servant appeared
instantly, rushing out to see what the arrival meant.
Almost before the carriage had come to a stand-still,
Berenice put her head out of the window and called
as cheerily as she could : —

"All right, grandmamma."

She could not keep her voice steady, and she could
only try to carry off her emotion by a laugh which
was rather shaky and hysterical. She could not rise,
for Wynne's head was on her shoulder. The carriage door was torn open, and she felt her grandmother's arms about her in the darkness.

"My darling! My darling!" she heard murmured
in a sobbing voice.

"Look out, grandmother," she said, embracing Mrs. Morison with her one free arm; "I 've brought a man with me, and he 's hurt. I think he 's fainted."

There is nothing so efficacious in restraining the outpouring of emotion as the necessity of attending to practical details. The need of getting Wynne out of the hack and into the house as speedily and as safely as possible restored Mrs. Morison to calmness, and although for the rest of the evening and for many days after she and her granddaughter had a fashion of rushing into each other's arms in the most unexpected manner, they now devoted themselves to the unconscious young deacon.

Wynne revived again when he was lifted out of the carriage, and when he had been, with the friendly aid of the driver, got into the house and given a little brandy, he came once more to his complete if somewhat shaken senses. He was too weak from the shock and the loss of blood to resist anything that his friends chose to do to him, and although he feebly protested against being quartered upon Mrs. Morison, his protest was not in the least heeded.

"Say no more about it," Mrs. Morison said, with a quiet smile. "You are here, and you are to stay here. There is nowhere else for you to go, even if you don't like our hospitality."

"That is n't it," he began feebly; "only I 've no claim " —

"There, that will do," Berenice interposed with decision. "Do you suppose, grandmother, that it 's possible to get anybody to come and see his arm?"

"I 'm afraid not, dear," was the answer. "Everybody 's at the wreck. I 've been cowering down in the corner of the fire for what seemed to me years

since Mehitabel came rushing in with the news; and
all the time I 've heard people driving past the house
on their way out of town."

"There ain't a man left," put in Mehitabel, a severe
elderly servant, who had the air of being personally
responsible for her mistress, and of being bound to
fulfill her duties faithfully, even if the effort killed
her. "I see Dr. Strong go gallopin' past first, and
the other doctors was all after him; even to that little
squinchy electrical image that 's round the corner on
Front Street."

"Electrical image?" repeated Berenice.

"She means the eclectic physician," explained Mrs.
Morison. "I 'm sure that there 's no use in sending
for the doctors now. Later we will see. We must
manage the best we can. If I hurt you, Mr. Wynne,
you must tell me."

Berenice looked on, sick with the sight of the
blood, while her grandmother examined the wounded
arm. Wynne shrank a little, but Berenice noted that
he bore the pain pluckily. The sleeve was cut to the
shoulder, and his arm laid bare. A jagged cut was
revealed reaching from the wrist to the elbow; a cut
so ugly in appearance that the girl went faint again.

"There, there, Miss Bee," old Mehitabel said, taking her by the shoulder. "You 've had enough of
this sort of thing for one night. You 'll dream gray
hairs all over your head if you don't get out."

But Berenice refused to give up her place. She
stood beside Wynne while her grandmother examined
the arm, handing the things that were wanted; fighting with the faintness that came over her in waves.

"No, Mehitabel," said she. "I 'm made of better
stuff than you think."

In her heart she had a half unconscious feeling
that she had been inclined to hold this man in contempt because of his priestly garb; and that she
owed him this reparation. She did not know what
had occurred in that overturned car; but she looked
back to it as to a horror of great darkness in which
Wynne had risked his life for hers. She felt that
she could not do less than to stand by while the
wound he had received in her service was being
attended to. It was Wynne himself who put her
away.

"You are too kind, Miss Morison," he said; "but
you are not fit to do this. I beg that you'll not stay.
Your face shows how hard it is for you."

The first thought that shot through her mind was
one of relief that she now might properly leave her
self-inflicted task; the second was a pang of self-reproach that she should wish to leave it; the third
and lasting was a sense of pleasure that even in his
pain he had not failed to note her face and divine
her feelings.

"Mr. Wynne is right," Mrs. Morison added decisively. "Mehitabel can help me, my dear. Go into
the other room and let Rosa get you a cup of tea."

"It won't be much of a cup of tea," Mehitabel
commented grimly. "That fool of a girl's got it
into her head that it's a good time to cry for her
doxy, because he's a brakeman on some other train."

Berenice smiled at the characteristic crispness and
the absurd speech of the old servant. She remembered Mehitabel from the days when in pinafores
she used to visit here, and when she looked upon the
tall, gaunt woman with an awe which was saved from
being terror only by the fact that she had learned to

associate with that abrupt speech an after gift of crisp cakes. Mehitabel was to her as much a part of the establishment as were the tall chairs, the lion-headed fire-dogs, or the silver which had belonged to her grandmother's grandmother.

Passing into the dining-room Berenice summoned the afflicted Rosa, who came with face all be-blubbered with tears, and who sniffed audibly as soon as she caught sight of the visitor.

"How do you do, Rosa? I would n't cry, if I were you," Berenice said. "Mehitabel says that this was n't his train."

"Oh, I know it, Miss," responded Rosa, with more tears; "but I can't help thinking how dreadful it would be if it was; and me not to know whether he was dead or alive. It don't seem to me I could ever marry him, not to be able to tell whether he 'd come home any day dead or alive. I 'll have to give him up, Miss; and he 's real kind and free-handed."

Her tears flowed so freely at the thought of giving up her lover that they splashed on Berenice's hand as Rosa leaned over to reach for something on the table.

"Well, Rosa," Miss Morison remarked, smiling at the absurdity of the maid, and wiping her hand, "I 'm sorry that you feel so bad; but I don't like to be deluged with tears."

"Indeed, Miss," Rosa returned penitently, "I did n't mean to cry on you; but tears come so easy in this world. We 're all born crying."

Berenice laughed in spite of herself.

"If we are born crying," she said," "that 's reason enough for our smiling when we 've outgrown being babies."

" That's all well enough for you," Rosa retorted
with fresh tears. " You've got your man here all
safe if he is hurt a little ; and I don't know " —

Berenice broke in with indignant amazement, feeling her face burn.

" My man ! " she exclaimed. " How dare you
speak to me like that ! Mr. Wynne is nothing to
me. He's only a clergyman that was hurt saving
my life."

She broke off with a laugh somewhat hysterical.
Her nerves were not under control yet.

" I'm sure I did n't mean," wailed the girl, " to say
anything wrong."

" There, there, Rosa," the other interrupted. " We
are both upset. You should n't take so much for
granted, or talk to me about ' men.' "

But in her mind the phrase repeated itself vexatiously : " your man."

XI

THE power of self-torture which the human heart possesses is well-nigh infinite. When one considers how futile are self-reproaches, self-examinations, remorses for faults and weaknesses; how vanity puts itself upon the rack and conscience inflicts envenomed wounds; how self tortures self until the whole man writhes in anguish, and in the end nothing is altered by all this pain, one might almost thank the gods for moral insensibility. Yet New England was founded upon the principle that this temper of mind develops manlihood; that inward struggles are the only discipline which can fit a human being for the outward conquest of life. The Puritans had power to subdue the wilderness, to overcome whatever obstacles interposed to the founding of a state and the establishing of the truth as they conceived it, because all these difficulties were accidents, outward and of comparative insignificance when set against the real life, which was within. If a heritage of self-consciousness has come down with the noble gifts which the forefathers have left to their children, it is at least part of the price paid for great things.

To Maurice that night only the pain and misery of his Puritan inheritance made themselves felt. Through the long hours he lacerated his heart and soul with repentance, with remorseful self-reproaches,

enduring agony intense enough to be the reward meet
for a crime. Fevered with the loss of blood, racked
with the smart of bodily wounds, bruised and sore
from the injuries of the accident, unable to move
without torture in every joint, he yet forgot physical
in mental suffering.

The weakness and disorder of his body confused and
distorted his thoughts, but it was in any case inevitable that with his training he should be wrung with
bitter self-condemnation. He flushed and thrilled at
the remembrance of the pressure of Berenice against
his breast; the warmth of her breath, the odor of
her hair, seemed to come back to him even out of the
tumult and reek of the burning car. He remembered
how it had seemed to him — to him, a priest — sweet
to die if he might die clasping unrebuked this woman
in his arms. The blood throbbed in his temples as
he recalled the wild thoughts that had swirled in a
mad throng through his brain in those moments which
had seemed like hours; the blood throbbed, too, in his
wounded arm, so that a groan forced itself through
his parched lips. He was constantly throwing himself
to and fro as if to escape from some teasing thought,
always to be by the sharp pang in his wound brought
to a sense of his condition. The whole night passed
in an agony of mind and body.

There were moments, too, when he seemed to
stand outside of himself and judge dispassionately
this human creature, wounded, broken, rent in body
and in soul; moments in which he sometimes seemed
to smile in supreme contempt of the wretch so weak,
so wavering, so utterly to be despised; sometimes to
protest in angry pity against the unmerited anguish
which had been heaped upon the sufferer. He had

instants of delirious clearness and exaltation in which
he felt himself lifted above the ordinary weaknesses
of humanity; to see more clearly, and to take a view
broader than any to which he had ever before at-
tained.   It shocked and startled him to realize that in
these intervals which seemed like inspiration, — intervals in which he felt himself illuminated with inner
light, — he cast from him the ideals which he had
hitherto cherished. As if for the first time seeing
clearly, he felt that men should not be hampered by
dogmas which cramp and restrain. A line he had
seen somewhere, and which he had put aside as irreverent and irreligious, kept repeating itself over and
over in his head —

> " He had crippled his youth with a creed."

Life stretched out before him futile and meaningless unless love should light it, unless he could win
Berenice; and he protested feverishly against any
vow that would thwart or restrain him. He had
crippled his youth with a creed unnatural and de-
forming; it was time for the manhood within him to
shake off its fetters and assert its strength. He told
himself wildly that now for the first time he saw life
as it was; that now first he understood the meaning
of existence, and that life meant nothing without freedom and love.

The beliefs of years, however, or even those habits
which so often pass for beliefs, are not to be done
away with in a night. Even love cannot completely
alter the course of life in a moment. At the last,
worn out with the conflict, but with a supreme effort
to regain spiritual calm, Maurice flung his whole soul
into an agony of supplication, as he might have

flung his body at the foot of a cross, and prayed to be
delivered from this too great temptation. He would
renounce; he would pluck up by the roots this passion which had sprung and grown in his heart; at
whatever cost he would tear it up, and be faithful to
his high calling. As a child casts itself upon the
bosom of its mother, he cast himself upon the Divine,
and with an ecstatic sense of pardon, of peace, of
perfect joy, he fell asleep at last.

Maurice awoke in broad daylight, with a confused
sense that the world was falling in fragments about
his ears, and that his name was being shouted by the
angel of the last trump. He found that the physician
who could not be had on the previous night had now
been brought to his chamber by Mehitabel.

"Here's the saw-bones at last," was the characteristically uncompromising introduction of the woman.
"Dr. Murray's come to tell you that all Mis' Morison
did last night was wrong, and that probably you'll
have to have your arm cut off 'cause of it."

Wynne sat up in bed dazed and uncomprehending,
but the smile of the doctor brought him to a sense of
where he was. The latter was not in the least surprised by Mehitabel's manner of speech.

"If you'd had anything to do with it, Mehitabel,"
was Dr. Murray's comment, "I've no doubt the arm
would have had to go; but when Mrs. Morison does a
thing, it's another story."

"Humph!" sniffed she. "You've got some small
amount of sense, if it ain't much. Now, young man,
set your teeth together and put out your tongue —
your arm, I mean."

Maurice smiled, not so much at the humor of the
error as at the fact that it was so evidently inten-

tional on the part of the elderly virgin, who cunningly
glanced at him and at the doctor to discover if the
rare stroke of wit were properly appreciated.

"Jocose as ever, Mehitabel," observed the doctor,
going to work at once with swift and delicate pre-
cision. "You've a nasty cut here, Mr. Wynne; but
you're lucky to get off with nothing worse. It's a
good deal to come through such an accident without
a permanent injury."

"That's true," Maurice responded cheerfully. "I
dreamed in the night that I was all in bits."

"Plenty of poor fellows were. It was the most
terrible smash-up for years."

"How is Miss Morison?" Wynne asked, wondering
if his voice betrayed the inward agitation without
which he could not pronounce her name.

"Oh, she's all right. Nervous and shaky, of
course; but she's a sound, wholesome creature, and
it won't take her long to recover her tone."

"Yes; I brought her up," interposed Mehitabel,
with grim self-complacency. "Don't pull that band-
age so tight, doctor. You want to have me running
over after you in an hour to come and loosen it."

"That's it, Mehitabel; teach your grandmother to
suck eggs. I come here, Mr. Wynne, chiefly to learn
my profession from her."

"She seems willing to teach you," Wynne replied,
and then, with a boyish doubt if she might not take
offense, he added, "which of course is very kind of
her."

Mehitabel chuckled in high good-humor.

"Kind it is and unappreciated it is; and little is
the credit he does to his training. Men are all alike;
if they owned half they owe to women they'd be too
ashamed to show their heads in daylight."

The droll airs of the old woman entertained Wynne so greatly that he bore with exemplary fortitude the painful attentions of the physician, the harder to bear because the wound had had time to inflame. The arm was dressed at last, and the doctor took himself away with a parting passage of arms with Mehitabel.

"The thing for you to do, young man," she said, when Dr. Murray had departed, "is to stay in bed where you are, and that's reason enough for a man to want to get up."

"I'm not fond of staying in bed," Maurice responded with a smile; "and besides that I must get back to Boston."

She regarded him with an expression of marked disfavor.

"Humph," said she. "Quarters ain't good enough for you, I suppose."

"On the contrary, it is I who am not good enough for the quarters."

Mehitabel went on with her work of arranging the curtains and putting the room to rights as she answered : —

"Well, I dare say you ain't; but what special thing 've you done?"

"Special thing?" Maurice repeated, somewhat confused. "Oh, I see. The fact is, I don't think I 've any right to impose on the hospitality of Mrs. Morison."

"Well," assented she again, "I dare say you ain't; but if she 's willing, you ain't no occasion to grumble, 's I see. She ain't a-going to hear of your starting out hot-foot, 's if she would n't keep you. It 'd look bad for the reputation of the family."

"But," began he, "I" —

"Besides," the old woman continued, ignoring his attempt to speak, "you ain't got much to wear. Them petticoats you come in, which ain't suitable for any man to wear, without it's the bearded lady in the circus if she's a man, which I never rightly knew, is so torn to pieces by the grace of heaven that you can't go in them, and all the rest of your clothes are all holes and blood."

"I suppose my clothes were pretty well used up," he replied, divided between a desire to laugh and a feeling that he should resent the affront to his clerical garb; "and of course my baggage is nowhere. Can I get clothing here, or shall I have to send to Boston?"

"You can't get men's petticoats," Mehitabel retorted uncompromisingly, "nor none of them Popish things. If it's good, plain God-fearing pants and such, there ain't no trouble, and the price is reasonable."

"Plain God-fearing trousers and coat will do," Maurice answered, bursting into a laugh. "Do you think that you could send for some if I give you the size?"

She was evidently pleased at the success of her attempts to be funny, for her face relaxed, but she set her mouth primly.

"I'd go myself," was her reply. "I'd trust myself to pick out things, and it might give the girls ideas to go traipsing round buying pants and men's fixings."

When she was gone Maurice lay in a pleasant half-doze, smiling at the absurd old servant with her labored determination to be thought witty, and wondering at the caprices of existence. He was interrupted by the arrival of his breakfast, and after that had been disposed of he received a visit from Mrs.

Morison. She was a fine old lady with snowy hair, her sweet face wrinkled into a relief-map of the journey of life, her eyes as bright and sparkling as those of her granddaughter. Wynne could see the family likeness at a glance, and said to himself that some day when time had wrinkled her smooth cheeks and whitened her hair Berenice would be such another beautiful dame. Mrs. Morison brought with her an air of brisk yet serene individuality, as of the fire which on a winter evening burns cheerily on the hearth, warming, invigorating, suggesting wholesome and happy thoughts. She was so kindly and yet so thoroughly alive to the very tips of her fingers that her age almost seemed rather a merry disguise like the powdered hair of a young girl.

"Good-morning," she greeted him cheerily. "The doctor says that you are doing well. I hope that you feel so."

"Thank you," he answered. "I don't seem to have as many joints as I used to have, but I 'm doing famously, thanks to the skillful treatment I had last night."

"It was not too skillful, I 'm afraid; but Dr. Murray says I did no harm, and that 's really a good deal of a compliment from him."

"I cannot thank you enough for your kindness," Maurice said. "It is so strange to be taken care of "—

He broke off suddenly, awkward from shyness and genuine feeling. He looked up, however, to meet a glance so reassuring that he felt at once at ease.

"It is time that it ceased to be strange," she returned. "We must try before you go to make you more accustomed to being looked after a little."

He returned her kind look with a grateful smile.

"You are too generous," he said. "I must not trespass on your good-nature. I think that I could manage to get back to Boston to-day if the trains are running."

"The trains are running, but that is no reason why you should think of running too. We mean to mend you before we let you go."

"But "—

"There is no 'but' about it," Mrs. Morison declared, speaking more seriously. "Berenice and I have settled it, and we are accustomed to having our own way. You are selfish to wish that we should be left with all the obligation on our shoulders."

"Obligation?" repeated he. "How on earth is there any obligation but mine?"

"Do you think that there is no obligation in owing to you Bee's life?"

He stared at her in complete confusion. He made a vain effort to recall clearly what had happened in the car. He remembered the crash, the din, the pain, the horrible clutch on his arm, the choking reek of the smoke, his frantic fear for Berenice, but all these things seemed blurred in his mind like a landscape obscured by a night-fog. Only one memory stood out clear and sharp; that was the joy of holding Berenice clasped in his arms, and of thinking that they would die together. He felt the blood mount in his cheek at the thought, and he hastened to speak, lest his hostess should divine what was in his mind.

"Why do you say that?" he asked. "It was not I that saved her. I was not even conscious when she was taken out."

Mrs. Morison smiled, and touched lightly with

the tip of her finger the bandaged arm which lay on the outside of the coverlid.

"We won't dispute about it," said she. "The proof is here. Let it go, if you like; but we shall remember."

"But," protested Maurice, "it wouldn't be honest for me to let you think that I did anything for Miss Morison. I should have been only too glad to help her, but I couldn't. I wish what you think could have been true; but since it isn't, I can't let you think it is."

Mrs. Morison let the matter drop, but her kind old eyes were brighter than ever. She contented herself with saying that at least he was to remain with them, and need not try to escape; then she led the talk to more indifferent matters. Her hand, worn and thin, the blue veins relieved under the delicate skin, lay on the white coverlid like a beautiful carving of ivory. As Maurice looked at it, it brought into his mind the hand of his mother, as in her last days, when he sat by her bedside, it had rested in the same fashion. The tears sprang in his eyes at the memory, half-blinding him. As he tried to brush them away unseen he caught the sympathetic look of his hostess, and its sweetness overpowered him still more. Meeting his glance, she leaned forward tenderly, taking his fingers in her own.

"What is it?" asked she softly.

"Your hand," he answered simply. "It looked so like my mother's."

"Poor boy," she murmured.

He returned the pressure of her clasp, and then the masculine dislike for effusiveness asserted itself.

"I'm afraid I'm weaker than I thought," he said shamefacedly. "I'm almost hysterical."

She glanced at him shrewdly, and smiling, rose.

" For all that," she returned, "you are to get up. Dr. Murray says that it will be better, and you would get hopelessly tired of bed before to-morrow morning. I'll send you something in the way of clothing, and we'll let you play invalid in a dressing-gown to-day. If Mehitabel can help you, you've only to ring. I dare say that you can do something with one hand."

"One never knows until he tries," Wynne answered.

Maurice wished to ask for a barber, but could not pluck up courage. When he was alone he gazed ruefully into the mirror at his stoutly sprouting black beard, which so little understood the exigencies of the situation that it persisted in growing as vigorously as ever.

" If I stay here a couple of days without shaving," he mused, " I shall simply be hideous. Well, my vanity very likely needs a lesson. What did Mrs. Morison mean by my saving Miss Morison's life? I certainly could not have said so when I was unconscious. It must be from something she herself has said. If I could only remember what did happen after the car went over!"

His bath and toilet were difficult and unsatisfactory enough. The linen with which he was provided, however, smelled sweetly of lavender, and the odor seemed to bear him away into a pleasant reverie, in which he was chiefly conscious of the pleasure of being near — of being near, he assured himself, so delightful and sympathetic an old lady as Mrs. Morison. A feeling of well-being, of content, saturated him. Behind his thought of his hostess and his denial to himself that the presence under the same

roof of Berenice was the true source of his happiness,
lay the consciousness that the latter regarded him as
her preserver. He resolutely thrust the thought down
deep into his heart, but he could not forget it.

Before he was ready to leave his chamber Mehitabel brought him a telegram from Mrs. Staggchase, to
whom he had sent a line announcing his safety. It
was merely a friendly word with an offer to come to
him if he needed her ; but it changed the whole current of his thoughts. He seemed to see the mocking
smile of his cousin as she read that he was staying
with the Morisons, and to hear again her words about
his period of temptation. He resolved, however, to
put the whole question of the future out of his mind.
Somehow there must be a way to steer safely between
his duty and his inclination. He failed to reflect
that he who decides to compromise between duty and
desire has already sacrificed the former.

Berenice greeted him on his appearance in the
library, whither he descended rather shakily. She
held in her hand a telegram when he entered under
the escort of Mehitabel, and her cheeks were flushed.
Instantly into his mind came the feeling that her
color was connected with the message which the yellow paper brought, and he became jealous in a flash.
There was no possible reason why he should scent a
rival in the mere presence in his lady's hand of a telegram, unless there were an intangible shade of self-
consciousness in her manner. He had come down-
stairs eager to see her and to assure himself that she
was really no worse for the accident, but the sight of
the paper instantly changed his mood. In crossing
the half-dozen steps from the door to the fire Maurice
shifted from frank eagerness to aggrieved distrust.

He said good-morning as he entered in the tone of a
lover; he spoke as he reached the hearth with the
formality of an acquaintance.

He was too keenly alive to the change in his feelings not to know that he showed it. He endeavored
to hide his perturbation under an appearance of simple politeness, but he was sure that she watched him
and that she was puzzled.

"Well," she said, as she arranged a cushion in the
big easy-chair beside the crackling wood fire, "you
have the genuine scarred veteran air."

"Please don't bother to wait on me, Miss Morison," he answered, trying to speak naturally, and
painfully aware that he did not succeed. "I 'm all
right, except for the scratch on my arm."

"Scratch, indeed," she returned with a smile which
almost disarmed him. "How many stitches did the
doctor have to put in?"

"'Bout enough for a week's mending," interpolated
Mehitabel, putting him into the chair with an air of
authority, and preparing to retire. "There, now
stay there till you want to go upstairs again, and
then send for me."

"Indeed," he protested, laughing, "I am not helpless. You can't make a baby of me just for a disabled arm."

"I suppose," Berenice said, "that I ought to be
willing to say that I had rather the wound were in
my back, where it would have been but for you; only
as a matter of fact I shouldn't be telling the truth.
I am sorry for you, Mr. Wynne; but I can't help
being glad for myself."

She seemed to be setting herself to win him from
his ill-humor, and he had to look into the fire away

from her lips and eyes to prevent himself from yielding. He fortified his resistance, which he felt to be
weakening, by the reflection that it was his duty not
to be carried away by her charm. He called upon
his religious scruples to aid him in holding to his
passion-born jealousy.

"There," Miss Morison said, when he had been
properly ensconced and Mehitabel had departed,
"now it is my duty to entertain you. What shall
I do? My accomplishments are at your service.
I can read, without stopping to spell out any except
the very longest words. I can play two tunes on the
mandolin, only that I 've forgotten the middle of one
and the other has a run in it that I always have to
skip. The piano is too far off across the hall to be
available ; so that the little I can do in that way
does n't count. I can — let me see, I can teach you
three solitaires, or play cribbage, or — I beg your pardon, I forgot."

"You forgot what?" he asked, so intent upon
watching the sunlight filtering through her hair that
he had hardly noticed what she said.

She looked at him questioningly.

"You don't play cards, perhaps ?" she said tenta-
tively.

"No," he answered. "In the country in my boyhood they were n't held in high repute, to say the
least ; and naturally we don't play at the Clergy
House."

There was a brief interval of silence, during which
he watched her, while she in her turn looked into the
fire. When she spoke again it was in a different tone.

"I know," said she, "that you must think me
frivolous, and that I can't be anything else ; but " —

"Oh, no," he interrupted, "I never thought you frivolous."

She made an impulsive little gesture with one of her hands.

"Oh, you would n't put it in that way, I dare say. You 'd call it being worldly, I suppose; but it comes to much the same thing."

Wynne could not understand what was the direction of her thoughts, and he was taken entirely by surprise when she leaned forward impulsively and took in hers his free hand.

"At least," she said, quickly and eagerly, "I can't forget that you saved my life, and I thank you from my heart if I don't know just how to do it in words."

He returned the pressure of her fingers, longing to cover them with kisses.

"I 'm afraid," responded he, "that I 've very little claim to glory on account of anything I did for you. I certainly don't deserve the credit of having saved you. I only wish I did."

She laughed gayly, springing up from her seat, and he realized that his voice had lost all trace of unfriendliness. He told himself recklessly that he did not care; that if he were a thousand times a priest he could not but be kindly to Berenice.

"Come," she laughed, "we have been through a real adventure; and that 's more than happens to most people if they live to be a hundred." Suddenly she became grave. "I can't bear to think of it, though," she added. Then she turned toward him, and spoke with seriousness. "At least, Mr. Wynne, I am not so flighty that I do not thank God for my escape yesterday."

"Amen," he responded.

She walked over to the window, and stood looking out at the sunny day. The fire burned cheerfully on the wide, red hearth, and Maurice looked into its glowing heart thinking gratefully of his preservation and of the friendly refuge into which he had been brought. No reverent man can come face to face with death and escape without some feeling of awe and of gratitude to the power which has preserved him; and Maurice was filled with a sense of how great had been the hand which could bring him through such peril, how kind the protection which had preserved Berenice unscathed. Humility and tenderness overflowed his heart, and the inward thanksgiving which his spirit breathed was as sweet and as unselfish as if a personal passion had never invaded his breast.

"It seems to me," Berenice remarked from her place by the window, "that the woods on the hills over there are already beginning to show signs of spring. There is a sort of delicate change of color in them that means buds beginning to grow."

Before he could reply, the door opened, and Mehitabel presented herself with a card.

"Oh," said Berenice, as she received it, "already!"

There seemed to Maurice something of impatience or dismay in her tone. She excused herself and went out, leaving the old servant with Wynne. As soon as the door closed, Mehitabel turned upon him at once.

"Do you know him?" she demanded.

"Know whom?"

"This sprig that's come from Boston to see Miss Bee?"

Maurice looked at her with a sharp sense that he ought not to allow her to go on, yet with a desire to know more so burning that he could not refrain.

" I did n't even know that anybody had come from
Boston to see Miss Morison," he replied ; " so that it
is n't easy to say whether I know him or not."

" His name is Parker Stanford, and he 's all the
signs of being better 'n his grandfathers and knowing
it through and through. He 's too fond of his looks
to suit me."

" I don't know him," Maurice answered, " except
that I 've heard my cousin, Mrs. Staggchase, mention
his name. He 's very rich, I believe, and a good deal
of a leader in society."

" Humph," sniffed Mehitabel. " He may be a
leader in society, but he 's as selfish as a sucking calf ! "

" You seem to know him pretty well," commented
Maurice. " I suppose you 've seen him often."

" Never saw him in my life till this minute. Young
man, I 'll tell you this, though. Every woman with
any brains knows what a man is the minute she claps
eyes on him ; only if he 's good-looking, or awful
wicked, or makes love to her, or forty thousand other
things, she 'll deny to herself that she knows any bad
about him."

" Then it seems to be much the same thing as if
your sex were n't gifted with such extraordinary
insight," Maurice responded, laughing.

" If women did n't cheat themselves there would n't
be no marriages," Mehitabel retorted, grinning, and
retired in evident delight over her success in repartee.

As for Maurice, he became wonderfully grave the
moment he was left alone.

XII

To be is an irregular verb in all languages, but
always regular is the verb *to love*. There are many
sides to the existence of mortals; but to love is the
same for high and low. Any mortal knows little
enough about himself; but a mortal in love knows
nothing. Love is a bewildering and a bedazzling fire,
wherewith the eyes of youth are so blinded that they
are able to see clearly neither within nor without.
Often it happens, indeed, that the first intimation the
heart has of the presence of the divine flame is the
bewilderment which fills the mind.

Berenice had long been contentedly and unenthu-
siastically convinced that she was to marry Parker
Stanford. She approved of him; he was wealthy, wellborn, agreeable enough, and apparently very fond of
her. She had not, it is true, become formally engaged
to him. When he had asked her to become his wife
she had teasingly asked for time for deliberation;
but this was not because she felt any especial doubt
about ultimately accepting him. She was pleased,
maiden-like, to dally, and shrank from being formally
bound. Her pulses had not yet stirred with the unrest which love awakens. Her vanity had been
pleasantly aroused, and for the rest she was in all
the ignorance of those whom passion has not yet made
wise. She regarded marriage rather as an abstract

thing; she was familiar with the idea that it was a
matter of social arrangement and necessity, to be
looked upon as a part of life. She had, it is true,
some vaguely sentimental notion that love was a
necessity, and being persuaded that the match before
her was a desirable one, was persuaded also that
she was in love with Stanford. At least she was sure
that he was in love with her, and as she liked him,
that answered. To find a man amusing, agreeable,
handsome, and fulfilling the social requirements of a
desirable husband seemed to her unsophisticated mind
to love him. She was pleased with her lover; she
was not insensible of the triumph of having won the
attentions of one of the most sought-after men in her
set; to pass her life in the well-ordered establishment
which he would provide seemed to her a decorous and
desirable method of fulfilling the destiny of a woman.
She was willing that the event should be postponed
indefinitely, it is true; and the man himself in her
considerations of the future was something of a shadow;
a shadow pleasant enough, yet so remote as to count
for nothing intimately important. She was somewhat
less sophisticated than most modern girls, inheriting
that New England nature which is slow to understand emotion and endowed with the power rather of
tenacity than of spontaneity of passion.

When on the day previous Stanford had come to
the train to see Berenice off, she had been especially
gracious. She had been in particularly good spirits,
full of amusement that Mr. Wynne was to be her
neighbor on the train, and that he did not know it.
She had chanced to send for tickets with Mrs. Wilson,
the pair had laughingly planned the arrangement, and
Berenice had promised herself some entertainment in

teasing the young cleric on the journey. It pleased her, too, that Stanford should take the trouble to come to the station, especially as Kate West, who had tried so hard to secure him despite the fact that she was ten years his senior, chanced to be meeting a friend and to be there to see. She allowed herself to smile on her lover with more warmth than usual, and was a little vexed as well as a little amused by it afterward. On the train she reflected that if she were to be so gracious Stanford would press his suit more warmly than she wished; yet on the other hand it occurred to her that if she were to be engaged to him, she might as well get it over. Why not marry in the spring and go abroad? She wished much to go to Bayreuth for the Wagner operas in the summer, and the aunt with whom she had hoped to travel was not willing to go. Besides, she really could not afford the trip, and at least Stanford had plenty of money. The idea of marrying with a thought to his wealth was distasteful, and she at once said to herself that she could not do that; but if she were to marry him — As the train rolled on she had filled in the talk with Wynne with speculations whether it might not be as well to let Stanford propose once more, and have matters settled.

These cogitations, however, she interspersed with reflections that her traveling companion had a beautiful eye and a finely cut nostril; that he was on the whole a fine-looking man, handsome and well made, if he were not disguised in that detestable clerical garb; and that his hands were distinctly those of a gentleman. She liked the tones of his voice and the carriage of his head, smiling to herself at the thought that in the latter there was hardly so much meekness as was to be expected in one of his profession. She laughed at him almost openly, for to the young woman of to-day there is apt to be something bordering on the ludicrous and unmanly in a youth who is preparing to take orders, no matter how great her respect for the completed clergyman. Berenice felt something not entirely free from a trace of good-natured contempt for deacons in the abstract, not dreaming that she might be led to make an exception in favor of this especial deacon in the concrete. She became more and more alive to the attractions of Wynne, although up to the time of the accident she hardly realized the fact.

From the moment, however, that the rescuer said to her that Maurice had saved her life, her feeling was changed. She felt that she had failed to do Wynne justice; that she had allowed his cassock to be the sign of a lack of manhood; she accused herself of having wronged him. She began now to exalt him in her thoughts, and to regard him as a hero. She had long been aware of the effect that she had on him. From the morning when she had encountered him at the North End, and had met the quick, troubled glance of his eye, full of doubt and of fire, she had been conscious that he was not indifferent to her presence. She had not reasoned about it; but it gave her pleasure. It was a passing breath of homage, pleasing like a breath from some rose-bed passed in a walk. Up to the moment, however, when she said to herself that he had risked his life for her, Berenice had never consciously thought of Maurice as a lover. When she saw him lying insensible, depending upon her, a new feeling kindled in her breast. She would not think of it; she shrank from it, and refused to acknowledge it to herself. Yet for her the world was

altered, and however she might try to hide the fact
from her heart, secretly she felt it fluttering and
throbbing deep within her breast.

When the telegram came in the morning announcing the visit of Stanford, her first thought was one of
gratification. The act was friendly, and it gave her
a pleasant sense of importance. The reaction came
instantly. The purport of the visit flashed upon her.
She remembered how she had smiled on Stanford yesterday, — yesterday that now seemed so far away that
she looked back to it over distances of emotion which
made it strangely remote. She felt that she must
receive him; but she found herself seeking for the
means of making him understand that what he hoped
was forever impossible. She certainly could never
marry him. She was sure that the thought could
never have been seriously in her mind. The idea of
belonging to him, of having no right to think of another man with tenderness, became all at once too
repugnant to be endured. She would not consider
why her attitude was so different from that of yesterday; she only insisted vehemently in her thought that
now first she really knew her own mind. Her cheek
burned at the reflection that Stanford was probably
sure of her consent to be his. It seemed to give him
a claim upon her; to shut the door upon all other
possibilities; to smutch the whiteness of her soul and
render her unworthy of any man whom she might
some day come to love. To remember that in her
secret thought she had actually contemplated being
Stanford's wife made her cringe.

She stood by the window with the telegram in her
hands, twisting it to and fro, wondering what it was
possible for her to do. She thought of excusing her-

self from her visitor when he should come, but the
evasion seemed to her unworthy, and she was eager
to free herself from even the suspicion of belonging
to him. She felt that she could not breathe freely
until she were clear of the faintest shadow of any
claim, even in Stanford's secret thought. She must
belong once more to herself.

It was at this point in her musings that Wynne
came into the library. He was pale and sunken-eyed,
and the tinge of his sprouting beard gave to his face
a certain virility which startled her. It imparted a
trace of something perhaps remotely animal and brutal, subtly altering his whole expression. He became
in appearance at once more vigorous and more human.
For the first time Berenice saw a suggestion of the
possibility that this man might be a master; and the
strength in man that makes a woman tremble also
makes her thrill. Some inward voice cried in her
ear: " Here is the reason why Parker Stanford is repugnant!" But she denied the accusation indignantly
in her mind, putting the thought by, and refusing to
see in Wynne anything more than the man to whom
she had cause to be grateful. Yet in that part of her
mind where a woman keeps so many things which she
declines to confess to herself that she knows, Berenice
from that moment kept the fact that this man before
her had touched her heart.

She made a strong effort to greet Wynne frankly,
and to conceal from him the feeling which his coming
excited. She would have died rather than show him
how glad she was that he had come. She saw the
eagerness of his glance when he entered, and she felt
the warmth of his greeting. She noted the change in
his manner, and fancied it arose from his fear lest he

betray himself. She set herself to overcome his re-
serve; and when she had succeeded she sprang up
with a gay laugh, light-hearted and full of a delicious,
incomprehensible pleasure. She wanted to break out
into singing, so sweet is the delight of new love un-
recognized save as simple joy in living.

The entrance of Mehitabel with the card of Mr.
Stanford brought her back to earth.

"Already?" she said, feeling as if she were de-
frauded that thus her moment of enjoyment was cut
short.

She could not trust herself for more than a word of
excuse to Wynne, but hurried to her chamber to collect her thoughts and to examine her toilet before she
descended to her visitor. Some inward personality
seemed to be trying properly to frame the speech by
which she should make Stanford understand that it
was idle for him to hope longer; while all the time
she was thinking of the man whom she had just left.

Stanford was holding out his hands to the blaze in
the fireplace when she entered the parlor, for the
morning was a sharp one. Berenice saw with appreciation how satisfactory he was in all his appointments and in his bearing; how well kept and how
well bred. She felt, however, for the first time that
he was perhaps a little too faultlessly attired for a
man, and she glanced at his cleanly shaven cheek with
an acute memory of the stout black stubble on the
face she had left behind her, yet carried still in the
eye of her mind.

"Good-morning," she said, giving the visitor her
hand, and making her manner at once as cordial and
as unemotional as possible. "It was too good of
you to come all the way up here in this cold weather,
just to see me."

He pressed her hand with eagerness, and so meaningly that the color flushed into her cheeks. His air seemed to her to have in it a suggestion of intimacy which was irritating beyond endurance.

"There was nothing good about it," he answered. "I had to assure myself by actual sight that you were safe; and, besides, it gave me an excuse for coming, and I was only too glad of that."

"Sit down," Berenice said, ignoring the compliment. "It really was frightful; but I came through safe. Grandmother would n't let me see the paper this morning; but I know the details must have been horrible."

She grew grave as she spoke. She seemed again to see the whole terrible sight. The wreck, thrusting out tongues of fire, the dead and the dying strewn about on the snow; Wynne, at her feet, insensible and ghastly in the uncertain light. She shuddered and drew in her breath.

"Oh, don't let's talk about it!" she exclaimed. "I can't bear to think of it, and I feel as if I should never get it out of my head!"

Stanford was silent a moment, pulling his mustache as if trying to find the right word.

"It must have been awful," he said hesitatingly; "and I'll never speak of it again if you don't wish. Only I must say that it was dreadful to me too. The thought of how near I came to losing you is more than I can stand."

She leaned back in her chair, suddenly chilled, yet moved by the feeling in his voice. Her conscience reproached her that she had allowed a false hope to grow up in his mind. She felt as if he were establishing a claim upon her, and that at any cost she must make him see things as they were.

" You are very kind," she responded, trying to keep her tones from being too cold; " but of course we always feel a shock when any friend has been through a great danger."

Her eyes were cast down, but she could divine his regard of disquiet and surprise.

" And especially those we love," he added, leaning forward, and endeavoring to take her hand.

" Oh, of course, Mr. Stanford," she said hastily. " That is of course true. Were people in Boston much excited about the accident? "

She felt herself a hypocrite, yet she could not help this one more effort to avoid the explanation she dreaded.

" I suppose so. I don't know. I was so taken up with thinking about you, that I paid very little attention to anything else."

" I 'm afraid I did n't deserve it. I was n't thinking of anybody but myself. It was very good of you."

" Of course you were n't thinking of anybody," Stanford responded, pulling his mustache more furiously than ever; " but I was at the club instead of being in a burning car. I was half crazy at the thought that my future wife " —

" Stop! " Berenice broke in. " You must n't say such things. I 'm not your future wife! "

" Forgive me. I know I have n't any right to say that when you have n't promised; but I can't help thinking of you so, and " —

" Oh, please don't! " she cried.

A wave of humiliation, of repulsion, of terror, swept over her. That this man had thought of her as his wife seemed almost like an inexorable bond.

She shrank away from him with an impulse too strong
to be controlled.

"But, Berenice, I "—

She sprang up and faced him.

"I have never promised you!" she declared with
hurried vehemence. "I never will promise you! I
can't marry you. If I've made you think so, I didn't
mean to. I didn't know my own mind. I thought
— O Mr. Stanford, if I have deceived you, I beg
your pardon. I "—

The tears choked and blinded her. She broke off,
and put her handkerchief to her eyes; but when she
heard him rise and hurry toward her, she went on
hastily.

"I've let you go on thinking I'd marry you; I
know I have. I thought so myself; but I've found
out that it's all a mistake. I didn't realize what I
was doing. I'm so sorry. I do hope you'll forgive
me."

He regarded her in amazement not unmingled with
indignation.

"You have let me think so," he said. "Now I suppose there's somebody else."

"Oh, I shall never marry anybody," she answered
quickly.

"When a girl tells one man she never'll marry,"
retorted he bitterly, "there's sure to be another man
in her mind."

She felt herself burn with blushes to her brow; and
then in very shame and anger to grow pale again.
Her first impulse was to leave him; but she controlled herself. He was her guest, he had come all
the way from Boston to assure himself that she was
safe, and more than all she was sorely aware that she

had not treated him well. To have injured a man is
to a woman apt to be an excuse for continuing to
treat him ill; but when the opposite occurs she can
be very forbearing.

"There is no other man," she said with dignity.
Then she added, more mildly: "Badly as I may have
treated you, I don't think you've quite the right to
say such a thing as that to me."

"I have n't," he acknowledged contritely. "I beg
your pardon; but I surely have a right to ask what
I've done to change you so. You were not like this
yesterday."

Berenice forced herself to meet his eyes, but she
ignored his question. She sank back into the chair
from which she had risen to face him.

"Come," said she, trying to speak lightly, "I don't
see why we need stand. We are not rehearsing private theatricals. It was very kind of you to take the
trouble to come all the way up here, but you must see
that my nerves are all on edge. The shock has completely upset me."

"Poor girl!" he said.

There was a genuine ring in his voice which irritated while it touched her. She hated to feel that he
was really hurt. It made her seem the more deeply
guilty, and she unconsciously desired to discover in
him some excuse for her own shortcomings.

"Oh, it 's over now," she responded. "Let 's talk
of something else."

"I 'd be glad to," Stanford replied, "but I can't
seem to. I want to know how you escaped. I won't
ask you to tell me now, but I keep thinking about
it."

"I 'm afraid I can't tell you much. I remember

a tremendous crash, and being thrown against Mr.
Wynne " —

" Mr. Wynne ? "

The tone showed Berenice that Stanford did not
attach especial importance to the question, but asked
only from a natural curiosity. Nevertheless she could
not keep her voice from hurrying a little as she answered : —

" Mr. Wynne is a young clergyman who was in
the seat next to mine. He 's a cousin of Mrs. Staggchase."

" Oh, a clergyman," Stanford echoed.

The tone seemed to her excited mood to be full of
intolerable superiority.

" He may be a clergyman," she retorted with unnecessary warmth, " but he is a gentleman and a
hero. He saved my life ! "

" Oh, he did ! "

The exclamation stung her beyond endurance. She
sprang up with flashing eyes.

" Mr. Stanford," she exclaimed, " I don't know
what you mean to insinuate, but you will please to
remember that you are speaking of the man that
saved me, and of my grandmother's guest."

" Your grandmother's guest ? Do you mean that
he is staying here ? "

" Certainly he is. Why should n't he be ? "

The young man rose, and stood looking at her a
moment; then he began to pace up and down, his
gaze fixed on the floor. Berenice felt herself being
swept away by tumultuous feelings which she could
neither compel nor understand. Her mind was in
confusion, out of which rose most definitely the desire
that Stanford would go and leave her in peace.

"There is no reason why I should question the right of Mrs. Morison to choose her own guests," said Stanford at length, pausing, and speaking with an evident effort to be entirely calm; "and as I know nothing of this Mr. Wynne, I should n't in any case have a right to say anything about him. You can't wonder, though, that I 'm jealous of him for having had the luck to save your life, or that when I come here and find you so suddenly different and this man staying in the house and a hero in your eyes " —

"I wish that you would n't keep calling Mr. Wynne 'this,'" she interrupted hastily. "It sounds dreadfully superior. Come," she added, softening her tone, and pleased at having prevented him from going on, "there is no need that we should quarrel about him. He is a priest, or going to be, and he 's to take the vows of celibacy, so that it is absurd for anybody to think of being jealous of him. If I seem different to-day, it is n't any wonder after what I 've been through."

"I beg your pardon," he said, coming quickly forward and extending his hand. "I 'm awfully selfish. Of course I understand that what you 've been saying is n't to be taken seriously. We stand as we did before. Only," he added, his voice deepening, "you are to remember that the danger of losing you has shown me how fond I am of you. Good-by."

He stooped and kissed her hand, and before she could speak, he was gone. She stood where he had left her, hearing him leave the house, and the tears came into her eyes.

"Oh," she moaned to herself, "I 've made it worse than it was before. I wanted to be honest, and he would n't let me !"

She stood a moment disconsolately, then she shrugged
her shoulders as if to throw off all care.

"Well," she told herself, " I 've given him fair
warning.   Now it is time to go and entertain grandmother's guest."

XIII

WHILE the advocates of Father Frontford were laboring, the friends of other candidates were not idle. By the middle of January, however, the contest had practically narrowed itself down to a struggle between the supporters of the Father and those of the Rev. Rutherford Strathmore. Other names had been suggested, but in the end it was felt that there was no doubt that one or the other of these men would succeed to the vacant bishopric. Even church politicians are human, and most divisions are sure sooner or later to arouse the vanity of contestants. The struggle, which begins without consciously personal motives, is apt to be strongly tempered by the determination not to be beaten. For thousands who can accomplish the difficult feat of triumphing humbly, there is hardly one who can submit to defeat generously; and against the humiliation of failure the human being instinctively strives with every power. Those who upheld the rival candidates were undoubtedly convinced that they had the best interests of the church at heart; but that meant the election — even at some cost! — of their favorite.

There could be no question that Mr. Strathmore was the more generally popular candidate. He was a man who appealed strongly to the common heart, both by his sympathy and by flexibility of character and temperament which made it impossible for him to be repellantly stern or austere. He preached the high ideals which are dear to the best thought of the children of the Puritans; he demanded high purpose and high life, noble aims and unfailing charity; while he laid little stress on dogmas, and allowed an elasticity of individual interpretation of doctrine which made the creed easy of adoption by all who believed anything. His enemies — for he was by no means so insignificant as to be without enemies — declared that he carried the doctrine of " mental reservations " to the extent of rendering the articles of faith mere empty forms of words; his defenders protested that he was but wisely conforming in non-essentials to the progressive spirit of the age. Bitterly attacked by the more conservative members of his own denomination, he was looked up to by the general public as a great spiritual leader, and loved with an affection exceedingly rare in this unpriestly age. Those who urged his elevation had the support of the body of the laity, and also of the public outside of the church, which for once was interested in church politics on account of affection and reverence for the candidate.

Mr. Strathmore himself had the discretion not to express himself freely in relation to his own feelings in the matter. The enthusiastic assertions of his friends that no one save him could fill the vacant office he had answered by observing with a smile that the church was indeed fallen upon evil times if there was in it but one man fit to be made a bishop. He had added, it is true, that if it were the will of Providence that he be the one chosen he should accept the office as a duty given him by Heaven, and should devote himself to it with all his ability. It was by no

means the least of Mr. Strathmore's gifts that he had
the grace of speaking always without any suggestion
of cant. There was an impression of candor and
enthusiasm in everything he said, so that words which
might on the lips of another sound conventional or
meaningless became on his spontaneous and vital.
" He is too modest and self-forgetful to wish for the
honor," his friends commented now ; " but he is too
conscientious not to put aside his personal preferences
for the good of the church. He may shrink from the
high places, but he is the ideal man for them." As
much of this sort of thing was said in the public print,
it is not impossible that the Rev. Rutherford Strathmore was aware of it; but he had the good taste to
ignore it, even in conversation with his nearest friends,
and the tact to carry himself without self-consciousness
or the appearance of humility with which a smaller
man would have shown that he knew that he was being
praised.

Of friends he had a host well-nigh innumerable.
He had an especial liking for young men, and a great
influence over them. He had the art of arousing in
them an emotional enthusiasm toward a higher life, so
that he had never lack of efficient helpers among the
laymen in whatever projects he undertook. He had
also that invaluable attribute of the priest, the gift of
inspiring confidence and opening the heart. He did
not seem to seek confidences, yet they always came to
him. Young men in trouble, young women in woe,
lads in the impressionable period when sentimental
experiences assume importance prodigious, youth of
both sexes bewildered between physical and religious
sensations, the sick and the poor, the ignorant and
the cultivated, all found in him that sympathy which

opens the heart, and which, most of human qualities, endears a man to his fellows.

Mr. Strathmore and Father Frontford might not unfairly be said to represent the two extremes of modern theology: on the one hand the relaxing of creeds, the liberalizing of thought, the breaking down of barriers which have divided the church from the world, and, above all, acquiescence in individual liberty of thought; on the other hand, the conservative element taking the position that individual liberty of interpretation means nothing less than a practical destruction of all standards, and that what is called the liberalizing of thought can result in nothing less than the utter overthrow of the church. Undoubtedly either would have declared that he held the other to be a devout and godly man ; but he must inwardly have added, a mistaken and conscientiously mischievous one. If Mr. Strathmore was right, Father Frontford was little less than a mediæval bigot, unhappily belated ; if the Father was correct, then Strathmore, despite all his influence, his popularity, his power of attracting great congregations, was little better than a dangerous and pestilent heretic.

One morning Mr. Strathmore sat in his study talking to a visitor in clerical dress. The room was luxuriously appointed, for Mr. Strathmore's belongings were always of a sort to minister pleasantly to the sense. The walls were lined with books in sumptuous bindings, the windows hung with heavy curtains of crimson velvet, the floor covered with rich rugs. A bronze statuette of Savonarola stood on an ebony pedestal between two windows, consorting somewhat oddly with the velvet draperies which swept down on either side. Indeed, there might be thought to be something in the thin, spiritually impassioned face of the monk, in the eagerly imperative gesture with which he pointed with one hand to the open Bible he held in the other, not entirely consistent with the somewhat worldly air of the room. The handsome carved chairs, cushioned with fine leather, the beautiful landscape by Rousseau above the mantel, the bronze and silver of the writing-table, had been given to the popular pastor by enthusiastic admirers, however, and perhaps the Savonarola better expressed his own inner feelings. Mr. Strathmore's face, it is true, was in itself somewhat unspiritual. The clergyman was of commanding presence, and while neither unusually tall nor exceptionally large, he somehow gave, from the air with which he carried himself, the impression of size and importance. His eyes were keen and piercing, neither study nor the advance of years having dimmed their clear sight or reduced him to the necessity of wearing glasses. He was still handsome, although his face was too full, and he was too generously provided with chins. As he talked, his face would have seemed almost blank and expressionless had it not been for his keen eyes, full of alert intelligence and abundant vitality. His glance was acute and searching, and yet nothing could exceed its kindliness and sympathy.

The visitor who sat talking with Mr. Strathmore was almost ludicrously his opposite. Mr. Pewtap was a small, ineffectual creature, with inefficiency oozing out of his every pore. He was conspicuously the incarnation of well-meaning and exasperating incompetence; one of those men who might be forgiven everything but the fact that their stupidities are invariably the result of the best intentions. It was evident at a glance that this man had used the church as a genteel pauper asylum, wherein his ineptitude might be devoted to the service of Heaven since nothing gifted with the common sense of earth would tolerate it. His very attitude was an excuse, and the way in which he handled his hat might have provoked profanity in any saint at all addicted to nerves. Mr. Pewtap was more than usually crushed in his appearance, and toed in more than was his custom, because he had come on an awkward errand, and had been telling his host that he could not vote for him in the coming election.

Mr. Strathmore had received this declaration with good-humor, and even with no appearance of disapproval.

"Of course, Mr. Pewtap," he said, "I am human, and it would be disingenuous for me to pretend that I am not pleased by the fact that my name has been mentioned in connection with the bishopric. I can conscientiously affirm, however, that the good of the church is more dear to me than ambition. Even were it not, I hardly think that I am capable of being offended with any man who felt it his duty to vote against me."

He smiled with winning warmth. The other moved in his seat uneasily, becoming momentarily more apologetic until he seemed to beg pardon for existing at all.

"I have always felt," he said confusedly, "that you ought to be chosen. That is, I mean that when Bishop Challoner was taken from us I said to Mrs. Pewtap that you were sure to succeed him."

Mr. Strathmore smiled, but he did not offer to help his visitor out of the tangle in which he was evidently involving himself.

"It is n't the good of the church, exactly," Mr. Pewtap stumbled on, turning his seedy hat about like a slow wheel which had some connection with grinding out his speech, "that I — Yes, of course I mean that the good of the church must be considered first, as you say."

Speechlessness seemed to overcome him, and he looked upon his host with a piteous appeal in his face.

"I understand that it is not an easy thing for you to tell me that it seems best to you not to vote for me," Mr. Strathmore said kindly. "I appreciate your coming to me on an errand so hard for you."

Mr. Pewtap sighed eloquently.

"If circumstances," he interpolated eagerly, "if circumstances were different" —

"Of course," the other responded with a genial laugh. "As they are, however, it seems to you best to vote for Father Frontford, and you have a kindness for me that makes you come and tell me your reason. I 'm glad you do me the justice to believe that I won't misunderstand."

"Oh, I was sure you would n't misunderstand. You see, Mrs. Frostwinch has been so good to my family. I have seven children, Mr. Strathmore, all under ten."

The eye of the host twinkled, but he was otherwise of admirable gravity.

"And my chance might be better if you had n't so many?" he suggested.

"Oh, we never could have had so many if it had n't been for Mrs. Frostwinch," Mr. Pewtap responded eagerly. "I mean, of course, that we could n't have taken care of them all. She has for years given Mrs.

Pewtap a little annual income, — little to her, I mean, of course; but it does n't take much to be a great deal to us."

Mr. Strathmore picked up a paper-knife of cut silver and played with it a moment in silence, as if waiting for the other to go on.

"Do I understand," he said at length, "that Mrs. Frostwinch has something to do with your decision in regard to the election?"

"Yes; she wrote to me that she was sure that I'd vote for Father Frontford, and that she was greatly interested in his being bishop. It's the only thing she ever asked of me, and she has been so generous that I don't see how I can refuse when Father Front-ford is so good a man, and so earnest for the upbuild-ing of the church."

"You must certainly follow your conscience," Strathmore commented blandly.

"Oh, I should n't have any conscience against voting for you, Mr. Strathmore; I could n't possibly have. Besides, it would be my inclination if circum-stances were different. I wanted to explain to you that it is not because I fail to appreciate how kind you have been to me that I vote for him. When I was told yesterday that the vote was likely to be close, and that my vote might make a difference, I assure you I was quite distressed. I told Mrs. Pewtap last night in the night that I could n't feel comfortable till I'd seen you and explained."

"It is most kind of you," Strathmore put in, his face inscrutable, but his eyes still kindly.

"I wanted to explain that under the circumstances I had no choice."

"I understand. It is not necessary to say any

more about it. Of course in a case of this sort a man has only to follow his conscience, and let the consequences take care of themselves."

"That is what I said to Mrs. Pewtap," was the enthusiastic reply. "I said to her that you would understand that this is a matter to be decided by conscience and not by individual preferences. Otherwise I should have been very glad to vote for you. I am sure you understand that I personally wish you all success."

He rose as he spoke, his face lighted with an expression of relief.

"I am very much obliged to you, I'm sure," he ran on. "I knew you wouldn't blame me, but these things are always so hard to state properly so that there sha'n't be any misunderstanding. You have taken a great weight off of my mind. Of course, as you say, in such a case there is nothing to do but to act according to one's conscience, and let the consequences be cared for by a higher power. Only personally, you know, personally I shall be delighted if you are successful."

When Mr. Pewtap was gone Mr. Strathmore stood a moment in thought, his forehead wrinkled as if with doubt. Then his face melted into a smile, as if he were amused at the peculiarities of his visitor. He shrugged his shoulders, and sat down to write a note. At that moment there was a tap at the door, and his colleague came into the room.

"Good morning, Thurston," Mr. Strathmore greeted him. "I shall be ready to go with you in a moment. I am writing a note to Mrs. Gore."

The Rev. Philander Thurston was a short, brisk, worldly-looking divine, with shrewd glance. Nature

had evidently been somewhat too hasty or careless
in the making of his face, for she had cut his nostrils unpleasantly high and set his eyes much too near
together.

"I saw Mrs. Gore yesterday," Thurston responded.
"She thinks that she can answer for those votes of
which we were speaking. She says that the vote of
Mr. Pewtap will depend upon Mrs. Frostwinch."

"He has just been here," Strathmore said smiling.
"He told me in so many words that he is to vote for
Frontford. His conscience will not allow him to run
the risk of depriving his children of the annuity Mrs.
Frostwinch gives his wife. I'm sure I'm not in-
clined to blame him."

"It is outrageous that he should fail you after all
you've done for him," Thurston declared with some
heat. "I never had any confidence in him."

"Oh, he acts according to his nature," was the
good-humored response, "and I'm afraid there isn't
substance enough to him for grace to get a very
strong hold to change him. If Mrs. Frostwinch is
taking an active part in this matter there are others
she can influence."

"Yes," the colleague said. "I thought that she was
too much taken up with that mind-healing business;
but she evidently wants to help bring the church back
to the formalities of the Middle Ages. Frontford
would have the whole diocese going to confession if
he had his way."

"He could do nothing of the kind if he did wish
to do it," Mr. Strathmore answered quietly. "The
worst that he could bring about would be to give
the impression to the world that the church was retro-
grading instead of progressing. He would be entirely

opposed to individual liberty of conscience every-where, and that seems to me to be in opposition to the spirit of the age."

" It undoubtedly is," assented the young man eagerly.

" The gravest harm that he could do in the church," pursued the other, " would be to encourage the sub-stitution of form for spirit. The more religious faith is shaken, the greater is the temptation to supply its place by a ritual, and this temptation seems to me the most imminent and deadly peril of the church to-day."

" It certainly is," confirmed the colleague.

" Besides," Strathmore added emphatically, rising as he spoke, " the deepest need of any time can be met only by a church which is in sympathy with the tendencies of the time."

" You put it admirably," the other murmured.

Strathmore regarded him keenly, almost as if he suspected some hidden thought behind the words.

" It is time for us to go," he said in his usual genial tone.

The two clergymen left the house and went down the street together, talking of parish business, until they came to the street-corner where they were to take a car. As they stood waiting for this convey-ance, a lady came quickly forward and spoke to Mr. Strathmore, who greeted her cordially, expressing much pleasure in seeing her.

" You were so kind to me," she said. " I have been thinking of all you said to me last week, and it seems to me that I can bear my burden better. I want to thank you with all my heart."

" There is nothing to thank me for," he answered

with grave tenderness. "The blessing is mine if I
have been able to help you."

" But there was no one else," she said, tears springing in her eyes, " that I could have talked to so freely.
You understood and sympathized.   It was like talking
to a brother."

He took her hand with an air perfectly unaffected
and unobtrusive, yet which was almost paternal in
its benignity.   Her look was one almost of reverence
as she hurried on her way with bowed head.

" Thurston," Mr. Strathmore asked, as they took
the car together, " do you know the name of that lady
who spoke to me on the corner? "

" I did n't notice, sir.   I was watching for the car."

" She seemed to know me perfectly," Strathmore
said rather absently, " and yet I can't place her.   By
the way, did you bring that letter from the church
committee in New York?   There is a passage in it
that I may want to read at the meeting."

" I brought it, sir.   There is likely to be a good
deal of difference of opinion at the committee meeting
to-day," Mr. Thurston said with an air of craftiness
which was like an explanatory foot-note to his character, " so I judged that it was well to be provided
with documents."

The other made no reply, but fell into deep thought,
making no further remark until they left the car near
the place where they were to attend a meeting of the
Charity Board.

" I think," he observed dispassionately, " that there
are four clergymen whose votes Mrs. Frostwinch may
be able to control."

XIV

HE SPEAKS THE MERE CONTRARY
Love's Labor 's Lost, i. 1

ASHE had in these days been dallying with temptation. He contrived not to confess it to himself, but by a variety of ingenious devices to cheat his conscience into the belief that he was serving the church by his consultations with Mrs. Fenton, his services to her charity work, and his continual thought of her views in regard to the election. It is amazing how clever even a dull man may be when it comes to inventing excuses for his own beguiling; and Philip struggled with such desperation to convince himself that he was acting disinterestedly that he all but succeeded. He could not, however, achieve what is impossible; and there was a pain in the heart of the young man which testified that his sense of right was sore despite all his cunning.

At the meeting of the Charity Board to which Mr. Strathmore had been going, Ashe sat beside Mrs. Fenton. His obvious excuse was that she was to make a report, and that he, as a visitor in her district, was able to support her in case there were any discussion. The session had been looked forward to with much interest, from the general feeling that there would probably be something like a conflict between the Frontford and Strathmore factions. There had for a long time been a growing division on the subject of the method of conducting church charities;

and it was expected that at this meeting the feeling
would break out openly. It would not be easy to say
how it was known that anything of the sort was to
occur. There was no announcement of business which
differed materially from that of the ordinary sessions
of the board. The time did not seem propitious for
a discussion, and there were evident reasons why the
followers of either candidate might be supposed to
wish to avoid arousing antagonism; yet it was certain
that the meeting would not close without some sort
of a demonstration. There are times when public
feeling seems to demand and force declarations of
principle or of purpose which policy would gladly
suppress; and such a time had arrived in the Charity
Board. Ashe was so strongly moved by the possibilities of the situation that even the proximity of Mrs.
Fenton did not absorb his attention; although he
was not for a moment unconscious of being beside
her.

The business routine was gone through, and after
that half an hour passed in the ordinary fashion. At
the end of that time Mr. Thurston, with apparent
unconsciousness, threw a spark into the combustibles.

"The fact seems to be," he said, "that there has
been too much the air of proselyting in our charity
work, and that has brought it into discredit with the
class which we most wish to reach."

He sat down with a face admirably controlled.
Mr. Strathmore showed in his benignant countenance
nothing save charity for all and general approval of
the remarks of his subordinate. The audience stirred
nervously, realizing that the critical moment had
come. Father Frontford, pale, ascetic, austere, rose
with grave deliberation.

" What has just been said," he began, " brings up a
subject which has been in the minds of many for some
months, — the question whether there is or should be
any difference between the charity work of the church
and that of the city or the world in general. As far
as I understand the position of the last speaker, I
take it to be his opinion that there is, or at least that
there should be, no such difference. He believes in
alleviating misery, and he would have religion kept in
the background, lest the poor should feel that they are
being fed for the sake of being led to a better life. I
do not myself see the objection to their thinking so.
I am by no means sure that they do ; but I am convinced that they look for a motive, and it seems to me
better that they should believe the object of missionary work to be proselyting — I think that that was the
word — than that they should embrace the too preva-
lent and most dangerous idea that charity is a bribe
from the rich to keep the poor quiet. There is not a
little feeling nowadays that philanthropy is encoura-
ging socialism. The poor echo incendiary orators in
saying that the rich dole out a little of what they
know to belong to the poor so that they may be
allowed to keep the rest unmolested. I believe that
this feeling is a menace to the State, and that philanthropy which nourishes such a belief is working hand
in hand with treason."

He paused a moment, and there arose a faint murmur. Ashe looked at his companion, and encountered
a glance which seemed to express something of his
own surprise at the boldness of Father Frontford's
words. That the speaker should be uncompromising
was to be supposed, but this was an attitude unexpected and astonishing. One or two men started up

as if to reply, but the Father went on again. His
voice was thin and incisive, with a vibrating quality
when it was raised which affected the nerves. It was
easy to dislike his tones, but it was not easy to resist
their influence. He passed to another point, and his
words had a keener emphasis.

"Neither have we escaped the accusation that we
use the poor simply as a means of self-improvement.
An old Irish woman in a tumble-down tenement house
once said to me: 'Ye 'll have no chance to work out
your salvation doing for me.' I believe that there are
many of the poor who more or less consciously have
the same idea. They think that we make visiting
them a sort of penance, and they resent it. I am not
sure that I can find it in my heart to blame them."

"He is either sacrificing himself completely, or
making one of those bold strokes that are irresistible," Ashe whispered to Mrs. Fenton; and she
nodded assent.

"What should be," the speaker proceeded, amid a
deep hush which showed the keen interest which his
words had aroused, "is that we should dare to be
consistent. As individuals and as churchmen we
should exercise the virtue of charity, but both as individuals and as churchmen we are bound to see to it
that we make our charity effective for the glory of
God and the salvation of men. There is no stronger
instrument in our hands than philanthropy, and not
to utilize it for the good of the church is to be culpably negligent. I believe that charity should be the
instrument of evangelization. The poor will have a
reason for our interest in them. Let them have this.
Let them believe, if they will, that we purchase their
spiritual acquiescence by ministering to their bodily

needs. Certainly I believe that we should limit our
work to those who can be spiritually influenced.
There are more of these than we can at present attend to, and I am in favor of boldly and consistently
taking the position that as administrators of the
bounties of the church we feel bound to use them for
the advancement of the church. To aid the corrupt,
the evil, the hardened without any attempt to draw
them into the fold and without any pledge that they
will be influenced, is simply to aid the avowed enemies
of religion and to strengthen their hands against
righteousness."

The air of the room was becoming electric. Philip
could see the exchange of glances all around him,
some of surprise, some of consternation, some — or he
was deceived — of triumph and scornful satisfaction.
He fancied that he saw Mr. Thurston shoot toward
Mr. Strathmore a flash of gratification, but the face
of the latter remained unmoved and inscrutable.
Ashe, full of uneasiness as to the result of the speech,
was greatly excited, but at the same time moved to
profound admiration for its boldness and its consist-
ency. He was in sympathy with the views expressed,
and he was more than ever convinced that Father
Frontford was the only man for the sacred office of
bishop.

"Even our Lord," Father Frontford went on, his
thin cheeks burning and his slender frame swayed by
the strength of his emotion, "did not many works in
places where he found unbelief. There was no limit
to his power; there was no limit to his mercy. It
was out of love for the whole of mankind that He refused to benefit individuals who would have hindered
the work He came to do. The example is one which

we shall do well to follow. We have more work than
we can do in aiding the faithful and in building up
the church. Let us accept the name of proselyters
which has been contemptuously flung at us, and wear
it as our glory. We are proselyters. We must be
proselyters. It is the highest joy and honor of our
lives that we are allowed of heaven to take this work
upon us. God will require it at our hands if we fail
in our private charities, and still more if we fail in
the administration of the revenues of the church to
be always ardent, consistent, unwearied proselyters!"

There was a good deal of applause when the speaker
sat down. The profound earnestness of the man carried the hearers away, at least for the moment. Ashe
saw Thurston look inquiringly at Strathmore, as if
to ask if the latter was not intending to reply, but
Strathmore sat silent.

"Don't you suppose Mr. Strathmore means to
speak?" Mrs. Fenton whispered. "He almost always does speak after Father Frontford, and he has
expressed very strong views about the charities."

"I cannot understand why he does n't speak,"
Ashe responded. "It may be he feels that the meeting is not with him, and does not wish to take the
unpopular side."

Several men did speak, however, among them Mr.
Candish. Their remarks were in accord with the
views expressed by the Father, yet they somehow lessened the effect of his words. Put into their plain
and sometimes even awkward language his position
seemed unpractical and hopelessly far from daily life;
so that even Ashe, warm partisan as he was, could
not but feel his enthusiasm somewhat chilled. Again
he intercepted a glance between Thurston and his

superior. Philip sat with the two men directly in his range of vision, and could not keep his eyes from watching them. He recognized that there was danger in the keen, crafty face of the colleague, thin-lipped and narrow-eyed; he wondered in troubled fashion how far it was possible that Mr. Strathmore was of the same nature as his assistant. Ashe was confident that Thurston was a born intriguer, and he instinctively watched for signs of understanding between Mr. Strathmore and the other. He could detect nothing of the sort. The Rev. Rutherford Strathmore bore a countenance as beneficent, as kindly, as guileless as ever; responding to the challenge of his colleague's eyes by no evidence of understanding or connivance. It was not until the talkers ceased and there fell a silence which indicated that the first force of admiration and enthusiasm had spent itself, that Strathmore rose.

"No one can possibly disagree with the sentiments which have just been expressed," he began in his cordial, frank manner. "There is no truth which we need in these days to keep more constantly before us than the duty of being always eager for the advancement of the church, and of employing all means to this end. The question which is of vital interest is how best to do this. When the caution was given that to the harmlessness of doves be added the guile of serpents, it might almost seem as if it was especially intended for our own day and case. There has certainly never been a time when wisdom was more needed than it is to-day. The growth of doubt, the overthrow of old traditions, old beliefs, old forms, in short of all that has been sanctioned by custom and by time, have gone on in every department of human knowledge and

endeavor. ⌈The spirit of the time is restless, progressive, liberal, even irreverent.⌋ The beautiful serenity
of the church, its reverent conservatism, its hallowed
enthusiasm for old ideals, are at variance with the
temper of the century. Since the church is the shrine
of truth it is impossible that it should alter with every
shifting of scientific thought, every alteration in the
fashions of human opinion ; and we stand face to face
with the trying fact that the age is not in sympathy
with the church."

IIe paused, looking down as if in thought. Ashe
regarded him closely, much impressed by the apparent spontaneity and candor with which this was said.
The hearers were closely attentive.

"The only thing upon which we seem to have some
possible disagreement," continued Mr. Strathmore, "is
in regard to the best method of meeting this want of
sympathy, this feeling which often seems to amount
almost to general indifference. Is it to arouse all the
suspicion and opposition possible ? Is it to seem to
justify the charges brought against us of narrowness,
of formalism, of repression, and of obstructing the progress of the race ? It does not seem to me that this
is the wisest course. I agree that it is our duty to
forward the interests of the church, and to make our
administration of charity a means to this end. It is
certainly a question whether open and avowed proselyting is the best means. Religion is no more to be
bought with a price than is love. The person who
conforms for a soup-ticket or a blanket has simply
added hypocrisy to his other failings, and has moreover gained for the church that contempt which men
always feel for those they have overreached. The
child that goes to Sunday-school for the Christmas

tree and the summer week has learned a lesson in deception which can never be blotted out. It is of
course proper that these means should be used; but
unless it is understood fully and frankly that they are
employed not as a bribe but as a persuasion, not as a
price but as a kindness, the evil that they do is more
than any good that it is possible to bring about
through their means. I do not believe that our charities should be conducted on the basis of bargain and
sale; nor do I believe that they should be put on a
sectarian basis at all."

He sat down quietly, with an unimpassioned air
which seemed to rebuke the emotional close of the remarks of Father Frontford. Strathmore could be
emotional and impassioned upon occasion, and this
deliberate, matter-of-fact mien affected Ashe as a cal-
culated stroke of policy. Philip felt that his leader
had suffered a defeat; and he was profoundly moved
by the thought. Other speakers took up the question,
but he paid little heed. He was occupied in speculating how the meeting would affect the chances of the
election. When he was walking home with Mrs.
Fenton after the session was over, he was so absorbed
that she rallied him on his absent-mindedness.

"I was thinking of the discussion," he said. "I
am afraid that Father Frontford injured himself this
morning."

"But how noble it was of him to say what he believed in spite of the chances," she responded. "I was
delighted with Mr. Candish for seconding him as he
did."

"Yes," Ashe said, a pang of jealousy piercing him
at the mention of Mr. Candish. "It was fine. What
I cannot make out," he added, "is whether Mr. Strath-

more is as simple and candid as he looks.   He always seems to speak sincerely and freely, and yet he somehow contrives never to say anything that might not have been thought out with the most clever policy."

"I cannot make out either," returned she.   "Mr. Fenton used rather paradoxically to say that Mr. Strathmore was too frank by half to be honest."

She sighed as she spoke, and instantly all thought of bishops and church matters vanished from the mind of Ashe.   He became entirely absorbed in wondering how warm was Mrs. Fenton's affection for her dead husband and in hating himself for the thought.

XV

INSTEAD of returning to Boston next morning, Maurice remained at Brookfield for ten days. Mrs. Morison decided the matter, and it is not to be supposed that he was entirely unwilling to be constrained.

He naturally saw much of Berenice, and he passed hours in brooding over thoughts of her. He was convinced that she was not engaged. She had spoken of Stanford's visit, and it had seemed to Wynne that she had conveyed the impression that her relations to the visitor were less intimate than might at first sight appear. If she were free — the thought made his heart beat, and he wondered if, had the circumstances been different, he might himself have won her. He tormented himself with all her ways and words; the smiles she gave him, the trifling attentions which were addressed to the guest, but which seemed to have a touch of something deeper, that might be due to her thinking of him as her preserver, but which might even go beyond that. There was a delicious torture in all this reverie, in these continual self-reproaches which involved the thought of her, the remembrance of how she had looked, how she had spoken, how she had moved. He became every day more hopelessly her slave, yet every day insisting more strongly to himself that he felt nothing more than warm friendship. Once for a moment he tried to believe that

his feeling was merely a desire for her spiritual good,
that his attitude was that which it was proper for a
priest to feel toward a beautiful and frivolous world-
ling; but the pretense was too ghastly, and he abandoned it with a shudder of disgust.   He had moments,
too, when he said to himself frankly, in defiance or in
sorrow as the mood might be, that he loved her; but
for the most part he tried to keep the assumption of
simple friendship between him and bitter thought.

He found great pleasure in Mrs. Morison.   She
was to him a revelation of possibilities of which he
had never dreamed.   It was a continual surprise to
him to find himself so impressed by the wit, the wisdom, and the sanity of this fine old lady.   He not
only felt himself an ignorant and inexperienced boy
beside her, but found himself shrinking from comparing with her the men whom he had followed as
leaders.)   The ease of her manner, the completeness
of her self-poise, her frank simplicity, high-bred and
winning, delighted him, while the extent of her mental
resources filled him with amazement.

Mrs. Morison opened to Wynne a new world in
her conversation.   At first she gave herself up chiefly
to entertaining him, telling him delightful stories of
famous folk she had known, of her life abroad and in
Washington.   She was full of charming little tales
which she had the art of relating as if she were not
thinking of how she was telling them, but as if they
came to her mind and bubbled into talk sponta-
neously.   She had a way, too, of putting in unobtrusive observations on character and events which
impressed Maurice.   The art of saying things tren-
chantly he had found in Mrs. Staggchase, but his
cousin had the air of being aware of her cleverness,

while Mrs. Morison said these things as if they were
of the natural and habitual current of her thoughts.
Mrs. Morison said clever things as if she thought
them; Mrs. Staggchase as if she thought of them.

It did not take the young man long to discover that
Mrs. Morison was not in sympathy with his creed.
She was too well-bred to bring the matter forward,
but he could not resist the temptation now and then
to touch upon it. She was of principles at once so
broad and so deep that he found himself as often surprised by her devoutness as he felt it his duty to be
shocked by her liberality. One day when Maurice
had made some allusion to a discussion over the doctrine of predestination which was agitating the English
church, Mrs. Morison said : —

"It always seems to me a pity that those who
believe in that dreadful doctrine do not remember
that if one were not one of the elect, he could at least
carry through eternity the realization that he was lost
through no fault of his own. God could not take
from him that consolation."

He was silent in mingled amazement and disapproval; yet he found his mind following out with
obstinate persistence the train of thought which her
words suggested. In this or in many another remark
it could hardly be said that her words convinced him,
but they awoke a swarm of doubts in his mind. He
found himself following speculations that were law-
less, wild, dangerous, and intoxicating. However
convinced he might be that the reasoning of Mrs.
Morison was fallacious, he did not find it easy to tell
just wherein the fallacy lay. He felt that as a priest
he should be able to refute her, and he was filled
with dismay to discover that he was rather himself
falling into the attitude of a doubter.

One subject which was constantly in his mind he did not touch upon until the day before he left Brook-field. He longed to sound Mrs. Morison on the subject of a celibate priesthood. He was well enough aware that she would not approve of it, and he was irritated by the knowledge that he secretly felt that her decision would be founded on strong common sense. He tried to assure himself that it was her dangerous laxity of principle that blinded her to the nobility and sanctity of asceticism ; but it was impossible to feel that such was the case. He was teased by a wish which he would not acknowledge that she might advance arguments which he could not controvert ; though to himself he said that she would be his temptation in tangible form, and that he would struggle against it with his whole soul.

His opportunity came while they were discussing the election of the bishop. Mrs. Morison was not immediately concerned in the matter, not being a churchwoman, but she had an intelligent interest in all questions of the day.

"I find it hard to understand," Mrs. Morison observed, "how any churchman can be so blind to the importance of conciliating public thought and the general feeling as for a moment to think of any other candidate than Mr. Strathmore. He is so completely in sympathy with the broadening tendencies of the time."

"But that means ultimately the destruction of creeds," Maurice objected, answering rather the implication than her words.

"I think that perhaps the highest courage men are called upon to show," she answered, "is that of giving up a theory which has served its use. The race forces us to do it sooner or later, but the men who are really great are those who are able to say frankly that their creeds have done their work; and that the new day must have new ones. You might almost say that the extent to which a man prefers truth to himself is to be judged by his willingness to give up a dogma that is outworn."

"But you leave no stability to truth."

"The truth is stable without effort or will of mine," she returned, smiling; "but surely you would have human appreciation of it advance."

He felt that there must be an answer to this, but he was not able to see just what it was, and he shifted the question.

"But Mr. Strathmore," he said hesitatingly, "is married."

"Yes," she assented. "'The husband of one wife.'"

"If you begin to quote Scripture against me," Maurice retorted, laughing in spite of himself, "I might easily reply to St. Paul by St. Paul. But letting that pass, it is certainly true that the church has always held that marriage absorbs a man in earthly things so that he cannot give the best of his thoughts to his work."

"When the church sets itself against marriage," Mrs. Morison responded quietly, "it seems to me to be setting up to know more than the Creator of the race."

Maurice colored, although he might not have been able to tell whether his strongest feeling was horror at this bold language or joy at the emphasis with which she spoke.

"Perhaps I should beg your pardon for saying so

frankly what I think," Mrs. Morison continued. "It
is n't the way in which one generally talks to a clergyman; but the subject is one for which I have n't
much patience, and of course I could n't help seeing
that you are in doubt yourself."

Maurice started.

"What do you mean?" he stammered. "I — I
in doubt?"

"I had n't any intention of forcing your confidence," returned she. "I am an old woman, and
sometimes I find that I don't make allowance enough
for the slowness of you young people in arriving at a
knowledge of self."

He cast down his eyes.

"Until this moment," he said, "I have never acknowledged to myself that I was in doubt. I see
what you mean, and it shows that I have been playing with fire."

She looked at him questioningly, then turned the
subject.

"Which is perhaps a hint that our fire is going
down. Sit still, please. Every woman likes to tend
her own fire."

"I should have learned that by this time," was his
answer. "I lost an inheritance once by insisting upon
fixing a fire."

"That sounds interesting. Is it proper to ask for
the story?"

"Oh, there is n't much of a story. I had a great-
aunt who was worth a lot of money, and who was
eccentric. She was in a way fond of me when I was
a child, and used to have me at the house a good deal.
I confess I did n't like it much. Things went by
rule, and the rules were often pretty queer. One of

them was that nobody should presume to touch the fire if she was in the room. I liked to play with the fire as well as she did, and when I was a boy just in my teens I used to do it. After she 'd corrected me half a dozen times I got into my foolish pate that it was my duty to cure her of her whim. So I set to poking the fire ostentatiously until she lost her temper and ordered me out of the house. Then she burned up the will in my favor and made a new one, giving all her money to the church."

"How unjust," commented Mrs. Morison, "and how human. Did you never make peace with her?"

"Yes, but of course I was careful that she should understand that I did n't do it for the sake of her money. She told my mother that she had made a new will in my favor, but it never turned up. My aunt's death was very singular. She was found dead in her bed, and the woman who lived with her, an old nurse of mine, had disappeared. Of course there was at once suspicion of foul play, but the doctors pronounced the death natural, and there was no evidence of theft."

"Did you never discover the nurse?"

"Never. We tried, for we thought she might give a clue to the missing will. She 'd been in the family so long that she was a sort of confidential servant, and knew all Aunt Morse's affairs. She was devoted to me."

"The romance may not be ended yet," Mrs. Morison suggested smilingly. "Who knows but the missing nurse will some day turn up with the missing will."

"I 'm afraid that after a dozen years there 's little enough chance of it."

His mind was so racked upon this wretched question of the right of a priest to marry, that he could not rest until he had drawn from Berenice also an expression of opinion on the subject. He made Mr. Strathmore again the excuse for the introduction of the topic.

" I don't see," he said to her, " how you can think that it's well to have a married bishop. His wife is sure to be meddling in the affairs of the diocese."

She looked at him with a mocking glance.

" Do you wish to drag me into a discussion of the wisdom of allowing the clergy to have wives ? " she asked cruelly.

He flushed with confusion, but tried to carry a bold front.

" Very likely it does come down to the general principle of the thing," he answered.

" Well then, the question of the marriage of the clergy does n't interest me in the least."

She looked so pretty and mischievous that he began to lose his head.

" But it is of the greatest possible interest to me," he returned, with a manner which gave the words a personal application.

She flushed in her turn, and tossed her head.

" That is by no means the same thing," she retorted.

" But what interests me you might try to consider ; just out of charity, of course."

" Oh, well, then, since you ask me, this celibacy of the clergy of our church is n't at all a thing that anybody can take seriously. Everybody knows that a clergyman may have his vows absolved by the bishop, so that after all he can marry if he wants to ; so that the whole thing seems " —

" Well ? " he demanded, as she broke off. " Seems how ? "

" Pardon me. I did n't realize what I was saying."

" Seems how ? " he repeated insistently.

He challenged her with his eyes, and he could see the spark which kindled defiantly in hers. She threw back her head saucily.

" Well, since you insist! I was going to say that it made the whole thing seem a little like amateur theatricals."

He became grave instantly.

" I beg your pardon," he said. " You do not seem to understand that what you are speaking of may mean the bitter sacrifice of a man's whole life. Even a clergyman is human, and may love as strongly, as completely " —

He choked with the emotion he could not control. He realized that he was telling his passion, and there came to him an overwhelming sense that he must never tell it save in this indirect manner. He hastened on lest she should interrupt him.

" Don't you suppose that a priest may know what it is to worship the very ground a woman walks on ? Don't you suppose he has had his heart beat till it suffocated him just because her fingers touched his or her gown brushed him ? A man is a man after all, and the dreams that come to one are much the same as come to another. The difference is that the priest has to tear his very heart out, and turn his back on all that other men may find delight in."

Berenice looked at him with shining eyes, not un- dimmed, he thought, by tears.

" If you really care for her so much," she said

softly, " you can give only a divided heart to your
work. It is better to own that to yourself, is n't it ? "

" For her ? " he echoed.

" Oh, there must be somebody," she returned hastily,
her color coming. " No matter about that."

" But think of giving up ! " he cried, leaning toward
her. " Even those who believe nothing despise a
renegade priest."

" That 's of less consequence than that he should
ruin his life and despise himself."

He held out his uninjured hand impulsively.

" Berenice ! " he whispered.

She flushed celestial red, and for an instant her
eyes responded to the love in his. Then she sprang
to her feet, with a laugh.

" There ! " she cried. " See what dunces we are to
get to discussing theology. I 'll never forgive you if
you try to inveigle me into another talk about such
subjects. Here is Mehitabel to say that she 's ready
to help you with your packing."

XVI

THE GREAT ASSAY OF ART

Macbeth, iv. 3

"I am sorry if I kept you waiting," Mrs. Wilson said to her husband, coming into the library one afternoon, "but the fact is that I was dressing for a comedy."

"Gad! you dress for a comedy every day, as far as that goes."

She made a mocking courtesy.

"Well, what is life without comedy?"

"Oh, nothing but a bore, of course. Is this comedy with some of your ministerial hangers-on?"

She sat down by the fire and stretched out her feet upon a hassock. She was radiant with beauty and mischief, and dressed to perfection.

"That isn't a respectful way to speak of the clergy."

"It's as respectful as I feel," he responded, lighting a pipe. "You do have a nice gang of them round. There's Candish, for instance. He looks like an advertisement for a misfit tailor, and he's fairly putrid with philanthropy."

Elsie gave a quick burst of laughter. Then she pretended to frown.

"Chauncy," she said, "you have the most abominable way of putting things that I ever heard. What would you say to the youngsters from the Clergy House that I have in train? They're perfect lambs, and they love each other like twins. Have you seen them?"

"Oh, yes; I've seen them. They seem to have been brought up on sterilized milk of the gospel, and to have Jordan water for blood."

"Oh, don't be too sure. You can't tell from a man's looks how red his blood is, especially if he's a priest. I suppose it's the men that have to hold themselves in hardest that make the best ministers."

"I dare say," he answered indifferently. "Priestcraft has always been clever enough to see that unless the things it called sins were natural and inevitable its occupation would be gone. However, as long as folks will follow after them they'd be foolish to give up their trade."

"Of course," his wife assented laughingly. "You won't get a rise out of me, my dear boy."

Dr. Wilson chuckled.

"You're a devilish humbug," he remarked admiringly; "but you do manage to get a lot of fun out of it."

She smoothed her gown a moment, half smiling and half grave.

"Of course it's of no use to tell you that in spite of all my fun I'm serious at bottom," she said slowly; "but it's a fact all the same. I don't take things with doleful solemnity like the old tabbies; but that's no sign that I'm not just as sincere. It's no matter, though; you won't believe it. What did you want to see me about?"

"Oh, it was about those mortgages. I saw Lincoln this morning, and he has heard from Mrs. Frostwinch. She insists upon paying them off."

"Then there isn't any truth in the story that that

Sampson woman is circulating that Anna is going to build a spiritual temple or something. I never believed that Anna could be such an idiot as to give her money for anything so vulgar."

" The whole thing is nonsensical on the face of it," was his response. " Mrs. Frostwinch can't build churches, let alone temples, if there 's any difference."

" Oh, in these days," Elsie interpolated, " a temple is only a church *déclassé*."

" She has only a life interest in the property," Wilson went on. " Berenice Morison is residuary legatee of almost everything, unless Mrs. Frostwinch has saved up her income."

The talk ran on business for a few moments, Wilson advising with shrewdness, and practically deciding the matter for his wife.

" I suppose," he said, when this was disposed of, " that Mrs. Frostwinch is too much wrapped up in faith-cure nonsense to take much interest in your holy war against Strathmore."

" She is n't so much wrapped up in that stuff as you think. Dear Anna has n't any sense of humor, but she 's a model of propriety, and she 's constantly shocked at herself for being alive by a treatment so irregular. She was mortified beyond words when that Crapps woman gave a treatment to Mrs. Bodewin Ranger's dog."

" That snarling little black devil that 's always under foot at the Rangers' ? Gad! I 'd like to give it a treatment ! "

" It got its ear hurt somehow, and Mrs. Crapps pretended to cure it. Mrs. Ranger was all but in tears over it, she was so grateful. Anna was entirely disgusted. She told Mrs. Crapps that she had n't known before that she was in the hands of a veterinary."

Dr. Wilson smoked in silence for a moment. The fire of soft coal purred in the grate, the smoke from his pipe ascended in the warm air. The thin sunshine of the winter afternoon filtered in through the windows, and made bright patches on the rugs.

" By the way," Wilson asked lazily, "how is the campaign going ? I have n't heard anything interesting about it for some time."

" Oh, things are moving on. The man I sent up to canvass the western part of the state — one of your sterilized milk-of-the-word babies, you know, — got smashed up in the accident ; but he 'll be back in a few days. Cousin Anna has brought her pensioners into line beautifully. There 's no doubt that we 'll carry the convention."

" What happens after that ? "

" The election has to be ratified by a majority of bishops ; but of course they 'll hardly dare to go against the convention, even if they want to."

" It would make things much more interesting if they 'd do it, and get up a scandal," commented the doctor. " You 'll get bored to death with the whole thing if something exciting does n't turn up."

" I had half a mind to get up a scandal myself with Mr. Strathmore," Elsie said with a laugh; "but I confess I should be afraid of that she-dragon of a wife of his."

" It 's devilish interesting to know that you are afraid of anybody."

" At least," she went on, " I could go to New York and see Bishop Candace. I can wind him round my finger. I 'd tell him what Mrs. Strathmore said about his Easter sermon last year. With a little judicious comment that would do a good deal. I never yet saw a man that could n't be managed through his vanity."

" I suppose that explains why I 'm as clay in your hands."

" Oh, you 're not a man; you 're a monster," she retorted, rising. " Well, I must go and prepare for my comedy."

He regarded her with a look of evident admiration; a look not without a savor of the sense of ownership, and, too, not entirely devoid of good-natured insolence.

" You are devilishly well dressed for it," he observed.

" Thank you," returned Elsie, sweeping him a courtesy again. " The wife that can win compliments from her own husband has indeed scored a triumph."

Dr. Wilson puffed out a cloud of smoke with a characteristic chuckle.

" I have to admire you to justify my own taste. But you have n't told me about the comedy."

She thrust forward one of her pretty slippers.

" Do you see that? " she demanded.

" I suppose you expect me to say that I see the prettiest foot in Boston."

" Thank you again, but I 'm not yet reduced to trying to drag compliments out of you, Chauncy. I sha'n't do that till the other men fail me. It 's the slipper I wanted you to notice, and these ravishing stockings."

" If the comedy has stockings in it," he began; but she stopped him.

" There, no impudence," she said. " Did you ever

see anything so entirely heavenly as those stockings
and slippers? I declare I 've wanted ever since I
put them on to keep my feet on the table to look at."

" You might do worse."

" Oh, I 'm going to."

" Indeed! It 's apparently getting time for me to
interfere. What 's your game ? "

" I 'm going to squelch that detestable Fred
Rangely."

" How ? "

" My slippers," Elsie said vivaciously, again thrusting one of them forward, " are ravishing."

" Gad," her husband returned, regarding her with
a look of the utmost amusement in his topaz-brown
eyes, " you have a good deal to say about them."

" Do you notice anything particular about my
hair ? " she asked.

" It looks as if it might come down."

" It will come down," she corrected, nodding. Then
she glanced at the clock. " It will come down in
about twenty minutes; all tumbling over my shoulders. I shall be so mortified and surprised ! "

Her husband stretched himself luxuriously back in
his chair, regarding her with laughing eyes. There
was an air of perfect understanding between the two
which might have been an effectual enlightenment for
any man who thought of making love to the wife.
Elsie went on, telling off on her slender fingers the
points as she made them.

" In fifteen minutes I shall be standing on the piano
in the drawing-room, straightening a picture. I never
can bear a picture crooked, and I had Jane tip it a
little this morning, just to vex me. Fred Rangely
will come in unannounced. Of course I shall be

dreadfully confused, and have to get down.   In my
maidenly confusion I am almost sure I can't help
showing my slippers, and just a trifle — a very discreet trifle, of course, — of these beautiful, beautiful
stockings.   Nothing vulgar, you know, but " —

" But just enough," interpolated Wilson with huge
enjoyment.   " You need n't apologize.   I don't be-
grudge the poor devil whatever satisfaction he can get
out of that."

" And then as he is helping me down, with his
heart in a flutter, — it will flutter, I assure you."

" You mean his vanity ; but it 's of no consequence.
He 'd call it a heart if he were putting the scene in
a novel."

" With his whichever it is in a flutter, by some
provoking accident down comes my hair and tumbles
over his shoulders."

Wilson regarded her with amused admiration.

" Five years ago," he observed placidly, " I should
have thought you were telling me half the truth to
cover the other half, and were really having a devilish
flirtation with that cad."

Elsie flushed, and into her gay voice came a strain
of seriousness.

" Five years are five years," she answered.   " Don't
go to dragging all that up again, Chauncy."

His laugh was not untinged with malicious delight,
but he put his hand on hers and patted her fingers.

" All right, old girl. Bygones are bygones. But
what in the world is all this fooling with Rangely
for ? "

" Why, don't you see? The fool is sure to say
something so silly that I can snub him within an
inch of his life. I 've only been holding off until

he had that thing written for the Churchman. Now I 've got that, I 'll settle him."

" Oh, the gratitude of women ! "

" Why, it is n't that. He need n't be smirking at me the way he does. I simply won't stand it. Besides, he makes eyes at me wherever I go, just to advertise the fact that he 's silly about me. He 's a cad, through and through. Would you come here as he does if I refused to invite your wife ? "

Chauncy Wilson laughed again, leaning forward to knock the ashes out of his pipe.

" He 's a fool, fast enough ; and I dare say you 're tired of his beastly spooning ; but all the same, the real reason for this circus is that you want to amuse yourself."

She drew up her head in mock dignity.

" Of course," she returned, " if my own husband does not appreciate how I resent " — She broke off in a burst of laughter. " Nobody ever understood me but you, Chauncy," she cried. " Good-by. It 's time I took the stage."

She threw him a kiss, and went to the drawing-room. Looking at her watch, she placed herself behind the curtains of a window which commanded the avenue. Presently she espied her victim, and with a last glance around to assure herself that everything was as she wished it to be, she mounted to the top of the piano. There she hastily tucked the hem of her skirt between the piano and the wall. The reflection in a great blue-black Chinese jar showed her when Rangely appeared between the portières, so that she was able to step back as if to view the effect of her work just as he reached the middle of the room.

" Be careful ! " exclaimed he, hurrying forward. " You almost stepped off backward ! "

She wheeled about quickly.

"O Mr. Rangely!" she cried. "How did you get into the room without my knowing? How horrid of you to surprise me like that!"

"But think how charming it is for me," he responded with an elaborate air of gallantry. "It is so delightful to see you on a pedestal."

"Meaning that I am no better than a graven image?" she demanded with a smile. "If that is the best you can do, I may as well come down."

She held out her hand for his, and then sat down, displaying one of the fascinating slippers, and the openwork instep of her silk stocking, through the meshes of which the pearly skin gleamed evasively.

"My dress is caught," she said, turning to conceal her face, and pretending to pull at her skirt. "I hope my slippers have n't damaged the piano."

"The piano is harder than my heart if they have n't!"

She gave a sly twitch at a hairpin.

"That is very pretty," observed she, giving her head a shake that brought her hair down in a rolling billow. "Oh, dear! Now my hair has" —

Before she could finish he had dropped her fingers, and gathered her hair in both hands, kissing it again and again.

"Mr. Rangely!" she exclaimed. "What do you mean?"

For reply he stooped to her foot, and kissed the mesh-clad instep fervidly.

"How dare you!" she cried, scrambling down hastily without his assistance.

But, alas, even trickery is not always successful in this uncertain world! The hold of the piano upon the hem of her gown was stronger than she realized. She tripped and stumbled, half-hung for a second, and then dropped in an inglorious heap at the feet of the man she wished to humiliate.

Elsie was on her feet in a minute. She did not take the hand which Rangely extended, but drew back, her eyes sparkling with rage.

"Oh, you find it laughable, do you?" she cried. "A gentleman would at least have concealed his amusement!"

He grew suddenly grave, and seemed not a little surprised.

"I beg your pardon," he said. "I hope you were not hurt."

She looked at him scornfully without replying, and then walked to the mantel, where there was a small antique mirror of silver.

"Thank you, not in the least."

Her tone was no warmer than an arctic night. She gathered her hair, and began to twist it up. He followed and stood behind her with an air at once deprecatory and insinuating.

"I should n't think you could see in that thing," he observed.

She took no notice of his words.

"If I laughed," continued he, "it was only from nervousness. I was carried away" —

"I observed that you were," she interrupted icily.

He stood awkwardly a moment, while she finished putting up her hair. Then, as she turned toward him, he smiled again, holding out his hand.

"Surely you are not angry with me," he pleaded. "I care more for your feeling toward me than for anything else in the world."

"It would amuse Mrs. Rangely to hear you say so, not to mention my husband."

He stared at her with the air of a man not sure whether he is awake or dreaming.

"What are they to us?" he asked, sinking his voice almost to a whisper.

"Mrs. Rangely may be nothing to you, but Dr. Wilson is still a good deal to me, thank you."

He looked at her again with perplexity in his glance, but with his face hardening.

"You surely cannot mean that you have ceased to care for me just for a second of meaningless laughter?"

She swept him a scornful courtesy.

"You do these things better in your novels, Mr. Rangely, which shows what an advantage it is to have time to think speeches over. I would n't have my hero say a thing like that, if I were you. It would make him seem like a conceited cad."

The insolence of her manner was such as no man could bear. Rangely crimsoned to the temples. He paced across the room, while she coolly seated herself in a great Venetian chair, and began to play with a little jade image. He came back to her, and stood a moment as if he could not find words.

"Why don't you go?" she asked, looking up at him as if he were a servant sent upon an errand.

"Because," he broke out angrily, "when I go I shall not come back; and I should like to understand this thing."

She shrugged her shoulders, and leaned back in her chair, looking him over from head to foot.

"Why you quarrel with me is more than I know," he went on. "You 've got tired of me, I suppose, and want to amuse yourself with another man."

The red flushed in her cheek.

"If my husband, who you say is nothing to us, were here," she said, "he would horsewhip you."

The other laughed savagely.

"He is not here, however, so you may digest my remark at your leisure."

Mrs. Wilson rose from her seat with an air of dignity which was really imposing.

"Mr. Rangely," she said, "it is not my custom to bandy words, even with my equals. I have allowed you the freedom of my house because I was willing to help you in your desire to be useful to Father Frontford. You have taken advantage of my kindness to insult me. This seems to me sufficiently to explain the situation."

He stared at her a moment in evident amazement. Then he burst into hoarse laughter.

"My desire to be useful to Father Frontford!" he echoed. "That is the best yet! You know I cared nothing about your pottering old church politics except to please you."

"I see that I was deceived completely," she responded coldly.

She crossed the room and pressed an ivory button.

"Deceived!" he sneered. "It would take a clever man to deceive you."

She looked not at him, but beyond him. He turned, and saw a footman in the doorway.

"The gentleman wishes to be shown out, Forrester," said she.

She held the tips of her fingers to Rangely.

"Thank you so much for coming," she murmured in her most conventional manner.

"The pleasure has been mine," he responded.

They both bowed, and Rangely followed the footman.

XVII

A BOND OF AIR

Troilus and Cressida, i. 3

"You have made a new man of me," Maurice
Wynne had said to Mrs. Morison in bidding her
good-by; and the words repeated themselves in his
mind as he came back to Boston, and as he once more
took up for a few days his home with Mrs. Staggchase.

There is nothing more inflammable than the punk
left by the decay of a religion, and any theology may
be said to be doomed from the moment when men
begin to ask themselves whether they believe it.
Maurice had been so strenuously questioning his belief that it is small wonder that he found his heart
full of fire. In the days of his stay at Brookfield,
moreover, he had been rapidly journeying on the road
toward a new view of life; and the idea of returning
to the Clergy House became to him well-nigh intolerable. It seemed like taking upon himself once more
the swaddling-clothes of infancy.

On the afternoon of his return, he hurried to see
Ashe, and found himself obliged to wait some time
for his friend's return from a committee meeting.
Mr. Herman chanced to be at home alone, and Maurice
sat with him in the library. Wynne had come to
know the sculptor fairly well, and had been warmly
drawn toward him. He was to-day struck more than
ever by the strength and self-poise which Herman

showed. The young man was seized with a desire to
appeal to the sanity and the kindliness of one who
seemed to possess both so aboundingly.

"Have you ever found yourself all at sea, Mr.
Herman?" he asked abruptly.

"Of course. I fancy every man has had that experience."

"But," Maurice hurried on, more impulsively yet,
"you can never have felt that you were a renegade
and a hypocrite. That 's where I am now."

The sculptor regarded him with evident surprise,
yet with a look so keen that Maurice felt his cheeks
grow warm.

"Does that mean," Herman asked with kindly
deliberation, "that you are tired and out of sorts, or
is it something deeper?"

Wynne was silent a moment. Now that he had
broken the ice, he feared to go on. It was something
of a shock to find himself on the brink of a confidence
when he had not intended to make one.

"I 'm afraid it goes deep," he answered. "The
truth is, Mr. Herman, that I 've come back with my
whole mind in a turmoil."

Herman seemed to hesitate in his turn.

"I 'm afraid I 'm a poor one to help you, Mr.
Wynne. Mrs. Herman does the mental straightening-
out for this family. Besides, we look at things so
differently, you and I, that I should n't know how to
put things to you if I tried."

"I 've no right to bother anybody with my troubles,"
Maurice said.

"That anybody could help you would give you a
claim upon him," Herman responded cheerily. "I
noticed, Mr. Wynne, that things were not going right

with you before you went away. May I give you a
piece of advice?"

"I shall be glad if you will."

"Then if I were you, I'd go and talk with Mr.
Strathmore."

"With Mr. Strathmore!" Maurice echoed in surprise.

"Oh, I know he isn't exactly of your way of thinking in church matters," Herman proceeded. "He's
still farther from my position, but he's the man I
should go to. He is so human, and so sympathetic,
that there isn't such another man in Boston for comfort and advice."

"But I've always been opposed," Maurice protested, "to all" —

"That's no matter. He's too big a man for that
to make any difference. Go to him as a fellow that's
in a hobble, and the only thing he'll consider is how
to help you. He's had experience, and he has the
gift of understanding."

No more was said on the subject, but the words
stuck in Wynne's mind. Since all things seemed to
him to be turning round, why should he not take this
one more departure from the old ways? Yet it was
in some sort almost like treason to Father Frontford
to seek aid and comfort from Strathmore. Although
the thing had never been so stated in words, it was
understood at the Clergy House that Strathmore was
to be looked upon in the light of an enemy to the
faith, and Wynne felt as if he had been enrolled to
fight the popular preacher under the banner of Father
Frontford. It seemed the more treasonable to desert
the Father Superior now that he was in the midst of
a desperate struggle. Maurice knew, however, that it

was useless to carry to his old confessor doubts which for the heart of the stern priest could not exist. He would simply be told that doubt was of the devil and was to be crushed; and the young man felt that this would leave him where he was now. If he were to seek aid, it must at least be from one who would understand his state of mind.

Wynne resumed his clerical garb on the morning after his return to Boston. His conscience reproached him for the strong distaste which he felt for the dress, and his spirits were of the lowest. About the middle of the forenoon, he started out to try the effects of a walk. It was a clear, brisk morning, with a white frost still on the pavements where the sun had not fallen. The air was invigorating, and Maurice began to feel its exhilaration. He walked more briskly, holding his head more erect, even forgetting to be irritated by the swish of his cassock about his legs. Without consciously determining whither he would go, he followed the streets toward the house of Mr. Strathmore, in that strange yet not uncommon state of mind in which a man knows fully what he is doing, yet assures himself that he has no purpose. When at last he found himself ringing the bell, Wynne carried his private histrionics so far that he told himself that he was surprised to be there.

The visitor was shown at once to the study of Mr. Strathmore, whose readiness to receive those who sought him was one of the traits which endeared him to the general public. Maurice felt the keen and inquiring look which the clergyman bestowed upon him, and found himself somewhat at a loss how to begin.

"I am from the Clergy House of St. Mark," he said, rather awkwardly.

"So I judged from your dress," Strathmore responded cordially. "Sit down, please. That is a comfortable chair by the fire."

The professed ascetic smiled, but he took the chair indicated.

"It is a beautiful, brisk morning," the host went on. "The tingle in the air makes a man feel that he can do impossible things."

Wynne looked up at him with a smile. He was won by the heartiness of the tone, by the bright glance of the eye, by some intangible personal charm which put him at once at his ease and made him feel that understanding and sympathy were here.

"And I have done the impossible," he said. "I have ventured to come to talk with you about the celibacy of the clergy."

He saw the face of the other change with a curious expression, and then melt into a smile.

"And what am I, a married clergyman, expected to say on such a topic?"

Maurice smiled at the absurdity of his own words, and then with sudden gravity broke out earnestly : —

"I am completely at sea. All things I have believed seem to be failing me. I don't even know what I believe."

"Will you pardon me," Strathmore asked, "if I ask why you consult me rather than your Superior?"

Maurice flushed and hesitated : yet he felt that nothing would do but absolute frankness.

"I will tell you!" he returned. "I was to be a priest. I went into the Clergy House supposing that that was settled. I see now that I really followed a friend. If he went, I couldn't be shut out. Now I have been among men, and " —

He hesitated, but the friendly smile of the other reassured him.

"And among women," he went on bravely; "and — and " —

"And you have discovered the meaning of a certain text in Genesis which declares that 'male and female created He them,'" concluded Strathmore.

Wynne felt the tone like a caress. He seemed to be understood without need of more speech. His condition, which had seemed to him so intricate and so unique, began to appear possible and human. He was not so completely cut off from human sympathy as he had felt.

"Yes," he assented; "I will be frank about it. I did not think that Father Frontford would understand what it meant to feel that life is given to us to be glorified by the love of a woman."

"If this is all that is troubling you," Strathmore remarked, "it seems to me that your position, though it may not be pleasant, is not very tragical. Our bishops are generally willing to absolve from vows of celibacy."

"I doubt if Father Frontford would be," Maurice commented involuntarily.

"That is perhaps one of his virtues in the eyes of his supporters," Strathmore suggested with a twinkle.

"I have not taken the vows, however," Maurice responded hastily, flushing, and ignoring the thrust.

"Then what is your trouble?"

"When I meant to take them, it was the same thing."

"Do I understand you that to intend to do a thing and then to change the mind is the same as to do it?"

"Oh, no ; not that ; but I am not clear that it is n't my duty to take them. I 'm not sure that it is right for a priest to marry — if you will pardon my saying so."

" And you come to me to convince you ? It seems to me that Providence has already done that through the agency of some young woman. If you really know what it is to love a good woman there is no real doubt in your mind as to the sacredness of marriage, — for the clergy or for anybody else. Is n't your trouble perhaps an obstinate dislike to seem to abandon a position once taken ? "

The words might have sounded severe but for the tone in which they were spoken.

" But that is not the whole of the matter," Maurice continued, feeling as if he were being carried forward by an irresistible current. " If I have been mistaken on this point about which I have felt so sure and so strongly, what confidence can I have in my other beliefs ? "

" Ah, it goes deep," Strathmore said with emphasis. " It is of no use to put old wine into new bottles. The effect of trying to make you young men accept mediævalism, like clerical celibacy, is in the end to make you doubt everything. Have n't you any respect for the authority of the church ? "

" Oh, implicit ! " Maurice responded.

" But," his host remarked with a smile, " because you begin to have doubts about a thing which the church does n't inculcate, you show an inclination to throw overboard all that she does teach."

Maurice was silent a moment, playing with a rosary which he wore at his belt. He was surprised that he had never thought of this ; and he was startled by

the doubt which had arisen in his mind as soon as he
had declared his implicit faith in the church. He
realized in a flash that while he had spoken honestly,
he had not told the truth.

"I am afraid that I'm not quite honest," he said,
"though I meant to be. I'm afraid that after all I
don't feel sure of all the church teaches."

"My dear young man," the other replied kindly,
"you are fighting against the age. You have been
taught to believe, — if you will pardon me, — that
the thing for a true man to do is to resist the light of
reason. There are, for instance, a great many things
which used to be received literally which we now find
it necessary to interpret figuratively. It would be
refusing to use the reason heaven gives us if we refused to recognize this. The teachings of the church
are true and infallible, but every man must interpret
them according to the light of his own conscience and
reason."

"But if this is once allowed I don't see where you
are to draw the line. The heathen are very likely
honest enough."

"I said the teaching of the church, Mr. Wynne.
If a man earnestly searches his heart and follows this
guide as he understands it, there can be no danger."

"Mr. Strathmore," Maurice said, "perhaps it seems
like forcing myself upon you, and then taking the
liberty of fighting your views ; but this is too vital
to me to allow of my stopping for conventionalities.
You seem to me to be inconsistent. You refer to the
church as the supreme authority, but you give into
the hand of every man a power over that authority."

The other smiled with that warm, sympathetic
glance which was so winning.

" Does it seem possible to you," asked he, " that two human beings ever mean quite the same thing by the same words? Isn't there always some little variation, at least, in the impression that a given phrase conveys to you and to me ? "

" Theoretically I suppose that this is true," assented Maurice ; " but practically it doesn't amount to much, does it ? "

" It at least amounts to this," was the reply, " that what one man means by a set form of words cannot be exactly the same that another would mean by it. The creed is one thing to the simple-minded, ignorant man, and something infinitely higher and richer to a Father in the church. You would allow that, of course."

" Yes," Maurice hesitatingly assented, " but I shouldn't have thought of it as an excuse for laxity of doctrine."

" I am not recommending laxity of doctrine. I am only saying that since absolute unity of conception is impossible, it is idle to insist upon it. I am not excusing anything. A fact cannot need an excuse in the search for truth."

The young deacon felt himself sliding into deeper and deeper waters, though the mien of Strathmore seemed to inspire confidence. He was more and more uncertain what he believed or ought to believe.

" But is this the belief of the church ? " he persisted.

" What is the belief of the church if not the belief of its members ? "

" I do not know," Maurice answered. " I came to you to be told."

He tried to grasp definitely the belief which was

being presented to him, but it appeared as elusive as a shadow in the mist. Mr. Strathmore's look was as frank and clear as ever. There was in his eyes no sign of wavering or of evasion; his smile was full of warmth and sympathy.

"My dear young friend," the elder said, "I don't pretend to speak with the authority of the church; but to me it seems like this. We live in an age when we must recognize the use of reason. We are only doing frankly what men have in all ages been doing in their hearts. Men always have their private interpretations whether they recognize it or not. Nothing more is ever needed to create a schism than for some clear thinker to define clearly what he believes. There are always those who are ready to follow him because this seems so near to what many are thinking."

"But that is because so few persons are ever able to define for themselves what they do believe," Maurice threw in.

"Then do they ever really appreciate what the doctrines of the church are?" Strathmore asked significantly.

Maurice shook his head. He seemed to himself to be entangled in a net of words. He could not tell whether the man before him was entirely sincere or not. There seemed something hopelessly incongruous between the position of Mr. Strathmore as a religious leader and these opinions which seemed to strike at the very foundations of all creeds; yet the manner and look with which all was said were evidently honest and unaffected.

"Don't suppose that I think it would be wise to proclaim such a doctrine from the housetops," con-

tinued Strathmore, answering. Maurice felt, the doubt
in the face of the latter. "I speak to you as one
who is face to face with these facts, and must have
the whole of it."

Maurice rose with a feeling that he must get away
by himself and think.

"Mr. Strathmore," he said, "I am more grateful
than I can say for your kindness. I'm afraid that
I've seemed stupid and ungracious, but I haven't
meant to be either. I see that every man must work
out his own salvation."

"But with fear and trembling, Mr. Wynne."

The smile of the rector was so warm and so winning that it cheered Maurice more than any words
could have cheered him; Mr. Strathmore grasped the
young man warmly by the hand and added : —

"Don't think me a heretic because I have spoken
with great frankness. Remember that the good of
the church is to me more dear than anything else on
earth except the good of men for whom the church
exists. God help you in your search for light."

XVIII

THE afternoon was already darkening into dusk one day late in January when Philip Ashe stood in the hallway of a squalid tenement house, looking out into a dingy court. The place was surrounded by tall buildings which cut off the light and made day shorter than nature had intended, an effect which was not lessened by the clothes drying smokily on lines above. In one corner of the court yawned like the entrance to a cave the mouth of the passageway by which it was entered. In another stood a dilapidated handcart in which some dweller there was accustomed to carry abroad his rubbishy wares. The windows were for the most part curtainless, rising row above row with an aspect of wretchedness which gave Ashe a sense of discomfort so strong as almost to be physical. Here and there rags and old hats did duty instead of glass; some windows were open, framing slatternly women.

These women were stupidly quiet. Ashe wondered if they would have talked to each other across the court if he had not been in sight, or if the gathering dusk silenced them. One of them was smoking a short black pipe, and once let fall a spark upon the head of another idler a couple of floors below. The injured woman poured forth a volley of oaths, and Ashe expected a war of words. Nothing of the sort occurred. The figure above was so indifferent as hardly to glance down where the offended harridan was steaming with a fume of curses.

Philip began to be uneasy. He looked up at the darkening sky, and backward to the gloom of the stairway behind him. No gas had been lighted in the building, and he wondered if any ever were. It was certainly too late for Mrs. Fenton to be poking about in these dangerous places. They had been doing charity visiting together, and she had insisted on coming to this one house more before going home. He had remonstrated, but she had laughed at his fears.

"I don't believe any of these places are really dangerous," she had declared. "I've been coming here for years, and nobody ever troubled me."

"By daylight it is all very well," he had answered, "but it's a different thing after dark. I have been here once or twice to see some sick person in the evening, and it is a rough place."

"But it isn't after dark," she had persisted, "and it won't be for an hour."

She had had her way, but Ashe reflected uneasily that if harm came to her it would be his fault. He should have insisted upon her going home. The light was fading fast, and the locality was one of the worst in town. He wondered why the mere absence of daylight gave wickedness so much boldness. Men who by day were the veriest cowards seemed to spring into appalling fearlessness as soon as darkness gave its uncertain promise of concealment. The thought made him turn, and begin slowly to walk up the stairs.

He was not sure what floor she meant to visit. She was going, he knew, to see a woman whose husband got drunk and beat her. She had told him about the

poor creature as they came along. She was sure Mrs.
Murphy must have known a decent life. She set her
down as having been a housekeeper or upper servant
who had foolishly married a rascal. The woman,
Mrs. Fenton had added, was evidently ashamed of her
present condition, and afraid that those who had
known her in her better days should discover her.

"It is pitiful," Mrs. Fenton had said musingly, "to '
see how she clings to her husband. She pulls down
her sleeves to cover the bruises, and tells how good he
was to her when they were first married. She says
he does n't mean to hurt her, but that he 's the strongest man in the court, and does n't realize what he is
doing. She 's even proud of his strength."

"Strength is apt to impress women," Ashe had
answered, not without a secret sense of humiliation to
lack this quality.

As he walked gropingly up the dark stairway, a
man came clumsily after, and presently stumbled
past him. A strong smell of liquor enveloped the
newcomer, and he lurched heavily against Ashe without apology. Philip heard his uneven steps mounting
in the gloom, and followed almost mechanically. He
paused in one of the hallways to listen to a babble of
words in one of the rooms. It was chiefly profanity,
but it hardly seemed to be ill-natured. It was simply
a family cursing each other with well-accustomed
vehemence. He grew every instant more and more
uneasy, and thought of knocking at every door until he
found his friend. What right had philanthropy to
demand that a beautiful, noble woman should be exposed to the chances of a nest of ruffianism and vice?
He was indignant at the committee for not delegating
such work to men. Then he remembered that Mrs.

Fenton was herself on the committee, and that it was
by her own insistence that she was here.

" She is capable of any sacrifice to what she believes
to be right," he said to himself ; " but she is too good
for such work ; she is too delicate, too " —

Suddenly a noise arose on the floor above him. A
man's voice, thick with anger or drink, was pouring
out a stream of words, half oaths ; a woman was
shrilly entreating. Ashe sprang quickly upstairs,
and as he did so he heard Mrs. Fenton scream. The
sound was behind a door, and without stopping to
deliberate he tried to open it. The latch yielded, but
he could not open.

" Let me in ! " he cried fiercely. " What is the
matter ? "

The voice of a man who was evidently against the
door answered him with blasphemies. A woman
within cried to the man to stop, while Mrs. Fenton
called to Ashe for help. Philip set his shoulder
against the door and strained with all his might to
force it. He remembered then what Mrs. Fenton had
said about the strength of the husband of her pen-
sioner.

" Go to the window, and call the police," he
shouted.

" He's holding me ! " Mrs. Fenton cried back pant-
ingly.

Philip strained more desperately, and as he did so
he heard the window within flung open, and the voice
of a woman yelling for the police. The man inside
sprang forward with an oath, the door yielded, and
Philip plunged headlong into the room.

As Philip fell upon his knees, he saw a man seize
the woman who from the window was calling for help,

and fling her to the floor. The sound of her fall,
with her wild shriek beaten into a choking gasp by
the force with which she struck, turned his heart
sick; but his fear for Mrs. Fenton kept him up. He
scrambled to his feet, and as he did so she ran toward
him.

"Your cassock is all dust!" she cried hysterically.
"Oh, come away!"

The absurdity of the words made him burst into
nervous laughter; yet he saw that the drunken man
was coming, and he instinctively put her behind him
and took some sort of a posture of defense.

"Save yourself," he cried hastily. "He's killed
the woman."

All this passed with the quickness of thought.
There seemed to Philip hardly the time of a breath
between the opening of the door and the blow which
now fell upon the side of his face. Fortunately he
partly evaded it, but he reeled and staggered, feeling
the earth shake and the air full of stinging points of
fire. He saw the figure of his assailant towering between him and the light; he had a glimpse of Mrs.
Fenton rushing to the window to call again for help;
he realized with a horrible shrinking that that hammer-
like fist was again striking out for his face; he was
conscious of a sickening impulse to run, a humiliating
and overwhelming sense of his inability to cope with
this brute and of even his ignorance how to try; yet
most of all he felt the determination to defend Edith
or to die in the attempt. In a wild and futile fashion
he dashed against his assailant, striking blindly and
furiously, crying with rage and weakness, but throwing all his force into the fight. He felt crushing
blows on his head and chest. Once he was struck on

the side of the throat so that he gasped for breath with the sensation that he was drowning. Now and then he felt his own fist strike flesh, and the sensation was to him horrible. He fought blindly, doggedly, inwardly weeping for the shame and the pity of it, wondering if there would never be any end, and what would happen to Mrs. Fenton if he were beaten helpless. Surely if aid were coming it must have arrived long ago. He had been fighting for hours. He kept striking on, but he felt his strength failing, and he could have laughed wildly at the pitiful feebleness of his blows. He was knocked down, and scrambled up again, amazed that he was not killed or disabled. His one hope lay in the fact that the man was evidently much the worse for drink, and often struck as blindly as himself. If he could but occupy the brute's attention until help came, Mrs. Fenton would be saved.

Suddenly he was aware that the roaring in his ears was not all from the ringing in his head, but that heavy steps were sounding from the stairway. In a moment more screaming women were swarming in, and the din become intolerable as they scuttled about him, calling out to his opponent to stop and not to do murder. Men followed, and a couple of policemen came in their wake. Ashe saw through heavy eyelids the shine of brass buttons, and felt that the wearers of the uniforms to which these belonged had seized upon his assailant. He staggered against the wall, sick, faint, and dizzy. The two policemen were having a severe struggle to subdue their prisoner, and it seemed to Philip that all the inhabitants of the neighborhood were crowding in at the narrow door. The wife lay where she had been dashed to the floor, and Mrs. Fenton bent over her.

" Oh, Mr. Ashe," the latter said, coming to him,
" you must be terribly hurt! I think Mrs. Murphy's
killed."

He tried to smile, but his face was swollen and un-
manageable.

" It 's no matter about me," he managed with difficulty to say, " if you are not hurt."

The realities of life came back. The whirling rush
of the swift moments of the fight seemed already far
off. The crowd examined him with frank curiosity,
commenting on him as " the dude that 's been scrappin'
with Mike Murphy." He saw some of the women
busy over the prostrate form of Mrs. Murphy, lifting
her from the floor to the bed.

" Well, Mike," one of the policemen said, " I guess
this job 'll be your last. You 've done it this time."

The prisoner seemed to have become sober all at
once, now that he was in the hands of the law. He
went over to the bed, between his captors, and examined the injured woman with the air of one accustomed to such occurrences.

" Oh, the old woman 'll pull round all right," he
growled. " She ain't no flannel - mouth charity
chump."

Without a word Ashe put his hand upon the arm
of Mrs. Fenton, and led her toward the door. The
insult cut him more than all that had gone before.
What had passed belonged to a drunken and irrational
mood. This taunt came evidently from deliberate
contempt and ingratitude. Philip had a bewildered
sense of being outside of all conditions which he could
understand. This shameless effrontery and brutality
seemed to him rather the distorted fantasy of an evil
dream than anything which could be real. His one

thought now was to get his companion away before she was exposed to fresh insult.

They were detained a little by the police; but after giving their addresses were allowed to go. Ashe felt shaky and exhausted, but the hand of Mrs. Fenton was on his arm, and the need of sustaining her gave him strength. They got with some difficulty through the crowd and out of the court, and after walking a block or two were fortunate enough to find a carriage.

" Mr. Ashe," Mrs. Fenton said, as they drove up Hanover Street, " I'm afraid you're terribly hurt; and it is all my fault."

" No, no," he replied with swollen lips. " The fault was mine. I shouldn't have let you go into that place."

" But you did try to stop me; only I was obstinate. Oh, I don't know how to thank you for coming as you did."

" But what happened before I came ? "

Mrs. Fenton shuddered.

" Oh, I don't think I know very clearly. That great drunken man came in, and asked me for money. Of course I didn't give it to him; and his wife tried to get him to let me go. Then he struck her on the mouth ! "

" The brute ! " Ashe involuntarily cried, clenching his bruised fists.

" Then he caught me by the waist, and I screamed; and in another minute I heard you at the door."

" But it was the woman that called the police."

" Yes; and when she did that I was fearfully frightened. I knew that if she called the police against her own husband she must think that he'd really hurt me."

Philip leaned back in the carriage, dizzy with the overwhelming sense of the peril that had beset her, — her! Then, mastered by an overpowering impulse, he threw himself forward and caught her hands, covering them with kisses.

"Oh, my darling!" he gasped. "Oh, thank God you are safe!"

She dragged her hands away from him, and shrank back.

"Mr. Ashe!" she cried. "What is the matter with you? What are you doing?"

He did not attempt to retain his hold, but drew himself back into the darkness of his corner of the carriage. A strange calmness followed his outbreak; a sort of joyous uplifting which made him master of himself completely.

"I am sinning," he answered with a riotous sense of delight. "I am laying up remorse for all my future. I am telling you I love you; that I love you: I love you! I love you and I have saved you; and I shall brood over that, and do penance, and brood over it again, and do penance again, all my life long!"

"Oh, you are confused, excited, hurt," she cried. "You don't know what you are saying!"

"I know only too well what I am saying. I am saying that I" —

"Oh, for pity's sake, don't!" she moaned, putting out her hand.

He caught her wrist, and again kissed her hand passionately.

"Yes, I know that I ought not to say this now when you have had to bear so much already; that I ought never to say it; but it is said! It is said! You'll forget it, but I shall remember it all my life.

I shall remember that you heard me say that I love you!"

He threw himself back into his corner, and she shrank into hers, while the carriage went rattling over the pavement. Aching and sore, Philip yet knew a wild exhilaration, a certain divine madness which was so intense a delight that it almost made him weep. It was like a religious ecstasy, recalling to his mind moments in which he had seemed to be lifted almost to trance-like communion with holy spirits.

"I ought to ask you to forgive me, Mrs. Fenton," he said as they drew near her house, "but I cannot. I did not mean to do this; but I can't regret it. I am sorry for you; I am sorry — I shall be sorry, that is — for the sin of it; but the sin is sweet."

He wondered at his own voice, so even yet so high in pitch.

"Oh, what shall I do?" Mrs. Fenton cried sobbingly. "Is it my fault that this happened?"

"Oh, nothing can be your fault. It is all mine! But you must love me, I love you so!"

"No, no," she exclaimed vehemently. "I don't love you! I cannot love you! For pity's sake don't say such things!"

She buried her face in her hands and burst into sobs. Philip set his lips together, smiling bitterly at the pain it gave him. He controlled his voice as well as he was able.

"I beg you will forgive me," said he. "I have been out of my head. Forget my impertinence, and " —

He could not finish, but the stopping of the carriage at her door saved him the need of farther effort. He assisted her to alight, rang the bell, and said goodnight in a voice which he was sure did not betray him to the coachman.

XIX

Poor Ashe got home more dead than alive. His passion had shaken him like a delirium. He had been swept away by his emotion, and had thrown to the winds past and future. He felt as the carriage drove away from Mrs. Fenton's as if he had been swung up and down on some monstrous wave and dashed, broken and bleeding, on a rough shore. He could not think; and fortunately for him he was even too benumbed to feel greatly.

He reached the Hermans' in a sort of half-stupor, in which indifference, keen joy, and bitter contrition were strangely mingled. The contrition, however, seemed somehow to belong to the future; it was what he must endure when the time should come for repentance; the joy was a present blessing, tingling in his every fibre.

He met Mrs. Herman in the hall. She exclaimed when she saw him, and he stood smiling at her, swaying as if he were intoxicated.

"What has happened?" she cried. "What have you done to your face?"

The room and his cousin swam before him in a golden mist. He felt that he was grinning idiotically, yet he could not stop. He tried to speak, but his lips seemed too swollen to form words. He put out his hand to grasp a chair, and perceived that he could not reach it.

" I — fall ! " he managed to ejaculate.

Mrs. Herman caught him, and supported him to a chair. He felt her arm around him, and he wondered how he came to be thus embraced. He tried to grope back into the dusk of his mind to tell what had happened, and the fiery glow of the moment in which he had kissed the hand of Mrs. Fenton came back to him. He sat suddenly erect.

"Cousin Helen," he said, with husky fervor, " I have been a wretch, and I rejoice in it ! I have found out how sweet it is to sin ! I am lost, lost, lost ! "

He buried his face in his hands, almost hysterical. He felt his cousin's hand on his shoulder.

" Philip," she said decisively, " you must stop this, and tell me what has happened."

" I beg your pardon," he answered, dropping his hands. "Mrs. Fenton was attacked by a drunken man in the North End, and I fought him. I am afraid that I am pretty disreputable-looking."

" Yes, you are. I hope that is the worst of it."

She took him by the arm and led him into the library, where she established him in an easy-chair by the fire.

" I 'll send for a doctor to look you over," she said, "and meanwhile you are to take what I give you."

She left him, and Philip sat looking into the coals.

" Ah, if the glove had been off ! " he murmured half aloud.

He flushed hotly, and struck his clenched hand against his breast, rubbing it back and forth until the haircloth within stung and smarted.

" No, no," he said to himself fiercely. " I will not think about it ! "

Helen came back with a tumbler of something hot

and fragrant, which made his eyes water as he drank.
It sent a strange sensation of warmth through him,
and seemed to restore his energy. The doctor, who
came in soon after, found nothing serious the matter.
Ashe was temporarily disfigured, but had luckily
escaped without worse injury. He was sent to bed,
and despite his expectation of passing the night in an
agony of remorse, he sank almost immediately into a
dreamless sleep.

When Philip awoke his first sensation was that of
stiffness and soreness, — soreness such as he had felt
once when he had slept on the floor with his arms
extended in the form of a cross. The thought of
penance performed gave him a thrill of happiness,
but to this instantly succeeded the remembrance of
the events of yesterday, and his brief satisfaction
vanished.

His face was discolored, and as he set out after
breakfast to seek his spiritual adviser he felt a grim
satisfaction in going abroad thus marked. It was in
the nature of a mortification and a penance. He
repeated prayers as he walked, his eyes cast down,
his bosom pricked by haircloth. He felt that he had
already begun the expiation of the sin of yesterday.

He found Father Frontford at home, but so occupied as to be unable to listen to him. It would have
been impossible for Philip to do as Maurice had done,
and go to a man like Strathmore; and indeed, he had
come to his Father Superior partly because of the
sharpness with which he felt that his offending would
be judged. Where Maurice would question, Philip
would submit blindly and with ardent faith.

"Good-morning," the Father greeted Ashe kindly,
holding out his left hand, while the right held sus-

pended the pen which had already produced a heap of
letters. " I am very glad to see you; but you find
me extremely busy. There are so many things to be
thought of just now, and so many letters to be written."

" Yes ? " Philip responded absently.

" The election is so near at hand now," the other
continued, " that we cannot leave any stone unturned.
I am writing to some of the country clergy this morning. By the way, I wanted to speak to you about
Montfield."

Philip wondered at himself for the remoteness
which the affairs of the church had for him, so absorbed had he been in his own experiences.

" It seems to me," Father Frontford went on with
fresh animation, " that perhaps you can do something
there. Can't you go down and talk with Mr. Wentworth ? He's inclined to support Mr. Strathmore.
You should be able to influence him; you are his
spiritual son."

Mr. Wentworth was the rector in Philip's native
town, and under him both Ashe and Wynne had
come from Congregationalism into the Church.

" It is possible," Philip said doubtfully. " Mr.
Wentworth is, however, rather inclined to disagree
with me nowadays. He is completely carried away
by Mr. Strathmore."

A strange look came into the face of the old priest.
He laid down his pen, and pressed together the tips
of his white fingers, thin with fasting and self-denial.

" Did you not once tell me," he asked, " that Mr.
Wentworth has hoped for years that he might bring
your mother also into the fold ? "

" Yes."

" And you are her only child ? "

" Yes."

Father Frontford cast down his eyes; then raised them to flash a glance of vivid intelligence upon Ashe. Then again he looked down.

" I think that you had better run down and see your mother," he said. " It is possible that she may be even now leaning toward the truth; and in any case you might arouse Mr. Wentworth to fresh activity. It is of much importance that the country clergy should be pledged not to support Mr. Strathmore in the convention."

Philip went away confused and baffled. He said to himself that his feeling was caused solely by his disappointment that he had found no opportunity to talk with the Father Superior about his own affairs; but it was impossible for him to put out of his mind the way in which his mission to Montfield had been spoken of. He was willing to go down and do what he could to arouse Mr. Wentworth to the gravity of the situation, but he could neither forget nor endure the hint that he should make of the hope of his mother's conversion to the church a bribe. He could not think of this without being moved to blame Father Frontford; and he set himself to argue his mind into the belief that there was no harm in the suggestion. He walked along in a reverie as deep as it was painful, trying to see that the occasion called for the use of all lawful means, and that it was natural for the Father to suppose that Mrs. Ashe might be influenced more readily if the rector yielded to the wishes of her son in voting for Frontford.

" My dear Ashe, what have you been doing to yourself ? " a strong voice asked him.

He came with a start to the consciousness of where
he was, and that he had almost run into the Rev. De
Lancy Candish. The thought flashed through his mind
that Father Frontford had been too deeply absorbed in
his plans to notice the bruised face of his deacon.

"How do you do?" he exclaimed impulsively.
"Providence has sent you to me. Can you spare
me a little of your time?"

"Certainly," the other answered, with some appearance of surprise. "I'm on my way home now."

They walked in silence toward the home of Mr.
Candish, Ashe trying to frame some form of words
by which he could confess the sin of his heart without betraying Mrs. Fenton. He wondered if Maurice
Wynne could have helped him, and reflected how they
had been in the habit of confiding everything to one
another. Now he shrank from opening his heart to
his friend, and was almost seeking out a confidant in
the highways and hedges.

"You have not told me what sort of an accident
you have had," Candish observed, as he fitted the
latch-key into the lock of his door.

"I was attacked by a man in the North End,"
Philip answered, obeying the wave of the hand which
invited him to enter. "He had insulted Mrs. Fenton, and " —

"Mrs. Fenton!" echoed Candish.

The tone made Ashe turn quickly. Into his mind
flashed the words of Helen and of Mrs. Wilson connecting the name of Candish with that of Mrs. Fenton. In his longing for comfort and advice he had
seized upon the rector of the Nativity without remembering that he was the last person to whom he should
come.

" Ah," he said, " it was true ! "

Candish did not answer, and they went into the study in silence. The host sat down in the well-worn chair by his writing-table, while Philip took a seat facing him.

" What a foolish thing for me to say," Ashe broke out; then surprised at the querulousness of his tone he stopped abruptly.

" Mr. Ashe," Candish said gravely, " if there is anything I can do for you will you tell me what it is ? "

Philip rose quickly, and took a step towards him, leaning down over the thin, homely face.

" I have found you out ! " he cried with exultation. " I came to confess my sin to you, and I find that you love her too ! "

" Don't be hysterical and melodramatic," was the cool response. " Sit down, and let us talk rationally if we are to talk at all."

The manner of Candish recalled Philip to himself. He sat down heavily.

" I beg your pardon," he said. " Since that fight I have been half beside myself. I am like a hysterical girl."

The other regarded him compassionately.

" Mr. Ashe," responded he, " there is no good in my pretending that I did n't understand what you meant just now. You and I are both given to the priesthood. If we both love a woman " —

" I love her," burst in Philip, half defiantly, half remorsefully, " and I have told her so ! I have condemned myself " —

" Stop," Candish interrupted. " First you have to think of her."

Philip stared in silence. It came over him how entirely he had been thinking of himself, and how little he had considered Mrs. Fenton in his reflections upon the events of the previous evening. Here was a man who could love her so well as to think of her first and himself last.

"But I have given her up," Philip stammered.

"Was she yours to give up?"

There was nothing bitter or sneering in the words; they were said simply and dispassionately.

"No," Philip answered, dropping his voice; "she was not mine."

The older man rose and walked to the fire, where he stood looking down at the flaming coals.

"After all," he said, "we are pretty much in the same plight. I knew her when her husband brought her here a bride, the loveliest creature alive. Arthur Fenton was a clever, selfish, wholly irreligious man; and I could not help seeing how completely he failed to understand or appreciate his wife. She was kind to me, and when her trouble came she turned to me for comfort and sympathy. It is my weakness that I love her; but she will never know it."

"And does she love nobody?" demanded Ashe jealously.

Candish turned upon him a look of rebuke.

"What right have you or I to ask that question?" he retorted sternly. "I do penance for loving her, and God is my witness how carefully I have hidden it. It is not for me to question her right to love if she please."

Philip rose, and went to the other, holding out his hand.

"Mr. Candish," said he earnestly, "you have taught

me my lesson. I have been a weak fool, and worse.
I will pray for strength to lay my passion on the altar
and forget it."

The rector took the extended hand, looking into
Philip's eyes with a glance so wistful, so humble, and
so tender that the remembrance went with Ashe long.

" And forget it ? " he repeated. " I do not know
that I could do that ! "

He dropped the hand of Ashe, and shook himself
as if he would shake off the mood which had taken
possession of him.

" Come," he declared resolutely, " this will not do.
This is not the sort of mood that makes men. Let
me give you a single piece of advice, — I am older,
you know ; don't pity yourself, whatever else you do.
In the first place, that would be equivalent to saying
that Providence does n't know what is best for you ;
and in the second, it spoils all one's sense of values."

As Ashe that afternoon journeyed down to Montfield, he recalled all the details of this interview. The
more he considered the more he respected Candish
and the less satisfaction he found in his own conduct.
Yet perhaps the human mind cannot cease self-justi-
fication at any point short of annihilation, and Philip
still had in his secret thought a deep feeling that the
church should more absolutely settle the question of
the celibacy of its clergy, so that there might be no
more doubts. He honored the attitude of Candish,
and he resolved to imitate it. He who has never
shaken hands with the devil, however, can have little
idea how hard it is to loose his grasp ; and Philip
groaned at the thought of how far he was even from
wishing to put his love out of its high place in his
heart.

His mind was calmer as he sat that evening talking
with his mother. Mrs. Ashe was a plain, sweet-faced
woman, with gray hair brushed smoothly under her
cap of black lace. There was in her pale, faded face
little beauty of feature or coloring; yet the light of
her kindly and delicate spirit shone through. Maurice
Wynne had once said that she was like a sweet-pea, —
born with wings, but tethered so that she might not
fly away. Philip, with his exquisite sensitiveness,
found an unspeakable comfort in her presence; a
soothing sense of rest and peace so blissful that it
seemed almost wrong. There are even in this worldly
age many women who hide under the covering of un-
eventful, commonplace lives existences full of spiritual
richness, — women who find in religion not the mechanical acceptance of form, not a mere superstition which
encrusts an outworn creed, but a vital, uplifting force;
a power which fills their souls with imaginative warmth
and fervor. The worth of an experience is to be esti-
mated by the emotional fire which it kindles; and to
the lives of such women the dull, colorless round of
their daily existence gives no real clue. Theirs is
the life of the spirit, and for them the inner is the
only true life. It is when the sunken eye shines
with a glow from deep within; when the thin cheeks
faintly warm with the ghost of a flush and the blue
veins swell from the throbbing of a heart stirred by
a spiritual vision, that the observer gets a hint of the
realities of such a life.

Mrs. Ashe was a type of the saintly woman that
the spirit of Puritanism bred in rural New England.
Such women are the living embodiment of the power
which has inspired whatever is best in the nation; the
power which has been a living force amid the worldli-

ness, the materialism, the crudity that have threatened
to overwhelm the people of this yet young land, so
prematurely old. In her face was a look of high
unworldliness that marks the mystic, the inheritance
from ancestors bred in a faith impossible without mys-
ticism in the very fibres of the race. The heroic self-
denial, the persistent belief, the noble fidelity to the
ideal which is the salvation of a nation, shine in such
a countenance, and make real the high deeds of a past
generation the narrowness of whose creeds too often
blinds us to-day to the greatness of their character.

She smiled a little on hearing the object of her son's
visit.

" I am glad to see you on any terms," she observed, " but I cannot say that I think your coming
very wise."

" But, mother," he urged, " don't you see that it is
a matter of so much importance that we ought not
to neglect any chance ? "

" My dear boy," questioned she, " do you really
think that it is of so much importance who is bishop ? "

" It is of the greatest possible importance," he
returned earnestly. " Of course you don't agree with
me as to the importance of forms of worship, but suppose that it were your own church, and the question
were of having a man put into a place so influential.
Wouldn't you be troubled if one were likely to be
chosen who taught what you regarded as heresy ?"

She smiled on him still, but he saw the seriousness
in her eyes.

" Yes," she said, " I suppose I should ; but doesn't
it ever occur to you, Philip, that we are all too
much inclined to feel that everything is going wrong if
Providence doesn't work in our way ? We can't help,

I suppose, the habit of regarding our plans as some-how essential to the proper management of the universe."

He laughed and shook his head.

"You always had a most effective way of taking down my conceit," he responded. "I don't mean that it is necessary that Father Frontford shall be bishop because I want him, but "—

"But because you believe in him," his mother interrupted with a little twinkle in her eye. "Well, we cannot do better than to follow our convictions, I suppose."

She ended with a sigh, and Philip knew that it was because into her mind came the sadness she felt at his defection from the faith of his fathers.

"Yes, you trained me from the cradle to do what I thought right without considering the consequences."

They fell into more general talk after that; and after the news of the family and the neighborhood had been pretty well exhausted, Mrs. Ashe said : —

"I have asked Alice Singleton to make me a visit."

"Alice Singleton! Why, mother, I cannot think of a person I should have supposed it less likely you would want to stay with you."

"I'm afraid that I don't want her very much ; but she wrote me that she was very lonely, that she had n't any plans, and that Boston seemed to her a very home-sick place. Her mother was my nearest friend, you know ; and if Alice needs friendship it's very little for me to do for her."

"I did n't know she'd been in Boston," Philip commented thoughtfully. "She never seemed to me honest, mother. I never could be charitable to her at all."

The sweet face of his mother took on a curious expression of mingled amusement and contrition.

"If I must confess it, Phil," she said, "neither could I; and I'm afraid that there was more notion of doing penance in my asking her than of real hospitality. She is after all not to blame for her manner, and no doubt we do her wrong."

"If you have come to doing penance, mother, there's no knowing how soon you will be with me."

"No, Phil," she answered softly, "do you remember what Monica told her son? 'Not where he is, shalt thou be, but where thou art he shall be.'"

He shook his head, sighing.

"I ought not to have touched on that matter, mother. You know that I am trying to follow my conscience."

"Yes, I cling to that. I should be miserable if I did not believe that your way and my way will come together somewhere, on this side or the other; and I bid you Godspeed on whatever way you go with prayerful conviction."

A sudden impulse leaped up within him, and it was almost as if some voice not his own spoke through his lips, so little was he conscious of meaning to ask such a question.

"Even if the way led to Rome?"

Mrs. Ashe grew paler, but her eyes steadfastly met those of her son.

"I trust you in the hands of God," she said.

Late that night Philip woke from a heavy sleep into which fatigue had plunged him. He reached out his arm, and drew aside the curtain near his bed, so that he might see the window of his mother's chamber. A faint light was shining there; and he knew that the beams of the candle fell on his mother on her knees.

XX

THE two deacons were together again in the Clergy
House. Maurice frankly confessed to himself that he
did not like it, and he wondered if Philip were also
dissatisfied. It was a question too delicate to ask, however; and he contented himself with watching his
friend to discover, if possible, whether the stay outside
had affected Ashe as it had him. They returned late
in the afternoon, and their greeting was of the warmest.

" Dear old boy," Maurice cried, " you don't know
how glad I am to get at you again. Where in the
world have you kept yourself ? "

" Just at the last," Philip responded, " I 've been
down to Montfield."

" Down home ? Have you really ? How is everybody ? I hope your mother is well."

" She is very well, and I do not remember anybody
that we know who is n't. I went down to see Mr.
Wentworth, and found that he is already pledged to
Mr. Strathmore."

" Is he really ? How did that happen ? "

" It seems that he is a cousin of that Mrs. Gore
where we heard that heathen, and she is greatly interested in Mr. Strathmore's election. Mr. Wentworth
promised her his vote. How people are carried away
by that man. Mr. Wentworth told me that he looked
upon him as the greatest man in the church to-day."

"It is strange," Maurice assented absently ; " but
he is a man of great personal fascination."

" To me," Philip retorted, " he is a whited sepulchre.
His doctrine of mental reservation amounts to nothing
less than that a priest is at liberty to believe anything
he pleases if he will only conform outwardly."

Maurice was secretly much of the same opinion,
but they came now to the dinner table, where silence
was the rule. Wynne had a feeling of dishonesty
from the fact that he concealed from his friend that he
had sought an interview with Strathmore, yet he felt
that he could not confess the visit. While they sat at
table a brother read aloud, and the reading chanced to
be to-night from the book of Job. The words of the
splendid poem mingled in the mind of Maurice with
the most incongruous and unpriestly thoughts. He
chafed at the routine into which he had fallen as into
a pit from which he had once escaped ; the meagre
repast seemed to him pitifully poor ; and most of all
he was angry with himself that he could not feel joy
at his return to the house which was the symbol of
the consecrated work to which he had given his life.
After dinner came an hour and a half of recreation,
and in this he was called to the study of the Father
Superior.

"You returned so late in the day," the Father said
with a smile, " that you will not mind giving up recreation to-night. I wish to speak with you on a matter
of importance."

Maurice took the seat toward which the other waved
his hand. He felt alien and strange. He recalled
the attitude of submission and reverence with which
he had once been accustomed to enter this room, the
respect with which he had heard every word of the

Father; and he blamed himself bitterly that he now took rather a defensive mood, and felt an instinctive desire to escape. He reflected that he had been poisoned by the world ; yet he could not wholly shut out the consciousness that he had no genuine desire to be freed from the sweet madness which had seized him. He tried to put all thought of these matters by, however, and to give his whole attention to what the priest might say to him.

"I think that you have met Mrs. Frostwinch," the Father said.

"I went to her house once," Maurice answered, surprised at the remark, and feeling his pulse quicken at the remembrance of his first sight of Berenice.

"I remember that you mentioned it in confession," was the grave reply. "Satan sets his snares in the most unlikely places."

The words seemed almost a reply to Wynne's secret thought. His first impulse was to resent this open allusion to a sacred confidence whispered in the confessional. It was like a stab in the back, or a trick to take unfair advantage ; and the matter was made worse by this allusion to a snare of Satan, which could mean nothing else but Berenice herself. Maurice flushed hotly, but habit was strong in him, and he cast down his eyes without reply.

"Have you heard that Mrs. Frostwinch is on her way home? " Father Frontford went on.

"No."

"It is said that her faith-healing superstition has failed her, and she is coming home to die."

"To die? " echoed Maurice.

He recalled Mrs. Frostwinch as he had seen her, gracious, high-bred, apparently brilliantly well ; and

it appeared monstrously impossible that death should
be near her. She had seemed a woman who would defy
death, and live on simply by her own splendid will.

"So it is said," the Father assured him. "Do you
know how important it is to us to have her influence
in the election?"

"I know that there are certain votes that she
may influence, and that she is in"—he almost said
"your," but he caught himself in time—"our interests."

"There are three and perhaps four votes which
depend upon her. Three are sure to go over to the
other side if she is not able to stand behind them.
They are all dependent upon her for support in one
way or another."

"But surely," Maurice suggested, "they would not
vote unconscientiously? They would n't sell their
convictions for her support?"

"They would not vote unconscientiously," was the
dry response, "but they believe that the support
which she gives to them and to their missions is of
more importance than that the man they really prefer
should be chosen."

"But what can be done?"

Father Frontford sat leaning back in his chair, his
face in shadow, and the tips of his thin fingers pressed
together in his habitual gesture.

"Perhaps nothing," he answered.

His voice had dropped into a soft, silky half-tone,
insinuating and persuasive. Maurice began to have
an uneasy feeling as if he were being hypnotized; yet
the words of the other came to him with a quality
strangely soothing and attractive.

"Perhaps," the priest went on after a pause of a
second, "perhaps everything that is necessary."

It seemed to Maurice that there was something significant in the tone which the words did not reveal. He looked keenly at the shadowed face, but without being able clearly to make out its expression. He could see little but the bright eyes holding and dominating his own.

"It is for you to do this work," Father Frontford continued; "and it is wonderful how Providence brings good out of all things. Here is an opportunity for you not only to expiate your fault, but to serve the cause of the church."

Without understanding, Maurice began to tremble with inner dread lest the name of Berenice should again be brought up between himself and this pitiless priest.

"I do not see that there is anything that I can do," he said coldly.

"On the contrary. Do you chance to know anything about the Canton estate? I suppose you are not likely to."

"Nothing whatever. What is the Canton estate?"

"Mrs. Frostwinch was a Canton. Her father was a brother of old Mrs. Morison."

Maurice could not see how all this involved him, but he became more and more uneasy.

"The estate of old Mr. Canton," the Father went on in the same smooth voice, "was, as I have just learned from Mrs. Wilson, left to his daughter for life and to her children after her. If she died childless it was to go to Miss Morison."

"And she is childless?"

"She is childless. If she is taken away now, the property will all be in the hands of Miss Morison."

There was a moment of stillness in which the

thought most insistent in the mind of Maurice was
that in this fortune fate had raised another wall between himself and Berenice.   He spoke to escape the
reflection.

"But all this is surely not my concern."

"It is your concern if it shows you a way in which
the votes of those clergymen may be assured, although
Mrs. Frostwinch should not recover."

"It shows me no way."

Maurice tried to speak naturally and without evidence of feeling, but his throat was parched and his
heart hot.   He hated this inquisition.   The long reverence and admiration which had bound him to the
Father melted to nothing in the twinkling of an eye.
Who was this Jesuit that sat here making of Berenice
and her fortune pawns in his game; involving her in
a web of intrigue unworthy of his sacred office; and
forcing his disciple to listen through a knowledge of
facts stammeringly poured out in the confessional?
Absence from the Clergy House and from town, and
after that a growing reluctance, had prevented Maurice from confessing anything beyond his first attraction to Miss Morison, but he had written to the Father
Superior of the accident, and had mentioned that he
was thought to have been of assistance in saving her.
It came to him now that he was being repaid for the
accursed vanity which had led him to make this boast;
and he became the more animated against his director
from his anger against himself.

"Whatever Mrs. Frostwinch has done with the
property," Father Frontford said, "of course Miss
Morison may do if she pleases."

"I should suppose so; but I know nothing about
it."

"Then if Miss Morison will promise to continue the donations of Mrs. Frostwinch, the position of the beneficiaries will be the same toward her as toward Mrs. Frostwinch."

Maurice bent forward quickly, unable longer to maintain an appearance of calm.

"Father Frontford," he exclaimed, "you certainly cannot ask this of Miss Morison! It would be sheer impertinence! I beg your pardon, but I cannot help saying it. Besides, there is something horribly cold-blooded in talking about what shall be done with the property of Mrs. Frostwinch when she is dead. Miss Morison would not listen to anything of the sort."

"The circumstances justify what otherwise would be inadmissible. It is necessary, Mrs. Wilson thinks, to be able to tell those men that their situation is not changed by the death of Mrs. Frostwinch, which is almost sure to take place before the convention. You must explain that to Miss Morison."

"I!"

"The obligation which she is under to you," the Father said, ignoring the exclamation, "will naturally incline her to listen."

"But I cannot" —

"I had thought that it was mine to decide what you could and should do."

"But, Father, this is so extraordinary, so impossible, so" —

"Miss Morison is to be in Boston in a couple of days. Mrs. Wilson will let us know when she arrives. I know how strange this looks to you, and how repugnant it must be. Do you think that it is any less hateful to me? Do you think that it is easy for me to be working for what is to be my own personal exal-

tation if we succeed? I give you my word, Wynne,
that the severest sacrifice that any one can be called
on to make in this matter is that which I make when
I take these steps toward putting myself in office. I
am not naturally humble, and it humiliates me to the
very soul; but I do what seems to me to be for the
good of the church, and try to put my personal feeling
entirely out of the matter. It is for you to do the
same."

It was impossible for Maurice to doubt the sincerity
with which this was said. He had no answer to
give.

"Go now, my son," the Father concluded, "and do
not forget to thank God that the weakness of your
heart may be turned into a means by which the
church may be served."

Maurice retired to his room in a whirl of conflicting
thoughts. He was summoned almost immediately to
vespers and complines. The familiar ritual soothed
him, and he was able to join in the chants in much
the old way. His feeling was that he would gladly
have had the service last into the night. He would
have liked to go on with this half·emotional, half
mechanical devotion, which kept him from thinking,
and which put off the dreaded hour when he must
face the proposition which had been made to him.

It was the rule of the house that all the inmates
should preserve unbroken silence among themselves
from complines until after nones the next day. Maurice knew therefore that he was free from intrusion
of human companionship, which it seemed to him he
could not have borne. Even the talk of dear old
Phil, to a chat with whom he had looked forward as
the one pleasure in coming back to the Clergy House,

would have been intolerable while this nightmarish
trouble lay upon him. He went at once to his chamber, a cell-like room, and sat down to think. Could
he do it? How would Berenice regard this imperti-
nent interference with her private affairs? How could
he go to her and say: "It is necessary for church
politics that you assume to dispose of the property
which now your cousin holds, and over which you
have no rights until she is in her grave." He could
see her eyes sparkle with indignation and contempt,
and he grew hot in anticipation. He could not do it,
he thought over and over. It was impossible that in
this age of the world anybody should dream of having
such a thing done. If he were almost a priest, he
told himself fiercely, he had not yet ceased to be a
gentleman!

The stricture which this thought seemed to cast
upon the priesthood made him pause. He had not
yet shaken off the dominion of old ideas and old
habits. He apologized to an unseen censor for the
apparent irreverence of his thought. It was not the
priesthood, it was— He came again to a standstill.
He was not prepared to own to himself that he disapproved of the Father Superior. He had vowed obedience, and here he sat raging against a decree because
it sacrificed his personal feelings to the good of the
church. The blame should be upon himself. There
was nothing in all this revolt except his own selfish-
ness and wounded vanity. He had transgressed
by allowing his thoughts to be entangled in earthly
affection, and this misery and wickedness followed
inevitably. The fault was in him entirely; it was his
own grievous fault. The familiar words of the office
of confession made him beat his breast, and fall in

prayer before the crucifix which seemed to waver in the flickering candlelight. He repeated petition after petition. He would not allow himself to think. It was his to obey, not to question. He would regain his old tranquillity, his old docility. He would submit passively. It was his own fault, his most grievous fault.

The ten o'clock bell rang, calling for the extinguishing of lights. He sprang from his knees, blew out the candle, threw off his clothes in the dark, and hurried into his hard and narrow bed. He was resolved not to think. He said the offices of the day; he repeated psalms; and at last, in desperate attempt to control his mind and to induce sleep, he began to multiply large numbers. All the time he was resolutely saying to himself: "It is my fault; my most grievous fault!" And all the time some inner self, unsubdued, was persistently replying: "It is not! It is not! I am right!"

XXI

THIS "WOULD" CHANGES

Hamlet, iv. 7

MAURICE woke next morning to a deep sadness, as if some bitter calamity had befallen. In a moment the conversation of the previous evening rushed to his mind, and his gloom rather deepened than grew less. The rising-bell had rung, and he rose languidly in the cold, gray twilight. So long had he tossed restlessly in the night unsleeping that he felt worn out and miserable, and after the hours which he had necessarily kept at the house of his cousin half past five seemed hardly to be day. He shivered with a discouraged disgust as he made his toilet, endeavoring to forget.

The routine of the morning followed : meditation, lauds and prayers ; mass ; breakfast ; prime ; then the study hours before luncheon ; and so on to nones. All this time the rule of the house protected him from speech, but now that the hour for recreation came he was in the midst of questioning fellow-deacons. They had all so much to tell, however, of the manner in which they had passed their time during their absence from the Clergy House that Maurice was able for the most part to listen instead of speaking. He watched with curiosity to see that they appeared glad to return to seclusion. They had been troubled by the sensation of finding themselves out of their accustomed groove, and had found the world confusing. Most often they seemed to him to have been oppressed by the need of deciding what they should do, and how they should meet trifling unforeseen emergencies.

"It is impossible to be spiritually calm except in seclusion," one of them said.

Involuntarily Maurice looked at the speaker, feeling that this must be mere cant. It struck him as non-sense, yet one glance at the serene, honest face of the deacon who spoke, with its tender, candid eyes, like those of a pure girl, was enough to convince him of the entire sincerity of the words. He sighed, and turned away; as he did so he caught the eye of Philip, who was watching him with solicitous attention. Maurice put his hand on the arm of his friend, and led him away.

"Why did you look at me that way, Phil?" he asked. "Does it seem to you that spiritual calm is the best thing in life?"

Ashe was silent a moment. Maurice noted that he looked thinner than of old, and reproached himself that he had seen so little of his friend during their absence from the Clergy House.

"I was thinking," Philip replied at length, hesitating and dropping his voice, "that I feared both you and I had discovered that something more than seclusion is needed to give it, however good it may be."

Maurice laid his hand on the back of Philip's, grasping it tightly.

"You too?" was his response.

They stood in silence for some moments, looking out of a window over the dingy back yards which formed the prospect from the rear of the house. Wynne was wondering how it was that for the first time in his life it was impossible to be frankly confidential with Philip, and how far it was probable that his friend would be in sympathy with him in his trouble. He longed for counsel, and the force of old habit pressed him to tell everything.

"Phil," he said, "will you go out with me for a walk this afternoon?"

"Of course," Ashe answered. "Don't we always go together?"

Wynne laughed, turning to look at his companion as if from afar.

"I doubt," he observed, "if anything I could tell you directly would give you so good an idea of how upset I am, and how completely out of the routine of our life, as the fact that I seem to have forgotten that there ever were any walks before."

"I am afraid that I am a good deal out of touch with the life here," Ashe responded seriously. "I have been troubled, and tempted, and— Oh, Maurice," he broke off suddenly, "Maynard is right: no spiritual calm is possible in the world outside!"

"Even if that were true," returned Maurice, "I don't know that I am prepared to agree that calm is the best thing in life."

"It is the highest thing."

"I don't believe it. It isn't growth."

The bell for study sounded, and ended their talk. Maurice went to his work uneasy, perhaps a little irritated. He was disquieted that Philip should be so monastically out of sympathy, and he was annoyed with himself for being out of key with his friend. He felt as if he had returned to his old place in the body without being here at all in the spirit. He had while at Mrs. Staggchase's looked into many books which in the Clergy House would never have come in his way; he had more than once been startled to encounter

thoughts which had been in his own mind, but which
he had felt it wrong to entertain. Here they were
stated coolly, dispassionately, with no consciousness,
apparently, that they should not be considered with
frankness. He had heard opinions and ideas which
from the standpoint of the religious ascetic were not
only heretical but little short of blasphemous, yet
they were evidently the ordinary current thought of
the time. It was impossible that these things should
not affect him; and to-day as he sat in lecture he
found himself trying all that was said by a new stand-
ard and involuntarily taking the position of an ob-
jector. He·was able to see nothing but flaws in the
logic, faults in the deduction, breaks in the argument.

"I am come to that state of mind when I should
see a seam in the seamless robe," he groaned in spirit.

Father Frontford lectured that afternoon on church
history. Sometimes in the long hour Maurice studied
the priest, wondering at him, trying to comprehend
the working of his mind. Sometimes he would ask
himself whether it were possible that this man were
wholly sincere, whether it were possible that an intel-
lect so acute could really believe the things which
were the foundation of the teaching of the day; but he
came back always to faith in the complete conviction of the Father. Maurice, indeed, said to himself
that Frontford was quite capable of taking his spiritual
self by the throat and compelling it to believe; and
then the young doubter asked himself if this were
the secret of the faith which showed in every word
and look of the speaker. He told himself that Father Frontford was his Superior, and as such to be followed, not criticised; he resolved not to think, but
endeavored to give his whole attention to the lecture.

Here however he did little better. The glories of
the church upon which the speaker dwelt seemed to
Wynne in his present mood poor and paltry triumphs
of dogmatism, — or even, why not of superstition
indeed ? He was startled by the sin of his questioning, yet it seemed impossible to silence the mocking
inner voice.

" This is one of the incidents," he at last became
aware that the Father was saying to close, " which
strikingly illustrate the need of implicit obedience.
If the church were a simple organization of man, if it
were for the accomplishment of worldly ends, if its
object were the aggrandizement of individuals, nothing
could be more dangerous than the establishment in it
of what seems like arbitrary power. As it is directed
from above ; as its aim is nothing less than the spiritual
uplifting of the race ; as, indeed, upon it rests the salvation, under God, of mankind, the case is different.
It is necessary that no energy be lost ; that all the
power of the church be used to the best advantage ;
that the hand assist the head and the head have complete control of the hand. Obedience is of all the
lessons which you have to learn perhaps the hardest.
It is no less one of the most essential. In an age
which is lacking not only in obedience but even in
that reverence upon which obedience must rest, it is
for the true priest to be an example of reverence
and obedience alike. Revere and obey, and you have
done noble service."

The deacons buzzed together as they left the lecture-
room. They were but boys after all, and some of
them light-hearted enough. Maurice heard one or
two of them commenting upon the lecture or upon
indifferent things. A curly-haired young deacon, a

Southerner with the face of a cherub, was laughing lightly to himself. He was the youngest of them all, and Maurice had for him that liking which one might have for a pretty kitten.

"I say, Wynne," he remarked, looking up into the face of the other with a twinkling eye, "the Dominie gave us a good preachment to-day in support of his authority. It almost made me resolve to rebel the next time I was told to do anything."

"Then I suppose that you don't agree with him," Maurice responded rather absently.

"Oh, it is n't that. I do agree with him. I mean to be a bishop myself some day, and then the doctrine will come in all right. I 'll work it. Down South we understand that sort of thing better than you do up here."

"Then what did you object to in the lecture?"

"I did n't object to anything; only when anybody proves that you ought not to do a thing is n't it human nature to want to do it, just for the fun of it?"

Maurice felt how far from serious was the temper of the boy, and that it would be utterly unreasonable to expect from him anything like reverence.

"Then how do you expect anybody to hold to the doctrine of implicit obedience?" he questioned, smiling.

"Oh, everybody expects to wield the authority sometime," was the light answer. "Nobody 'd hold to it otherwise."

Maurice instinctively glanced at Ashe. In Philip's pale, enrapt face was an expression of self-surrender which made Wynne feel how completely the teaching to which they had just listened must appeal to the temperament of his friend.

"To obey for the sake of obeying is precisely what Phil would delight in," he thought. "How entirely different we are! Yet if it hadn't been for him I should never have come here. Haven't I strength enough to follow my own convictions?"

The hour for walking was four, and a few minutes after the clocks had struck, Maurice and Philip started out. It was a dull and lowering afternoon, and the narrow street was already gloomy with shadows. Half unconsciously Wynne found himself casting about in his mind for topics of conversation which should be free from the personal element. Now that the time for confidences had come, he shrank from words. He reproached himself, and then half peevishly thought: "I seem nowadays to do nothing but to find fault with myself for things that I can't help feeling!"

"I am glad Father Frontford said what he did to-day," Ashe remarked after they had walked in silence for a little. "It was just what I needed. I've got so in the habit of following my own will since we have been out in the world that I needed to be reminded that there is something better."

Maurice felt a faint irritation that the talk was begun in precisely the key he would most gladly have avoided, but honesty would not let him be silent.

"I am afraid, Phil," he said, "that I'm not entirely in sympathy with you. I didn't like the lecture. Since we are given will and reason, I believe that it was intended that we should use them."

"Of course. If I had no reason, how could I bring myself to give up my own will to one that I know to be higher?"

Maurice smiled unhappily.

" Well," was his answer, " when you begin with a paradox like that it is evident that I could n't go on without getting into a discussion darker than the darkness of Egypt. I 'd rather just talk about common everyday things. Where shall we go ? "

" I want to go to the North End. There is an old woman there that I thought of visiting. I had trouble with her husband the other day ; he threw her down and hurt her."

" What sort of trouble ? "

" He struck me, and we had a sort of struggle. He was n't sober."

" Were you on the street ? "

" No ; in his room. I — I broke in."

" Broke in ? "

" Yes." Ashe hesitated, and then added : " Mrs. Fenton was there, and he tried to rob her."

" Mrs. Fenton ? Why did n't you tell me about it ? When was it ? "

" The day before I went down home. You were n't here, you know. There was not much to tell."

Maurice questioned eagerly, and his friend related briefly what had happened.

" Why, Phil, you 're a hero ! " Wynne exclaimed. " You 've quite taken the wind out of my sails. I counted for something of an adventurer simply by having been in a smash-up ; but you rushed in and had a real adventure. I never thought of you as a defender of dames."

The other turned toward him a face contracted with a look of pain.

" Don't, Maurice," he protested. " I can't joke about it. It was not anything to be proud of ; and nobody knows better than I how far I am from being a hero,"

"Oh, you're modest, of course. That's like you; but I call it stunning. Mrs. Fenton must have admired you tremendously."

"Do you suppose she did?" Philip demanded impetuously. Then his voice altered. "Oh, she knows me too well!" he added.

The intense bitterness of his tone gave Maurice a shock.

"Phil!" cried he.

His companion apparently understood the thought which lay behind the exclamation. He dropped his head, and for a little distance they walked in silence.

"I may as well tell you," Ashe said in a moment. "It is true, what you guess. I — I have been thinking of her more than was right. That is one reason why I am glad to get back to the Clergy House."

"To give her up?"

"She was not mine to give up."

"But do you mean not to try to — Oh, Phil, does n't it ever come to you that all this monkish business is a mistake? We were a couple of foolish boys that did n't know what we were about when we went into it; and" —

Ashe turned and looked at him with eyes full of reproach, and of almost despairing determination.

"Is that the way you help me?" he asked.

Maurice drew a long, deep breath, and set his strong jaw with a resolve not to abandon so easily the endeavor to bring his friend out of his trouble. It hardly occurred to him for the moment that it was his own cause that he was defending.

"Phil," he persisted, "is n't it possible that after all we may be wrong in making ourselves wiser than the church by taking vows that are not required?"

" Do you suppose that the devil has forgotten to say that to me over and over again ? " was the response.

" Meaning that I am the old gentleman ? " Maurice retorted, trying to be lightsome.

" Oh, don't joke. I can't stand it. I 've been through so much, and this is so terrible a thing to bear anyway."

Wynne seized his rosary with one hand, and struck it across the other so hard that the corner of the crucifix wounded his finger.

" Phil, old fellow," he said gravely, " I never felt less like joking. It cuts me to the quick to see you suffer ; and I know how hard you will take this. I know what it is, for I 'm going through the same thing myself, and I 've about made up my mind that we are wrong. I begin to think that celibacy is only a device that the early church somehow got into when it was necessary to hold complete authority over the priest, or when men thought that it was. It belongs to the Middle Ages ; not to the nineteenth century."

" Then you don't see how marriage would be sure to interfere with a man's zeal for his work ? "

" But it would certainly bring him into closer sympathy with humanity."

Ashe shook his head.

" You don't seem to realize," he said with a certain doggedness which Wynne had seldom seen in him, " how it must absorb a man, and take possession of his very reason. Why, see me. I know it is a sin to think of her, and yet " — He broke off and choked. " Besides," he resumed presently, " you say yourself that you feel as I do, and that means that you are not looking at the thing fairly. You are trying to

make your conscience come round to the side of your
desires."

They walked on up the dingy street into which
they had come, and for some time nothing more was
said. Maurice recognized that it was idle to attempt
to reply to the charge of his companion. He had
made it to himself and succumbed to it; but now
that another stated it, he instinctively found himself
refusing to yield. He repeated to himself that he
was not trying to befool his conscience, but merely
acting with human sanity.

Presently they came into a dusky court, and crossing it, found themselves at the door of an ill-smelling
tenement house. Here Ashe turned suddenly, and
faced his friend, his face full of strange excitement.

"Do you suppose," he said, in a voice which, though
low, was full of feeling, "that I do not know how
absorbing a thing it is to give up life to a woman?
Here I am, when she is nothing to me, when I do not
mean ever to see her again, going into this place
simply because here she was half a minute in my
arms, because here for two minutes she looked at me
as her preserver. It is sin, and I know it; but it
is too strong for me."

"But, Phil," Maurice exclaimed in astonishment,
"there is surely no harm in going to see a sick
woman."

The other laughed bitterly.

"So I told myself, and so I kept saying over and
over till the talk we've had forced me to stop lying
to myself. I'm not going to see a sick woman. I'm
going to stand where she stood that day."

"If you feel that way about it," Maurice said, putting his hand on the other's arm, "you ought not to
go in."

" I will go in."

" But obedience, Phil. Think what you were saying about the lecture."

" Nobody has forbidden me," Ashe responded defiantly. " I will go in. I had made up my mind before I came. Oh, I shall do penance enough for it; you need not be afraid of that. I shall suffer enough for it."

He started up the stairs, and Maurice followed blindly, full of sympathy and dismay.

XXII

THEY found the old woman in bed, attended by a slatternly half-grown girl, who was reading by the dying light a torn and dirty illustrated paper. There was little furniture in the chamber; merely the frowsy bed, a bare table, a single broken chair besides the one in which the girl was sitting. The floor was bare and dirty; one of the window-panes was broken and stuffed with a bundle of paper. There were a rusty stove, a few dishes on the shelf, a kettle and a tin tea-pot. On the window-sill by the bed were a medicine bottle and a cup.

"How do you do, Mrs. Murphy?" Ashe asked. "Are you any better to-day?"

"No better, thank yer riverince. I'll never be better again. My back is broke, and the pain in me is like purgatory already."

The slatternly girl laid her paper on her knees, but she neither rose nor spoke. To Maurice she seemed to have an air of contempt.

"I am sorry to hear it, Mrs. Murphy," said Ashe. "I thought that I would drop in and ask after you."

Maurice involuntarily glanced at him, surprised by the indifference of the tone. Enlightened by the passionate words which had been spoken below, he could see that Philip was preoccupied, and gave to the sick woman no more than the barest semblance of attention. Ashe mechanically inquired about Mrs. Murphy's wants, his thin cheeks glowing and his eyes wandering about the room. He was apparently reacting the scene of the fight, and presently he made a step or two backward, so that he stood near the middle of the chamber. Here he took his stand, and seemed to become lost in reverie.

"Might as well set," remarked the girl, looking toward the unoccupied chair.

Maurice made a slight gesture inviting Philip to the seat; but Philip remained where he was. Wynne realized that his companion must be standing where he had supported Mrs. Fenton in his arms; and so touching was the expression of Ashe's face that he felt his throat contract. He turned away and looked out of the dim window over the chimney-pots and the irregular roofs.

"I 'm used to falls," the sick woman said. "I 've had plenty of 'em. I left a good home and them as was good to me, to be beat and starved, and murdered in the end. Women are all like that. If a man asks 'em, they 're always ready to cut their own throats. Sorry was the day for me I ever left old Miss Hannah."

Maurice turned toward the bed, his attention suddenly arrested. The name was that by which his aunt had usually been called, and he seemed to perceive in the talk of the woman something familiar. The possibility that this battered old creature might be his nurse came to him with a shock, so broken, so altered, so degraded was she; and as he looked at her he rejected the idea as preposterous.

"But your husband will be punished for his brutality," Ashe remarked absently.

He spoke like a man in a dream, as if his whole intent were fixed upon something so widely apart from the present that he hardly knew what was passing about him.

"Who wants him punished?" cried out the sick woman with sudden shrill vehemence. "That's what you rich folks are always after. Who asked the lady to come here with her purse in her hand to tempt him when he wasn't himself to know what he was doing? First you get him into a scrape, and then you punish him for it! What for do I want Tim shut up and me left to starve in me bed? If Tim's a little pleasant when he's had a drop more'n would be handy for a priest, whose business is it but mine? It's little comfort he gets, poor man; and he only takes what he can get to keep up his spirits in these poor times, and me sick and can't do for him."

"That's what I say too, Mrs. Murphy," the slatternly girl aroused herself to interpose. "Them as never had no hard times in their lives is always ready to jump on a poor man when he's down."

Maurice began to feel as if he were entangled in a strange and uncanny dream. Philip seemed more and more to retire within himself, and Wynne felt that he must do something to attract attention from his friend's conduct.

"We haven't anything to do with punishment, Mrs. Murphy," he said soothingly, coming forward as he spoke. "We came only to see if there is anything we can do to make you more comfortable."

The old woman answered nothing, but she stared at him with wild eyes.

"We may be able to make you more easy," he went on cheerfully, "if we can't fix things for you just as they were at Aunt Hannah's."

He used the name half unconsciously as the result of the suggestion of old association and half with an impulse to prove the faint possibility that this might be Norah Dolen. As he spoke Mrs. Murphy raised herself on one elbow, stretching out a lean hand convulsively toward him.

"Master Maurice!" she cried. "Holy Mother of Heaven, is it yourself?"

He went to her quickly, and took the outstretched hand.

"Yes, Norah. It is I."

She gazed at him a moment with haggard eyes, and then a look of deep tenderness came into the worn old face.

"Blessed be the saints!" she murmured. "It's me own boy!"

She drew her hand out of his grasp to stroke his arm and the folds of his cassock. He sat down by her on the bed, and she fell back upon the dingy pillow, breaking into hysterical tears. She caught one of his hands and carried it to her lips, kissing it in a sort of rapture.

"My own baby," she chuckled. "My Master Maurice so big and fine! I always said you'd be taller than Master John."

The allusion to his half-brother, dead nearly a dozen years, seemed to carry him back into a past so remote that he could hardly remember it. He smiled at Norah's enthusiasm, more moved by it than he cared to show.

"I've had time to grow big since you deserted us, Norah."

A look of terror came into her face.

"It wasn't my fault," she gasped, sobbing between

her words. "Don't believe it against me, me darling.
I never went to hurt old Miss Hannah in me life, and
the saints knows how she died."

"I never laid any blame on you," he answered.
"I knew you would n't hurt a fly."

She broke into painful, hysterical laughter.

"No more I would n't. To think it's me own
baby boy that I 've carried in me arms, and him a
priest!"

The attendant, who had been watching in stupid
and undisguised curiosity, gave an audible sniff.

"Oh, he ain't a real priest," she interrupted with
brutal candor. "They 're just fakes. They ain't
even Catholics."

A pang of irritation shot through Maurice at the
girl's words, but his sense of humor asserted itself,
and helped him to smile at his own weakness.

"But, Norah," he said, ignoring the taunt, "I want
to know about yourself. We 've often tried to find
you," he added, a sudden perception of the possible
importance of this recognition coming into his mind.
"You know we depended on you to tell us a lot of
things at the time of Aunt Hannah's death."

"He told me you 'd be after me," Norah exclaimed
with rising excitement. "He said you 'd be laying it
to me; but, Master Maurice, by the Mother of Mercy,
I never " —

"I know that," he interrupted, to check her excitement; "but why did you go off in that way?"

"She told me to go. She ordered me out of the
house like a dog, just because I would n't give up
Tim when she 'd accidentally seen him when he 'd
had one drop more than the full of him, — and any
poor body might take a wee drop more 'n he meant to

take beforehand. She was that hot in her way when her temper was up, rest her soul, — and that nobody knows better than yourself, — that the devil himself could n't hold her with a pair of red-hot tongs, — saving the presence of your riverinces for mentioning the Old Gentleman."

Her momentary discomposure at having mentioned the arch fiend in the presence of those who were his professional enemies gave Wynne a chance to interpolate a question. He could easily understand that the violent excitement of a quarrel with her old servant might account for the sudden death of his aunt. He perceived in a flash how Norah, terrified by the newspaper reports which had openly accused her of making way with her mistress, would without difficulty be induced by her husband to conceal herself. The matter to him most important, however, had not yet been touched upon.

"But what became of her will?" he asked. "You told me she made a new one."

"She did that, Master Maurice. Was n't I night and day telling her she 'd treated you scandalous, and upside down of all reason; and did n't she send for old Burnham, with the squinchy eyes and the wife that had a wart on her nose, and have it all writ over."

"So he said. But what became of it?"

"Ain't you ever had it?"

"No; we could never find it."

"Why did n't you look under the bottom of her little desk?" Mrs. Murphy demanded in much excitement.

"Under the bottom of her desk?" he repeated.

"The double bottom. The little traveling-desk

with the little pictures on the corners. She was that contrary that she was n't willing you should find it all fair and open. She wanted to tease you a while before you found out she 'd changed her mind and give in."

"Maurice," Ashe broke in, "we have overstayed our time."

Wynne rose at once, the habit of obedience being strong. Mrs. Murphy clung to his hand, mumbling over it with tears of delight, and could hardly be persuaded to let them go. It was only when he had promised to return on the next day, and the slatternly girl had peremptorily ordered her patient to lie down and stop acting like a buzz-headed fool, that he escaped. He hurried down the dark stairway and out of the house with a step to which excitement lent speed, while Philip followed in silence.

As they were leaving the court they encountered a middle-aged priest, evidently an Irishman, with a kindly face and a bright eye.

"Can you tell me," he asked in a rich brogue, greeting them in friendly fashion, "where Mrs. Tim Murphy lives?"

"In the house we came out of," Maurice answered. "She 's on the fifth floor, at the front."

The priest regarded him with some surprise in his look, and something, too, of uncertainty.

"You have n't been there, have you?" he asked.

"Yes; we 've just come from her place."

"Then perhaps she won't want me," the priest remarked. "It 'll save me a good bit of a climb."

"But we went only as friends," Maurice explained. "She might wish the consolations of religion."

"Then you did not" —

"We are not of your church," Maurice interrupted, flushing.

The priest looked at them with a puzzled air.

"But surely," he said, "you are Catholic. Haven't you been to me at the confession?"

Maurice had not at first recognized the priest to whom he had been in the habit of confessing at St. Eulalia, but he had known him before this announcement made Philip stare at him with a face of astonishment.

"Yes," he responded steadily. "I have confessed to you at St. Eulalia, but I am not of your communion."

He turned, and walked away quickly, not looking at Phil. He resolved not to bother his head about this unchancy encounter. It was awkward, and the fact that he had never confided in Ashe seemed to give to these visits to St. Eulalia an air almost of underhandedness; but there was nothing wrong, he told himself, and he would not be vexed at this moment when he was full of delight at the probability of discovering the missing will. He was certainly in no danger of becoming a Catholic. He smiled to think how little likely he was to exchange the too strict rule of the Clergy House for one which might be more rigid still. The keen thought now was the remembrance of the wealth which he hoped soon to possess.

"Phil, old man," he said joyously, "I believe I shall get Aunt Hannah's money after all. I always felt that it belonged to me."

"Yes," Ashe replied, so dully that Maurice turned to him quickly.

"Come, Phil, don't answer me like that. What are you moping about?"

There was no answer for a moment. Maurice, full of a fresh vigor born of the discovery of the afternoon, was yet rebuked by the silence of his friend.

"Of course, Phil," he went on, "you know I don't mean anything unkind. I am no end obliged to you for taking me there this afternoon. When we go to-morrow" —

"I shall never go there again," Ashe interrupted.

"Nonsense! Why not?"

"I went to-day to say good-by to my sinful folly. I shall not go again."

A prickling irritation began to make itself felt in the mind of Maurice. Even so slight a contact with the material realities of life as this interest in the will had put him completely out of tune with the monkish mood.

"Oh, stuff, Phil!" he exclaimed. "For heaven's sake don't be so morbid. You talk like a mediæval anchorite."

Ashe regarded him with a look of pain.

"It does n't seem possible that this is you, Maurice."

"It is I," was the sturdy answer; "and it is I in a sane frame of mind, old fellow. Come, it 's no sin to be human; and as far as I can see that 's the only fault you 've committed."

"Maurice," Ashe retorted in a voice of intense feeling, "have you thrown away everything that we believe? Are n't you with us any more?"

The pronoun which seemed to separate him from the company to which his friend belonged struck harshly on Maurice's ear. He felt himself being forced to define for Philip thoughts which he had thus far declined to define for himself.

"Phil," he said determinedly, "I insist that your

way of looking at this whole matter is morbid; and I
won't get into a discussion with you. I 'm in too good
spirits to let you upset them. To think I shall get
my property after all."

"But our lives are devoted to poverty."

Maurice turned upon his friend, more exasperated
than he had ever been with him before in the whole
course of their lives.

"Look here, Phil," he declared, "if you want to be
as mopish as a mildewed owl yourself, that is no
reason why you should try to make me so too."

There was no response to this, and in silence they
went toward the Clergy House. Just as they reached
the door, Maurice turned quickly and held out his
hand to his friend. Ashe grasped it so hard that it
ached; and Maurice went to his room with a sigh on
his lips, while in his heart he said to himself, "Poor
Philip!"

Maurice went next day to see Mrs. Murphy, and
for a number of days thereafter. Norah was sinking, and clung to him with pathetic tenderness. He
learned not much more about the will. She was sure
that it had been concealed under the false bottom of
a little traveling-desk which he remembered, but beyond that she knew nothing. Maurice wrote to Mr.
Burnham, the family lawyer, and the question now
was, what had become of the desk? The effects of
the testator had been sold at auction, but as they had
been largely bought by relatives, Maurice believed
that it would not be difficult to trace the missing document.

The interest and excitement of this new business
so occupied the thoughts of Maurice that he almost

ceased to think of religious matters. Perhaps there was more danger to his monastic profession in this indifference than in the most poignant doubt. He went through his duties at the Clergy House cheerfully because he thought little about them. They were part of the routine of life, and when the hour for recreation came he laid all that aside. He even on one occasion wrote a hurried note to Mr. Burnham in the hour for meditation, and it amazed him when he thought of it that his conscience did not protest. He reflected with a certain naïve pleasure that it was possible after all to modify the strict rules of the house without suffering undue contrition afterward. The discovery might have seemed to Father Frontford a dangerous one.

XXIII

THIS DEED UNSHAPES ME
Measure for Measure, iv. 4

So much was Maurice absorbed in his thought of the will and his inquiries after it that he gave little consideration to the disquieting plan of Father Frontford for the securing of Miss Morison's coöperation in the election schemes. Several days having gone by without farther allusion to the matter, he decided that his remonstrances had been effective, and was greatly relieved to be freed from a task so repugnant under any circumstances and made intolerable by his feeling for Berenice. It was with a most painful shock, therefore, that he one day received from the Father the information that Miss Morison had returned to Boston. He met the Father Superior in the hall one morning after matins, and although it was a silent hour the latter spoke.

"It is better to see her at once," he added. "Mrs. Frostwinch is very low, and the sooner the thing is settled the better."

"But," stammered Maurice, "I " —

"I think," the other went on, ignoring the interruption, "that it will be best for you to call on her this afternoon at exercise hour. She is likely to be at home then, and it will be rather early for other visitors."

Maurice struggled with himself, endeavoring to shake off the influence which this man always ex-

ercised over him. He determined to speak, and to
decline the hateful errand.

"Father Frontford," he said with an effort, "I
cannot undertake this."

"My son," the other responded with gentle severity,
"you forget that this is a silent hour. Although I
may speak to you on affairs concerning the church,
that does not give you the right to answer irrelevantly."

"It is not irrelevantly," Maurice protested, feeling his growing irritation strengthen his resolve.
"I "—

The voice of the old priest was more stern as he
interrupted.

"You seem to forget entirely your vow of obedience. There is little merit," he added, his tone softening persuasively, "in service which is easy and
pleasant. It is in the sacrifice of self and our own
inclinations that we gain the conquest of self. Go,
my son, and pray to be forgiven for pride and insub-
ordination. Do you think that you would be object-
ing if it were not for the wound to your vanity which
this work inflicts? You may repeat ten *paters* for
having violated the rule of silence."

Maurice moved away, feeling that he dared not
trust himself to speak again. To be thus treated
like a willful child galled his pride and quickened all
the obstinacy of his nature.

"The rule of silence!" he said to himself angrily
as he went. "Are we in the Middle Ages?"

It came to him as a sort of jeer from an outside
intelligence that after all they were trying to ape
mediæval discipline. He had been for weeks coming
to the point where the whole monastic life seemed to

him fantastic and theatrical; and now that his personal liberty was so sharply assailed, his self-respect so threatened, he was prepared to see everything in the most unfavorable light. He laughed bitterly in his mind at the tangle he was in, and contempt for himself and for the community took hold of his very soul.

Yet he was not ready to throw off allegiance. The bonds of habit are strong; the power of old belief is stronger; and strongest of all is that vanity which holds a man back from the avowal that he has been mistaken in his most ardent professions. It is one thing to change a conviction; it is quite another to acknowledge that a belief formerly upheld with ardor is now outgrown. It is not simply the ignoble shame of fearing the opinion of others that is involved in such a case, but that of losing confidence in one's own judgment, of standing convicted of error in that inner court of consciousness where all disguises are stripped away and all excuses vain. To see that even the most passionate conviction may have been mistaken is to feel profound and disquieting doubt of all that human faith may compass; it is to seem to be helpless in the midst of baffling and sphinx-like perplexities. Maurice was already at the point where he could hardly be regarded as holding his old opinions, but he had not reached that of being ready to confess that he had been wrong in a matter so vital that error in it would involve the whole reordering of his life and leave him with no standards of faith.

He was, moreover, noble in his impulses, and he had too long been bred in introspection not to perceive now that he was greatly influenced by his inclinations. He was too honest not to be aware that there was as much passion as reason in his revulsion from the monastic life, and that Berenice Morison's perfections weighed as heavily in the scale as any shortcomings of theology. He reproached himself stoutly, in thoroughly monkish fashion, and ended by resolving that obedience was a duty; that the errand on which he was sent was one which would abase his sinful pride and must be executed for the benefiting of his spiritual condition.

He said this to himself sincerely, yet he was human, and behind all was the consciousness that in this bad business there was at least the consolation that he should be face to face with Berenice. If humiliation was doubly bitter by being wrought through his love, at least his love might find some scanty comfort in the very means of his humiliation.

When the hour for exercise, four in the afternoon, came, Maurice set out on his mission. He had blushed at himself in the mirror for the solicitude with which he regarded his image, but he had tried to believe that this arose only from a disinterested anxiety to appear at his best in behalf of the object which he was sent to accomplish.

Miss Morison was living with Mrs. Frostwinch, and as Maurice walked buoyantly along, forgetting his errand and only remembering that he was to see her, he recalled how on the day when they had first met he had walked home with her from Mrs. Gore's. He recalled the pretty, willful turn of her head and the saucy side-glance of her eyes, the proud curve of her neck, the color on her cheeks delicate as the first peach-blossom in spring. That he had no right thus to be thinking of a woman perhaps added a certain piquancy to his thought; but he quieted his conscience with the reflection that he was in the path of duty, and of a duty, moreover, which was likely to prove sufficiently hard and humiliating.

Miss Morison was at home, and would see Mr. Wynne.

The high reception room in which he waited for her had a gloomy formality, a sort of petrified respectability, most discouraging. On the wall was a large painting, evidently a copy from some famous original, although Maurice did not know what. The picture represented a painter with a model in the dress of a nun. The artist was evidently engaged in painting a saint for some convent, a beautiful sister had been chosen as his model, and he was improving the opportunity to make love to her. Her reluctant and remorseful yielding was evident in every line of her figure as she allowed the painter to steal his arm around her waist and bend his lips toward hers. Wynne looked at the picture with vague disquiet. Here was the struggle of the natural human impulse against the constraint of ascetic vows; the irresistible yielding to nature and to the call of a passion interwoven with the very fibres of humanity. The sombre Boston parlor vanished, and he seemed to be in some old-world nunnery with the unknown lovers. He felt all their guilty bliss and their scalding remorse. He sighed so deeply that the soft laugh behind him seemed almost an echo. Turning quickly, he found Berenice watching him with a teasing smile on her lips.

" I beg your pardon for startling you," she said, holding out her hand, " but you were so absorbed in Filippo and his Lucretia that you paid no attention to me."

"I beg your pardon," he responded, taking her hand cordially. "I was looking at the picture and wondering what it represented."

"It is that reprobate Filippo Lippi and Lucretia Buti, the nun that he ran away with. Why it pleased the fancy of my grandfather, I'm sure I can't imagine. Sit down, please. It is a long time since I have seen you, and now that Lent is coming, I suppose that you will be lost to the world altogether."

He sat down facing her, but he did not answer. His voice had deserted him, and his ideas had vexatiously scattered like frightened wild geese. He looked at her, beautiful, witching, full of smiles; then without knowing exactly why he did so, he turned and looked again at the Lucretia. Berenice laughed frankly.

"Are you comparing us?" she asked gayly. "Or are you trying to decide what I would have done in her case? I can tell you that."

"What would you have done?"

"Done? I would have run away from him and the convent both! Do you think I was made to be cooped up in a nunnery if I could escape?"

"No," he answered with fervor, "you were certainly not made for that."

"That is an unclerical answer from a monk."

"I am not a monk."

She put her head a little on one side with delicious coquetry.

"Would it be rude to ask what you are, then?"

He regarded her a moment, and then with explosive vehemence he broke out:—

"I am a deacon who has not taken the vows, and I am a man who loves you with his whole soul!"

She paled, and then flushed to her temples. She cast her eyes down, and seemed to be struggling for self-control. He did not offer to touch her, although his throat contracted with the intensity of his effort to maintain his outward calm. Then she looked up with a smile light and cold.

"We are not called upon to play Filippo and Lucretia in reversed parts," she said. "I am not trying to tempt you away from your calling. Would n't it be better to talk about the weather?"

He was unable to answer her, but sat staring with hot eyes into her face, feeling its beauty like a pain.

"It has been very cold for the season during the past week," she went on.

"Miss Morison," he retorted hotly, "I had no right to say that, but you need n't insult me. It is cruel enough as it is."

Her face softened a little, but she ignored his words.

"Tell me," she remarked, as if more personal subjects had not come into the conversation, "what are the chances of the election? I hear so many things said that I have ceased to have any clear ideas on the subject at all."

Maurice sat upright, throwing back his shoulders. This girl should not get the better of him. He lifted his head, his nostrils distending.

"It is too soon to speak with certainty," he responded; "but it is in regard to that that I came — that I was sent to see you this afternoon. We are under vows of obedience at the Clergy House."

He said this defiantly, fancying he saw in her face a smile at the idea of his servitude.

"You will regard what I say as the words of a messenger."

" All? " she interrupted.

He flushed with confusion, but he was determined that he would not again lose control of himself.

" All that I *shall* say," he responded. " What I have said is to be forgotten."

" By me or by you? " she asked, dimpling into a smile so provoking that he had to look away from her or he should have given in.

" By you," was his reply; but he could not help adding under his breath : " If you wish to forget it."

She laughed outright.

" I will consider the matter. But this errand from the powers that be at the Clergy House; I am curious about that."

" You will remember," he urged, his face falling, " that it is only a message for which I have no responsibility."

" Certainly; although you would of course bring no message of which you did n't approve."

" I am not asked whether I approve or disapprove. It is the decision of the Father Superior that it should be said; and that is the whole of it."

" Well," she inquired, as he paused, unable to go on, " after this tremendous preamble, what is it? "

It seemed to Maurice that he could not say it; but he cleared his throat, and forced himself to look her in the face.

" It has to do with your inheritance of the — your inheritance through Mrs. Frostwinch."

" My inheritance? What do you mean? " she demanded, suddenly becoming grave.

As briefly as possible he explained to her the errand which had been given to him. He could see indignation gathering in her look.

" But who has told Father Frontford that Mrs. Frostwinch is so ill?" she broke out at last. " Cousin Anna is not so well since she came from the South, but that is all. It is shameful to be speculating on her death and disposing of her property as if she were buried already! I wonder at you!"

Wynne smiled bitterly.

" I have already said that I had nothing whatever to do with the matter," he answered.

" You had no right to come to me with such a message. It puts me in the position of waiting for her death! Oh, it's an insult! It's an insult to me and to Cousin Anna! What will she think?"

" She will think nothing," he said, roused by a sense of her injustice, " because she will never know."

" Why will she not?"

" Because if it is cruel for me to say a thing which harms nobody except me for bringing the message, it would be a thousand times more cruel for you to tell your cousin that her death was counted on."

He rose as he spoke, and stood looking down on her with the full purpose of constraining her to his will. She sprang up in her turn.

" Very well; I will not tell her. You may say to Father Frontford from me that it will be time enough for him to undertake the disposal of my property when it is mine. I thank him for his officiousness!"

" You are unjust to Father Frontford. I have made his wish seem offensive by the way I have put it, I suppose. At any rate, he is simply seeking the good of the church."

" And to have himself made bishop."

" He would vote to-morrow for any man that he thought would do better than he can do. He would support Mr. Strathmore himself if he believed it well for the church. I do not find myself in sympathy with everything that he does, but I know him, and of one thing I am sure: he would be burned alive in slow fires to advance the good of the church."

She looked at him curiously. Then she turned away in seeming carelessness, and began to arrange some pink roses which stood in a big vase on a table near at hand.

"Good-by," he said. "I am sorry to have offended you."

"Must you go?" responded she with a society manner which cut him to the quick. "Let me give you a rose."

She broke one off, and handed it to him. He took it awkwardly, wholly at a loss to understand her.

"They are lovely, are n't they?" she said. "Mr. Stanford sent them to me this morning."

He looked at her until her eyes fell. Then he laid the rose on the table near the hand which had given it to him, and without further speech went out.

XXIV

ALTHOUGH Ashe had said that he should not go
again to the poverty-stricken dwelling of Mrs. Murphy, he found himself a few days later beside her bed.
Word had been brought to him that she was dying,
and that she begged to see him before her death.
There was no resisting a call like this, and on a gloomy
afternoon he had gone down to the dingy court, torn
by memories and worn with inward struggles.

He found the old woman almost speechless with
weakness. The room was more comfortable, and he
knew that Maurice had been at work. The slatternly
girl was in attendance, and there was also the pleasant-
faced priest whom Philip and Maurice had encountered
in the court. The priest had come with an acolyte
to administer the last rites, and the woman had made
her confession. So intent, however, was Mrs. Murphy upon the purpose for which she had summoned
Ashe that she cried out to him as he entered, and
apparently for the moment forgot all else.

Ashe looked at the priest in apology, but the latter
said kindly : —

"Let her speak to you, and then she will be done
with things of this earth."

It was the safety of her husband for which the poor
creature was concerned. It was on her mind that
Ashe and Mrs. Fenton could save him from punish-

ment if they chose. She pleaded piteously with Philip to have the prisoner set free.

" He 'll be all alone of me," she moaned. " That 'll be more punishment than you 're thinking, your riverince. He 'll come out of jail sober, and he 'll remember how he had me to do for him night and day these long years. He 'll not be liking that, your riverince; and he 'll be uneasy to think maybe he had some small thing to do with it himself. Not that I say he did," she added hastily. " His little fun would n't be the cause of harm to me as is used to his ways, but maybe he 'll be after thinking so. It 's the fever I have, from poor living, and maybe from being so long without Tim and worrying the heart out of my body for him, and he there in jail. Only if you 'll promise to let him go, you and the sweet lady that very likely did n't know his pleasant ways when he had a drop too much, you 'd make it easier dying without him."

She gasped out her words as if every syllable were an effort, her eyes appealing with a wildness which touched his heart. The girl went to the bed and leaned over, taking in hers the thin, withered hand.

" There, there, Mrs. Murphy," she said, " of course the gentleman 'll do it. He could n't have the heart to resist your dying prayer."

" I am ready to do all I can, Mrs. Murphy," Philip stammered, struggling with his conscience to promise as much as he could ; " and I 'll see Mrs. Fenton. I 'm sure she won't wish to have anything done that you would not like."

The sick woman burst into weak tears, stammering half inarticulate blessings.

" I don't know," Philip began, feeling that it was not honest to give her the impression that he could set her husband free, " how much " —

The priest crossed to him and laid a hand quickly on his shoulder.

"Whist!" he said in Philip's ear. "There's no need of troubling her with that. You'll do what you can, and the rest's with heaven that is good to the poor."

Mrs. Murphy had not heard or heeded what Ashe said, and still mumbled her thanks while the Father prepared to administer the viaticum. The acolyte and the girl looked at Ashe as if expecting him to withdraw.

"May I remain?" Philip asked, looking at the priest with deep feeling.

The other regarded him benignly.

"Remain, my brother; and may the Holy Virgin bless the sacrament to your soul as well as to hers."

Ashe could not have told why he had yielded to the impulse to stay. He had for months been coming more and more to feel that the church of Rome was his true refuge, yet he hardly now dared confess this to himself. He had been deeply affected by the discovery that Maurice had been to confession at St. Eulalia, and he longed himself to follow the example of his friend. To Ashe, however, it seemed like trifling with sacred things, and he could not do it. Now as he knelt on the unclean and uneven floor of that sordid chamber he experienced a peace and a security such as he had never before known. He was moved almost to tears; yet he would not yield.

"It is not Rome," he insisted to himself. "It is the simple faith of these poor souls. That is beautiful and holy. It would be easy for me to think that I was becoming a Catholic."

He left as soon as the rite was concluded, but the memory of it remained.

He saw Mrs. Fenton on the afternoon following. He had not been alone with her since his mad declaration of love. He wished now to meet her calmly, yet the moment he entered her house his heart quickened its beating. He was no longer a priest bent on an errand of mercy; he was an ardent lover, acutely conscious that he was in the rooms through which she passed day by day, that in a moment he should see her, hear her voice, perhaps touch her hand. He was shown into the library where she was sitting, and she rose to greet him frankly and simply.

" She was not touched by what happened in the carriage," Philip said to himself, with the woeful wisdom of love, " or she could not so completely ignore it."

" How do you do, Mr. Ashe ? " she said with perfect calmness. " You are just in time for a cup of tea. I am having mine early, because I came in a little chilled."

He was too confused with the joy of her presence to decline.

" I have come on an errand which is not over pleasant," he remarked, watching her handling the cups, " and I am afraid that it is useless too."

" Does that mean that it is something you wish me to do but think I 'm too hard-hearted or selfish to agree to ? "

" It is not a question of willingness so much as of power. Mrs. Murphy is dying, — very likely by this time she is not living, — and she begs us to save her husband from being punished."

" But how could that be done ? "

" I doubt if it could be done ; but I promised her that I would speak to you. I suppose that if we did not give evidence there would not be much that could be told; but I hardly think that we have the right not to."

Mrs. Fenton thoughtfully regarded the fire a moment; then seemed to be recalled to the present by the active boiling of the little silver teakettle.

"I'm afraid women would drive justice out of the world if they had their way," she said with a smile.

He smiled in reply, full of delight in her mere presence. They talked the matter over, arriving at some sort of a compromise between their sympathy for the dying woman and their feeling that a man like Murphy should be dealt with by the law. They came for the moment to seem to be on the old footing of simple friendliness, while she made the tea and they discussed the situation.

"One lump or two?" Mrs. Fenton asked, pausing with tongs suspended over the sugar.

"Two," answered he. "I am afraid I am self-indulgent in my tea, but then I very seldom take it."

"So small an indulgence," she said, handing him his cup, "does not seem to me to indicate any great moral laxity."

"It is the principle of the thing," Philip returned, smiling because she smiled.

Mrs. Fenton shook her head.

"Come," she said, "this is a good time for me to say something that has been in my mind for a long time. You may think that it isn't my affair, but I can't help saying that it seems to me you have allowed yourself to get into a frame of mind that is rather — well, that isn't entirely healthy. I hope you don't think me too presuming."

"You could not be," was his reply; "but I do not understand what you mean."

She had grown graver, and leaned back in her chair with downcast eyes.

" I hardly know how to say it," she began slowly, " but you seem to me to be feeling rather morbidly about the virtue of personal discomfort. If you will pardon me, I can't think that you really believe it to be any merit in the sight of heaven that a man should make himself needlessly uncomfortable."

" But if the mortification of the flesh helps us to " —

She put up her hand and interrupted him.

" I am a good churchwoman, but I am not able to believe in scoring off the sins of the soul by abusing the body. The old monks scourging themselves and the Hindus swinging by hooks in their backs seem to me both pathetically mistaken, and both to be moved by the same feelings."

" Then you do not believe in asceticism at all ? "

"Mr. Fenton used to say that asceticism was the most insolent insult to Heaven that human vanity ever invented."

" But if we are to follow the devices and desires of our own hearts," Ashe broke out, his inner excitement bursting forth through his calmness, " if we are to give way to the joys of this life, if — Do you not see, Mrs. Fenton, that this covers so much? It goes down into the depths of a man's heart. It comes almost at once, for instance, to the question of the marriage of priests."

She flushed, and her manner grew perceptibly colder.

" That is naturally not a subject that I care to go into," she said; " but I have no scruple against saying that I do not believe in a celibate priesthood. In our church and our time, it is out of place."

"But it is the supreme test whether a man is willing to give up all his earthly joy for the service of Heaven."

She frowned slightly, and he realized how significant his manner must have been.

"The marriage of the clergy is not a subject that it seems to me necessary for us to discuss," she said.

"Mrs. Fenton," Philip said, "I have given you too good a right to be offended with me once, but I must say something that I fear may offend you again. It is not about myself. It is about a better man."

She looked at him in evident surprise and disquiet.

"I asked what you think of the marriage of the clergy," he went on, "because it seems to me right to tell you that Mr. Candish loves you."

She flushed to her temples, starting impulsively in her seat.

"Mr. Ashe," she said vehemently, "what right have you to talk to me of such subjects at all?"

"None," he answered, "none at all, — unless — None that you would recognize; but I wish to atone for the wrong I did in speaking to you, and to say what he would never say. If it were possible that you cared for him, I should perhaps help you both."

"You forget, I think, that I have been married."

"I do not forget anything," Philip returned desperately. "It is only that he is a good man, a noble man, a man that would never have fallen under his weakness as I did, and if you cared for him, he is too fine to be allowed to suffer. He loved you long before I ever saw you."

"He has never given me any sign of it."

Her flushed cheeks and something in the way in which she said this seemed to him to indicate that she

did love Candish. He had been moved by the most
sincere desire to sacrifice his own will and happiness
to the well-being of the woman he loved, and if it
were that she loved his rival he had been ready to
forget everything but that. Now by a quick revulsion
it seemed to him that he could not endure the success
of this man whose cause he had been pleading.

"Ah!" he cried, bending toward her, "you love
him!"

She rose indignantly to her feet.

"Your impertinence is amazing!" she exclaimed.
"It is time that somebody told you the truth. It is
hard for me to say unkind things to one who has
saved my life, but you ought to know how you appear.
You have got yourself into a thoroughly unwholesome
state of mind and body; and unless you get out of it
you will ruin your whole career. Does it seem to you
that a man who has so little control over himself is a
fit leader for others? Can't you see that you have
brooded over this question of celibacy until you are
completely morbid? Find some wholesome, right-
minded woman, Mr. Ashe; love her and marry her,
and be done with all this wretched, unwholesome
mawkishness. As for me, when I married once, I
married for life. My son will never be given a second
father."

He had risen also, and his self-possession had returned to him.

"I have annoyed you," he said with a new dignity.
"You are perhaps right in saying that I am morbid,
but in what I said to-day I was trying to put self
entirely out of the question. There is only one thing
more that I want to say; and that is that it is not
fair to judge our order by me. I know only too well

how natural it is that you should think all the men at
the Clergy House weak and despicable like me; but
that is not so. They are sincere, self-forgetful fellows. You have seen my friend Wynne. He, for
instance, is as manly and fine and honest as any man
alive."

" I do not misjudge them or you, Mr. Ashe. I only
feel that in these past weeks you have not been yourself. We will forget it all, and I hope that you will
forgive me if I have hurt you."

" I have nothing to forgive. It is you who must do
that. Good-by."

He went away with the remembrance of her beautiful eyes looking in pity into his, and once more the
phrase of the Persian came into his mind like a refrain: " O thou, to the arch of whose eyebrow the
new moon is a slave! "

XXV

WHOM THE FATES HAVE MARKED
Comedy of Errors, i. 1

MAURICE soon heard from his lawyer that the missing desk had passed into the hands of his sister-in-law, Mrs. Singleton, and that that lady was staying at Montfield as the guest of Mrs. Ashe. He determined to go down himself, feeling unwilling to trust business so important to any other. In order to leave the Clergy House, it was necessary to have permission from the Father Superior, and on Monday of Shrove week Wynne requested what the deacons jestingly called among themselves a dispensation. He did not think it honest to conceal the reason for his wishing leave of absence, and briefly related the story of his finding his old nurse and of her revelation.

"Poor old Norah is dead," he concluded, "but I had her affidavit taken, and if the will can be found there should be no difficulty in establishing it. The other witnesses are alive."

They were sitting in the Father's study, a room severely plain in its furnishings, like all the apartments in the Clergy House. The table by which the Superior sat was covered with papers and letters, the signs of the large correspondence which Wynne knew Frontford to keep up with members of his order in England and this country. The furniture was stiff and uncompromising, the windows covered only by plain shades, while the bookshelves took an austere air from the dull leather of the bindings of their tall, formal volumes. Father Frontford leaned back in his uncushioned chair and pressed together his thin finger-tips in the gesture which was habitual with him, regarding the young man with keen eyes.

"This property, if I understand you rightly, is now in the possession of the church?"

"It was given by the will that was found to the church and to missions. Some of it went to the founding of a home for invalid priests. My aunt was the one of my relatives who was a churchwoman."

"And if you succeed in finding and establishing this new will, you mean to divert the money to your own use?"

"If the will is valid, is not the money mine?"

The Father looked at him a moment before he answered. Then he sighed.

"My son," he asked, "would you have put that question six months ago?"

Maurice flushed, but he did not wish to show that he understood.

"Why not?" he demanded.

"There was not then in your heart a wish to wrest property from the church that you might enjoy it yourself."

"I have n't any wish now to take from the church anything which is not mine already."

"By divine right or by human?" the Father inquired with cold inflexibility.

Maurice began to be irritated. He felt that he was being treated with too high a hand.

"Have I no rights as a man?" demanded he warmly.

The other sighed once more, and a look of genuine pain came into his face.

"My son," he said with a gentleness which touched Maurice in spite of himself, "when you gave yourself to the church, did you keep back part of the price? Was not your gift all you were and all you might possess?"

Maurice was silent. He could not for shame answer that he did not then know that he had so much to give, and he realized too that this would then have made no difference. He felt as if he were now being held to a pledge which he had never meant to make, yet he could not see what reply there was to the words of the Superior. He cast down his eyes, but he said in his heart that he would not yield his claim; that the demand was unjust.

"I have for some time," Father Frontford went on, "in fact ever since your return, seen with pain that your heart is no longer single to the good of the church. An earthly passion has eaten into your soul. Your confessions are evidently attempts to satisfy your own conscience by telling as little as possible of the doubts which you have been harboring in your heart. Now there is given you an opportunity to see for yourself, without the possibility of disguise, what your true feeling is. The question now is whether you are seeking your own will or the good of religion. Will you fail us and yourself?"

Maurice was touched by the tone in which this was said. While he had been growing to be less and less in sympathy with Father Frontford and with the ideals which the brotherhood represented, he had never for an instant ceased to believe in the sincerity of the Superior. He might think him narrow, mistaken, even at times so blinded by desire for the success of the brotherhood as to become almost Jesuitical

in method; but he felt that the Father lived faithful
to his belief, ready, if the cause required, to sacrifice
himself utterly. He could not but be moved by the
appeal which the priest made, and by the genuine feeling which rang through every word.

"Father," he said, raising his eyes to the face of
the other, "I cannot deny that I am less satisfied
about our faith than I used to be. I can see now
that I perhaps have not been entirely frank in confession, though I had n't recognized it before. I cannot
go into a discussion of my doubts now. I am not in
a mood to talk with you when we must look at so
many things from different points of view. I have n't
hidden from you anything that has happened, and you
could not be persuaded that all the change in me has
not come from the fact that I — has not come from
my feeling toward — my feeling about marriage.
This is not true. Everything has changed; and
while I may be wrong. I have been trying to act conscientiously. I feel that it is right for me to follow
up this matter of my aunt's will; and if I cannot
make you share my feeling, I can only say that I
don't wish to do anything that seems to me wrong."

The other smiled sadly.

"What does that mean in plainer words?" asked
he. "It means that you do not wish to do wrong
because whatever you desire will seem to you right."

"You are unjust!" Maurice retorted, flushing.

The face of the Father grew stern.

"Since when did the rule of the order allow you to
use such language to your superiors? If you are not
thinking of evading your vows, you do evade them
daily; and the throwing them off can be nothing but
an affair of time."

Maurice felt that he could not endure this longer without breaking out into words which he should afterward repent. He rose at once.

"Will you permit me to retire?" he said. "I shall be glad of your answer to my request for leave of absence, but I cannot go on with this conversation."

The other stretched out his hand with a gesture infinitely tender.

"My son!" he entreated. "Do not stray into the wilderness!"

Maurice looked at the outstretched hand. His eyes moistened, but he could not yield. He felt tenderness for Father Frontford, but he was more and more at war with the Father Superior. For an instant they remained thus, and then the thin hand dropped.

"You are then still resolute in asking leave?" the Father said, in his coldest voice.

"It seems to me my duty to see that if possible the last wishes of my aunt be carried out."

"Is that your only motive?"

Maurice flushed hotly, but he looked the other boldly in the face.

"I must allow you to impute to me any motive you please. The point is whether I am to have your permission."

"Under the circumstances I do not feel justified in granting it. We will speak of the matter again, when you have examined your heart more carefully."

Maurice bowed and left the room in silence, his spirit hot within him. That he should be denied had not entered his mind. He was now confused by the conflict in his thoughts. To disobey would be equiva-

lent to nothing less than a defiance of the authority
of the Father Superior. To assert his right to decide
this matter could only mean a resolve to break away
from the brotherhood altogether. He was hardly prepared for a step so extreme ; yet he could not but ask
himself whether he were willing to accept the conditions involved in remaining. He realized for the
first time what the vow of obedience meant. He had
received the slight sacrifices involved thus far in his
novitiate as right and proper ; simple things which
had marked his willingness to yield to the authority
which by his own choice was above him. Now he
said to himself that to continue this life was to become
a mere puppet ; to give up independence and manhood itself.

On the other hand, he had not been bred in theological subtilties without having come to see that the act
cannot be judged without the motive, and he had been
more nearly touched by the words of Father Frontford than he would have been willing to confess. He
knew that he had been hiding from his confessor the
extent to which a longing for the world had taken
possession of him ; that there was in this wish to
secure the will and through it the property an eagerness to be independent of control and to take his
place in the world as a man among men. The
thought that the money was now in the hands of the
church to which he had pledged himself tormented
him. There came into his mind the question what he
would do with the wealth if he obtained it. He had
vowed himself to poverty, at least in his intention.
If he had this fortune and became a priest, he would
be pledged to endow the church with all his worldly
goods.

He faced his inner self with sudden defiance, as if he had thrown off a disguise cunningly but weakly worn. He confessed with frankness that he had secretly desired this money that he might be in a position to gain Berenice. He pleaded with himself that he did not mean to abandon the priesthood ; that he had simply discovered that he had not a vocation for the existence he had contemplated. He tried to see some way in which he might gain the end he desired without giving up the faith he professed ; and in the end he succeeded only in getting his mind into a confusion so great that it seemed impossible to think of anything clearly.

He had an errand at Mrs. Wilson's on Shrove Tuesday, and she invited him to accompany her to midnight service at the Church of the Nativity. When he repeated the request to Father Frontford, he was given permission to go.

"It is an unusual, and even an extraordinary request," the Superior said ; "but Mrs. Wilson is so deeply interested in the welfare of the brotherhood that it is better to make a concession. What time are you to meet her ? "

"She is to send her carriage for me at half past eleven. She was so sure that you would not object that she told me not to send any word."

"It is not well to have her treat so great a departure from rules as a matter of course," the Father answered gravely. "I will send her a note which will show her this. You have permission not to retire at the usual hour."

The carnival season was celebrated at the Clergy House with a meal better than usual, and with some gayety on the part of the young deacons. The light-

hearted Southerner improved to the full the permission to talk at dinner, and chatted away with a
volubility which seemed to Maurice to indicate a
nature too buoyant or too shallow to be deeply stirred.
Father Frontford was absent, and there was nothing
to throw a shadow of restraint over the feast, the
other priests being almost as boyish as the deacons.

"Here's Wynne," the Southerner said laughing,
"is as glum as if he were Lent incarnate, come six
hours too soon. You must have a good deal on your
conscience to be so solemn."

Maurice smiled, trying to shake off his depression.

"It isn't always what is on one's conscience," he
retorted, "so much as how tender the conscience is."

"Good! He has you there, Ballentyne," one of
the deacons cried.

"Oh, not at all. If a conscience is tender, it must
be because it is harrowed up. Now Wynne has probably vexed his so that it is habitually sore."

Maurice was out of the mood of the company, but
he tried to answer with a light word. The jesting
seemed to him trifling; and his companions, compared
to the men he had seen during his stay with Mrs.
Staggchase, appeared like boys chattering at boarding-
school. He wondered where they had been for their
absence; then he remembered that they had all told
him, and that he had forgotten. He had had no real
interest in them after all, he reflected; and at the
thought he reproached himself with egotism and a
lack of brotherliness. He glanced at Ashe, and was
struck by the paleness of his friend. His look was
perhaps followed by Ballentyne, for the latter commented on the downcast aspect of Philip.

"Ashe," the young man said, "looks ten times more

doleful than Wynne. What have you fellows been doing? One would think that you had been eating the bitterest of all the apples of Sodom."

"They have been in the gay world," another re-joined.

"Then they might be set up as a warning against it," was the retort.

Laughter that one cannot share is more nauseous than sweets to the sick ; and this harmless trifling was intolerable to Maurice. He got away from it as soon as it was possible, and passed the heavy hours in his chamber, waiting for the coming of the carriage. He tried at first to read and then to pray ; but in the end he abandoned himself to bitter reverie.

He did not attempt to reason, he merely gave way to gloomy retrospect, without sequence or order. Seen in the light of his experiences during the past weeks, his life looked poor, and dull, and misdirected. It was little comfort to assert that he had at least been true to ideals high, no matter how mistaken.

"It is not what one does," he thought, "but the in-tention with which he does it. Only that does not excuse one for being stupid, and raw, and ignorant. When a man is a weakling and a fool, he always takes refuge in the excuse that he is at least fine in his intentions. Bah! No wonder she laughed at me! I have shut myself up with ideas as mouldy as a mediæval skeleton, and when I come to daylight all that I can say is that I meant well. I suppose an idiot means well from his point of view!"

He looked about for something which should divert him from thoughts so tormenting. His eye fell upon his Bible, and he took it up half mechanically. On the title page was written the name of his aunt, to

whom it had once belonged. The name brought back
the interview with Father Frontford, and the refusal
of his request for leave of absence.

"Nothing belongs to me," he said to himself. "I
am a thing, a sort of thing like a numbered prisoner.
How could she care for a chattel, a creature without
even identity! I will go down to Montfield. I am
not yet so completely out of the world that I can't
have a word in the disposition of my own property."

He threw himself on the bed and tried to sleep, but
sleep was impossible. He only thought the more hotly
and wildly. The hours stretched on and on inter-
minably before he heard the bell ring, and knew that
the carriage had come. Rising hastily, he adjusted
his cassock and his tumbled hair, and went down.

"Perhaps I may find peace at the mass," he sighed
with a great wistfulness.

The fresh, cool air of night was grateful, and as he
was driven along the quiet streets, a new hopefulness
came to him. He had supposed that he was to be
taken to Mrs. Wilson's, and when the carriage stopped
was surprised to find himself before a large building
which he did not recognize.

"But I was to meet Mrs. Wilson," he said doubtfully to the footman who opened the carriage door.

"Mrs. Wilson is here, sir," was the answer. "She
said to carry you here. James is inside to tell you
what to do."

A footman was indeed within, waiting for him.

"Mrs. Wilson says will you please come to her, sir,"
the man said, and led the way upstairs.

The sound of gay music, growing louder as he advanced, filled Wynne's ears. He began to feel disquieted, and once half halted.

"Are you sure there is no mistake?" he asked.

"Oh, no mistake at all, sir," his guide answered. "Mrs. Wilson has arranged everything. Leave your hat and cloak here, sir, if you please."

Maurice mechanically did as requested, but as he threw off his outer garment the opening of a door let in a burst of music which seemed so close at hand that he was startled. He was in what was evidently a coat-room, the attendant of which regarded him with open curiosity; and he realized suddenly that he must be near a ball-room.

"Where am I?" he demanded.

"It's the ball, sir, that they has to end the season before Lent. It's Lent to-morrow, sir, as I thought you'd know."

Maurice stared at him in amazement and anger.

"There is a mistake," he said. "Give me my cloak."

"Indeed, sir," the man said, holding back the garment he had taken, "Mrs. Wilson said, sir, that I was to say that she particular wanted you to come fetch her in the ball-room, sir; and I was to bring you without fail."

"You may send her word that I am here."

"Please, sir," the man returned, in a voice which struck Maurice as absurdly pleading, "she was very particular, and it's no hurt to go in, sir. She'll blame me, sir."

Maurice looked at him, and laughed at the solemnity of the man's homely face. A spirit of reckless-ness leaped up within him. He said to himself that at least Mrs. Wilson should not think that he dared not come.

"Very well," he said. "Show me the way."

"Thank you, sir," the servant said, as if he had received a great favor. "It's not easy to bear blame that don't belong to you."

He opened a door into an anteroom thronged with people laughing and chatting. The sound of the music was clear and loud, with the voices striking through its cadences. Across this he led Wynne, to the wide door of a ball-room flooded with light and full of moving figures.

XXVI

THE brilliant glare of lights, the strident sound of dance-music, the enlivening sense of a living, vivaciously stirring company of gayly dressed merry-makers, assailed Maurice as he followed his guide across the anteroom. At the door of the ball-room he was for a moment hindered by a group of men who were lounging and chatting there. All his senses were keenly alert, and he perhaps unconsciously listened to hear if there were any comment on his appearance in such a place. He had not realized what he was coming into, and now that it was too late for him to withdraw without sacrificing his pride, he saw how incongruous his presence really was. Almost instantly he caught a name.

"By Jove!" one of the men said. "Isn't the Wilson in great form to-night! That diamond on her toe must be worth a fortune."

"She saves the price in the materials of her gowns," another responded lightly. "I never saw her with quite so little on."

"No material is allowed to go to waist there," put in a third.

"She has two straps and a rosebud," yet another voice laughed; "and nothing else above the belt but diamonds."

"Her very smile is *décolleté*," some one commented.

"This is one of her nights. When I see Mrs. Wilson with that expression, I am prepared for anything."

Maurice felt his cheeks burn at this light talk. It seemed to him ribald, and he was outraged that the name of a woman should be bandied about so carelessly. He raised his head and set his square jaw defiantly; then began to push his way through the group, keenly conscious of the stare which greeted him.

"Hallo! What the devil's that?" he heard behind him.

"The skeleton at the feast," responded one voice.

"Oh, it's some devilish trick of Mrs. Wilson's, of course," put in another.

All this Maurice heard with an outraged sense that there was no attempt to prevent him from hearing. He might have been a servant or a piece of furniture for any restraint these men put upon their speech. He was troubled with the fear of what absurdity Mrs. Wilson might intend. Now that he was here, however, he would go on. The natural obstinacy of his temper asserted itself, and if there was little pious meekness in his spirit at that moment, there was plenty of grit.

The ball-room was garlanded with wreaths of laurel stuck thickly with red roses; women in white and in bright-hued gowns, with fair shoulders and arms, were floating about in the embraces of men; the music set everything to a rhythmic pulse, and gaily quickened the blood in the veins of the young deacon as he looked. The throbbing of the violins made him quiver with an excitement joyous and bewildering. He was dazzled by the bright, moving figures, the shining colors, the sparkling of gems, the lovely faces, the alluring creamy necks and arms; a sweet

intoxication began to creep over him, despite the defiance of his feelings toward the men he had passed
in the doorway. Half blinded by the glare, dazed
and fascinated by the sights, the sounds, the per-
fumes, he followed the footman down the hall.

He was obliged to skirt the room, even then hardly
evading the dancers. His progress was necessarily
slow. The footman so continually paused to apologize for having brushed against some lady in his
anxiety to avoid a whirling pair of dancers, that it
began to seem to Maurice that they should never
reach Mrs. Wilson. He cast his eyes to the floor,
resolved not to look at the worldly sights around him.
Country bred and trained in the asceticism of the
Clergy House, he could not see these women without
blushing; and more than ever he wondered that he
had been so blindly obedient as to allow himself to
be brought to such a place.

He heard a man clap his hands. He looked up to
see a flock of dancers hurrying to the upper end of
the room. Among them, with a shock so violent that
his heart seemed to stand still, he recognized Berenice
Morison. He saw her go to a table and pick up
something; then she and her companions turned and
came glancing and gleaming down the hall like a
flock of pigeons which fly and shine in the sun. Fair,
flushed softly, more beautiful than all the rest in his
eyes, Berenice came on, her hair curling about her
forehead, her eyes shining with laughter and pleasure.
She was dressed in white, and at one shoulder, crushed
against her bare, creamy neck, was a bunch of crimson
roses. Maurice trembled at the sight of her beauty;
he reddened at the consciousness of her dress; over
him came some inexplicable sense of fear.

Suddenly he perceived that she had caught sight of him. He could see the look of amazement rise in her face, give place to one of amusement, then change instantly into sparkling mischievousness. He moved on toward her, abashed, bewildered, feeling as if he were running a gauntlet. He could not withdraw his gaze from her, as she came quickly onward, dimpling, smiling, her face overflowing with saucy fun, her glance holding his.

" Good-evening, Mr. Wynne," she said lightly, coming up to him. " This is an unexpected pleasure."

" Good-evening," Maurice responded, hardly able to drag the words out of his parched throat.

" Of course you came for the german," Miss Morison went on, more mockingly than before. " I am so glad that I happen to have a favor for you."

She leaned forward, swaying toward him her white shoulders, dazzling him with the hint of the swell of her bosom, bewildering him with the perfume of her dark hair, the alluring feminine presence which brought the hot blood to his face. Before he guessed her intention, she had pinned to his cassock a grotesque little dangling mask which swung from a bright ribbon.

" There," she commented, drawing back as if critically to observe. " The effect is novel, but striking."

A burst of amusement, light and blinding as the spray from a whirlpool, went up from the women around. The music, the voices, the laughter, seemed to Maurice so many insults flung at him in idle contempt. He looked around him with a bitter anger which could almost have smitten these laughing women on their red mouths. Then he turned back to Berenice. He saw that she shrank before the wrath of his look ; he felt with a thrill that he had at least power to make her fear him. He bent toward her full of rage made the wilder by the impulse to catch her in his arms and cover her beautiful neck with kisses.

" Shameless ! " he hissed into her ear.

He saw her turn pale and then flush burning red ; but he hastened on after the footman without waiting for more. Presently he reached the head of the hall, where Mrs. Wilson stood laughing and talking with several men. Her dress was of alternate stripes of crimson silk and tissue of gold, and since it had excited comment from the loungers at the door, it is small wonder that to the unsophisticated deacon, almost convent bred, it appeared no less than horribly indecent. He cast down his eyes ; but his glance fell upon the foot which just then she thrust laughingly forward, evidently in answer to some remark from Stanford, who stood at her right hand. Upon the toe of her exquisite little shoe sparkled a great diamond like a fountain of flame.

" It gives light to my steps," she laughed.

" The service is worthy of it," Stanford returned with a half-mocking bow.

" Thank you," Mrs. Wilson retorted, sweeping him a satirical courtesy. " If you say such nice things to me, what must you say to Berenice ! "

It seemed to Maurice that the devil was exerting all his infernal ingenuity that night to have him tormented at every turn. He came forward hastily, eager to stop the talk.

" Ah," cried Mrs. Wilson, " have you come, ghostly father ? "

The men stared at him in careless surprise and

open amusement. Maurice could not trust himself to speak, but only bowed in silence.

"I am called, you see," Mrs. Wilson said gayly. "Now I must go to penance and confession."

"Surely you will need so little time for confession," one of the men said, "that there 's no necessity of going so early."

"You must have been more wicked this winter than I ever suspected, Elsie," put in the even voice of Mrs. Staggchase. "Or is it that you only mean to be?"

Maurice turned quickly, and found that his cousin was sitting behind the table near which he stood. In front of her were heaps of trinkets of all sorts of fantastic devices.

"Good evening, Cousin Maurice," she greeted him. "Are you dancing? What sort of a favor ought I to give you?"

"Mrs. Wilson's wickedness," Stanford answered Mrs. Staggchase, "is of the sort so original that I 'm sure the recording angel must always be too surprised to put it down."

"What a premium you put on originality!" responded Mrs. Staggchase. "That is all very well for her, but how is it for her victims?"

"Oh, the honor of being her victim is compensation enough for them."

Mrs. Wilson laughed, and shook her head, twinkling with diamonds which dazzled the eyes of the young deacon.

"You are all worldly," she retorted. "Brother Martin and I are too unsophisticated to understand you."

Maurice winced at the name. He felt that he must

be a picture of confusion. To stand here among these sumptuously dressed women, to endure the glances which he knew were watching him from all parts of the room, to be pricked with this monkish title by a woman who was making of him and of the whole incident a sport and a spectacle, stung him to the quick. He thought of Berenice, and he cast at Mrs. Staggchase a look of defiance, lifting his head proudly in assertion of his hurt dignity.

" I am at your service, Mrs. Wilson," he said with cold sternness.

" Well, we will go then. Unless, that is, you are dancing, Mr. Wynne. I see that you have a favor."

He glanced down at the grotesque little mask, dangling by its red ribbon. With unbroken gravity he detached and laid it upon the table in silence. He would have given much to hide it in his pocket, since it came from Berenice ; but even as he put it down a bevy of girls swept up for favors, and one of them bore it away.

" He has abandoned his opportunity," Mrs. Staggchase observed. " The favor goes to Mr. Stanford."

The girl who had taken up the mask was indeed pinning it to the coat of that gentleman, with whom she quickly danced away. Maurice felt his heart grow hot, but he looked at his cousin with face hard and determined.

" It was never mine," he said, " except by the chance of a misunderstanding."

A maid now came forward with a black domino, which Mrs. Wilson slipped into gracefully, drawing up her glittering draperies. The big diamond on the toe of her slipper glowed fantastically, peeping from beneath the penitential robe.

"Hallo," Dr. Wilson exclaimed, coming up at this moment, "what's in the wind now? Is this turning into a masquerade?"

"Your wife is about to retire from the world," Mrs. Hubbard answered, laughing.

"With a man," Mrs. Staggchase added, her eyes shining on her cousin.

Wynne stabbed her with a glance of indignation.

"No, with a priest," corrected Mrs. Wilson, adjusting her domino about her face.

"Elsie, how devilishly fond you are of making a fool of yourself," Dr. Wilson observed jovially. "Well, good-night."

Mrs. Wilson swept him a profound courtesy, with her hands crossed on her bosom.

"My lord and master, good-night. Ladies, remember that it will be Lent in ten minutes."

She took Wynne's arm, and together the black-robed figures went down the length of the room. The music had for the moment stopped, and it seemed to Maurice as if his presence had brought a chill to the whole gay scene. He was inwardly raging, angry to have been used by Mrs. Wilson as an actor in her outrageous comedy, furious with Berenice for her part in the play, full of rage against the men who stood around grinning and laughing at the whole performance. Most of all, he assured himself, he was righteously indignant at the trifling with sacred things. He looked neither to the left nor to the right, but with Mrs. Wilson sweeping along by his side he strode toward the door.

"He looks as if he belonged to the church militant," he heard one of the men say as he passed out.

"Even the church militant is nothing against a

woman," another replied, catching the eye of Mrs. Wilson, and laughing.

In the vestibule stood a footman bearing Maurice's cloak, and a maid with fur over-shoes and an ermine-lined wrap for Mrs. Wilson. Maurice said not a word except to reply in monosyllables to the questions of his companion, and almost in silence they drove to the Church of the Nativity.

XXVII

THE music of the Church of the Nativity was most elaborate, the very French millinery of sacred music. The selection of a new singer was debated with a zeal which spoke volumes for the interest in the service of the sanctuary, and the money expended in this part of the worship would have supported two or three poorer congregations. The church, moreover, was appointed with a richness beautiful to see. The vestments might have moved the envy of high Roman prelates, and the altar plate shone in gold and precious stones.

It was no wonder, then, that a midnight service at the Nativity attracted a crowd. Mrs. Wilson and Wynne had to force a path between ranks of curious sight-seers in order to make their way to the guarded pew of the former, which was well up the main aisle. It came to Maurice suddenly that in his angry mood he was pushing against these worshipers rudely, and that he was venting upon them a fury which had rather increased than diminished in his ride to the church. He was seething with anger; anger against Mrs. Wilson for having put him in a ludicrous position, at Berenice for her mockery, at Mrs. Staggchase for her satire, and at all the frivolous fools who had stood around, grinning to see him made ridiculous. His hurt vanity throbbed with an ache intolerable, and as he forced his way between the crowding spectators he felt a certain ugly joy in thrusting them aside.

He was recalled to self-control by the expression in the face of a girl whom he pressed back to give Mrs. Wilson passage. She turned to him with a look of surprise and pain, and to his excited fancy her hair in the half shadow was like that of Berenice.

" You hurt me! " she exclaimed.

" I beg your pardon, " he answered with instant compunction. " I did not mean to. Come with me."

He yielded to the sudden impulse, and then reflected as they passed down the aisle that he had no right to bring a stranger into Mrs. Wilson's pew. Having invited her, however, it was impossible to retract, and he showed her into the slip after Mrs. Wilson. As the latter turned to sit down, she became aware of the stranger. She paused, and looked at her with haughty surprise.

" I beg pardon," she said, " this is a private pew."

The girl flushed, looking inquiringly at Maurice. His masculine nature resented the insolence of the glance with which Mrs. Wilson had swept the stranger, and he came instantly to the rescue.

" I invited her, " he said, leaning forward, speaking with a determination at which his hostess raised her eyebrows.

" Oh, very well then, " Mrs. Wilson murmured.

She sank into her seat, and inclined her head on the rail before her. As Maurice did the same there shot through his mind a wonder at the change there must be in the mental attitude of the woman who spoke with haughtiness almost insulting to the stranger, and the penitent who bent to ask pity and forgiveness from heaven. He tried to fix his thoughts on his own

prayer, but the words ran on as mechanically as might
water flow over a stone. The serious danger of a rit-
ualistic religion must always be that the mere repeti-
tion of words shall come to answer for an act of worship; and to-night Maurice might have exclaimed with
King Claudius : —

"My words fly up; my thoughts remain below."

The service went on with its deep, appealing prayers
for pardon, for help, for uplifting, and Maurice followed it only half consciously. It was as if he were
drugged, so that only now and then a phrase pene-
trated to his real consciousness, — words which in
their instant and particular application were so poignant that he could not avoid their force.

"'From all inordinate and sinful affections,'" repeated the rich voice of Mr. Candish, thrilling the
church from floor to vaulted roof, "'and from the
deceits of the world, the flesh, and the devil.'"

"'Good Lord, deliver us!'" swelled the response
of the congregation; and on the lips of the deacon
the words were almost a groan.

He lost himself then in a flood of bitter repentance
and prayer, hardly realizing where he was or what
was passing around him. The music swelled and
eddied; there was a genuine "Kyrie," wherein a
single voice, a rich contralto, wailed and implored in
a passion of supplication until the whole congregation quivered with the fervor of the music. Maurice
felt himself swayed and lifted upon the rising tide of
emotion. He lost his anger, he swam in billows of
celestial delight; a blessed peace soothed his troubled
soul; he knew again some of the old-time ecstasy.
Yet in all this religious fervor there was some subtle

consciousness that it was unreal. He was not able
so completely to give himself up to it as to fail to
watch its growth, its progress, its intensity ; he was
vexed that he should trap himself, as it were, glory-
ing in the susceptibility to religious influences which
such excitement showed. He had even a whimsical,
momentary irritation that the part of his mind which
was acting the devotee could not do it so well that
his other consciousness could not detect the unreality
of it all. Then he struggled to forget everything in
the service ; to steep himself in the spiritual intoxication of the hour.

The girl whom he had introduced into the pew
dropped her prayer-book. He turned, startled by the
sound, and saw her sway toward him. He realized
that the crowd, the heat, the excitement, the odor of
incense with which the air was heavy, had overcome
her, and that she was fainting. He rose instantly,
and, lifting her, assisted her into the aisle. She was
half in his arms as he led her down the nave, and her
hair, the hair which had seemed to him like that of
Berenice, brushed now and again against his shoulder.
He recalled the wreck, when Berenice had been in
his arms, and his religious mood vanished as if it had
never been. His cheek flushed ; he thrilled with anger
at himself. He had been playing a part here in the
church. He had never for an instant wished to be
set free from his bondage to Berenice, — Berenice
who had to-night mocked him and his profession in
the eyes of all the world.

The way to the door seemed interminable. He was
eager to get rid of this stranger and escape. Fortunately the party to which the fainting girl belonged
were at hand to take charge of her ; and presently

Maurice had made his way out of the church. He hardly gave a thought to Mrs. Wilson. She was abundantly able to take care of herself, he reflected with angry amusement; or, if not, the very pavement would spring up with troops of men to assist her. She was the sort of woman whose mere presence creates cavaliers, even in the most unlikely places.

The cool outer air seemed to wake him from a bad dream. He walked hastily through the quiet streets toward the Clergy House, full of disordered thoughts, wondering whether the ball were yet over, or if Berenice were still dancing in the arms of other men. The blood flushed into his cheeks at the thought. He hated furiously the partner against whose shoulder her white, bare arm might be resting. He looked back with ever growing anger to the scene at the dance, tingling with shame at the humiliation, at the thought of standing before the women who had laughed when Berenice had fastened upon his breast the tawdry trinket which seemed chosen purposely to mock him. He wished that he had kept the toy, that he might now throw it down into the mire and tread on it. Yet grotesque and insulting as the thing had been, he was conscious that if the little mask were still in his possession he should not have been able to trample on it, but should have taken it to his lips instead. He remembered that now Stanford wore it. He looked up to the shining stars and felt the overwhelming presence of night like a child; his helplessness, his misery, his hopelessness swept over him in bitter waves.

Late as it was when he reached his room he did not at once undress. He sat down heavily, staring with hot eyes at the crucifix opposite. From black

and unknown depths of his heart welled up rage
against life and its perplexities. He threw upon his
faith the blame of his suffering. What was this
religion which made of all human joys, of all human
instincts only devilish devices for the torture of the
very soul? Why should the world be filled only with
temptations, with humiliations, with desires which
burned into the very heart yet which must be denied?
Was any future bliss worth the struggle? He realized with a shudder that he might be arraigning the
Maker of the world; then he assured himself that he
was but raging against those who misunderstood and
misinterpreted the purposes of life.

He flung himself down on his knees before the
crucifix in a quick reaction of mood, extending his
hands and trying to pray; but he found himself
repeating over and over: "For Thine is the kingdom and the power and the glory." He felt with the
whole strength of his soul the force of the words.
This deity to whom he knelt might in a breath change
all his agony; might out of overflowing power and
dominion and splendor spill but one unnoted drop,
yet flood all his tortured being with richest happiness.
The contrast between his weakness, his helplessness,
his insignificance, and the superabundant resources
of the Infinite crushed him. He was transported
with aching pity for himself and for all poor mortals.
He repeated, no longer in entreaty but with passionate
reproach: "For *Thine* is the kingdom and the power
and the glory." It seemed an insult to the clemency
of Heaven to call so piteously when it were a thing
lighter than the puffing away of a flake of swan's
down for One with all power to help and to comfort.
If he were in the hands of a God to whom belonged

the universe, why this agony of doubt? Then he cried out to himself that this was the temptation of the devil. He cast himself upon the ground, beating his breast and moaning wildly: "Mea culpa! Mea culpa!" With quick histrionic perception he was affected by the intensity and the effectiveness of his penitence, and redoubled his fervor.

Then in a flash came over him the sickening realization that this devotion was a sham; that it was hysteria, simple pretense. He ceased to writhe on the floor. It was like coming to consciousness in a humiliating situation. He blushed at his folly, and rose hastily from before the crucifix.

"I have been acting private theatricals," he muttered scornfully; "and for what audience?"

He threw himself again into his chair, burying his face in his hands. He plunged into a reverie so deep and so self-searching that it could have been fathomed by no plummet.

"I do not believe," he said at last aloud, raising his face as if to address the crucifix. "I have never believed. I have simply bejuggled myself. I have been a contemptible lie in the sight of men, not even knowing enough to be honest to myself."

He was silent a moment, a smile of bitter contempt curling his lip.

"I have not even been a man," he added.

Then he rose with a spring to his feet, and looked about him, stretching out his arms as if to embrace all the world.

"But now," he exclaimed with gladness bursting through every syllable, "at last I am free!"

XXVIII

WHEN Maurice Wynne's bitter word stung her, Berenice Morison stood for a second too overwhelmed to speak or move. She felt the blood mount to her temples, and she could see reflected in the eyes of acquaintances around a mingled curiosity and amusement. Wynne passed on, and she shrank into her seat, which fortunately was near.

"Who in the world is that, and what did he say to you when you gave him that favor?" exclaimed her neighbor. "I don't see how you dared to do it!"

A gentleman took the speaker away, so that Berenice was spared the necessity of answering. She watched Wynne advance to the group of which Mrs. Wilson was the centre, and she understood well enough that his being here was some contrivance of the latter's. She was angry with Wynne and humiliated by the insult that he had flung at her, yet she had room in her heart for rage against the woman who had brought him there. She looked at Mrs. Wilson laughing and jesting, she watched the comedy proceed as the black domino covered the white shoulders and the gown of gold and crimson, yet most of all was she conscious of how straight and strong Maurice stood among the gay group which surrounded him. The sternness of his mouth, the gravity and indignation of his look, seemed to her most manly and noble.

She felt that he had by his bearing mastered the absurd circumstances in which he was placed; she smiled bitterly to think how poor and flippant had been her own thoughtless jest. When Maurice threw the favor on the table, Berenice saw Clara Carstair take it up and give it to Parker Stanford. She watched Wynne and Mrs. Wilson leave the hall, two solemn, black-robed figures passing like shadows among the dancers. When they had disappeared she sat with eyes cast down, her thoughts in a whirl of regret, anger, and confusion.

"Well, did you ever know Mrs. Wilson to get up a circus equal to that before?" queried her partner, coming back to his place beside her. "She gets more amazing every day."

"She certainly gets to be worse form every day. It's outrageous that everybody lets Mrs. Wilson do anything she chooses, no matter how bad taste it is."

"Oh, she amuses folks," Mr. Van Sandt said. "Nobody takes her seriously."

"It is time that they did," answered Berenice rather sharply. "Such a performance as this to-night makes us all seem vulgar, — as if we were her accomplices."

"Oh, you take it too seriously; besides, I thought that you helped it on a bit."

Berenice was silenced, but she was none the happier for that. She was vexed with herself for having any feeling about the incident; but the word of Wynne came afresh into her mind, and brought the blood anew to her cheek. She said to herself that she hoped that she should meet him soon again, that she might wither him with a glance of burning contempt, ever after to ignore him.

" You think I would n't do it," she sneered to some inner doubt; " but I would ! "

She was interrupted by a partner, and went whirling down the bright hall to the tingling measures of a new waltz ; yet all the while she was thinking of the moment she had stood face to face with Maurice. She scoffed at herself for giving so much weight to a thing so trifling ; she made a strong effort to appear gay, only the more keenly to realize that at heart she was miserable.

Mrs. Staggchase, on her way out of the hall a little later, stopped and spoke to her.

" Come, Bee, it is time for you to go home. You don't seem to profit by the godly example of Elsie Wilson at all."

" Heaven forbid that I should take her as my exemplar ! " Berenice flung back with unnecessary fervor.

" Well," Mrs. Staggchase observed good-humoredly, " there are things in which it is conceivable that you might find a better model. By the way, what did Cousin Maurice say to you when you gave him that german favor ? Of course I have n't any right to ask, but you see I am interested in bringing the boy up properly."

Berenice flushed with confusion and vexation.

" It was something no gentleman would have said ! "

" Ah," the other returned with perfect calmness, " that is the danger of doing an unladylike thing. It is so apt to provoke an ungentlemanly return. Men, you know, my dear, have n't the fine instincts that we have. However, I 'm sorry that Maurice did n't behave better than you did. Good-night, dear."

Mrs. Staggchase had hardly gone when Parker Stanford came up with a favor.

"I am tired, Mr. Stanford," Berenice said. "Thank you, but you had better ask some one else."

"I 'd rather sit it out with you," he answered.

"Nonsense; one does n't sit out turns in the german."

"They do if they wish."

"Well, instead of sitting it out," she said, rising, "let us go and get a cup of bouillon. I feel the need of something to hold me up."

"Here is your favor," remarked Stanford, as they passed down the hall.

It was an absurd Japanese monster, with eyes goggling out of its head.

"How horrible!" cried Berenice. "It looks exactly like old Christopher Plant when he is talking about his last invention in sauces. Don't you know the way in which he sticks out his eyes, and says: 'It is the greatest misfortune in nature that the nerves of taste do not extend all the way down to the stomach!'"

Stanford laughed gleefully.

"Jove, I don't know but he's right. Think of tasting a cocktail all the way down to the stomach!"

"Or a quinine pill!" returned she with a grimace. "Thank you, no. Things are bad enough as they are."

At the door of the supper-room they encountered Dr. Wilson, with a bud on his arm.

"Well, Miss Morison," he exclaimed, with his usual jovial brusqueness, "I thought that my wife was the cheekiest woman in Boston, but you ran her hard to-night."

"Oh, even if I surpassed her," Berenice retorted in sudden anger, yet forcing herself to speak laughingly, "she is entirely safe to leave the reputation of the family in the hands of her husband."

Dr. Wilson chuckled with perfect good-nature.

"Oh, we men are not in it with the women," laughed he.

He passed on with his companion, and Berenice, with feminine perversity, avenged herself upon the girl he was escorting.

"How stout Miss Harding is," she commented. "It is such a pity for a bud."

"But she is pretty," Stanford returned.

"Oh, yes, in a way. She has the face of an overripe cherub."

He laughed and led her to a seat.

"Take your picture of Mr. Plant," said he, "and I will get you the bouillon."

"No, I can't have anything so hideous. Give me one of yours instead. I'll have that little fat monk."

"All that I have is at your service," he responded with seriousness sounding through the mock gravity, as he unpinned the little mask and put it into her hand.

"Thank you, but I don't ask your all. I hope that you didn't value this especially."

"Not that I remember. I haven't an idea who gave it to me."

"You don't seem to value a gift on account of the giver."

"That depends," returned he. "Now there are some givers whose favors I cherish most carefully."

He took from his breast-pocket a little Greek flag

of silk, neatly folded. Berenice flushed, recognizing
a favor which she had given him early in the evening.

"Now this," he said, "I put away next to my heart,
you observe."

"The giver would be flattered," Berenice observed.
"Was it Clare Tophaven?"

He looked at her, laughing; then seemed to reflect.

"I don't know that it is right to tell you," he returned; "but if you won't mention it, I'll confide to
you that it must have been Miss Tophaven. Sweet
girl."

"Very. Are congratulations in order?" Berenice
inquired.

She was pleased that the talk had taken this ban-
tering tone, and secretly determined to keep it away
from dangerous seriousness.

"Somewhat premature, I should say," Stanford replied. "You see she has no suspicion of my devotion, and her engagement to Fred Springer is to come
out next week."

The bit of gossip served Berenice well. She had
heard it already, but it was easy to feign surprise,
and to chat lightly about the match, as if she had not
a thought beyond it in her mind. To her amazement
and disconcerting Stanford cut through the light talk
to demand with sudden gravity: —

"And when may our engagement be announced,
Berenice?"

She regarded him with startled eyes, but she held
herself well in hand, managing to use the same jesting
tone in which she had been speaking.

"Certainly not before it exists," was her answer.

He leaned toward her eagerly. The room was

almost deserted, and they sat in the shelter of a great palm, so that she felt herself to be alone with him.

"Don't try to put me off," he pleaded. "I am in earnest."

She rose quickly, setting her cup down in the tub of the palm.

"Come," she said, "you forget that I am dancing the german with Mr. Van Sandt. He will have no idea what has become of me."

Stanford stood before her, barring her way.

"Hang Van Sandt! You should be dancing with me, only I had to do the polite to this everlasting English girl. I wish she was in Australia. I wonder why in the world an English girl is never able to learn to dance."

"That I cannot answer. Perhaps their feet are too big; but you must go back to her all the same, whether she can dance or not."

"Not until you answer me. You know you are keeping me on hot coals, Berenice. You know I love you."

She flushed, drew back, grew pale.

"I have answered you already," she replied, hurriedly but firmly. "Why must you make me say it again? I don't love you, and that is reason enough why you should n't care for me."

"It is n't any reason at all. I should be fond of you anyway. Why, even if you made a guy of me before everybody as you did to-night of that clerical thing" —

"Stop!" Berenice interrupted, her color rising and her eyes shining. "I will not have you speak of Mr. Wynne in that way. What I did was bad enough."

"Berenice," demanded Stanford, regarding her keenly, "do you mean to marry *him?*"

" You have no right to ask me whom I mean to marry! I am not going to marry you, at least! "

" A clergyman. A man in petticoats! Well, I must say " —

She drew herself up to her full height, looking at him with anger and excitement in her heart so great that they seemed to choke her.

" Do you see this ? " she asked, holding up the little mask dangling from her finger. " I fastened this to his cassock to-night. I insulted him in the sight of everybody. Does that look as if " —

" Is that the same mask ? " broke in Stanford. " You begged it of me afterward ! "

She could not command her voice to reply. Shame, grief, indignation, struggled in her heart; yet her strongest conscious feeling was a determination that the tears in her eyes should not fall. She slipped past him, and moved toward the ball-room. With a quick step he gained her side.

" I beg your pardon," he said contritely. " I did n't mean to hurt you. You used to be nice to me, but lately " —

She mastered herself by a strong effort. She was fully aware that there were too many curious eyes about her to make any demonstration safe.

" Let me take your arm," she answered. " Folks are watching. We need not make a spectacle of ourselves. I have n't meant to treat you badly. A girl never knows how a man is going to take things, and I only meant to be pleasant. As soon as you began to show that you were in earnest " —

She was so conscious that her words were not entirely frank that she instinctively hesitated.

" I have always been in earnest," interpolated he.

"But you will get over it," murmured she, desperately.

They had come to a group of palms, where they paused to let a bevy of dancers pass.

"Do you really mean," Stanford asked, in a hard voice, "that there is really no hope for me?"

"There is no hope that I shall ever feel differently about this."

"Then I shall certainly get over it," returned he with a touch of anger in his voice. "I don't propose to go through life wearing the willow for anybody."

She raised to his her eyes shining with shy but irresistible light.

"Ah," she half whispered, "that is the difference. I know he would n't get over it."

"He!"

The monosyllable brought to her an overwhelming sense of the confession which her words had carried. She pressed the arm upon which her finger-tips rested.

"I have trusted you," she whispered hurriedly. "Be generous. Ah, Mr. Van Sandt," she went on aloud, "I hope you did n't think I had deserted you. Mr. Stanford found me incapable of dancing, and had to revive me with bouillon."

XXIX

STRANGELY enough the thought which most strongly impressed Maurice Wynne on the morning following the Mardi Gras ball was the simplicity of life. He had heard in the early dawn the bell for rising; he had started up, then upon his elbow realized that he had freed himself from its tyranny. He had slidden back into his warm place, smiling to himself, and fallen into a sleep as quiet as that of a child. About eight he was roused by a brother sent to see if he was ill, his absence from early mass having been noted. Maurice sent the messenger away with the explanation that having been out to the midnight service he had slept late; then, being left alone, he made his toilet with deliberation. He seemed to himself a new man. There appeared to be no longer any difficulty in life. He reflected that one had but to follow common sense, to live sincerely up to what commended itself to his reason, and existence became wonderfully simplified. He no longer experienced any of the confusing doubts and perplexities which had of late made him so thoroughly miserable.

He hesitated to don again the dress of a deacon, but he reflected that to do otherwise would be to expose himself to the curiosity and comment of his fellows. With a smile and a sigh he put on for the last time the cassock, recalling the contemptuous terms in which

at the time of the accident Mehitabel Durgin had re-
ferred to the garment. He wondered at himself for
ever finding it possible to appear before the eyes of
men in such a dress, and blushed to think how incongruous the clerical livery must have looked in the ball-
room.

Breakfast was already half over when he appeared,
and the reading of Lamentations was accompanying
the frugal meal. He sank into his seat in silence,
casting his eyes down upon his plate lest they should
betray the joy he felt. He knew that he could have
no talk with Philip until after nones, and he was not
willing to leave the house without bidding his friend
good-by. While he went on with his breakfast he
was busy planning what he would do when he had
left the routine of the Clergy House behind him. He
determined to go to Mrs. Staggchase for advice, and
to ask her to direct him to some quiet boarding-place
where he might reorganize his scheme of life.

In the study hour which followed breakfast Wynne
went boldly to the room of Father Frontford, and
knocked at the door. When he heard the voice of the
Father Superior bidding him enter he was for the first
time seized with an unpleasant doubt. The long habit
of obedience half asserted itself, so that for an instant
he was almost minded to turn back. With a smile of
self-scorn he shook off the feeling, and opened the
door.

The Father looked up in evident surprise at sight
of the deacon who came unsummoned at such an hour.
He was alone, a fact which Maurice noted with satisfaction.

"Good morning, Wynne," he said. "Did you wish
to see me?"

" Yes, sir," Maurice answered, closing the door, and standing before it. " I came to tell you that I have decided to leave the Clergy House."

The abruptness of the communication evidently startled the Superior. Wynne watched him as he laid down his pen, the lines about his thin lips growing tense.

" Sit down," he said gravely.

Maurice obeyed unwillingly. He would have been glad to retreat at once, his errand being done; but he knew this to be of course impossible. He sat down facing the other, meeting with steadfast eyes the searching look fastened upon him.

" Since when," Father Frontford asked, " have you held this determination ? "

" Since last night."

" Is it founded upon any especial circumstance connected with your going with Mrs. Wilson to midnight service? "

Maurice looked down for a moment in thought, then he met the eyes of the other frankly.

" Father," he said, " I don't think that I could tell you all that has led to this decision if I would; and I do not see that it would be wise for us to go into the matter in any case. It seems to me that the fact that I have decided, and decided absolutely, is enough."

The face before him grew a shade sterner.

" You seem to forget that you are speaking to your Superior."

" Perhaps," the young man returned with calmness, " it is you who forget that I have ended that relation."

Father Frontford's face darkened.

" I do not recognize that you have authority to end it."

Maurice tried to repress the irritation which he could not but feel; and forced himself to speak as civilly as before.

"Will you pardon me," he said; "I do not wish that our last talk should be bitter. I owe you much, and I shall never cease to respect the unselfishness with which you have tried to help me. That I cannot follow your path does not blind me to the fact that you have worked so untiringly to make the way plain and attractive to me."

He was not without a secret feeling that he was speaking with some magnanimity, yet he was entirely sincere. He realized with thorough respect, even at the moment of breaking away, how complete was the devotion of the Father. There was in his mind, too, some satisfaction at the tone he had unconsciously adopted. It flattered him to find that he should be almost patronizing his Superior.

Father Frontford regarded Maurice with a look in which were mingled surprise, disapprobation, and regret. As the two sat holding each other's eyes, the face of the older man changed and softened. Into it came a smile of high and spiritual beauty, of nobility and unworldliness, of tenderness most touching. All that was most winning in the character of the man was embodied in the look which he fixed upon his recreant disciple, a look pleading and wistful, yet full of dignity and strength. He leaned forward, laying the tips of his thin fingers almost caressingly on the arm of the other.

"My son," he said, "it is not what I have done that you remember; it is what I represent. The truth and sweetness of religion is what has touched you. I am only the representative; and no one knows better how unworthy I am to be so looked on. If the grace of divine love seems to you good shining through me, think what it is in itself. Oh, my son," he went on, the tears coming into his eyes, " I have loved you, and I love you more now that I see you tempted and bewildered. Turn back to the bosom of the church before it is too late."

Maurice sat silent with look downcast. His firmness was not shaken ; he had no inclination to reconsider his decision, but he was deeply moved by the emotion of the other. He could not bear to meet pleading so affectionate with a cold negative.

" It is for yourself that I appeal to you," the priest went on. " It is for the good of your own soul, and for your happiness in this world and the world to come. Think of your mission. Think how men need you ; of the sin and the error that cry out to Heaven, and of how few there are to do the Lord's work. You have been confused by the temptations of the world, and in all of us there is a selfish spirit that may lead us to do in a moment of madness what we shall repent with tears of blood all our lives."

Still Maurice could not answer; and the Father, bending still nearer, taking one of the young man's hands in both his own, still pleaded.

" You have said that you felt my interest in you. Do not give me the bitterness of feeling that I am a careless shepherd who has lost a lamb to the wolves. If you have gone astray it must be in part my fault; it must be my negligence. Oh, my son, don't force me to stand guilty before God to answer for your lost soul."

It seemed to Maurice that he was being swept away by the simple power of the emotion of Frontford. He

felt the tears in his eyes, and almost without his voli-
tion his hand responded to the pressure of the hand
that clasped it. He made a strong effort to call back
his will.

"Father," he responded, "we must each stand or
fall alone. It is not your fault that I can't see things
as you do, or that I can't any longer remain here. I
am changed. If I stayed, it would be against my
convictions."

"Ah," was the eager reply, "but you could submit
your convictions to the church."

Maurice drew back.

"I am a man, to think for myself. I must be
honest with my reason. The church cannot take for
me the place of honesty and conviction."

The Father Superior dropped the hand he held.

"Then you insist on putting your own will and
your own wisdom above that of the church?"

"I must do the thing that seems to me right."

The priest's face hardened. It was as if over the
surface of a pool a film of ice formed. He sank back
in his chair, and when he spoke again it was in a
voice so hard and cold that the young man started.

"When do you leave?" the Father Superior asked.

"I meant to wait until after nones so as to say
good-by to Philip."

"I prefer that you should go at once."

"You mean that you prefer that I should not see
him?" Maurice demanded quickly.

"I merely said that I prefer that you should go at
once," was the cold reply.

Maurice rose briskly. His impulse was to retort
sharply, but he held himself in check.

"Very well," he answered. "I shall take it as a

favor if you will let Philip know that I did not willingly leave him without a word. It would hurt him to think that."

"The wounds of earth," the Father Superior said gravely, "are the joys of heaven."

Maurice stood an instant with a keen desire to reply, to break down this icy statue of religion; then he drew back.

"I will not trouble you longer," he said. "Good-by."

"Good-by, Mr. Wynne," the other responded with the manner of one addressing a stranger.

Maurice went to his chamber thoroughly aroused and excited. The restraint which he had put on himself during the talk with Father Frontford brought now its reaction. He rehearsed in his mind the telling and caustic things which he might have said, then laughed at himself for his unnecessary fervor. He packed his belongings, and, leaving them to be called for, set out for the house of his cousin. To go out from the Clergy House seemed to him like the ending of a life.

Mrs. Staggchase was fortunately at home. It seemed to Maurice that her keen eyes took in the whole story from his secular dress. He blushed as she gave him her hand.

"Well, my dear boy," she observed, "you have come to luncheon, I suppose, because the fare at the Clergy House is so poor in Lent. Sit down, and give me an account of your doings last night. I trust that you saw Mrs. Wilson safe home."

"I left her in the church."

"Ah! And what did you do then?"

"I went home and fought it out with myself. You

were right in saying that things were not concluded when I became a deacon. I have given up the whole thing."

" What do you mean by the whole thing ?"

" I mean," he returned earnestly, " that I found out that I was acting a part. That I did n't believe even the first principles of the religion I was getting ready to teach. I have broken down in the temptation, Cousin Diana."

She looked at him closely. The buoyancy of his morning mood was gone, and it was hard for him to endure her searching look. It came over him that he was an apostate ; one who had abandoned all that he had vowed to uphold ; his vanity smarted at the thought that she must think him weak and unstable as water.

" I am only what I was," he went on. " The difference is that I have discovered what you probably saw all the time, that I don't believe the things I have been taught. I am as free from the old creeds as you are. I don't even pretend to know that there is a God."

" My dear boy," she responded, shrugging her shoulders, " you run into extremes like a schoolgirl. I beg you won't talk as if I could be so vulgar as not to believe in a deity. Don't rank me with the crowd of common folk that try to increase their own importance by insisting that there 's nothing above them. Really, an atheist seems to me as bad as a man who eats with his knife."

He changed countenance, but her words left him speechless. He could not hear her speak in this way without being shocked. He might be without creed, but his temper was still devout.

"If you 've thrown overboard all your old dogmas," she went on with unruffled face, "you 'd better go to work to get a new set. I 've just heard of some sort of a society got up by women out in Cambridge, where they deduce the ethnic sources of prophetic inspiration — whatever that means! — from the 'Arabian Nights' and 'Mother Goose.' You might find something there to suit you."

He could not answer her; he could only wonder whether she disapproved of what he had done, or if she were vexed with him for coming to her.

"It 's possible," she went on mercilessly, a fresh note of mockery in her voice, "that Berenice might help you. Very often a woman wins converts where a priest fails. After last night " —

He came to his feet with a spring.

"Don't!" he exclaimed. "I can't stand any more. Do you think that it 's been easy for me to find out the truth about myself; to have to own that I 've been a cheating fool, without honesty enough to know my own mind? As for Miss Morison " —

His voice failed him. He was unnerved; the reaction from his long vigil, from his interview with Father Frontford, overcame him. The simple mention of the name of Berenice made him choke, and he stood there speechless. His cousin rose and came to him softly. Before he knew what she was doing, she bent forward and kissed his forehead.

"You poor boy," she said in a voice half laughing, yet so gentle that he hardly recognized it, "don't take my teasing so much to heart. You are only finding out like the rest of us that it is impossible not to be human."

He could answer only by grasping her hand,

ashamed of the weakness which had betrayed him, and touched deeply by her kindness.

"Come," Mrs. Staggchase said, moving to the bell, and speaking in her natural tone. "I have helped you to break your life into bits; I must try to help you to put the pieces together into something better. You must stay here for a while, and we'll consider what is to be done next. Will you tell Patrick how to get your things from the Clergy House? Take your old room. I'll see you at luncheon."

And as the servant appeared at one door she withdrew by another.

XXX

BERENICE had abundant leisure to reflect upon her attitude toward her lovers, for Mrs. Frostwinch was soon so seriously ill that it was evident to all that the end was at hand. Berenice devoted herself to the invalid, although there was little that she could do. The sick woman did not suffer; she seemed merely to be fading out of life; to have lost her hold upon something which was slipping from her loosened grasp.

"The fact is, Bee," Mrs. Frostwinch said one day, "that the doctors say I 'm dead. I 'm beginning to believe it myself, and when I 'm fully convinced, I suppose that that 'll be the end."

"Oh, don't joke about it, Cousin Anna," cried Bee. "It is too dreadful."

"It won't make it any less dreadful to be solemn over it," the other answered. "However, death should be spoken of with respect; even one's own."

Berenice longed to know what had taken place between her cousin and Mrs. Crapps, but she hardly liked to ask. That there had been a disagreement of some kind, and that Mrs. Frostwinch had lost faith in the woman, she knew; but beyond this she was in the dark. One afternoon, however, her cousin explained matters.

"It is so humiliating, Bee, that I can hardly bear

to think of it, the way things turned out. My conscience will be easier, though, if I tell you the whole of it. It is so vulgar that it makes me creep. We were at Jekyll's Island, and she had an ulcerated tooth."

"I thought she could n't have such things?"

"She thought or pretended that she could n't. I must say that she fought against it with tremendous pluck; but the face kept swelling, and the pain got to be more than she could bear. When she gave out she went to pieces completely. She literally rolled on the floor and howled. I could n't go on believing in her after that. She 'd actually made herself ridiculous."

"But," began Berenice, "I should think " —

"If it had been something dangerous, so that I had had to think of her life," went on her cousin, not heeding, "I could have borne it; but that common thing! Why, her face looked like a drunken cook's! I can't tell you the humiliation of it!"

"But if she could help you, why not herself?"

Mrs. Frostwinch smiled wanly.

"I 've tried to think that out," answered she. "It was always said of the old witches, you know, that they could n't help themselves. It is faith in somebody else that is behind the wonders they do. I 've grown very wise in the last few weeks, Bee. I don't pretend that I understand all the facts, but I do know pretty well what the facts are. I believed in Mrs. Crapps, and that belief kept me up. When I could n't believe in her, that was the end of it."

There seemed to Berenice something uncanny and monstrous in this calm acquiescence. She could not comprehend how her cousin could give up the struggle

for life in this fashion, after having succeeded so long
in holding death at bay.

"But surely," she protested, "you can't be willing
to let everything depend upon her. You 've proved
the possibility " —

"I 've proved the possibility of depending upon
somebody else; that 's all."

"Then find another woman that you can believe
in."

"It is too late. I can't have the faith over again.
I should always be expecting another humiliating
downfall of my prophetess."

She was silent a moment, and then continued : —

"Do you know, Bee, it seems to me after all that
my experience is like almost all religion. There are
a few men and women who believe in themselves in
that self-poised way that makes it possible for them to
get on with just ethics ; and there are those who can
take hold of unseen things ; but for the rest of us it 's
necessary to have some human being to lean on. I
hope I don't shock you. I lie awake in the night a
good deal, and my mind seems clearer than it used to
be. All the religions seem to have a real, tangible
human centre, a personality that human beings can
appreciate and believe in. Mrs. Crapps was so real
and so near at hand that I could have faith in her ;
now that that is gone there is n't anything left for me.
I can't believe in her, and she has destroyed the possibility of my believing in anybody else."

Berenice put out her hand in the growing dusk,
caressing the thin fingers of the sick woman.

"But — but," she hesitated, " she has n't destroyed
your faith in — in everything, has she ? "

"No, dear; she has n't touched my belief in God;

but it makes me ashamed to see how different a thing it is to believe in what we see and touch, from having a genuine faith in what we do not see. I have a faith in my soul still; the other was only a faith of the body. Perhaps it had only to do with the body, and it is not so bad to have lost it."

"Oh, Cousin Anna," Berenice murmured, tears choking her voice, "I can't bear to see you getting farther and farther off every day, and to feel so helpless."

"There, there, Bee," responded the other with tender cheerfulness, "you are not to agitate yourself or to excite me. I've lived half a year more now than the doctors allowed me, and I've enjoyed it too. Besides, think of the blessedness of not having any pain. Do you know, the night after Mrs. Crapps had that scene in the hotel, I was in a panic of terror lest my old agony should come back; but it didn't. Then I said to myself: 'Of course I couldn't suffer; I'm really dead!' You can't think what a comfort it was."

"Oh, don't, don't!" cried Bee. "I can't bear to have you talk like that."

"Well, then, we won't. There's something else I want to speak to you about while I am strong enough. Do you realize that when I am gone you'll be a rich woman?"

"I haven't thought about it. I've hated to think."

"Yes, dear, I understand; but when you are older you'll come to realize that half of the duty of life is to think of things which one would rather forget."

"But it could do no good to think of this."

"Perhaps not; but I want to ask you something.

I know you 'll forgive me. It 's about Parker Stanford."

" You may ask me anything you like, of course, Cousin Anna. As for Parker Stanford, he 's nothing more than the rest of the men I know, only he 's been more polite. We are very good friends."

" No more ? "

" No more ; and we never shall be."

" But he surely wished to be ? "

The day had darkened until the room was lighted only by the flames of the soft coal fire which sputtered in the grate. The cousins could hardly see each other's faces ; but in the dim light Berenice turned frankly toward Mrs. Frostwinch.

" That is all over now," responded she. " Of course to anybody else I should n't own that there ever was anything ; but whatever there may have been is ended. He understands that perfectly."

For some minutes Berenice sat smoothing the invalid's hand, the firelight glancing on her face and hair.

" How pretty you are, Bee," Mrs. Frostwinch said at length. Then without pause she added : " Is there anybody else ? "

Bee sank backward into the shadow with a quick, instinctive movement, dropping the hand she held.

" Who should there be ? " she returned.

Her cousin laughed softly.

" You are as transparent as glass," she said. " Come, who is it ? "

Berenice hesitated an instant, then threw herself forward, bending over the hand of her companion until her face was hidden.

" There is n't really anybody ; and besides I 've

insulted him so that he never could help hating me.
No, there is n't anybody, Cousin Anna; and there
never will be. I know I should despise him if he
was n't angry; and besides," she added with the air
of suddenly recollecting herself, " I hate him for what
he said."

"That is evident," the other assented smilingly.
" I could see at once that you hated him. But who is
it ? "

" Why, there is n't anybody, I tell you. Of course
I thought about him after he saved my life, but " —

" Oh," interrupted Mrs. Frostwinch. " Then it is
Mr. Wynne. But I thought " —

" He is n't a priest any more," Berenice struck in,
replying to the unspoken doubt as if it had been in
her own mind. " I heard yesterday that he has left
the Clergy House for good, and is staying with Mrs.
Staggchase."

" Have you seen him lately ? "

" He overtook me on the street yesterday."

Mrs. Frostwinch put out her hand with a loving
gesture.

" Bee," said she tenderly, " I want you to be happy.
You 've been like a daughter to me ever since your
mother died, and I 've thought of you almost as if
you were my own child. If this is the man to make
you happy " —

But Bee stooped forward and stopped the words
with kisses.

" I can't talk of him," she said, "and he will never
be anything to me. He is angry, and he has a right
to be. He " —

The entrance of the nurse interrupted them, and
Berenice made haste to get away before there was

opportunity for further question. In her anxiety to know something more of Mr. Wynne, Mrs. Frostwinch sent for Mrs. Staggchase, who came in the next day.

Mrs. Staggchase found her friend weak and frightfully changed. The high-bred face was haggard, the nostrils thin, while beneath the eyes were heavy purple shadows. A ghost of the old smile lighted her face, making it more ghastly yet, like the gleaming of a candle through a death-mask. The hand extended to the visitor was so transparent that it might almost have belonged to a spirit.

" My dear Anna," Mrs. Staggchase exclaimed, " I had n't an idea " —

" That I was so near dying, my dear," interrupted the other. " I am worse than that, I am dead, really ; but it does n't matter. I want to talk to you about Bee."

" About Bee ? " echoed the other, seating herself beside the bed. " What about her ? "

" I should have said that I want to ask you about Mr. Wynne. Do you know anything about his relations to her ? "

" The only relation that he has is that of a perfectly desperate adorer. He worships the ground she walks on, but he does n't cherish anything that could be decently called hope."

" Then he does care for her ? "

" My dear Anna, it almost makes me weep for my lost youth to see him. He has so wrought upon my glands of sentiment that this morning I actually examined my husband's wardrobe to see if the maid darns his stockings properly. Fred would be perfectly amazed if he knew how sentimental I feel. I even thought of sitting up last night to welcome him home

from the club, but about half past one I came to the
end of my novel and felt sleepy, so I gave that up."

Mrs. Frostwinch smiled with the air of one who understands that the visitor is endeavoring to furnish a
diversion from the dull sadness of the sick chamber.

" But Bee said he was angry with her."

" The anger of lovers, my dear, is legitimate fuel
for the flame. That's nothing. She's been amusing
herself with him, and if she thinks he resents it, so
much the better for him."

" But is he " —

She hesitated as if not knowing how best to frame
her question.

" He is a handsome creature, as you know if you
remember him," the visitor said, taking up the word.
" He is well born, he is well bred, if a little countri-
fied. He's been shut up with monks and other
mouldy things, and needs a little knocking about in
the world ; but I am very fond of him."

" Then you think " —

" I think that whoever gets Bee will get a treasure ;
but I am not sure that she is any too good for my
cousin. He hasn't much money, unless he gets a
little fortune that ought to have been his, and which
he has some hope of. I mean to give him something
myself one of these days, if he behaves himself ; but
of course he hasn't any idea of that."

" Bee will have all the Canton money, and can do
as she likes."

Mrs. Staggchase looked down at the carpet as if
studying the pattern.

" Perhaps," she returned.

" What do you mean by that ? "

" If I know Maurice Wynne, the fact that she has

money will make him very slow to speak. Besides,
he has a silly crotchet in his head now. He thinks
that if he tried to marry her it would look as if he
had given up his religion for her."

" Did he?"

" Bless you, no. He was simply led into the Clergy
House by being fond of a friend; one of those men
that young men and old women fall in love with.
Maurice never belonged there at all. I saw that the
first day he came to stay with me at the beginning of
the winter. I was abroad while he was in college, so
I never knew him except most casually before."

" But if he really cares for her he 'll get over those
obstacles."

" If she cares for him, he must be made to."

" I am convinced that she does," Mrs. Frostwinch
said. " I am so glad you speak well of him. I do
so want Bee to be happy."

There was a long silence in the chamber. The two
friends sat wrapped in thought. They had seen so
much of life, they had had so many blessings of fortune, culture, position, wealth, that there was a grim
irony in their sitting here helpless in the face of coming death. To their reverie, moreover, the mention of
love could not but give color. No woman has ever
come to speak of love entirely unmoved, though her
heart may have been deadened or crushed beyond the
power of thrilling or quickening at any other thought.
These two, who had led lives so happy, so protected,
so rich, sat there silent before the possibilities which
lay in the love of a girl; until at last both sighed,
whether with regret or tenderness perhaps they could
not themselves have told. Perhaps both remembered
their youthful days; remembered how one had lost

her first love by death and the other parted from hers in anger, making a marriage which seemed more a matter of affronting the man discarded than of affection for the man she chose. They knew each other's history so completely that there could be no disguise between them. Their eyes met, and for an instant there was a suspicion of wistfulness in the glance. Then Mrs. Frostwinch shook her head, and smiled sadly.

"At least," she said, "I shall be spared the pain of growing old."

"After all," the other responded, "the bitterness of growing old is to feel that one has never completely been young."

The sick woman regarded her with burning eyes.

"But we have been young, Di," she said eagerly. "Surely we had all that there was."

"Anna," Mrs. Staggchase murmured, leaning toward her, "we know each other too well not to say things that most women are afraid to say. We both married well, and we have cared for our husbands and been happy. But we both know that there was deep down a memory" —

"No, no, Di," her friend interrupted excitedly, "you shall not make me think of that! I have forgotten all that; and I am dying comfortably. You shall not make me think of him! Only, dear Di, I want you to help Bee to marry the man she loves with her whole heart; that she loves as we might have loved if" —

Mrs. Staggchase kissed her solemnly.

"I promise, Anna."

Then she rose, her whole manner changing.

"Do you know, my dear," she observed, in a tone

gayly satirical, "that I believe that Elsie Wilson is going to be beaten in her bishop steeplechase?"

"Do you mean that Father Frontford won't be elected?"

"I mean just that. However, things are still uncertain. It will be amusing to see what Elsie will do if she is defeated. She is capable of setting up a church of her own."

"There are two or three men with whom I have some influence that will go over to Mr. Strathmore if I am not here to look after them. I must write to them to-morrow and get them to promise to hold by our side."

But that night Mrs. Frostwinch died quietly in her sleep, and the letters were not written.

XXXI

HOW CHANCES MOCK
2 Henry IV., iii. 1

MAURICE had seen Berenice only once since his encounter at the ball. He had hoped and dreaded to meet her, but for more than a week after his leaving the Clergy House he had failed. One morning he saw her walking before him on Beacon Street; and while he instantly said to himself that he trusted that she would not discover him, he hurried forward to overtake her. His feet carried him forward even while he told himself that he did not wish to go. He was beside her in a moment, and as he spoke she raised those rich, dark eyes with a glance which made him thrill.

"Good-morning," he said with his heart beating as absurdly as if the encounter were of the highest consequence.

"Good-morning, Mr. Wynne," she responded, with a manner entirely abstract.

She had started and blushed, he was sure, on perceiving him; but if so she had instantly recovered her self-possession. He was disconcerted by the coldness of her manner, and began to wish in complete earnest that he had not overtaken her.

"I beg your pardon for intruding," he said, his voice hardening, "but" —

"The public street is free to anybody, I suppose," she returned, with an air of studied politeness. "I don't claim any exclusive right to it."

" I did n't apologize for being on the street, but for speaking to you."

" Oh, that," answered Berenice carelessly, although he thought that he detected a spark of mischief in her eye, " is a thing of so little consequence that it is n't worth mentioning."

" I venture to speak to you," he said, ignoring the thrust, " because I have wanted to beg your pardon for my rudeness when I saw you last."

She turned upon him quickly, her cheeks aflame.

" Your rudeness ?" she exclaimed. " Your brutality, I think you mean ! "

It was his turn to grow red.

" My brutality, if you choose. I beg your pardon for whatever offended."

" It was unpardonable ! It was a thing no woman could ever forgive ! "

Maurice turned pale. He stopped where he stood.

" In that case," he said, bowing with formality, " I have no business to be speaking to you now."

He turned and was gone before she could add a word.

This interview probably made neither of the young persons happy ; and Maurice it left entirely miserable. He was not without a proper pride, however, and in his present frame of mind was ready to call it to his aid. He bore a brave outward front. He resolved not to think of his love; yet he was not without the hardly confessed hope that if he could find the lost will he might be taking a step in the direction of the realization of his desires. He tried to forget Berenice in the very means he was taking to bring himself nearer to her.

He set out for Montfield one bright February day,

amused at himself for the difference in his attitude
toward the world from the mere fact that he had
discarded the ecclesiastical garb. It gave him a fresh
and delightful sensation to be traveling on business in
clothing like that of other men. He had no longer
any wish to be separated by his dress, and thought
with contemptuous amusement of the lurking self-consciousness which had always attached itself in his
mind to the fact that he was in a costume apart. He
realized now that he had from this derived a certain
satisfaction, half simple vanity and half the gratification of his histrionic instinct. He felt as if he had
been like a child pleased to attract attention by a
feather stuck in his cap, or a toy sword girt at his
side. Now that the whole experience was past he
could smile at it, but he had small patience with
those who still retained the clerical garb. Men have
usually little tolerance for the fault which they have
but newly outgrown ; and Maurice thought with a
sort of amazement of his late fellows at the Clergy
House, and of their manifest satisfaction in the dress
they wore. It was almost with a sensation of self-
righteousness that he enjoyed the habiliments of ordinary civilized man.

As the train sped on, and the scenery became more
familiar as he approached nearer to Montfield, Maurice naturally fell to thinking, in an irregular, detached fashion, of his youth. Both Wynne's parents
had died in his childhood, and there had been little
to keep firm the bonds of family. Alice Singleton he
had known, however, both as a girl and as the wife of
his half brother, but he had known only to dislike and
avoid her. He began now to wonder how she would
receive him, and whether she would allude to the scene

at Mrs. Rangely's when he had broken up her spirit-
ualistic deception.

The train of thought into which reminiscence had
plunged him carried him over his whole life. He
realized for the first time that his religious experiences
had been little more than a reflection of those of
Philip. It was Ashe who had interested him in
spiritual things, who had led him into the church,
who had practically determined for him that he
should become a priest. For the first time, and with
profound amazement, Maurice realized how completely his theological life had been the growth of
the mind of Ashe rather than of his own. The
thought brought with it a sense of weakness and self-
contempt.

"Have n't I any strength of character?" he asked
himself. "In everything practical Phil has always
relied on me. It was always Phil I cared for, not the
church."

Imperfectly as he was able to phrase it, Maurice
was not in the end without some reasonably clear
conception of the fact that in his life Philip had represented the feminine element. It was by love for
his friend that he had been led on. Now that his
reason was fully awake this emotional yielding to the
thought of another was no longer possible; now that
his heart was filled with a passion for Berenice his
nature no longer responded to the appeal of the
feminine in Ashe.

Maurice was half aware that his was a character
sure to be influenced greatly by affection; but he felt
that it would never again be possible for him so to
give up to another the guidance of his life as he now
saw that he had yielded it to his friend. He had

learned his weakness, and the lesson had been enforced too sharply ever to be forgotten.

He was coming now into the region of his old home. The forests were beginning faintly to show the approach of spring; the treetops were dimly warming in color, the branches thickening against the sky. Here and there Maurice looked down on a brook black with the late rains and with the floods from the snow-drifts still melting on the distant hills. Now he caught a far flash of the river where he had skated in winters almost forgotten, so fast does time move, where he had fished and bathed in summers so long gone that they seemed to belong to the life of some other. Yet once more and a distant hill, duskily blue against the bluer heavens, wakened for him some memory of his boyhood, seeming to challenge him to renew the old joys and to revel in the by-gone fervors.

All these things softened the mood in which Maurice came back to the old town, and as he walked up the village street, so well remembered yet so strange, he had a sense of unreality. The very homely familiarity of it all made it appear the more like a dream. He felt his heart-beats quicken as he approached the Ashe place, wondering if he should see Mrs. Ashe. He had always, with all his affection, felt for Philip's mother a sort of awe, as if she were more than a simple human creature. He found it difficult to understand that Mrs. Singleton should be staying with her, so incongruous was the association in his mind of two such women. With Mrs. Ashe, Alice must at least be at her best.

He walked up to the house, passing under the leafless lilac bushes with a keen remembrance of how they were laden with odors in June. He wondered if the tansy still grew under the sitting-room window, and if the lilies-of-the-valley flourished on the north side of the house as of old. Then he knocked with the quaint old black knocker, and with the sound came back the present and the thought that he had before him an interview which might be neither pleasant nor easy.

Mrs. Singleton herself opened the door.

" I saw you coming," she greeted him, " and there is nobody at home but me."

Maurice tried not to look disappointed.

" Then Mrs. Ashe is not at home ? "

" No ; she is out, and the girl is out. Will you come in ? You probably did n't come to see me."

" But I did come to see you."

She led the way into the long, low sitting-room, with its many doors and its wide fireplace, so familiar that he might have left it yesterday.

" I can't imagine what you want of me," Mrs. Singleton said, waving her hand toward a chair. " The last time I saw you you did n't seem very fond of me."

She seated herself by the side of the fire in a great old-fashioned chair covered with chintz and spreading out wings on either side of her head.

" You are still angry, Alice, I see," he rejoined. " Well, I can't help that. I did what was right. How in the world could you make up your mind to fool those people so ? "

" They wanted to be fooled ; why not oblige them ? "

He regarded her with astonishment. He had expected her to deny that her deception was deliberate, to claim that the manifestations were real. Her frank

and cynical speech disconcerted him. He had no
reply. She broke into a sneering laugh.

"There," she said, "you did n't come here to talk
about that séance. What did you come for?"

"I came to ask you if you still have Aunt Hannah's desk."

She regarded him keenly.

"The little traveling desk?"

"Yes."

"What if I have?"

"But have you?"

"Oh, I don't mind telling you that. I don't see
that it can do you any good to know that I have it.
I always carry it round with me. It's so conven-
ient."

"Will you sell it to me?"

"Certainly not. If you did n't want it, I might
give it to you; but if you do you can't have it."

Maurice began to feel his anger rising. He felt
helpless before this woman, with her innocent, baby
face, this woman with the guileless look of a child and
a child's freedom from moral scruples, who faced him
with a smile of pleased malice. It might be unwise
to tell his real errand, but she surely could not do any
harm greater than to be disagreeable. There must be
some method, he reflected, of getting at the thing
legally; but what it was he was entirely ignorant;
and now that he had shown a desire for the desk he
was confident that Mrs. Singleton would persist until she had discovered the truth. He could think of
nothing to do but to make a clean breast of the whole
matter. He nerved himself to the task, and told her
of the finding of Norah and of what followed.

"Have you ever discovered that the desk had a
false bottom?" he asked in conclusion.

" No, brother Maurice. The spirits had n't revealed it to me. But then I never asked them about that."

There was an air of triumphant glee in her manner, an open and mocking sneer, which dismayed him. He was sure that he had erred in telling her his secret; yet he reflected that he could hardly have done otherwise, and that she surely would not dare to refuse to give up a legal document so important.

" Will you let me examine the desk ? "

" I am so happy to oblige you," she returned. " Though whether your story is true or not must depend, you know, upon the unsupported testimony of the medium — I mean of the speaker."

Maurice rose and went toward her, facing her squarely.

" I understand, Alice," he said, " that you don't love me, and I have n't come to ask favors. This is a matter of simple honesty. I certainly don't think you would willfully keep me out of my property."

" Thank you for drawing the line somewhere. It was so noble of you to interfere at Mrs. Rangely's! You did n't in the least mind robbing me of my good name, and them of the comfort of believing it was real. Besides, I did see things ! I swear to you that I did ! I am a medium in spite of whatever you say. I can call up spirits ! "

Her voice rose as she went on, and he feared lest she should work herself into one of her furies of excitement and temper which he had seen of old.

" Why should we go back to that ? " he said, as gently as he could. " That is past, and I only did what I thought was my duty."

" Oh, you did your duty, did you ? " she sneered.

"Well, I 'll do mine now. Stay here, while I go and empty that old desk. I 'll match you in doing my duty ! "

She hurried tumultuously from the room, leaving Maurice in anything but an enviable frame of mind. He began to walk up and down, assailed by old memories at every turn, yet so disturbed by Mrs. Singleton's words and manner that he could not heed the recollections. The minutes passed, and Alice did not return. It seemed to him that she took a long time to remove her papers from the desk. Then he smiled to himself in bitter amusement and impatience. Of course his sister-in-law was trying to discover the secret of the double bottom. She would probably persevere until she had gained the precious document of which he had come in search. She would read it, and then — He broke off in his reverie with an exclamation of impatience. What a fool he had been to attempt to deal with this woman alone ! He had, it was true, expected to find Mrs. Ashe, but he should have sent a lawyer. What did he, a puppet from the Clergy House, know of managing the affairs of life ? He felt that he had failed in his match with Mrs. Singleton ; and he had almost made up his mind to go in search of her, when he heard her returning.

She came in with her face flushed, her eyes shining, and an air of triumph which struck dismay to the heart of Maurice.

"I am sorry to have kept you waiting so long," she said, " but I had to light a fire in the parlor, I was so cold. However, I have something to show you that will interest you."

" Is it the will ? " he asked eagerly.

She answered with a laugh, but led the way across

the narrow front entry into the parlor. The pleasant noise of a crackling fire sounded within, and as he entered the room he saw that the fireplace was filled with a ruddy blaze. Then he rushed forward with a cry. There on the top of the blazing logs were the unmistakable remains of the desk, eaten through and through by tongues of red flame. He seized the tongs, and dragged the burning mass to the hearth, but even as he did so he saw that he was too late.

"It is kind of you to want to save my old desk, Maurice," jeered his companion; "but I had the misfortune to put the poker through the bottom of it before I called you, so that I'm afraid it really isn't worth saving."

He saw that the wood had indeed been punched through and through, and that it was reduced almost to a cinder. It was easy to see that the bottom had been double, and burned flakes of paper were visible among the remains; whether of the will or not it was obviously impossible now to discover. He looked at the burned bits of board falling into ashes and cinders at his feet, realizing that here was an end to all his dreams of regaining his aunt's fortune; that with this dream ended, too, his visions of being in a position to offer Berenice — His wrath blazed up in an uncontrollable force.

"You are a fiend!" he cried, facing the woman who smiled beside him. "You are a thief, a shameless, deliberate thief!"

She stood the image of mirthful, innocent girlhood, her smooth forehead unclouded, her eyes gleaming as if with the merriment of a child.

"It is a pretty fire, isn't it, Maurice?"

Then her whole expression changed. Into her dark,

dewy eyes came a look of rage, visible murder in a glance.

" You called me a liar, there in Boston," she said hissingly. " I am not surprised to have you add thief now. I have only done what I chose with my own property ; but I would have been cut into little bits before you should have had that will through me ! "

He could not trust himself to reply. He felt that if he spoke he might break out into curses, and he was conscious of an unmanly longing to strike her, to mar that beautiful, false face, childlike and pure in every line, — for the expression of rage had melted as quickly as it had come, — to feel the joy of seeing her limbs slacken and her red lips grow white. He clinched his hands and turned resolutely away.

" I 'm sure I don't know that there was anything there that you had any interest in," she pursued lightly. " I tried as long as I dared to get the bottom open, and I could n't, so I decided that it was n't any of my business. Only when I put the poker through there seemed to be papers there."

Maurice could endure no more. He started toward her so fiercely that she recoiled, a sudden pallor blanching her rosy loveliness. Then he turned abruptly away again, and got out of the house.

XXXII

INTEREST in the question who would be bishop increased as Lent waned and the time for the meeting of the convention approached. The general public could not be expected to be greatly concerned about a matter so purely ecclesiastical, but the wide popularity of Mr. Strathmore gave to the election a character of its own. The question was generally held to be that of the prevalence of liberal views. Many who cared nothing about the church were interested in seeing whether new or old ideas would prevail. The age is one in which there is a keen curiosity to see what course the church will take. It is partly due, undoubtedly, to the inherited habit of being concerned in theology; it is perhaps more largely the result of unconscious desire for a liberalism so great that it shall justify those who have been so liberal as to lay aside all religion whatever.

The papers had entered into the discussion with an alacrity quickened by the fact that at this especial season there was not much else in the way of news. Rangely wrote for the " Daily Eagle " a glowing editorial in which he urged the choice of Strathmore on the ground that the new bishop should be not the representative of a faction, but of the whole church, and as far as possible of the people. It insisted that only a man liberal himself could have breadth to understand and sympathize with all shades of feeling. Others of the secular press had taken up the discussion, and Mrs. Wilson declared that the devil was contributing editorials to the papers in his keen fear that Father Frontford would be elected.

Lent wore at last to an end, and the festivities which follow Easter came in with all their usual gayety. One evening, about a week before the election, a musicale was given at the house of Mrs. Gore. Mr. and Mrs. Strathmore were present, the figure of the former being conspicuous in the crowd which after the music surged toward the supper-room and later eddied through the parlors. Fred Rangely came upon the clergyman at a moment when he had detached himself from the admiring women who usually surrounded him, and taken refuge in the shadow of a deep window.

"Good-evening, Mr. Strathmore," Rangely said. "Are you making a retreat? I thought Lent was the time for that."

The other smiled with that kindly benevolence which was characteristic.

"Ah, Mr. Rangely," he responded, extending his hand. "I am glad to see you. Will you share my retirement?"

"Thank you," Rangely answered, stepping into the recess. "A retreat is especially grateful to a journalist. We get so tired that even a moment of respite is welcome."

Mr. Strathmore smiled more genially than ever.

"Yes; you journalists are expected to know everything, and it must be wearing to have to learn all that there is to know."

"Oh, it's easy enough to learn instead how to appear to know."

The clergyman regarded him with a quizzical look.

" Is that the way it is done? I 've often wondered at the infallibility of your guild."

"A trick of the trade, I assure you. We have to seem to be infallible to secure any attention at all, you see ; and we soon learn the knack of it."

The clergyman, as if unconsciously, drew back a little farther into the shadow of the heavy draperies veiling the nook in which they stood.

" I dare say," he observed, as if speaking at random, " that one of your clever professional writers would be able, for instance, to give the reader quite an inside view even in church matters."

Rangely's face changed, and he in turn altered his position by leaning his elbow against the heavy middle sash of the window. The two men were thus not only concealed from the passing crowd, but stood with faces screened from each other by the shadow.

" Oh, even that might be possible," Rangely returned lightly.

" There is so much interest in church matters now," the other continued dispassionately. " I noticed that the ' Churchman' had rather a striking article two or three weeks ago on a layman's point of view of the bishop question. Did you see it ? "

" I seldom see the ' Churchman,' " Rangely replied in a voice not wholly free from constraint.

" It is a pity you did n't see this, it was so well done. It is true that it proved me to be all sorts of a heretic ; but if I am, of course it should be known."

There was a pause of a moment. Outside in the drawing-room rose the constant babble of speech, unintelligible and confusing. Then above it Rangely laughed softly.

" The wisdom of the journalist," he remarked, " is as nothing compared to that of the clergy. How did you discover that I wrote it?"

" Discover? Is n't that a word applied to finding things by seeking?"

" What of that?"

" I was merely thinking that you give me credit for more leisure and more curiosity than I possess if you suppose me to have tried to find out about that article."

Rangely laughed again.

" Mr. Strathmore," he said with a new resolution in his tone, " will you pardon me if I am frank? I want to ask you what I can do to help you to secure the election."

" Don't think I am given to word-splitting, Mr. Rangely, but I 've no wish to *secure* it. If the church needs me — but, after all, we need not quibble. Will you pardon me if I say that your question is rather remarkable coming from the author of the ' Churchman ' paper."

" Although I wrote the ' Churchman ' article, I wrote also the ' Eagle ' editorial," was the reply. " I see things in a different light. The fact is that I was trapped into writing that stuff for the ' Churchman,' and now I 'm anxious to undo any harm I may have done."

" I am glad that you do not really think me as bad as that article made me out," Strathmore said. " There have been some queer things about this election. Mrs. Gore has a letter that a woman has written which illustrates how injudicious some of those interested have been."

" What sort of a letter?"

"A letter that is amusing in a way. Of course I only mention the thing confidentially. Very likely, though, Mrs. Gore might be willing to let you see it if you are interested. It was written to a clergyman in the western part of the State by Mrs. Wilson."

"Mrs. Wilson?"

"Mrs. Chauncy Wilson. Of course you know that she is much interested in the matter. It is n't a very discreet document. I shall be much relieved when the whole thing is settled. It causes too much excitement, especially for us who have been named in connection with the office."

"It can't be pleasant," Rangely assented.

"It is not, I assure you. Now it is my duty to be talking to ladies and helping Mrs. Gore. She told me that she depended on me."

He moved forward as he spoke, and the two were soon in the company again. Rangely weltered through the crowd to Mrs. Gore and asked about the letter.

"It is a trump card," she said. "I am glad you spoke about it. I was wondering how it could be used to the best advantage. Mr. Strathmore talks about its being a private letter, but I have a shrewd suspicion that he would n't mind if somebody else used it. Come in to-morrow about five, and we 'll talk it over."

Maurice Wynne was naturally not entirely at home in this sort of a gathering. He had not overcome his shyness and want of familiarity with social usages, so that he was especially relieved when he found himself comfortably seated in a corner with Mrs. Herman, to whom he could talk freely.

"Is n't there something that can be done for Phil,

Mrs. Herman?" he asked earnestly. "I have n't seen him since I left the Clergy House. I had to come away without saying good-by to him, and in answer to my letter he says that Father Frontford advises him not to see me for the present."

Mrs. Herman sighed, playing with her fan.

"Life is hard for a nature like his," answered she. "He is born to be a martyr. He has the martyr temperament. It 's part of our inheritance from Puritanism, I suppose."

Maurice smiled, looking up impulsively.

"I can't see why you lay so much stress on Puritanism," he said. "What has Puritanism resulted in? Its whole struggle has come to an end in doubt and agnosticism and flippancy. Intellectual curiosity has taken the place of spiritual stress; ethical casuistry or theological amusements seem to me to stand instead of religious conviction."

Mrs. Herman regarded him with an inquiring smile.

"You make me feel old," she interposed; "it is so long since I went through that stage. Will you pardon me for saying that you are not quite a disinterested observer?"

"It is the eyes newly open that see most clearly," he responded, throwing back his head with a little laugh. "The Puritan came into the wilderness to establish a city of God. Time has shown that he dreamed an impossible dream. The result of that effort has been the establishment of a religious liberty" —

"One might almost say a religious license, I own," she interpolated.

"A religious liberty or license as you like, but at any rate something that would have seemed to them appallingly wicked, — a thousand times worse than anything they fled from into the desert."

Mrs. Herman was silent a moment while he waited for her answer. Her eyes grew darker, and the color flushed in her cheeks.

" It is odd enough for me to be the champion of Puritanism," she said at length, " and yet it seems to me that after all they did their work well, and that it was permanent. They left on the land the stress of sincerity and earnestness. Creeds fall away just as leaves drop from the trees, but each leaf has helped. Religions decay, but the salvation of the race must depend upon human steadfastness to conviction."

" Then I suppose that you think Phil is nearer to the heart of things than I am."

" Not in the least. The difference between you is superficial rather than real so long as you are both true to your convictions."

" But it seems to me," Maurice objected, " that Phil is looking at truth as a sort of fetish. He seems to feel that the root of the matter is in a dogma, and a dogma is only the fossil remains of a truth that is gone by."

She laughed appreciatively.

" Have you caught the fever for making epigrams? I'm afraid there's a good deal of truth in what you say about Cousin Philip. He can't help looking at religion as an end rather than a means."

" Has it ever struck you that he might finish by going over to the Catholics?"

" No," she answered, " I confess I'd never thought of it; but I see what you mean."

" It will seem to him a moral catastrophe, a sort

of ecclesiastical cataclysm," Maurice continued, " if
Father Frontford is n't elected ; and as far as I can
judge there is n't much chance of that."

" No," she assented, " I don't think there is much
chance."

" He said to me one day," added Maurice thoughtfully, " that in the Catholic Church there never could
have been any danger of the election of a heretic
bishop. I am afraid this will decide him."

Mrs. Herman regarded him with a smile, studying
him as if she were reading the working of his mind.

" You think that a misfortune," she commented.
" You feel that it is a step farther into the darkness."

" It is to narrow rather than to broaden his horizon,
is it not ? "

She played with her fan a moment, smiling to herself in a way which he did not understand, and looking
down as if considering some old memory. Then she
met his glance with a look at once kind and wistful.

" It is n't of much use to argue the matter, I suppose," were her words. " It seems to me as if in
talking to you I see my old mental self in a mirror,
if you 'll pardon me for saying so. When we come
out from any conviction, and most of all from a
religious belief, it seems to us a profound misfortune
that any man should still believe what we have decided is false. By and by I think you will see that
the chief point is that a man shall believe. What
he believes does n't so much matter. It must be the
thing that best suits his temperament."

" Then to outgrow a dogma is to weaken our power.
It certainly weakens our faith in general."

" Yes," she assented, " that is the price we must
pay for freedom ; but if Philip can still believe, I

have long ago passed the place where I should regret it. Perhaps he is to be envied."

Maurice shook his head.

" We may feel like that in some moods," he concluded with a smile, " but certainly nothing would induce you to change places with him."

" Oh, no," she cried; " certainly not. But that is mere womanly lack of logic ! "

XXXIII

THE disappointment of Maurice at the failure of his effort to secure his aunt's fortune was perhaps rather more than less keen because the property had never tangibly been his. The title of the fancy is that of which men are most tenacious, and the thing which has been held in fee of the imagination is precisely that which it is most grievous to lose. Maurice returned to Boston completely overcome by the result of his expedition, his mind overflowing with chagrin and anger.

It was not only the money which he had missed, but he had to his thinking lost also the hope of being in a position to press his suit with Berenice. However intangible might be his plans for winning her, they none the less filled his mind. He refused to regard her coldness as enduring. He had in his thoughts imagined so many tender scenes of reconciliation in which he magnanimously forgave her for the sharpness of the repulse of their last meeting or humbly besought pardon for his own offenses, that he came to feel as if all misunderstanding had really been done away with. It had been in his mind that if he were but in a position to meet Berenice on equal terms in regard to fortune all might be well ; and to be deprived of this hope was infinitely bitter.

Meanwhile he had before him the problem of re-

shaping his life. It was necessary that he decide
what should take the place of the profession which he
had laid down. Fortunately the decision was not difficult, as former inclination had practically settled the
matter. The definite shaping of his plans came one
day in a talk which he had with his cousin.

" It is n't exactly my affair, Maurice," Mrs. Staggchase said, " but I want to know, and that always
makes a thing her affair with a woman, — what are
you going to do with your life now that you have
pulled it out of the mouth of the church? "

" It is good of you to care to ask, " he answered.
" I suppose I shall study law."

" May I talk with you quite frankly ? " she asked.
" Fred does me the honor to say that for a woman I
have a reasonably clear head."

" You may say whatever you like, Cousin Diana.
I shall only be grateful."

" Well, then, in the first place, how much have you
to live on ? "

" I 've about a thousand dollars a year. What was
left of the estate at mother's death amounts to about
that. I wanted to give it all to the church when I
went into the Clergy House."

" Why did n't you ? "

" Father Frontford would n't allow it. He said
that a continual sacrifice meant more than an act that
stripped me of power to decide, and which might be
regretted."

" That was a noble temper, " Mrs. Staggchase remarked thoughtfully. " A priest is a strange being.
As for you, you say you have never believed, and yet
you would have given up everything you possessed."

Maurice flushed, and looked a little shamefaced.

" I never did believe, so far as I can see now ; but I
thought I did, if you see the difference. My wanting
to give up everything was n't belief ; it was a sort of
instinctive desire to play fair. If I were to do the
thing at all, my impulse was to do it thoroughly.   It
is n't in my blood to do a thing half way.   I 'm afraid
the explanation does n't speak very well for my common sense ; but so far as I can understand myself
that 's the way of it."

" But if you did n't believe what were you there
for ? "

" I was there because Phil was.   I don't pretend
to understand why I, who led Phil in everything else,
who did all sorts of things that he could n't and had
to decide everything else for him, should have followed
his lead so in religion ; but I did.   It was part of my
caring for him.   It would have hurt him so much if I
had n't, that of course I had to."

Mrs. Staggchase regarded him keenly.   He turned
away his eyes, thinking of his friend and of the wide
gulf which had opened between them, so that he but
half heard and did not understand the comment she
made softly.

" The *ewigweibliche* in masculine shape, " she murmured, smiling to herself.   " When the real came, it
could n't hold its power any longer."

" What ? " he asked.

" Nothing.   I was speaking in riddles.   To come
back to business, — you say you 've decided upon the
law."

" Yes.   That was always my choice.   I read a
good deal of law while I was in college.   It was n't
till I graduated two years ago that I fell into theology.   It 's two years wasted."

"Oh, perhaps, and perhaps not. After all, experience in youth is generally worth what it costs, little as we think so when we pay the price. Well, then, you can easily live on your income if you choose. Mr. Staggchase and I will be glad to have you make this your home, and " —

"But, Cousin Diana, " he interrupted in astonishment, "there is certainly no reason why you should burden yourself with me. Not that I am not a thousand times obliged to you, but " —

"Be as obliged as you like, " interrupted she in turn, "only don't be foolish. Fred and I are not exactly sentimentalists, and we both know what we wish. He likes to have you to talk with, and when you have learned to smoke you will find him a very clever and agreeable companion after dinner. He knows the world, and he'll teach you a great many things that you'd be slow to find out for yourself. As for me, you amuse me, let us say. The gods have spared us the bother of children ; but the gifts of the gods are always to be paid for, and we begin to feel as if there were a sort of loneliness ahead of us with nobody to be especially interested in. To have somebody younger to care for is a luxury when you are young yourself, but it's a necessity to age. I assure you that we shouldn't have you here if we didn't want you, and that we shall turn you out without scruple when we are tired of you."

"Very well, then," he responded with a laugh, "I am rejoiced to remain to be a blessing."

They looked into the fire a little time as if they were considering what effect upon the future this new arrangement would have ; then Mrs. Staggchase glanced up with a smile.

" Just now," she remarked, " before you are plunged in the study of the law, you may do escort duty for me. I am going to call on Berenice Morison."

" On Miss Morison ? "

" Yes. Her grandmother is staying with her. Mr. Frostwinch has gone abroad, you know, and as the old house belongs to Bee, she is staying on there."

" But — but she won't care to see me."

" Very likely not," assented his cousin coolly, "but she'll endure you for my sake."

" I don't like being endured, " he retorted, between fun and earnest. " Besides, she 's so much money " —

" You are not such a cad as to be afraid of her money, I hope."

" Not in one way, but don't you see now that she has so much, and I have lost Aunt Hannah's " —

" Really, Maurice," she interrupted brusquely, " you must learn not to speak your thoughts out like that! I 'm not asking you to go to propose to Bee. You have the theological habit of taking things with too dreadful seriousness. Come with me for a call, and don't bother about consequences and possibilities."

Maurice blushed at his own folly in betraying his secret scruples, but his cousin spared him any farther teasing, and they went on their way peacefully. It seemed to him when he entered the stately Frostwinch house that it had somehow been transformed. Everything was much as it had been in the lifetime of Mrs. Frostwinch, yet to his fancy all looked fresher and more cheerful. He smiled to himself, feeling that the change must simply be the result of his knowledge that this was now the home of Bere-

nice; yet even so he could not persuade himself that
the alteration was not actual. He felt joyously alert
as he followed Mrs. Staggchase to the library, where
Bee was sitting with old Mrs. Morison.

He had never been in this apartment before. It
was high, and heavily made, with an open fire on the
hearth, and enough books to justify its name. Berenice came forward to meet them, and Mrs. Morison
remained seated near the fire.

" I am so glad to see you, Mrs. Staggchase," Bee
said cordially. " It is just one of those dreary days
when it proves true courage to come out."

" And true friendship, I hope," the other answered,
passing on to Mrs. Morison. " My dear old friend,
I wish I could believe you are as glad to see me as I
am to see you."

Berenice in the mean time gave her hand to Maurice
graciously, but with a certain grave courtesy which he
felt to put them upon a purely ceremonious footing.

" It is kind of you to come," she said. " Grandmother will be glad to see you."

Maurice tried hard to look unconscious, but he could
not help questioning her with his eyes. She flushed
under his eager regard, and drew back a little.

" I am very glad of the chance to see — Mrs. Morison," he answered.

Bee flushed more deeply yet. Then she turned
mischievously to Mrs. Morison.

" Grandmother," she said, " it seems that Mr.
Wynne came to see you and not me."

The old lady greeted him kindly.

" I am glad to see you looking so well, Mr. Wynne,"
she said. " I hope that your arm does not trouble
you at all."

" Not at all. I was too well taken care of at Brookfield."

Mrs. Staggchase laughed, spreading out her hands.

" There," said she gayly, " you see! He has only
been in my hands a few weeks, but I call that a very
pretty speech."

" He probably has a natural gift for pleasing
speeches," Berenice remarked meaningly.

Maurice crimsoned, but his education had not proceeded far enough for him to have any reply.

" Well, take him away, Bee, and give him tea or
gossip. I want to talk to your grandmother about old
friends, and you young people won't understand."

" He may have tea if he is tractable." responded
Bee. " We are evidently not appreciated, Mr. Wynne.
Will you ring the bell over there, please."

He did as he was directed, and then followed her to
the tea-table at a little distance from the fire. He was
full of a troubled joy, the mingled delight of being
with her and the consciousness that he had firmly determined in his own mind that he had no right to show
her his feelings. He said to himself that he could
bear anything else better than that she should think
of him as a fortune-hunter. Her wealth loomed between them as a wall which it were dishonorable even
to attempt to scale. His brain was busy phrasing
things which he longed to say to her, words seemed to
seethe in his head, yet he found himself strangely
tongue-tied and awkward. When most of all he desired to appear at his ease, he was most completely
uncomfortable and self-conscious.

A servant came with the tea, and he was able to
cover to some extent his uneasiness by serving the
ladies. When this was done, and he sat nervously

stirring his own cup, he found himself searching his
mind in vain for those things which it would be safe
to say. His brain was full of things which must not
be said. He could think only of things which it was
not safe to utter ; and his discomfiture increased as
he saw Miss Morison watching him with a half-veiled
smile.

" By the way," she said at length, when the silence
was becoming too marked, " I fulfilled your request."

" My request ? " he echoed, unable to remember
that he had made any.

" Yes. Have you forgotten that you came to ask
me " —

He put out his hand impulsively.

" Please don't ! " he interrupted. " It is bad enough
to remember what an unmitigated idiot I was without
the humiliation of thinking that you remember it too."

" I remember," she responded, with a sparkle in her
eye, " that you did not seem to relish the mission on
which you were sent. However, I accepted the intention, and I have promised the men a continuance of
their stipends." Her face grew suddenly grave, and
she added : "I can't joke about it, though. I really
did it because Cousin Anna would have wished it."

They were silent now because they had come so near
a solemn subject that neither of them cared to speak.
The thoughts of Maurice went back to the day he had
come to do the errand of Father Frontford, and his
cheek grew hot.

" I hope you will believe," he said eagerly, " that I
had really no idea of how very ill your cousin was.
She seemed so well when I saw her that it was all unreal to me. I wish I could tell you how sorry I have
been for you. I have thought of you."

She raised her eyes to his, and they exchanged a look in which there was more than sympathy. Maurice felt her glance so deeply that for the moment he forgot all else. Obstacles no longer existed. He was looking into the eyes of the woman he loved, and thrilling as if her heart was questioning his. It seemed to him that her very self was demanding how deep and how true had been his thought of her in her time of sorrow. He bent forward, sounding her gaze with his, trying to convey all the unspoken words which jostled in his brain. Her eyes fell before his burning look, and her head drooped. The room was darkening with the coming dusk, and they sat at some distance from the others. He laid his hand on hers.

" Berenice ! " he whispered.

She rose as if she had not noted.

" Don't you think it is time for lights, grand-mother ? " she said in a voice so unemotional that it sent a chill to his heart.

" It is certainly time for us to be going home," Mrs. Staggchase interposed, rising in her turn.

And far into the night Maurice Wynne vexed his soul with vain endeavors to decide what Berenice meant by her treatment of him.

XXXIV

WHAT TIME SHE CHANTED

Hamlet, iv. 7

THE grief which Philip felt over the apostasy of
Maurice overshadowed for a time every other feeling.
He sorrowed for his friend, praying and yearning,
searching his heart to discover whether his own influence or example had helped to bring about this
lamentable fall; he turned over in his mind plans for
bringing the wanderer back to the fold; he ceased to
think about the coming election, and thought of his
ill-starred love hardly otherwise than as a possible
sin which had helped perhaps to lead to this catastrophe.

Affection between two men is much more likely to
be mutual than that between two women. Men are
more generally frank in their likes and dislikes, they
are as a rule more accustomed to feel at liberty to be
open and to please themselves in their familiarities;
and it seems to be true that men are more constant in
friendship, as women are said to be more constant in
love. Affection between women, moreover, is apt to
be founded upon circumstance, while that between
men is more often a matter of character.

The fondness of Philip and Maurice for each other
was of long standing; it had arisen out of the mutual
needs of their natures, and was part of their growth.
Philip was the one most dependent upon his friend,
however, and now he felt as if he were torn away

from his chief support. He reasoned with himself that he had been letting affection for his friend come between him and Heaven; he tried to feel that Providence had interfered to break down his idol; yet to all this he could not but answer that Maurice had been always a help, and that it was impossible to believe that Providence would accomplish his good by the hurt of his benefactor. He did assure himself that his suffering was the will of a higher power, and as such to be acquiesced in and improved to his spiritual good. If the voice of his secret heart, that inner self from which we hide our faces and whose words we so obstinately refuse to hear, cried out against the cruelty of this discipline, he but closed his ears more resolutely. To listen would be to yield to temptation. He would not see Maurice; he hardly permitted himself to read his friend's letters. He answered these notes by fervid appeals to the wanderer to return to the fold, to be reconciled with the church, to take up again the priesthood he had discarded. Hard as it was, he still strove for what he felt to be the other's lasting good.

Lent ended, and the gladness of Easter came upon the land; the spring showed traces of its secret presence by a thousand intangible and delicate signs in sky, and air, and earth: there was everywhere a stir and a quickening, a blitheness which belongs to the vernal season only. Philip felt all these things by the growing sharpness of the contrast between his mood and that of the world without. His melancholy and unrest seemed to him to grow every day more intense and unbearable.

That Father Frontford did not more fully realize Philip's condition was probably due to the near

approach of the election.   As the time for the convention drew near, the supporters of the rival candidates
redoubled their exertions; there was hurrying to and
fro, writing of letters and continued consultation, all
of which inevitably distracted the attention of the
Father. He did perceive, however, that Philip was
troubled, and nothing could have been more tender or
considerate than his attitude. He did not talk to
Ashe about Maurice, but he contrived to make his
deacon understand that no blame was attached to him
for the apostasy of Wynne. Philip found a new
affection for the Father springing in his heart, so
soothing, so winning was the sympathy of the Superior.

The days passed on until the convention actually
assembled. Philip was feverishly anxious; yet he
persistently assured himself that he had no doubt in
regard to the result. He felt that the end had been
accomplished by the work which had already been
done; and the convention itself seemed to him somewhat unreal and unmeaning. It had in his mind not
much more than the function of announcing a result
which he felt to have been arrived at already in the
canvassing of lists of delegates in which he had taken
part at Mrs. Wilson's. Until the thing was formally
announced, however, it was impossible to be at ease.

The first day of the convention was mainly one of
organization and of preparation. Business was disposed of and all made ready for the election of the
morrow. Philip went into the convention in the hour
of recreation. He tried to be interested in matters
which he assured himself were of real importance;
yet he found his memory dwelling on Maurice and
the times they had talked of this convention. Even

his efforts to fix his thoughts on the election itself could not drive his friend from his mind. He walked home at last, saying passionately that he had ceased to care for the church, for its welfare, its fate; that he had cared only for his own selfish desires and interests. He looked back upon the convention which he had left, and saw mentally a picture of men who seemed strange and remote, concerned with matters which he did not understand, in which he had no interest. He felt completely out of key with everything; he longed for Maurice with unspeakable pain. He had rested on Maurice. In every mental crisis he had depended upon finding his friend at hand, sympathetic, strong, responsive; he had come to be as one unable to stand alone. It seemed impossible for him to go on longer without seeing his fellow, his friend, his confidant, his support. The convention and the Clergy House alike became misty and accidental in comparison with his own desperate need of Maurice.

A couple of blocks from the House he was joined by a fellow deacon.

" I say, Ashe," was the other's greeting, " did you ever know anything so unfortunate as that Wilson letter ? "

Philip turned upon him an uncomprehending face.

" What is the Wilson letter ? " he inquired absently.

" What ? Don't you know about it ? I saw you at the convention."

" I was there a little while; but there was nothing said about a letter, that I heard."

" Oh, there has been nothing said about it in the convention, but they say it will turn the scale."

" But what is it ? "

" It's a letter Mrs. Wilson — Mrs. Chauncy Wilson, you know — you must know who she is ? "

" Yes ; I know her."

" Well, this is a letter that she wrote to a rector in the western part of the State, — his name was Briggs or Riggs, or something of that kind. She said that if he did n't vote for Father Frontford she could get him out of his parish."

" What ! " exclaimed Philip. " She could n't have written such a thing ! "

" There's a fac-simile of it in the hands of every member of the convention."

" But how did it get out ? "

" They say," answered the other, eager to impart his information, " that a man named Rangely had it printed, and sent it around. I don't know who he is, but he 's a newspaper man, I believe."

" I know who he is," Philip returned, " but I thought he was a friend of Mrs. Wilson. I 've seen him at her house. How did he get the letter ? "

" I 'm sure I don't know ; but he had it. He 's written a circular to go with it. He says that that is the way the friends of Father Frontford are trying to secure the election. There is a great deal of feeling about it."

" But will it make much difference ? "

" They say that it will turn the scale. There are a number of men who were in doubt, and this is likely to be enough to insure Mr. Strathmore's election."

" What a disgraceful trick ! " Philip cried indignantly. " Father Frontford is n't responsible for what Mrs. Wilson did. Besides, it does n't change the real facts of the case. It does n't make Father Frontford any the less the right man."

" Of course it does n't," was the reply. " But I 've been talking with my uncle. He 's a delegate from Springfield. He says that he 's sure it will get Mr. Strathmore elected."

The news gave Philip a shock, but it seemed impossible that a trivial, outside trick like this could alter the conscientious vote of the candidates. He was uneasy, but he seemed to have lost all vital care about the election, and even this disconcerting event did not greatly change his feeling. He reproached himself that he cared so little; yet his personal misery so absorbed him that his thoughts wandered even from this new cause for self-reproach.

After supper that night he was summoned to the Father Superior.

" I wish you to do an errand for me," Father Frontford said. " I presume that you have heard of the publication of Mrs. Wilson's letter. It may do harm, and whatever happens I want her to know that I do not blame her. She acted unwisely, no doubt; but her intention was good. Besides, I really became responsible when I trusted so much to her judgment. I shall be happier if I know that she is not thinking that I feel disposed to be vexed with her."

The tone in which this was said was too sincere for Philip to doubt that the Father uttered his true feeling. He looked into the face of the other, and was struck by the complete weariness, almost exhaustion, which marked it. He went on his way haunted by those deep-set eyes, so full of pain, of fatigue, and, it seemed to Philip, of self-reproach.

Mrs. Wilson was not at home, so that Philip had only to leave the note. He turned back, crossing the Public Garden in the soft evening. Overhead was

the mysterious darkness, quivering with stars. The
air was full of suggestions of advancing spring. He
felt in his veins an unreasonable restlessness, a stirring as of sap in the tree, a longing for that which
he could not define. He heard around him gay voices
and laughter, for the night was warm, and people
were sitting about on the benches or strolling along
the walks. He began to examine the groups he
passed, looking with a curious eye at the couples
sitting side by side in friendly or in loving companionship. He felt so utterly alone, and all these
about him were mated. The tones of women sounded
soft and sweet in his ear. Stray verses of Canticles
began to float through his mind as wisps of vapor
drift across the sky before the fog comes in from the
sea. He repeated the collect for the day, and through
it all he was thinking that it was possible to walk past
the house of Mrs. Fenton. The difference in the time
of his reaching the Clergy House would not be so
great as to attract notice; he might see her shadow
on the curtain; it was not probable, of course, but it
was possible; in any case, he should feel near to her.
He walked more quickly, and as he did so he heard
the notes of a guitar, and then the sound of a girl
singing. It was only the hard, coarse voice of a
street-singer, and the language was Italian. He did
not understand the words, but the music was seductive, the night of spring, star-lit and fragrant with
intangible odors, quickened his sense. Constantly
recurring in the song, as if set there for his ear, he
understood the magic word " *amóre, amóre*," strung
like beads down the necklace warm on a girl's bosom.
Surely he had a right to be human. All the world
had leave to love. He had given Mrs. Fenton up;

she was only a memory; he should never speak to her again; it could not be wrong simply to walk past her house. He had lost even his friend; if this poor act were a comfort, it surely was not sin. "*Amóre — amóre,*" sang the Italian girl over there in the warm, palpitating night. He had consecrated his love as an offering on the altar; surely he need not therefore deny it.

He had gained Beacon Street, and was walking rapidly, his cheeks hot and flushed, his heart on fire. Far down a neighboring street he heard the approach of a band of the Salvation Army. They were singing shrilly, with beating of tambourines and clanging of cymbals, a vulgar, raucous tune, redolent of animal vigor and of coarse passions, a tune as unholy as the rites of a pagan festival. As he stood still as with flaring torches they drew nearer. The blare of the brass, the vibrant, tingling clangor of the cymbals, the high, penetrating voices of the women, the barbaric rhythm of the air, made him in his sensitive mood tremble like a tense string. He shivered with excitement, nervous tears coming into his eyes so thickly that he turned away blinded, and stumbled against a man who was passing.

"My good brother," exclaimed a rich, Irish voice, jovial, yet not without dignity, "you don't see where you are going."

Philip recognized instantly the tones of the priest whom he had met at the North End; and without even apologizing he answered with an overwhelming sense of how true were the words in a figurative sense : —

"No, I cannot see."

The other was evidently impressed by the manner

in which the reply was given, for instead of passing on he stopped and examined Ashe closely.

" Can I do anything for you?" he asked.

" Providence has sent you to me, I think," Philip returned. Then he put his hand on the arm of the stranger, bending forward in his eagerness. " Where do you live?" he asked. " May I come to see you to-morrow afternoon? It may be that you can tell me where I am going."

XXXV

HOWEVER much or little the ill-starred letter of
Mrs. Wilson may have had to do with it, the fact
was that both houses of the convention elected Mr.
Strathmore by majorities sufficiently large to satisfy
even his friends. The lay delegates were more generally in his favor than the clergy, which circumstance
gave for a time some shadowy hope to the high-church
party that the House of Bishops might refuse to
confirm the election; but whatever consolation was
derived from such an expectation was of short dura-
tion. The election was ratified, and almost immediately preparations were begun for the consecration of
the new bishop.

Father Frontford remarked to an interviewer at
the close of the convention that "it was not the least
happy of the incidents of the election that Mr. Strathmore had been chosen by a majority so decided, since
it indicated clearly the wishes of the church;" and
he used his influence to prevent any attempt to induce the House of Bishops to oppose the choice of the
convention. As soon as the matter was settled he
called upon Mr. Strathmore and offered his congratulations in person.

"It is true that I would have prevented your election had I been able," he said frankly; "but that
was entirely a question of church polity. I hardly

need say how complete is my confidence in your sincerity and your ability."

"Brother," Mr. Strathmore replied, with that smile whose charm no man could resist, "I thank you for coming, and I thank you for your generous words. One thing we may be sure of and be grateful to God for. The church is certainly too great and too stable to be shaken by the mistakes of any one man. If we differ sometimes about the best way of showing it outwardly, we at least are one in wishing the best interests of religion and of humanity."

Father Frontford had had some difficulty in soothing Mrs. Wilson after the election. She declared vehemently that the House of Bishops should not confirm Mr. Strathmore.

"I will go to New York myself," she announced. "I know I can manage the Metropolitan. If he 's on our side we can prevent that infidel Strathmore from getting a majority."

It is possible that Father Frontford, with all his decision, might have been unable to prevent some demonstration, but Dr. Wilson quietly remarked to his wife : —

"Elsie, we 've had enough of this bishop racket. I 'm devilish tired of the whole thing, and I wish you 'd find a new amusement."

"But, Chauncy," she responded, "think how maddening it is to be beaten! And as for that Fred Rangely, I could dig out his eyes and pour in hot lead!"

Wilson chuckled gleefully.

"You played your private theatricals just a little prematurely. It was devilish clever of him to get back at you that way ; but that letter has made news-

paper talk enough about you, and you 'd better drop
church politics. Is n't it time to get your stud into
shape for the summer?"

Elsie shrugged her shoulders.

"I don't know. I hate to give it up while there 's
a fighting chance. The campaign has been a lot of
fun. However, I suppose you are right. You have a
dreadfully aggravating way of being. Besides, I am
pretty tired of parsons, and horses wear better."

She therefore managed to secure a visiting English
duke with a characteristically shady reputation, gave
the most brilliant dinner of the season in his honor,
and retired to her country place in a blaze of glory;
finding some consolation for all her disappointments
in the purchase of a couple of new racers with pedi-
grees far longer than that of the duke.

Easter came that year almost at its earliest, and it
was therefore found possible to have the consecration
of the new bishop in June. To it were assembled all
the dignitaries of the church. Boston for a couple
of days overflowed with men in ecclesiastical garb;
and if the general public was not deeply stirred by
the importance of the event, all those connected with
it were full of interest and excitement.

Mrs. Wilson surprised her friends by returning to
town and reopening her house for the consecration
week. She announced to her husband her intention
of doing this as they sat in the library at their country
place while Dr. Wilson smoked his final pipe for the
night. They had been dining out, and had driven
home in the moonlight, chatting of the people they
had seen and the gossip they had heard. Elsie was
in high spirits, amusing her husband by her satirical
remarks. At last she said : —

" I hope, Chauncy, you won't mind if I go off for a week."

" Off for a week? Where are you going?"

" Into town to open the house for the consecration of the great Bishop Strathmore."

" Well," her husband said, laughing, "I like your grit. If you can't win, you won't show the white feather."

She laughed in turn, as gleefully and as musically as a child.

" I'm going for revenge."

"Oh, that's it. Is Rangely to die?"

" Pooh, it isn't Rangely. He's too insignificant. I can snub him any time. It's better fun than that."

" Well, let's hear."

" You know that Marion Delegass is to end her season with a week in Boston."

" Well? You are not going to Boston to see her, are you? You've seen her in Paris and New York enough to last, I should think."

" Oh, no; I'm going to meet her."

" Marion Delegass, the most notoriously disreputable actress even on the French stage? Well, she'll be a change from your parsons."

" Luckily her last week is the week of the consecration of the heathen."

" Is she to take part?"

" Don't be flippant. I am to give Mlle. Delegass a luncheon. I've arranged it by letter. By one of the most curious coincidences in the world it comes on the very day of the consecration."

" That is amusing, but I don't see that it's much of a revenge."

" No?" Elsie responded demurely, casting down

her eyes. " I am so sorry that Mrs. Strathmore can't come."

" Mrs. Strathmore? You did n't ask her ! "

" Why, of course, Chauncy, I wanted to show that I had n't any ill feeling against the family of my bishop."

" To meet Marion Delegass ? "

" Of course. I thought it would liven Mrs. Strathmore up a little. She always reminded me of watergruel with not enough salt in it."

Dr. Wilson burst into a roar of laughter, leaning back in his chair and slapping his knee.

" Marion Delegass ! Why she 's left more husbands and lovers behind her than a sailor has wives ! Marion Delegass and that prig in petticoats ! Well, Elsie, you do beat the devil ! "

" Am I to understand that you know His Satanic Majesty well enough to speak with authority ? " she laughed. " What do you think now of my revenge ? "

" I don't exactly see where the revenge comes in. She won't come to the lunch."

" Come ? Oh, no; thank Heaven, she won't come. She 'd be like a death's head in a punch-bowl. She won't come, but she 'll tell that she was invited. She 'll be too furious not to tell; and everybody will know that I asked her. That 's all I care about."

Wilson laughed again.

" Well," he said again, " you are the cheekiest and the most amusing woman in town. You 'll shock all your relations, but they must be getting hardened to that by this time."

Whether the relatives were on this occasion more or less shocked than upon others was not a question to which Elsie devoted any especial thought. She gave

her luncheon, and all the world knew that she had
invited Mrs. Strathmore to meet Marion Delegass
on the day of the consecration. Mrs. Strathmore
was so enraged that she talked flames and fury, even
going so far as to wonder whether there were not
some possibility of excommunication; so that her tor-
mentor was enchanted with the success of her revenge.

The consecration took place on a beautiful June
day, and was as imposing a function in its line as
Boston had ever seen. Trinity was crowded to overflowing, and if the ceremony was less imposing than
would have been the induction of a Catholic bishop,
it was impressive and dignified. The sunlight filtering through the windows of stained glass splashed
fantastic colors over the long surpliced train which
wound through the aisles down to the chancel, singing processionals of joyous hope; the air was full of
the sense of solemn meaning; the organ pealed; the
noble words of the fine old ritual spoke to the hearts
of the hearers, and carried their message of a faith
which took hold upon the unseen. Above all the
circumstance, the form, the conventions, the creeds,
rose the spirit of the worshipers, uplifted by the
thrilling realization of the outpouring of the soul of
humanity before the unknown eternal.

Maurice had accompanied Mrs. Staggchase and
Miss Morison to the ceremony. It had been his
impulse not to go, but his cousin urged it, and it
needed little to induce him to go to any place where
Berenice was, even though it were a church. He
went with some secret misgiving lest the service
should move him more than he wished; but to his
satisfaction he found that while he felt æsthetic plea-

sure, he was inclined to be critical about the doctrine
of the ritual. His satisfaction, he reflected, would
have been thought amusing by Mrs. Staggchase; but
it at least assured him that he had not been mistaken
in his mental attitude toward the creed he had discarded.

The thing which most moved him was the sight of
Philip among the surpliced deacons in the procession. Philip's face seemed to him thinner and paler
than of old; he blamed himself that he had not disregarded his friend's injunction, and insisted upon
seeing him. To his repeated requests Philip had returned answer that he could not bear the meeting.
Maurice had come at length to feel something almost
of resentment at the wall which this prohibition put
between them; but to-day, seeing the white countenance, he experienced a pang of deep self-reproach.
He reflected how sharply his defection must have
weighed his friend down. He should have tried to
comfort him; at least he should have assured Phil
that in spite of whatever might come his affection
would remain unchanged.

He thought lovingly of the old days when he and
Phil were together, and of the plans they had sometimes made for keeping if possible together even after
they went out into the world to work. He had the impatience of one who has recently put a doctrine by
for the blindness, as it seemed to him, which kept
Phil still in the power of the old superstition; but
with his friend's white face, marked with mental suffering, there to soften him, he dwelt little on this, and
much on his affection for his friend and fellow.

As Maurice brooded, watching Philip moving
slowly down the aisle, Berenice bent forward to take

a book from the rack, and her face came between him
and his friend. The thought of Philip vanished as
a shadow before a sun-burst. He was conscious only
of Berenice, sitting there so near him, her dark eyes
serious with the solemnity of the occasion, her cheeks
tinged with a color so lovely that the lining of a shell
or the petals of a rose were poor things with which to
compare it. He forgot all else, and lost himself in a
delicious, troubled dream of what might be. Surely,
surely she must love him! He could not give her
up; it was not possible that he should not some day
win her. He fixed on her a look so ardent that it
seemed to compel her glance to meet his. The flush
in her cheek deepened, and he reflected with an ex-
ultant thrill that even in the absorption of a time like
this he could reach and move her spirit.

The rest of the service was little to Maurice. He
heard the music, listened now and then to the words
which were being spoken, thought for a moment here
and there upon the strangeness that these people should
be consecrating Mr. Strathmore and not recognizing
in the least that they were assisting at the breaking
down of the church; he gave a little reflection to his
own interview with the new bishop, unable completely
to satisfy himself how far Mr. Strathmore was sincere
and how far simply following out a policy; these and
other matters floated through his mind, but they were
mere trifles on the surface. His real thought was of
Berenice, always of Berenice. The fluttered, troubled
look which he had seen when his gaze had compelled
hers, a look which seemed to him full of confession
of things unutterable, full almost of appeal as if she
realized that she was betraying a feeling that she
feared to own even to herself, this look of a moment

so fleeting clocks could hardly have measured it, filled him with a wild, unreasoning bliss. He did not again try to challenge her eyes. He sat in a dream of happiness; a vague, intangible, ecstatic sense that all was well, that the universe was in tune, and that all things were but ministers of his joy.

When the ceremonial was concluded Mrs. Staggchase went home with Berenice to lunch with Mrs. Morison. Maurice put them into their carriage, feeling that he could not let Berenice go out of his sight. He stood on the curbstone watching the carriage as if it had set out on a voyage to regions unknown and far; then smiling at himself with a realization of what he was doing he turned back to go home himself. As he did so he came face to face with Philip.

XXXVI

THE HEAVY MIDDLE OF THE NIGHT
Measure for Measure, iv. 1

THE mind of Philip Ashe had not become more quiet as time went on, and the day of the consecration found him hesitating between his old life and a new one. Ever since the chance encounter with the Irish priest he had been going almost every afternoon to talk with this new friend, and one by one he had found his doubts about the supremacy of the Roman church fading away. Ashe was of a nature which must rely upon another, and since he was shut off from the companionship of Wynne it was inevitable that he should lean upon this great, hearty, healthy man, who with the possibility of adding a son to the church received him so warmly. Philip's nature, moreover, inclined him strongly toward a church which exercised absolute authority, and in doctrinal points he found himself surprisingly at one with his teacher. Nothing held him back but the force of habit and a natural hesitancy to break away from the faith which he had professed. Undoubtedly his feeling for Father Frontford counted for much; but the fact, that in the months which had preceded the election the Father Superior had been so much absorbed that intimacy between him and his deacons was impossible, had greatly lessened Philip's sense of loyalty to him. Very tenderly and wisely the priest led Ashe on, until he was in very truth a Catholic in all but name.

To his ardent, mystical mind, deeply responsive to the ritual of the older church, the ceremonies of the consecration seemed poor and thin. He craved symbolism and richly suggestive rites. He had been more than once in these latter days to the services of the Catholics, and his imagination came more and more to demand the embodiment in form of the aspirations of his soul. He tried to stifle the disappointment which assailed him as the function proceeded, but it was impossible for him not to realize that the ceremonial of his own faith left him cold and unsatisfied. He missed the warm emotional excitement of the music, the incense, the sonorous Latin, the sumptuous robes, and the romantic associations of the mass.

He felt keenly, moreover, that the man who was being to-day installed as the head of the diocese was of tendencies distinctly opposed to his desires. He mingled with disappointment that Father Frontford had not been chosen a genuine conviction that Strathmore would use his influence to carry church forms toward a worship ever simpler and more bare. He could not wholly smother an almost personal resentment against Strathmore, and a consciousness that it would be always impossible for him to regard the newly consecrated bishop with that respect and veneration due to one holding the office. He reflected that the church must itself be tending toward a dangerous liberalism if it were possible for this thing to have come about. He listened dully and confusedly to the service until the time came when the bishop elect made his vows. He heard the strong voice of Strathmore, vibrant, deliberate, penetrating, repeat with slow solemnity the promise of conformity and obedience to the doctrine and worship of the church. The words tingled through the mind of Ashe like an electric shock. To his excited feeling Strathmore was perjuring himself in the name of God, since it was impossible to feel that the new bishop followed or intended to follow either. He experienced a wild impulse to spring to his feet and protest; he wondered if he only of all the persons in this crowded church recognized the shocking irreligion of that vow. He reflected that in the Catholic communion it would have been impossible for popular suffrage to raise to the bishopric a man like this, a heretic and a perjurer.

The service went on, and Philip sat in a sort of dull stupor. He could not think clearly; he was only dreamily conscious of what was going on about him. The music, the prayers, the solemn words were to him so remote from his true self that he seemed to hear them through a veil of distance. He had ceased to have part in this rite; he ceased even to heed it.

Like one who is lost in idle musing, one who concerns himself with trifling thoughts lest he realize too poignantly a bitter actuality, Philip sat in his place, now and then glancing about the great church. Changing his position a little, he saw the face of Mrs. Fenton. He dwelt on it with mingled grief and pain. More and more he became absorbed in gazing, while love and anguish swelled in his heart. He forgot where he was; he saw her only; he felt only her presence in all the throng. His passion seemed to him greater than ever. He did not for an instant think of her as of one who could or would requite his affection; or even as one who belonged to his future life. He was filled with a sense of the completeness of his devotion to her; he felt that he had loved her more than Heaven itself; but he felt also that he was bid-

ding her good-by. He had not definitely said to himself that a change was before him ; yet looking at her
he felt it. The shadow of an eternal farewell seemed
to be over him. He was benumbed with suffering ;
he drank in her face greedily ; he seemed to himself
to be imprinting for the last time upon his memory
that which was dearer to him than life, yet which he
was to see no more.

The service ended at last, and once more the long
procession of which he was a part slowly made its way
out of the church. Philip found himself in the vestry
in the midst of a crowd of ecclesiastics from which
he extricated himself with all possible speed ; and got
once more into the open air. He threaded his way
among the groups standing on the sidewalks chatting
and hindering him. Suddenly a man turned close to
him, and Maurice stood before his face.

" Phil ! " he heard the joyful voice of his friend cry.
" My dear old Phil, how glad I am to see you ! "

The sound was like a charm which breaks a spell.
For the instant all else was forgotten in the pleasure
of being again with his heart-fellow. He could have
flung his arms about the other's neck and kissed him,
so keen was his delight. The doubts and distractions
which a moment earlier had bewildered and tortured
him vanished before Wynne's greeting as a mist before
a brisk and wholesome wind. He seized the hand
held out to him, and clasped it almost convulsively.

" Maurice ! " was all that he could say.

" I really ought not to recognize you," Maurice
said, in a great hearty voice which sounded to Philip
strangely unfamiliar. " Why in the world have you
refused to see me ? I assure you I 'm not contagious."

They were close to a group waiting on the sidewalk,

and with instinctive shrinking Ashe led the way down
the street. Soon they were walking in much the old
fashion, and Philip left his friend's question unan-
swered until they had gone some distance. Then he
turned with a smile not a little wistful.

"Certainly it was not because I did not long to see
you," he said.

Maurice smiled, but Philip sensitively felt a veiled
impatience in his tone as he replied : —

"Oh, Phil, if I could only get the ascetic nonsense
out of you ! "

Ashe could not answer. He could not reprove his
friend after the separation which to him had been
so long and so sorrowful, and he had a secret feeling
that they were to be more entirely divided. The pair
walked in silence a moment, and then Wynne spoke.

"Well, I'll not talk on forbidden subjects ; but,
surely, Phil, you are not going to throw me over entirely. I wouldn't drop you, no matter what happened."

"I'm not throwing you over," Philip answered with
a choking in his throat. "I would — Oh, Maurice,"
he broke out, interrupting himself, "it isn't for want
of caring for you, but if I am ever to help you, I
must keep my own faith. I have been so troubled
and so — There," he broke off again, "let us talk
of something else."

He felt that Maurice was studying him carefully.

"Phil, old fellow, you are hysterically incoherent.
What's the matter with you ? It can't be all my
going off. Can't you come home with me, and talk
it out ? "

Ashe shook his head. The more he was touched
and moved by the affection of his friend, the more he

shrank from him. This tender comradeship seemed to him the most subtile of temptations. He feared, moreover, lest he might reveal to Maurice too much of what was in his heart.

"Not now," he said. "I must go home at once."

"Then I'll walk along with you," rejoined the other. "I do wish you'd let me help you. You are evidently all played out physically, and half an eye could see that you've something on your mind. Is it the bishop?"

"That has troubled me a good deal," Ashe returned, feeling a relief in being able to say this truthfully.

"Well, Phil, if you worry yourself sick over what you can't help, what strength will you have for the things that you can do? I'm glad it isn't all my going that has brought you to this, for you look positively ill. I wish you'd get sick-leave, and go off a while."

Ashe shook his head again. He felt that if Maurice went on talking to him he should lose his self-command. He must get away; yet he could not bear to hurt his friend. He turned toward Maurice and held out his hand.

"Dear Maurice," he said, "don't be hurt; but I can't talk with you. I must be alone. I am upset, and not myself. It is not that I don't trust you, you know; but there are things that a man has to fight out for himself."

The other stopped, and regarded him closely.

"All right, Phil," he said. "I understand. If you've got a fight with the devil on hand nobody can help you. I only wish I could."

He wrung the hand of Ashe, and added:

"Good-by. I'm always fond of you, old fellow;

and you know that when there is a place that I can help there's nothing I would n't do for you."

Ashe tried to answer, but he could not command his voice. He could only return the warm pressure of Wynne's hand, and then, miserable and hopeless, go on his way to his conflict with the arch fiend.

Once in his chamber Ashe fastened the door, drew down the shades, and lighted the gas. He laid aside his cassock, and loosened his clothing so that his breast lay bare. He took from a drawer a little crucifix of iron. This he placed across the chimney of the gas-burner, and watched it until it was heated. Then he seized it with his fingers, but the stinging pain made him drop it to the floor. He bared his breast, wildly calling aloud to heaven, and flung himself down upon the crucifix, pressing the hot iron to his naked bosom. A fierce shudder convulsed him; he extended his arms in the form of a cross, and with closed eyes lay still an instant. A horrible odor filled the room; great drops of sweat dripped from his forehead; his teeth were set in his lower lip. For a moment he remained motionless; then in uncontrollable agony he writhed over upon his back and fainted.

The return to consciousness was a terrible sensation of misery and weakness. He was heart-sick and racked in body and mind. Feebly he rose, and gathered his scattered senses. Then with trembling he got to his feet. His wound gave him bitter agony, but the bodily pain made him smile. He took from the same drawer a picture of the Madonna, and knelt before it with clasped hands. His doubts, his passion, his self-reproaches, danced like demons before his distracted brain. The troubled, stormy thoughts of his distraught mind merged insensibly into prayers. He put aside the clothing and showed to the Virgin Mother his wounded breast, scarred and bleeding. He looked into her face with murmured words of contrition, of imploring, of faith. A gracious sense of her womanly pity, of her heavenly tenderness, stole soothingly over him. He seemed almost to feel cool hands on his hot forehead; it was as if in a moment more the heavens might open and grant to him the beatific vision. There came over him a wave of joy which was beyond words. The longing of his soul for the woman he loved was merged in the desire of his heart which yearned toward the blessed Virgin Mother. His prayers became more glowing, more ecstatic, until in a rapture of adoration, of bliss, of passion, he fell prostrate before the divine image, crying out with all his soul: —

"Thou ever blessed one! To thee I give myself! 'O thou, to the arch of whose eyebrow the new moon is a slave,' receive me, save me!"

He had no sense of incongruity to make the phrase unseemly or ludicrous. It was to him the formal transfer of his deepest allegiance from an earthly love to a heavenly. He had at last found peace.

XXXVII

THIS IS NOT A BOON

IT was Mrs. Wilson who was the immediate means
of bringing about an understanding between Maurice
and Berenice. Mrs. Wilson was never so occupied
that she was not able to attend to any new thing
which might turn up, and her interest in the spring
races did not prevent her from having a hand in the
affairs of the lovers. While she was in town attending to the luncheon for Marion Delegass she dined
with Mrs. Staggchase, and Maurice took her down.

"I understand that you are a renegade," she remarked vivaciously as soon as they were seated. "I
wonder you dare look me in the face."

"Because you are the church?" he demanded.

"Certainly not now that that Strathmore is bishop,"
she retorted, tossing her head. "However, I always
said that you were too good to be wasted in a cassock."

"Thank you. What would you say if I made such
a reflection on the clergy?"

"Oh, I 've no patience with the clergy!" she declared. "They bore me to death. There 's that
solemn-faced friend of yours, Mr. Ashe — his name
ought to be Ashes! — he actually lectured me on my
worldliness! *My* worldliness, if you please, and I
working myself to a shadow for the election of Father
Frontford!"

" He has imagination, you see," Maurice suggested, smiling.

" Now you are sneering, Mr. Wynne. I shall talk to the man on the other side."

She was good as her word, and left Maurice to devote himself to the lady on his right. He had the American adaptability, and a couple of months had sufficed to make him reasonably at ease at a dinner. The continuous delight he felt in his freedom, moreover, inspired him with an inclination to be frank and communicative, so that if he did not talk like the conventional man of the world, he managed not to sit silent. His neighbor to-night was Mrs. Thayer Kent, and he chatted easily with her about the West, where for a couple of years she had been living on a ranch. Something in Mrs. Kent's talk reminded him of Berenice, and he sighed inwardly that the latter's mourning prevented her from going out. As if the thought had been spoken aloud, Mrs. Wilson recalled herself to his attention by saying in his ear : —

" It is such a pity Berenice Morison is n't here. Have you seen her since the Mardi Gras ball ? "

" Yes," he answered, turning quickly, and vexed to feel himself flush. " I saw her yesterday at the consecration."

" Did you go ? How immoral ! I stayed at home and gave a luncheon for Marion Delegass."

" So I heard ; but everybody had n't such a moral thing as that to do."

" Oh, no ; very likely not. By the way, you have never apologized for deserting me in the middle of the service that night."

" I had to take care of that girl. She fainted."

" Oh, you did ? Who was she ? What did you do

with her? However, I don't care. It's none of my business. I wonder, though, what sort of a story you'd have told Berenice if she'd been there."

Wynne was too confused to answer this sally, although he wanted to say something about the cruelty of taking him into the ball-room. His confusion increased Mrs. Wilson's amusement.

"I think I should like to be in at the death," she said. "She is coming down to stay with me next week. Come down and make love to her. I won't tell about the girl you carried out of church in your arms."

More and more disconcerted and self-conscious, Maurice could only stammer that Mrs. Wilson flattered him if she supposed that Miss Morison would tolerate any love-making on his part.

"You are adorable when you blush like that," was the reply which he got. "I have almost a mind to set you to make love to me. However, that wouldn't be fair. I will take it out in seeing you and her. You must surely come down."

Maurice regarded the invitation as merely part of Mrs. Wilson's badinage, but in due time it was formally repeated by note. He opened the letter at the breakfast table, and was advised by his cousin to accept.

"Mrs. Wilson," she commented, "is like a banjo, more exciting than refined, but she isn't bad-hearted. She has the old Boston blood and traditions behind her."

"They are sometimes rather far behind," interpolated Mr. Staggchase dryly. "She wasn't a Beauchester, you know. However, she has her ancestors safe in their graves so that they can't escape her."

Mrs. Staggchase smiled good-naturedly at the little fling at her own family pretensions.

"You are wicked this morning, Fred," was her reply. "Elsie is something of a sport on the ancestral tree; but she is worth visiting. Berenice Morison is going down there sometime soon. Perhaps she will be there with you, Maurice."

"I thought," Mr. Staggchase observed, "that old Mrs. Morison did n't approve of Mrs. Wilson."

"Nobody approves of Elsie," was Mrs. Staggchase's calm reply. "I 'm sure I don't; but after all she is a sort of cousin of Berenice, and she can't very well refuse to visit her. Really, there is nothing bad about Elsie. She is startling, and she certainly does things which are bad form. That 's half of it because she married as she did."

Nothing more was said, and Maurice kept his own counsel in regard to the fact that he knew that Miss Morison was to be his fellow-guest. He was full of wild hopes. He reproached himself that he was wrong to forget that Berenice was rich and he was poor; yet not for all his reproaches could he keep himself from feeling Mrs. Wilson had not seemed to see any insurmountable obstacle to his wooing; that she had appeared rather to be ready to help his suit. He must not, of course, try to win Berenice; yet he was going to Mrs. Wilson's to meet her, to be with her, to revel in the delicious pleasure of hoping, of fearing, of loving.

The house of the Wilsons at Beverly Farms was on a bluff overlooking the sea. It was reached by a long avenue winding through pines mingled with birches and rowan trees; and stood in a clearing where all the day and all the night the sound

of the waves on the cliff answered the whispering of
the wind in the pine-tops. The broad piazzas of the
house looked out over the sea, and gave views of
the islands off shore, the ever-changing water, the
beautiful curves of the sea marge, now high with
defiant rocks, and now falling into sandy beaches. A
level lawn, velvety and green, stretched from the
house to the edge of the cliff, with here and there a
rustic seat or a century plant stiff and arrogant in
its lonely exile from warmer climes.

On this piazza Maurice found himself, just before
dinner on the evening of his arrival, walking up and
down with Berenice. It was still cool enough to
make the exercise grateful.

"It is so delightful to have the weather warm
enough to be out of doors without being all bundled
up," she said, looking over the sea, cold green and
gray in the declining light.

"The water does n't look very warm," Maurice responded, following her gaze.

"No, it is n't exactly summer yet," she replied
lightly. "Do you know," she added, turning to meet
his eyes, "I can't help thinking how different this
is from the last time we were together away from
Boston."

"When we were at Brookfield?"

"Yes."

"It is different; more different to me than you can
have any idea of. Then I was a cog in a machine;
now I am my own master."

They walked to the end of the piazza, turned, and
came down again. They were facing the light now,
and her face shone with the pale glow of the declining
day. In her black dress, with a soft shawl thrown

about her, she was dazzling; and Maurice found it difficult not to take her in his arms then and there.

"It must have been a strange feeling," she observed thoughtfully, "to know that you were not master of your own movements, but had to do as you were told, whether you approved of it or not."

"Strange," he echoed, a sense of slavery coming over him which was far stronger than anything he had felt while the bondage lasted, "it was intolerable!"

"Yet you endured it?" she returned, regarding him curiously.

"Yes, I endured it. In the first place, I thought that it was my duty; and in the second, it was not so hard until I had seen"—

"Well, until you had seen?"—

"Until I had seen you, I was going to say."

Berenice flushed, and tossed her head.

"You have caught a pretty trick of paying compliments, Mr. Wynne."

"No," he answered with gravity, "I have only the mistaken temerity to say the truth."

She regarded him with a mocking light in her deep, velvety eyes.

"And is it the truth that you have given up your religion because you have seen me?"

Maurice wondered afterward how he looked when she sped this shaft, for he saw her shrink and pale. She even stammered some sort of an apology; but he did not heed it. Although he was sure that he should sooner or later have come to the same conclusion whether he had met Berenice or not, he knew in his secret heart that there was in her words some savor at least of truth. He felt their bitterness to his

heart's core, and could only stand speechless, re-
proaching her with his glance. If they were true it
was cruel for her to say them. He regarded her a
moment, and then turned toward the long French
window by which they had come out of the house.
Berenice recovered herself instantly, and behaved as
if nothing had occurred to mar the serenity of their
talk.

"Yes," she said in an even voice, "you are right.
It is becoming too cold to stay out here."

He held open the window for her, and she swept
past him with a soft rustle and a faint breath of perfume. He did not follow, but drew the window to behind her and continued his promenade alone until he
was summoned to dinner. All his glorious air-castles
had fallen in ruins about his feet, and he rated himself as a fool for having come to Beverly Farms to
meet this girl who evidently flouted him.

The result of this conversation was to bring Maurice
to the resolution to return to town. All the doubts
which had been in his mind arose like ghosts ill ex-
orcised, more tangible and more insistent than ever.
He realized that he had come here fully persuaded in
his secret heart that Miss Morison must love him,
and with the hope of winning some proof of it. Now
he assured himself that she did not care for him and
that he had been a fool to indulge in a dream so
absurd. The obstacles which lay between them
presented themselves to him in a dismal array. He
decided that she could have no respect for him, or she
could not have thrown at him the implication that he
had apostatized from selfish motives. With all the
awful solemnity with which a man deeply in love
examines trifles, he recalled her looks and words,

deciding that he was to her nothing more than the butt of her light contempt; and secretly wondering when and where he should see her again, he decided to leave her forever.

He announced his determination next morning to his hostess. As he could not well give the real reason for his decision, and had no experience in social finesse, he came off badly when asked why he had come to this sudden decision. He could not equivocate; and when Mrs. Wilson asked him point-blank if Berenice had been treating him badly, he could only take refuge in the reply that it was not for him to criticise what Miss Morison chose to do. He persisted in his resolution to return to Boston, feeling obstinately that he could not with dignity remain where he was while Berenice was there. A man of the world would at once have seen the folly of such a course, but Maurice was not a man of the world.

"Well," Mrs. Wilson said, after she had argued with him a little, "you have retained the clerical obstinacy, whatever else you've given up. I am not in the habit of pressing my guests to stay if they are tired of my society. If you choose to go, of course you will go."

"Oh, it is not that I am tired of your society," poor Maurice put in eagerly.

"If I were a man," his hostess went on, "I never would let a woman see that I minded how she treated me. You'd soon have her coming down from her high horse if you showed her that you did n't care."

Maurice flushed painfully. It was impossible for him to talk to Mrs. Wilson about his feeling for Berenice.

"I am afraid that I had better go," he said, with eyes abased.

She regarded him with a mixture of impatience and amusement struggling in her face.

"By all means go," she retorted. "I'll tell Patrick to be at the door in time to take you to the three o'clock train."

She swept away rather brusquely, leaving him disconsolate and uneasy. He felt that he had bungled matters; but before he had time to consider Berenice appeared, and joined him on the piazza.

"I am sent by Mrs. Wilson," she announced, "to ask you to stay."

"You take some pains to clear yourself from the suspicion of having any interest in the matter."

"'I am only a messenger,'" she quoted saucily, seating herself on the rail of the piazza in the sunshine, and looking so piquant that Maurice felt resolution and resentment oozing out of his mind with fatal rapidity.

He flushed at her allusion to his ill-considered interview with her, but he could not for his life be half so indignant as he wished to be.

"Apparently an indifferent messenger. You evidently do not care whether I go or I stay."

"Why should I?"

"Why should Mrs. Wilson?" he retorted, not very well knowing what he was saying.

"Oh, Mrs. Wilson is your hostess. Besides," Bee went on, a delightful look of mischief coming into her face, "she said that she hated to have her plans interfered with, and that you were so handsome that she liked to have you about."

Maurice flushed with a strangely mixed sensation of pleased vanity and irritation, and was angry with himself that he could not receive her jesting unmoved. He bowed stiffly.

"I am very sorry," he returned, "that Mrs. Wilson should be deprived of so beautiful an ornament for her place."

"Then you will go?" Bee demanded, looking at him with mirthful eyes, a glance which so moved him that he could not face it.

"I see no reason why I should remain."

"There certainly can be none if you see none. Well, I want to give you something of yours before you leave us."

She drew from the folds of her handkerchief the little grotesque mask which she had pinned upon her lover's cassock at the Mardi Gras ball. Maurice flushed hotly at the sight.

"You are determined, Miss Morison, to spare me no humiliation in your power."

"Humiliation?" she echoed. "Why, I was humiliating myself. Seriously, Mr. Wynne, I have been ashamed of that performance ever since; and I most sincerely beg your pardon. The humiliation is mine entirely."

"But where in the world," demanded he, a new thought striking him, "did you get the thing? You know I threw it on the table."

"Miss Carstair gave it to Mr. Stanford, and I got it from him."

Maurice came a step nearer.

"Why?" he asked, his voice deepening.

"I — I did n't like to have him keep it," Bee murmured, with downcast face and lower tone.

"Why?" he repeated, so much in earnest that his voice was almost threatening.

She was for a moment more confused than ever, but rallying she held out the mask.

"Oh, that I might tease you with it again!" she laughed.

He took the absurd trinket in his hand.

"It is pretty badly dilapidated," he observed.

"Yes," she said demurely. "I crushed it in the carriage on the way home from the ball. I — I crumpled it up in my hand."

"Why?"

"You keep saying 'why' over and over to me, Mr. Wynne, as if I were on the witness-stand."

"Why?" he persisted.

He had forgotten all the doubts which had beset and hindered him, the scruples he had had about wooing, and the fears that she did not love him. He was conscious only that she was there before him and that he loved her; that her downcast looks seemed to encourage him, so that it was impossible to rest until he knew what was really in her mind. The unspoken message which he had somehow intangibly received from her made him forget everything else. He loved her; he loved her, and a wild hope was beating in his heart and seething in his brain. He could not turn back now; he must know. He saw her grow paler as he looked at her, standing so close that his face was bent down almost over her bent head. He felt that her secret, nay, the crown of life itself, was within his grasp if he did not fail now.

"Why?" he asked still again, hardly conscious that he said it, and yet determined that he would win an answer at whatever cost.

She raised her face slowly, shyly; her eyes were shining.

"Because," she said, hardly above a whisper, "I was determined to convince myself that I hated you. But then" —

Her words faltered, yet he still did not dare to give
way to the warm tide which he felt swelling up from
his heart. His voice softened almost to the tone of
hers.

"But then?"

The crimson stained her beautiful face, and faded.

"I think I — I kissed it," she murmured, so low
that the words were mere phantoms of speech.

He tried to answer, but the words choked in his
throat. He sprang forward, and gathered her into
his arms. It is an art which even deacons may know
by nature.

When the pair came in to luncheon an hour later,
Mrs. Wilson looked up at them, and then without
question turned to a servant.

"You may tell Patrick that we shan't need the
carriage for the station," that sagacious woman said
coolly.

Maurice was both surprised and touched by the
gratification which his engagement gave to his friends.
Mrs. Wilson might be expected to take satisfaction,
since any woman is likely to approve of any match
which she may be allowed to have a hand in pro-
moting; the Staggchases were delighted, and Mrs.
Morison received him with a kindness which moved
him more than anything else. Mrs. Morison treated
him much as if he were her son. She spoke wisely to
him about his future, and she had a word of warning
on the subject of his attitude toward religion.

"My dear Maurice," she said, after she had come
to call him by that name, "let me give you a caution.
The most fanatical belief is less evil than dogmatic
denial. If you are really the agnostic you claim to

be, your very confession that the truth is too great for human grasp binds you to respect the unknown."

" But one cannot respect dogmas," he objected.

" We were not speaking of dogmas," she responded with sweet and dignified earnestness, " but of the mystery of life and the great unknown that incloses it. The great fault and danger of this age is that it is all for breaking down. It reforms abuses and improves away old errors; but it seems to forget the need of providing something to take the place of what it clears away. Men can no more live without a belief than without air."

" But it is hard to have patience with what one sees to be false."

" What one believes to be false, you mean. It is n't easy to have patience with those who hold to theories that we 've laid by; but surely it is impossible not to respect the spirit in which any honest soul sincerely believes."

" Yes," Maurice assented, somewhat doubtfully; " but it is so hard to have patience with creeds that are entirely outworn."

The old lady smiled and shook her head.

" Again I have to say ' which seem to you outworn.' A creed is never really outworn so long as a single man sincerely believes in it. However, you may have as little patience as you like with them if you will only remember that after all the creed itself is nothing, while the attitude of the mind to truth is everything. If you respect conviction, that is all I ask."

Mrs. Staggchase at another time had also an ethical word for him. Maurice was deeply moved by the fact that Philip had gone into the Catholic church and entered a monastery at Montreal. Like his friend, Ashe had left the Clergy House as soon as he had come to the decision to which his doubts led. He had seen Maurice, and had talked to him unreservedly of his faith and of his plans. It was idle to attempt to move him; and it was after bidding the proselyte good-by that Maurice was talking of him to Mrs. Staggchase, and lamenting what occurred.

"My dear fellow," she observed in her faintly satirical manner, "I know that I'm growing old, because whereas my convictions used to be all right and my actions all wrong, now my actions are right enough, but my convictions have all evaporated. Mr. Ashe is still young enough to need convictions, and the more rigid they are the more contented he'll be."

"But with his training, to turn out in this way," responded Maurice. "It's amazing. Think of a New England Puritan turned Catholic!"

"On the contrary, it is the most natural thing in the world. His Puritan training is what has made him a Catholic."

Maurice thought a moment in silence.

"I suppose," he said at length, "that in this age there are only two things possible for a thinking man. One must go over to Rome and rest on authority, or choose to use his reason, and be an agnostic."

Mrs. Staggchase regarded him with a smile which made him flush a little.

"'No doubt but ye are the people,'" she quoted, "'wisdom shall die with you.' Yet I have known persons really of intellectual respectability who haven't found it necessary to do either."

He was too wise to answer her. He remembered

that it was time to keep an appointment with Berenice, and he smiled with the air of one too happy to be ruffled.

" I suppose," he remarked, as he rose to go, " that if I would give you the chance you would easily prove that Phil and I both are merely Puritans more or less disguised!"

The Riverside Press

CAMBRIDGE, MASSACHUSETTS, U. S. A.

ELECTROTYPED AND PRINTED BY

H. O. HOUGHTON AND CO.

www.ingramcontent.com/pod-product-compliance
Lightning Source LLC
Chambersburg PA
CBHW021333110726
47900CB00005B/1457